SHADOW ACCOUNT

*Also by Stephen Frey
in Large Print:*

The Day Trader
Trust Fund
Silent Partner
The Takeover

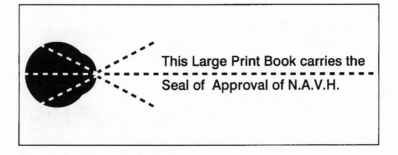

SHADOW ACCOUNT

Stephen Frey

Thorndike Press • Waterville, Maine

Published in 2004 by arrangement with The Ballantine Publishing Group, a division of Random House, Inc.

Thorndike Press® Large Print Core.

The tree indicium is a trademark of Thorndike Press.

The text of this Large Print edition is unabridged.
Other aspects of the book may vary from the original edition.

Set in 16 pt. Plantin by Ramona Watson.

Printed in the United States on permanent paper.

Library of Congress Cataloging-in-Publication Data

Frey, Stephen W.
    Shadow account / Stephen Frey.
      p. cm.
    ISBN 0-7862-6380-6 (lg. print : hc : alk. paper)
    1. Investment bankers — Fiction. 2. Corporate culture — Fiction. 3. New York (N.Y.) — Fiction.
4. Conspiracies — Fiction. 5. Finance — Fiction.
6. Large type books. I. Title.
PS3556.R4477S47 2004
813'.54—dc22   2004041190

SHADOW ACCOUNT

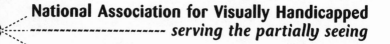

As the Founder/CEO of NAVH, the only national health agency solely devoted to those who, although not totally blind, have an eye disease which could lead to serious visual impairment, I am pleased to recognize Thorndike Press* as one of the leading publishers in the large print field.

Founded in 1954 in San Francisco to prepare large print textbooks for partially seeing children, NAVH became the pioneer and standard setting agency in the preparation of large type.

Today, those publishers who meet our standards carry the prestigious "Seal of Approval" indicating high quality large print. We are delighted that Thorndike Press is one of the publishers whose titles meet these standards. We are also pleased to recognize the significant contribution Thorndike Press is making in this important and growing field.

Lorraine H. Marchi, L.H.D.
Founder/CEO
NAVH

* Thorndike Press encompasses the following imprints: Thorndike, Wheeler, Walker and Large Pr int Press.

CHAPTER 1

"What are you looking at?"

Conner Ashby glanced up from his computer. "Did you say something?" He made it sound so sincere. Gave her that distracted tone and that puzzled expression. He had the routine down to a science, and he enjoyed playing with her head. It was one of those things they had in common.

Liz Shaw stood in the doorway of his cramped bedroom, hands on hips. She wore just an oversized blue-and-orange New York Knicks T-shirt that fell to her knees. "You're impossible," she said. "Answer me." From the doorway, she couldn't see the screen.

Conner grinned, impressed by Liz's ability to make casual cotton as sexy as black lace. She was gorgeous. Easily the most beautiful woman he'd ever been with. "I'm looking at my Schwab brokerage account."

"You're lying to me, Mr. Ashby."

Conner winced. It wasn't the accusation that bothered him. It was the fact that Liz *never* used his first name. Her means of maintaining a subtle yet effective distance. "What are you talking about?"

"You don't have a Schwab account anymore."

Conner fished an ice cube from a Bronx Zoo cup sitting beside his computer on the old desk, and ran it slowly across his bare chest. The air-conditioning had gone down a few hours ago, and he was wearing nothing but a pair of cargo shorts. "How do you know that?"

"I was on your computer last night before you got home. You closed your Schwab account. You, Mr. Ashby, are now an *Ameritrade* customer."

"Hey, as modest as this hovel is, it's *my* hovel," he reminded her, trying to sound annoyed. "I pay the rent here and you had no right to go snooping around my computer."

"Guilty as charged," Liz agreed, moving to the foot of the bed. "But I did. So I know you're lying." She gestured at the monitor. "Come on. *What are you looking at?*"

He glanced out the open window beside his desk at the lights of Manhattan's Upper East Side. They were burning hazy holes in the humid August night. "Some surf shop Web site. I'm gonna buy another board so I can —"

"I bet you're looking at *smut*."

Conner's eyes flashed to the screen. On it, a woman lay across a couch wearing a see-through teddy. She bore a strong resemblance to Liz — blond and slim with full, firm breasts straining at the frilly material.

"Turn the monitor this way," Liz demanded, crawling onto the bed.

Conner clicked back to his screen saver, a panoramic shot of a surfer emerging from the pipeline of a huge wave. But he was a second late.

"I knew it," she said triumphantly, kneeling upright as she reached the edge of the mattress. She'd caught a glimpse of the image on the screen. "Aren't I enough?" she asked, slipping the T-shirt over her head and dropping it in his lap. "Or are you like most men? Obsessive about enjoying as many of us as possible."

Conner let out a long, slow breath, admiring the work of art now on display. His eyes flickered down to the sapphire dangling from a gold ring in her navel. A body piercing seemed like the last thing a society girl would have, which was why he loved it. "I'm like most men," he confessed.

"At least you can admit it," she murmured, slipping her arms around his neck and kissing him.

Conner laughed softly as their lips parted.

"What's so funny?"

"What your father would say if he knew you were here."

"He'd be horrified."

"So he still thinks you're gonna marry Mr. Wonderful over at Morgan Sayers?"

"I still am."

She was always so damn blunt about it. At least she usually remembered to remove the other man's three carats when she was here.

"Morgan Sayers is one of the world's top investment banks, and Todd is one of its top investment bankers." She said the words as if they were a mantra. "Todd is what my father wants. He's the perfect son-in-law."

He hated it when Liz said the other man's name. He'd never laid eyes on Todd, but he could still picture the bastard. A tight-jawed, suspender-wearing snob who'd never really had to work for anything. "Then why are you here?"

Liz's expression turned distant. "Because of those beautiful blue eyes of yours, Mr. Ashby. Because you sing those Elvis songs to yourself all the time, even though you couldn't carry a tune if your life depended on it." She sighed. "Because you gave me flowers last month when I was sick, and Todd didn't even notice I had a cough. Because every time Todd makes love to me, I want it to be you." She hesitated. "Because you're what *I* want."

"Then why don't you tell Todd to — ?"

Liz cut him off with another kiss. "I can't," she murmured, running her fingers through his jet-black hair. "I've told you that so many times."

"But you've never told me *why*."

"I just can't," she whispered, pulling him down onto the bed with her. "I'm sorry."

"Yeah, sure."

"The wedding's still a year away," she reminded him. "Besides, this won't end after I'm married. I could never be without you."

He'd known early on what the deal was. She hadn't tried to hide her engagement. Their affair had begun as an instant physical attraction across a crowded room. Something he had no commitment to, and, he assumed, would end quickly. But it had lasted now for three months, and he couldn't figure out how. He didn't usually waste time on dead ends.

"I'm going to order out for Chinese," Liz announced, reaching for the cordless phone on the nightstand. "There's a place over on Second that's still open."

He caught her hand. "I'm tired of eating in front of the TV. Let's go out." He could count on the fingers of one hand the number of times they'd been out in public together. "Come on."

"No."

"Liz."

"No!"

"Dammit!" He rolled onto his back, frustrated.

She curled up next to him. "I'm sorry. I really am."

"If you were sorry, you'd do something about it."

Her expression turned sad. "I wish I could spend every night with you."

"You could. Just tell Daddy you've found somebody else. Tell him you don't want to marry that hemorrhoid at Morgan Sayers. If he loves you, he'll understand."

"Maybe that's the point. Maybe he doesn't love me."

"All the more reason to live life for yourself. Not for him."

"There's another thing," she kept on, ignoring Conner's irritation, "I'd be cut off from the money."

"So what?"

"Would you love me if I didn't have money?"

Conner rolled his eyes. "You must not think much of me if you have to ask."

"I'm just being realistic. If there's one thing I learned from Daddy, it's that you have to look at everything that way. Even love."

"Hey, I grew up in a run-down, three-bedroom ranch house a couple of blocks from a trashy beach. There was a 7-Eleven next door that got robbed once a week and a couple of sets of railroad tracks that ran right through my backyard. I mean, *come on*."

"Which is exactly why you wouldn't want a woman like me. I could never earn serious money. I don't have any real skills."

"Stop it," he ordered, pressing a finger to her lips. He hated it when she did that. "I just want . . ." His voice trailed off.

"You just want what?"

There it was. His inability to acknowledge how badly he wanted something. In this case, her. But badly enough to have her end the engagement? "I just . . . I just want you to admit that I do have a nice voice."

She laughed and kissed him on the cheek. "Oh, you do. As long as you don't try to sing."

"Hey, lots of people tell me I —"

The phone rang.

"Aren't you going to answer it?" she asked when he didn't pick up right away.

"Nah, it's probably just some telemarketer. Or my boss."

"You can't let a phone ring like that, Mr. Ashby. It's driving you crazy not to know who it is."

He reached for the phone. She was getting to know him too well. "Hello."

"Conner, it's Jackie."

"Hi there." He raised up on one elbow, turning his back to Liz. It was always nice to hear Jackie Rivera's voice. "How are you, Jo?"

Jackie had explained over a glass of wine one evening that she'd been named for Jacqueline Onassis because her mother had admired the former first lady very much. So he'd started calling her "Jo," short for Jackie O.

"I'm doing all right. But we haven't gotten together in a while. It's been almost a month. I miss you."

He'd been bad about keeping in touch with friends since meeting Liz.

"I left you a message at the office yesterday, Conner."

"I know. Sorry about not getting back."

"It's okay," she said cheerfully. "I'm sure you've been busy."

"I have. So, what's the thought for the day?" He asked her this question almost every time they spoke.

There was a short silence. "When the door doesn't open right away, do you pull harder, or push?"

Conner chuckled, thinking about the times he'd pulled harder when all he had to do was push. Understanding the deeper meaning. "Good one."

"Thanks. So, when are we getting together? I —"

"Let's — Ouch! Dammit!" Conner spun around on the bed, wrenching himself away from a painful pinch.

"Get off the phone," Liz hissed, staring at him with a steely expression.

Conner brought the receiver slowly back to his ear, still gazing into Liz's angry eyes. "Jo, let me call you tomorrow."

"Sounds like this might be a bad time."

"Yup."

"Okay," Jackie agreed with a sigh. "Talk to you then."

"What was that all about?" he demanded.

"You're with *me* right now, not her."

"Christ! *You're* the one who's engaged."

"I don't care. I don't like her."

"Why not?"

"She's after you."

"What! How can you say that?"

"Woman's intuition."

"Why would it matter to you if she was after me anyway?"

"Because I'm a jealous bitch."

Conner shook his head. "You're crazy."

"Maybe," Liz murmured, kissing him. Almost savagely this time. "I want you," she whispered, sliding one hand to his shorts.

But the phone rang again.

"Hello."

"It's Ginger. Is Lizzy there?"

Conner let out a frustrated breath. Ginger and Liz rarely had short conversations. "It's Ginger," he said, holding the phone out.

"Oh." Liz brightened. "Thanks."

But he pulled the receiver away. "If you're so worried about your father or Todd finding out about us, why give my phone number to *anyone?*"

"Ginger would never tell a soul," she assured him, leaning across his chest and grabbing the receiver.

"Sure she wouldn't." But Liz hadn't heard him. She'd already reclined onto the bed and started talking.

Liz and Ginger worked together at Merrill

Lynch, entertaining the firm's wealthy international clients when they visited New York City. At least, that was what Liz had told him. She never allowed him to come to the office.

Liz didn't really have to work, but her father believed everyone ought to have a job — at least until they were married. Conner had heard that many times. He'd heard about her trust fund, too. Left to her by her grandfather and controlled by her father until her fortieth birthday.

He watched her pull long blond tresses through her perfectly manicured fingernails as she lay on his bed. She was so comfortable being nude. God, he loved that.

More than once he'd considered confronting Todd to tell him about the affair. But then it would just end sooner, and she'd be gone for good. He was sure she'd cut their relationship off immediately if he did that. Besides, it wouldn't be easy to find Todd. Liz had never mentioned his last name, or what department of Morgan Sayers he worked in. And Conner had never asked.

The computer beeped softly, indicating the arrival of a new e-mail. Conner rose from the bed, sat down behind the desk, and clicked on the icon. He didn't recognize the sender's address, but scrolled down and began reading anyway.

Victor,
Update on Project Delphi. Been going through records in detail, like you told me to do, and we've got a problem. A big problem. They're pumping up earnings per share with phantom income from headquarters now too. Not just with the phony numbers out of Minneapolis. And it's still working. The stock hit sixty-two today. But how much longer before somebody gets a whiff and the whole thing blows up? The circle's getting bigger. You know what that means.

It doesn't stop with the EPS thing either. There are insider dealings with the board and the senior execs. Big expense accounts, undocumented loans, and tons of in-the-money option grants. Plus, the senior guys are hiring executive assistants who look like centerfolds but can't spell their own names. They're running the place like it's their personal Club Med.

If all this gets out, the stock tanks and people lose a ton of jingle-juice. There are heavy hitters in this puppy too. Big insurance companies and pension fund managers who are puking-sick of waking up to another headline about a company baking its books in the fraud oven. Guys who will make us pay. We're talking massive liabilities if a reporter with half a brain sniffs the stink. We'd be hauled up in front of Congress like all the other bozos. You know the deal.

One more thing. The Minneapolis operation is way out of hand. Which I'm sure is why they went to HQ for more. Looks like they tried to replicate the thing in Birmingham, Dallas, and Seattle, but the guys out there must have been too straight. Looks like they wouldn't play ball with the shadow account.

If we don't do something soon, the cat's gonna come crawling out of the bag. I'd give it a few months — at most.

So far the Washington office hasn't gotten dragged into what's going on out there in corporate America. We've managed to keep our noses clean here in D.C., but Delphi could be the one that screws us. And the big boys in New York would cut us loose in a heartbeat. We both know that.

What do you want me to do?

Rusty

Conner stared at Rusty's name for several moments, then scrolled up and rechecked the e-mail address.

"Mr. Ashby." Liz was on her side facing him, phone still pressed to her ear.

"What?"

"Be a doll and go get me some cigarettes."

Smoking was one of two habits she had that he hated. "Liz, you shouldn't —"

"I love you, Mr. Ashby."

Manipulating was the other.

Emerging from the lobby of his apartment building onto Ninety-fifth Street, Conner pressed the "light" button on his Casio and checked the time; 11:30. The deli up Third would be closed, this being a weeknight. But there was a twenty-four-hour place over on Second just north of Ninety-first, no more than five minutes away. He headed out into the darkness, humming "Burning Love."

He'd met Liz at a bar on the Upper West Side last May. She'd been sitting by herself, nursing a vodka and cranberry juice, when he'd come into the place with a few friends. He'd noticed her right away, drawn to her vixen eyes and those long legs beneath that short, black, come-get-me dress.

Thirty minutes later they'd left together, at her urging. She was waiting for someone she didn't really want to see, she said, and hadn't wanted things to get complicated when that person showed. She'd never told him who that "someone" was, but he knew. Now he saw her several nights a week, but never on weekends. Those days were reserved for Todd.

Conner entered the deli and pointed behind the counter at a stack of Marlboro Lights. When he understood the situation — why he couldn't see her whenever he wanted — he tried to end it, not returning her calls. But she'd been relentless, showing up at his apartment door late one night, dressed in a long raincoat and a dark, wide-brimmed hat pulled low over her eyes. Irresistible when she slowly opened her coat in the hallway to show him she wasn't wearing anything underneath.

He dropped a ten-dollar bill onto the counter and the elderly clerk scooped it up. On his way out of the apartment a few minutes ago he'd rifled through Liz's pocketbook, lying on the living room couch, to make certain she didn't already have a pack. To make certain she wasn't trying to manipulate him out of the apartment so she could laugh with Ginger about how much fun it was playing two men off against each other. He grabbed his change and headed out, irritated with himself.

When he hadn't found cigarettes, he'd continued to rummage through her purse. Searching for an address book, business cards, or scraps of paper with messages and phone numbers scrawled on them. Searching for anything that might explain why she'd been missing two nights last week. Nights he was sure she'd mentioned that Todd was going to be out of town. Perhaps he and Todd weren't the only men in her life. Perhaps she was involved with one of those wealthy Merrill Lynch clients too, he realized, staring down at the pavement as he walked.

He cursed under his breath. She'd gotten to him.

"Hello, Conner."

He glanced up, startled.

"Long time no talk."

Conner recognized the woman as she stepped into the glow of a streetlight. Amy Richards. A waitress at an Italian place down in Greenwich Village. A pretty, thirty-one-year-old blond who lived in a blue-collar section of Queens with her mother and five-year-old son, full of hatred for her ex-husband who'd run off with another woman. Conner had been seeing Amy off and on before meeting Liz. He'd never misled her about their relationship. Never told her it was serious for him when she'd told him it was for her. But he hadn't ended it very well.

"Why did you stop calling me?" Amy demanded.

"I got busy."

"Busy, right. With a *new* girlfriend, I'm sure."

Based on her tone, it wouldn't be wise to point out that she'd never been his *old* girlfriend. "What are you doing here?" Greenwich Village was toward the south end of Manhattan. Nowhere near here.

"I didn't know the Upper East Side was off-limits to me. I guess you don't think people from Queens should be let into the swanky part of town."

Bad question. Of course, any question he asked would probably trigger the same reaction. "It's nice to see you again, Amy," he said politely, trying to step past her.

"I got a new job last week," she volunteered, her tone turning friendly as she caught his arm. "Another waitressing gig. The place is only a couple of blocks away. I just got off."

"Oh?"

"You should come by. I'll comp you a few drinks."

"That'd be nice."

"But you never will," she said, bitterness creeping back into her voice. Her fingers curled tightly around his arm. "Will you?"

"Amy, I've got to be at work early." He pried her hand from his arm as gently as possible. "Are you still living with your mom?"

"Yeah."

"So I can reach you at the same telephone number? The one I have in my address book."

"Uh huh."

"Then I'll call you."

"When?"

"Soon."

"What does *soon* mean?"

"In a few days. Maybe this weekend, okay?" He tried stepping past her again.

Once more she caught his arm. "What's your hurry?"

Conner bit his lip. "I told you. I gotta be at work early."

"Didn't you like what you were getting?"

"Of course," he admitted, his voice dropping.

"You sure wanted it as much as you

could get it." She sneered. "Until somebody better came along, right?"

"Look, I —"

"I thought you cared."

"I did. *I do.*" he added quickly. "Please, Amy."

She gazed up into his eyes for several moments, then let her fingers slide slowly from his arm. "Fine. Fuck off."

"Thanks a lot," he muttered, finally able to get past her. "See you later."

"Oh, you'll see me, all right," she called.

He glanced back, wondering if that had been a chance encounter — or if he needed a new address. She'd turned to walk away, but her figure was still outlined by the streetlight. And he was struck by how much she resembled Liz from behind.

"Hi, Eddie." Conner nodded at the young doorman. Eddie hadn't been at the front desk on Conner's way out twenty minutes ago. "How you doing?"

"Fine, Mista Ashby. What's the good word?"

"You'll like this one," Conner said, grinning. "When the door doesn't open right away, do you pull harder, or push?"

Eddie broke into a wide smile. "That's a good one, Mista Ashby. A real good one.

Hey, how do you come up with this stuff?"

"Talent, my man. Raw talent."

As he stepped into the elevator, Conner thought about the errant e-mail from whoever Rusty was. Should he alert Rusty with a "reply" e-mail or do nothing? Sooner or later, Rusty would realize that the message had gone to the wrong person. When he asked, Victor would respond that the e-mail had never arrived, or Rusty would notice the mistake going through his "Sent Items" file. Then both he and Victor would panic.

Conner pressed the button for the seventh floor. If the e-mail was accurate, a large publicly held company was defrauding its shareholders, and now someone outside the tent knew about it. An investment banker, Conner knew that manipulating earnings per share was one of the cardinal sins a company could commit. EPS was the all-important number on Wall Street. The financial Holy Grail. A number that all investors, from multibillion-dollar fund managers to small town investment clubs, relied on to analyze a company's shares. When they heard that the outside accountants had blessed a company's fat EPS, they flocked to purchase its stock, driving up the price. In this case unaware that the actual figure should have been much lower. Unaware that the accountants were asleep at the switch — or on the take.

The elevator doors opened onto the seventh floor, and Conner stepped into the dimly lit hallway. He had no idea what company Rusty was referring to in the e-mail. If shareholders could lose a ton of money, the company must be large, maybe even *Fortune* 500. But he wasn't aware of any company in the *Fortune* 500 named Delphi. It had to be a code name.

The apartment door was ajar when he reached it. Conner hesitated, certain he'd shut it when he left.

He pushed it open, and his pulse spiked. The apartment had been destroyed. Notebooks from work had been ripped apart and papers lay strewn about the parquet floor. The couch and chair cushions had been sliced open, and the bookcase had been overturned, smashing the television. He stepped over the papers and moved quickly to the bedroom. Desk and bureau drawers were scattered on the floor and clothes lay everywhere. His computer was on the floor, too, hard drive removed.

"Liz!"

He was about to sprint for the kitchen

when he noticed something on the far side of the bed. He scrambled onto the mattress, then froze. Liz lay sprawled on her back in the corner of the room near the desk, her neck and chest a spattered mess.

"Oh, God." He reached for her. "Liz."

As his fingers touched her still-warm skin, he heard something over his shoulder and spun around. A man stood in the middle of the living room, staring at him. The man was huge, with dark, curly hair, a beard, and a zipper scar running down his temple.

Conner held his breath, his heart pounding so hard, his vision blurred with each beat. Their eyes locked and, for a moment, there seemed to be nothing but the intruder's cold, hard stare.

Then the man reached inside his jacket.

Conner lunged toward the open window by his desk and tumbled out onto the fire escape. Just as the sound of gunshots crackled in his ears.

CHAPTER 2

Conner was five years old the first time he beat his brothers at chicken. Diving the last few yards across the railroad tracks behind their run-down ranch house just in front of a blue-and-white Conrail GP-9 thundering down the main line. The smell of diesel smoke and creosote filling his nostrils as he picked himself up off the gravel ballast with skinned knees and a busted lip. Smiling triumphantly back through the open doors of empty boxcars flashing past at his brothers, who were still on the house side of the tracks. Furious that they lacked the speed and courage of their pint-size sibling wearing thirdhand Nikes.

Conner's extraordinary athletic ability had stayed with him as he grew up. Now twenty-seven, he was six feet three and weighed a muscular 220 pounds. He was strong *and* quick, and possessed an uncanny sense of balance. Which was why he'd taken to a surfboard like Jordan to a basketball the first time his oldest brother had allowed him out where the big breakers rolled. The varsity football and baseball coaches at his public high school had pleaded with him to play for their teams, but by ninth grade all he wanted to do was surf the turquoise waters off the South Florida beaches. Before and after school. Beneath the hot sun and the full moon. On cloudless days and even as hurricanes roared in. By sixteen, he was the best on the beach — no question.

After two years at a local Florida community college, Conner had maneuvered his way into the University of Southern California on a full scholarship by teaching the young son of an alumnus the finer points of catching a perfect wave. The alumnus, a prominent West Palm Beach surgeon who gave generously and often to Southern Cal, placed a few strategic calls to the admissions office, and the stark community college took its place in the rearview mirror of Conner's life. He'd gotten his first lesson in the importance of knowing the right people. It wouldn't be the last time he traded favors with the elite.

From Los Angeles, where he'd honed his skills on larger West Coast waves, he'd made it to Hawaii a few times to surf the

Banzai Pipeline, home to some of the biggest breakers in the world. It was on those breakers that he'd learned to control physical fear. Leaping across railroad tracks ahead of oncoming freight trains was one thing, but hurtling down the face of a twenty-foot wall of water standing on a slippery piece of fiberglass was quite another.

As he tore down the fire escape from his apartment, Conner used the lessons he'd learned on the Pipeline. *Always maintain control. Never panic. Quickly understand your physical limitations, given the parameters of the situation, and stay within them. Don't try to take seven steps at a time when you know the safe limit is six. Understand that, sooner or later, you will trip and fall if you try to take seven, and they will catch you. Be confident that your athletic ability is superior to theirs. Be confident that their safe limit is four steps at a time, so they can't catch you if you just stay on your feet.*

A bullet screamed past, pinging wickedly off the wrought-iron railing inches from his fingers.

Unless they have guns.

Just three more floors to the alley leading out to Ninety-fifth. As he rushed down the steps, he scanned the dimly lit

31

area below. Looking for anyone lurking in the shadows.

Another gunshot.

"Dammit!" Conner grabbed his left arm as he reached the second-floor landing. There was a burning sensation, as if someone had flashed a white-hot blow-torch across his skin. But the arm still worked.

The ladder from the second-floor landing to the alley was cranked off the pavement, and there was no time to lower it. He knelt, grabbed the bottom rung, swung himself out, and dropped nine feet to the ground. Spotting streams of blood coursing down his sweat-streaked forearm as he let go of the rusting metal.

He hit the pavement and rolled, then scrambled to his feet and sprinted away. When he reached Ninety-fifth, he glanced back. The guy was just picking himself up off the glass-strewn pavement, pistol clutched in his hand. Conner bolted toward Second Avenue, his lead a hundred feet.

A bullet slammed into a parked sedan beside him, shattering the rear window. So he zigzagged as he ran, trying to make himself a tougher target. Why had this man killed Liz, and want to kill him? Because he'd inadvertently intercepted the e-mail. That had to be the answer. Still, how could they have identified the e-mail's physical destination so fast?

Conner reached Second, hesitating as he rounded the corner of a building. Protected for a few fleeting seconds. Two cabs waited at a traffic light. He could go for the closer one, but the guy might get a clean shot at him before he could tumble inside and get away. The guy had already committed one murder tonight. Why not another? Or another *several*. Conner lowered his head and sprinted south toward Ninety-fourth.

It was after midnight, but the temperature still hovered around ninety and the humidity was 100 percent. Even at this late hour, there were usually pedestrians wandering the Upper East Side. But tonight the streets were deserted. People were inside trying to beat the heat.

He tore down Second until he reached Eighty-eighth, then turned right and headed up a rise to Third, continued across Third, then veered left onto Lexington at the next block. Searching for a cop. But they seemed to have beaten a retreat from the summer swelter, too.

Two blocks farther south, Conner raced

down into the 86th Street subway station, descending the grimy steps three at a time and jumping the turnstile. The woman inside the token booth had her nose in a magazine and didn't look up. Conner ran toward the south end of the desolate platform, checking the turnstiles several times, but there was no one. Maybe he'd lost the guy.

Now what? The answer was simple. Get back to the apartment. But he had to find a cop first.

He leaned over, hands on his shaking knees, sucking in air as perspiration poured down his face. He closed his eyes. Liz was dead. He'd only caught a quick glimpse of her sprawled on the floor, but there had been so much blood.

The headlight of an oncoming Number 6 local glimmered at the far end of the tunnel. At the same moment he heard footsteps rushing down the steps from the street. He leaped four feet from the platform and onto the tracks, not about to wait around and see who showed up at the turnstiles.

The headlight of the Number 6 loomed larger, and he ducked into the narrow space beneath the overhang of the station platform. The space was no more than two feet wide, and he flattened himself against the concrete wall. The lead car of the train roared into the station, shiny steel wheels hurtling past only inches from where he knelt. Decelerating rapidly as the train screeched to a halt. The smell of burning brake pads rising from the wheels as the train's warning signal echoed through the station, indicating that the doors were about to open.

Seconds later the signal sounded again, the doors closed, and the train accelerated out of the station toward Harlem.

Heels clicked on the platform above him as the roar of the train faded into the up-town tunnel. He'd been about to come out from beneath the overhang when he'd heard the footsteps. If the person on the platform had just gotten off the train, why stay down here where it was fifteen degrees hotter than on the street? And if this was the person who'd been rushing down the steps a few moments ago, why hadn't he or she boarded the train that had just pulled out? There'd been plenty of time to buy a token and make it through the turnstile.

Conner held his breath as the footsteps stopped directly above him. Beads of salty sweat dripped down his face to his top lip, then seeped into his mouth. He glanced at the streaks of blood on his arm, then up as the footsteps moved away. He exhaled silently and winced as his arm grazed the rough concrete wall. The bullet wound was starting to throb.

Several minutes later another train rumbled into the station past where Conner knelt. When it was gone, he listened for any sound, but there was nothing. Nothing except the far-off wail of a siren and the hum of the station's fluorescent lightbulbs. He rose cautiously, to a point where he could see above the overhang and onto the platform, when he spotted the man who'd broken into his apartment moving furtively down the platform on the other side of the station. Conner melted back into his hiding place.

Then his cell phone rang, the incoming call announced by the first few bars of "Hound Dog." The notes echoed throughout the quiet station like they were blaring through a megaphone. He yanked the phone from the cargo pocket of his shorts and quickly shut it off. Hoping the man on the platform hadn't heard it.

No such providence. The man whipped his pistol from his jacket, dropped down onto the tracks, and headed directly toward Conner. Conner bolted from his hiding place and sprinted into the tunnel, heading for the 77th Street station. Again he heard the ping of bullets ricocheting off metal as he tore through the darkness, the rancid smell of mildew heavy in the air.

A hundred yards into the tunnel, there was a commotion behind him. A yelp of surprise, then a loud groan of pain as his pursuer tumbled onto the tracks. Conner kept going, racing what remained of the nine blocks between stations until he reached the north end of the 77th Street station. There, he grabbed the yellow over-hang, hauled himself up onto the platform, hurried through the turnstile, and raced up the steps to the street.

Two police cruisers were parked at the corner of Seventy-seventh and Lexington as he emerged from the stairway, one directly behind the other. Two officers stood between the vehicles, talking, and Conner rushed toward them. Instinctively, they straightened up when they noticed him. One dropped his hand to his holster.

"Officers!" It was all Conner could do to speak. "I need your help!"

The larger of the two policemen put his hands out, motioning for Conner to stop. "What's your problem?" he demanded, stepping up onto the curb. He had a wide face and huge, hairy forearms.

"A guy just broke into my apartment," Conner gasped. "I went out to pick something up a few minutes ago, and when I got back, the place was destroyed. The guy had torn up everything. Smashed the television and sliced the furniture, and he —" Conner interrupted himself. His relationship with Liz would be difficult to explain as the policeman stared at her bloody body in the corner of the bedroom. There would have to be a story, and he hadn't come up with one yet.

"Why would he do that?" the cop asked suspiciously.

"Do what?"

"Why would he tear up everything."

Conner realized where the cop was headed with this. "I don't know."

"Sounds like he wasn't there to rob the place. Sounds like he was looking for something."

"Well —"

"What would he be looking for?"

Conner shrugged. "I don't know."

The other cop stepped up onto the curb. He was shorter and slimmer. His hand still rested on his holstered pistol, fingers nervously tapping the wooden handle. "This guy chase you?" he wanted to know, glancing at the bloody streaks on Conner's arm. "Is that why you're sweating so bad?"

"Yeah."

"What happened to your arm?" the big one asked.

"Huh?" Conner glanced at his arm. "Caught it on the fire escape when I ran. It's scratched up, but it's fine."

"You sure? You need to go to the hospital?"

"No, I'm *fine*."

The little cop glanced around, undoing the snap of the holster's leather strap. "When did you last see this guy?"

"In the subway. I lost him down there." Conner wasn't at all sure he'd lost the guy, but he wanted to get back to the apartment fast. He didn't want the cops going down there and wasting time. "I ran through the tunnel from Eighty-sixth Street."

"Where's your place?"

"Ninety-fifth between Second and Third."

"All right," the big one agreed, "we'll check it out." He nodded to the other cop. "Let him ride with you."

Conner followed the small cop back to the second squad car, pulling out his cell phone as he eased onto the backseat. He was going to call Eddie and warn him to watch out for anyone suspicious.

"Did you say Ninety-fifth?" the cop asked through the grate separating the front and back seats.

"Yeah." Conner took a deep breath. After twenty minutes of running for his life, he was finally beginning to calm down.

"Between Second and Third?"

"Right," he said, tapping out the number.

But the phone rang before he could finish. It was Gavin Smith, Conner's boss, calling from his Long Island mansion. Conner recognized the number on the phone's tiny screen. It showed up there constantly, late at night and on weekends. Gavin Smith was sixty-one, but he was still a workaholic. "Hello."

"Conner?"

Conner held the phone away from his ear. Gavin always talked loudly on the phone. "Yeah."

"Where are you?"

After being fired two years ago from Harper Manning — a bulge bracket New York investment bank — Gavin Smith had founded Phenix Capital, a boutique firm specializing in merger and acquisition work. Conner had joined Phenix last September and quickly come to realize that, in addition to being a workaholic, Gavin was a control freak. Manifested by his need to know where his key people were at all times.

"I'm out," Conner answered curtly.

"I know. I tried your apartment, but all I got was your answering machine, *pal*."

Pal seemed to be Gavin's favorite word. "Yeah, well I —" A mental alarm went off. Just like the living room, the bedroom had been a mess. Drawers and clothes scattered about the floor, table beside the bed turned over, and, yes, the phone on the floor, the cradle's cord ripped from the wall. He was sure of it.

"You out with that blond from Merrill Lynch?" Gavin asked, chuckling.

That was strange. Gavin had never met Liz. In fact, she'd never met *any* of his friends. She was too damn paranoid about being seen with him.

"What are you talking about?" Conner asked, as they pulled to a stop at a red light.

"Don't worry about it, pal. You're one of Phenix's rising stars. I need to know everything about you."

"Still —"

"I know it's late," the old man broke in, "but we need to talk about the presenta-

41

tion we're making Friday to Pharmaco. It's critical for us to win this mandate. It would go a long way toward putting my little firm on the map. And showing my old partners I can do it without them. I want to make certain we've anticipated *every* question before we walk into that boardroom. I thought of a few more things we should cover, and I want to go over them with you now while they're fresh in my mind."

The light turned green and the squad car squealed through the intersection.

"I can't talk now."

"Why not?" Gavin demanded. "Look, business takes precedence over everything. Especially *my* business, pal."

"Something's happened."

"Something?"

"My apartment was broken into," Conner explained, keeping his voice low. "I'm headed back there with the cops right now."

There was a moment of silence at the other end of the line. "That's terrible." Gavin's tone softened.

"I went out to pick up something. When I got back, I surprised the guy."

"You all right?"

"Yeah. He chased me, but I got away."

"Jesus. Well, call me when you've checked everything out. I'll be up late." Gavin paused. "Maybe you ought to come out here tonight. You sound pretty shook up."

"I'm fine."

"Still . . . you call me," Gavin instructed. "You understand?"

"I *understand*." Conner cut the connection as the cop turned onto Ninety-fifth. "This is it," he said, pointing at the building.

Minutes later he and the two officers were standing in the hallway outside his apartment door.

"This one?" the small one asked.

Conner nodded, surprised that the door was closed. It had been wide open behind the man in the living room. The image was still vivid in Conner's mind. The intruder wouldn't have had time to shut it and be so close behind him on the fire escape.

He stepped forward and tried to turn the knob, but it wouldn't budge. He pulled out his key and slid it into the lock.

"Get back," the big cop ordered, drawing his gun. "Move over there," he growled, motioning toward the opposite wall.

Conner stepped back as the small cop

43

turned the key, then pushed open the door and burst inside. When both policemen had disappeared, Conner followed, at first unable to comprehend. The living room was in perfect order. The bookcase was in its original position, beside the television — turned on without volume — and opposite the couch. His Phenix Capital notebooks were on the shelves, and the couch and chair cushions looked as good as new.

"My God," he whispered.

"I thought you said the place was destroyed."

"It was," Conner snapped, hurrying toward the bedroom.

Same scene there. The computer was back on his desk, hard drive reinserted. All of the desk and bureau drawers had been put back and the phone was on the nightstand, the cradle's cord plugged into the wall. The voice-mail indicator blinked a red *1*. Gavin Smith's message.

This was impossible.

Conner moved into the room, an eerie sensation crawling up his spine as he neared the desk. Liz's body was gone. So was the spreading pool of blood.

"Christ," Conner muttered. "What the — ?"

"Listen, buddy, we've got more important things to do than chase false alarms."

Conner turned to face the big cop who stood in the doorway. He'd replaced his gun in its holster. "I swear to you —"

"If this is some kind of insurance scam, I'll run you in."

"That's not what's going on."

"All clear," the small one announced, appearing at the bedroom doorway. "And it's neat as a pin in here."

The big cop glared at Conner. "We're outta here. I suggest you get a good night's sleep. You look like you could use it."

When they were gone, Conner walked around the bed past the desk to the corner of the room. He knelt down and stared at the spot where Liz's body had been. Touching the hardwood floor, searching for any traces of blood. But there was nothing.

He shook his head and moved to the desk, turning on the computer. He wasn't going to stick around long, but there were two things he wanted to check before he cleared out.

When the computer had warmed up, he opened his e-mail. The message from Rusty was gone. He clicked on the "Deleted Items" option. Gone from there, too. But he still remembered the sender's AOL address, which was probably what the in-

45

truder was worried about and why he'd tried to gun Conner down after killing Liz. Conner grabbed a pen and paper and jotted down the address.

When he'd put the paper in his wallet, he turned off the computer, then hurried to the kitchen and pulled a small bowl down from on top of the refrigerator. It was the sugar bowl Liz used for her morning coffee. His hands shook slightly as he placed it on the kitchen table and removed the top, digging into the smooth white crystals until his fingers struck gold.

Slowly he removed Liz's engagement ring. She always stashed it here so she'd be sure to remember it over her morning coffee. He blew a few granules from the band and held it up. The three carats sparkled in the rays of the overhead bulb.

CHAPTER 3

Lucas Avery was loyal to the president only by extension. Only because he was unfailingly loyal to the party, and the president was one of its leaders.

One of its leaders. The man in front of the cameras, but not necessarily the man pulling the strings. Over the last few months, that had become obvious.

Lucas gazed out the tinted window of the limousine into the predawn darkness. It was parked in the loading area of a strip mall somewhere in the Maryland suburbs of Washington, D.C. He wasn't exactly sure where, because he hadn't paid attention during the half-hour ride out here from his apartment in the city. He'd been too distracted.

The challenge was immense. No one seemed to know where the smoking gun was, whose fingerprints were on it, or what form it took. In fact, they weren't sure it existed at all. Still, he'd been ordered to make certain nothing came to light. With three months until the election, party leaders were terrified that the president's bid for a second term would be crippled if something came to light now.

A thrill coursed through Lucas's small body as a delivery truck rumbled past. This was his first major assignment and important pairs of eyes were watching. He could make his career in the next ninety days. He'd been waiting so long for this chance.

Fragile looking, Lucas was thirty-four and single. His passion was chess, which he played constantly against anyone willing to challenge him. Friends, strangers on the outdoor tables at Farragut Square, and anonymous opponents on the Internet. And he almost always won. He never tried to overpower an opponent with an early rush. Instead, he set his defenses during the initial moves, then waged a war of attrition. He was a marathon man of the sixty-four squares. A grinder, who methodically forced his foe into a corner. Then, and only then, did he attack. Crushing the opponent into submission with a final fury.

Lucas had followed the same kind of long-term strategy in his career. Biding his time until he saw an opening, then acting decisively when the opportunity presented itself. Unlike in chess, this patient strategy hadn't paid huge dividends in his career — until now.

His other passion was baseball, though he'd never once put a glove on and had a catch. He'd always been awkward, too uncoordinated to be any kind of athlete. His affection for baseball came from his love of statistics. They were everywhere in baseball. Batting averages, fielding averages, earned run averages. Myriads of categories to comb through every morning on the Web.

Lucas was self-conscious about his lack of athletic ability. And about his height. He was five eight, but people usually thought he was much shorter. Five five or five six, he often heard. Maybe it was because he was paper thin — he weighed only 140 pounds — or because he was balding. Without hair, he reasoned, he didn't have that extra half-inch or so of perceived height other men enjoyed.

It irritated him to no end when his Northwestern University roommates nicknamed him Shorty a month into his freshman year. Because, statistically speaking, he wasn't short. The average American male was five ten. So he was *slightly* below average, not short. But the nickname had stuck right away, and he'd carried it around like an anchor for four years. Fortunately, he'd been able to keep it out of Washington. But he worried every day that it might be resurrected by some arrogant intern.

Lucas was worth ten thousand dollars, most of that in a savings account earning a smidgen of interest. But it was safe there, protected by the federal government, and that gave him comfort. His family wasn't wealthy, and he'd spent his entire career in politics — traditionally a low-paying job. Several of his Northwestern roommates had gone to Wall Street after graduation and made millions. Roommates he knew he was smarter than. Roommates he'd lost touch with over the years because they took vacations that cost more than his life savings. And lived in homes he could only dream about. He'd gone to his five-year reunion, but not his tenth.

Once in a while, he thought about the money a Wall Street career could have provided. But he was convinced he would ultimately come out ahead if he stayed committed to his long-term strategy in politics. There was an inner circle he'd heard whispers about ever since coming to Washington. Party leaders who fed off the political system with help from private sector moneymen the same way investment bankers fed off the financial system. And Lucas wanted in on it.

He'd signed up for on-campus interviews with the New York investment houses during senior year, but hadn't heard back from any of them. So after graduation he'd come to the Hill to serve in the office of a newly elected Illinois senator. The son of a small-time Chicago lawyer, Lucas had a strong sense of national pride and political duty. His mother's father had been a six-term state senator from a county near Springfield. And, from the time Lucas was old enough to wave the flag at Fourth of July parades, his grandfather had instilled in him a responsibility to serve.

After two more Congressional staff tours and an administrative management position at party headquarters, Lucas had come to the West Wing to serve as deputy assistant political director to the president. Translated, that meant he had to be ready for anything. One day, he touched up a canned "Buy American" speech for the president to deliver to steelworkers in Pittsburgh. The next, he interfaced with the Secret Service, coordinating a European trip for the president. The next, he helped the First Lady plan a dinner. Important jobs that enabled him to interact daily with high-level members of the administration, and gain their trust.

Important, but tedious. Until two weeks ago, when he'd been summoned to the first of these meetings.

The call had come at one o'clock in the morning, distracting him from an intense chess match on the Web just as he was finally cornering a slippery opponent. The anonymous caller told Lucas to be on the southwest corner of Fourteenth and M Streets precisely at ten o'clock that morning, and to wait there for contact. He was told nothing else except that he was *not* to go into work that day. And that he was to be on the specified corner no earlier than five minutes before the specified time.

He would have brushed the call off as a hoax, except that the person at the other end of the line mentioned a photograph taped to the inside of his desk drawer at the West Wing. A photograph of the only girl he'd ever really cared about. A girl he'd dated during his junior year at Northwestern. Brenda Miller. Though not beautiful, Brenda was more attractive than the few other girls he'd dated. And she was nice, too. Apparently unconcerned with his lack of physical appeal and impressed with his IQ.

He'd feared the entire time they were together that she would figure out she could do better. When she left him, it had devastated him.

Lucas had been forced to watch her walk around campus senior year with other men, one in particular she'd started seeing second semester. All three of them had been in a psychology class together, and it had sickened him to watch Brenda holding hands with the guy during lectures. Lucas had followed Brenda to his apartment once, wishing he had the courage to do what he really wanted to do as he stood there knowing what was going on inside.

Now Brenda was in Washington, divorced and childless. A lawyer with a prominent firm in town. Here for a fresh start after leaving a physically abusive husband. He'd heard all this from a friend back in Chicago, but he hadn't called Brenda yet. She'd probably agree to have lunch or even dinner with him, for old times' sake. But then he'd have to endure that disappointed look when she first saw him. At least he'd had *some* hair back then.

The door of the limousine opened and

Franklin Bennett, the president's chief of staff, eased inside. "Morning," he said curtly, settling onto the leather seat opposite Lucas.

Lucas nodded back stiffly. "Good morning, sir."

Bennett was a decorated ex-Marine who kept his graying hair in the same crew cut he'd worn since basic training at Parris Island years ago. A man who routinely intimidated everyone from senior congressmen to the Joint Chiefs to network anchors. A man who commanded respect and had a fierce reputation as one who carried out swift political revenge.

"I have five minutes," Bennett announced. "Give me an update."

"Yes, sir. I've set up the place in Georgetown. It's ready to go. As we discussed, I'll move in full-time whenever you give me the order to go live."

"And only when *I* give you that order," Bennett spoke up. "I am the only one who does that. Got it?"

"Yes, sir."

"Someone else says something to you about this operation, you get word to me immediately. In the way that we discussed."

"Right."

"And *only* in that way."

Bennett was repeating himself. As he would to a child, Lucas realized. "Yes, sir."

"This is a very small cell. It must stay that way."

"I understand."

Bennett pointed at him. "And once you move into the apartment full-time, you do not come *home* until you're notified."

Home was code for the West Wing. "What will my story be?" Lucas asked.

"Story?" Bennett asked gruffly. "What are you talking about? You don't need a story. You shouldn't see anyone."

"Of course, of course, but when I come back, sir. That's what I meant. What will my story be when I come home? How will I explain my absence?" In the back of his mind it bothered Lucas that Bennett hadn't thought through the other side of this operation — his return.

"Oh." Bennett hesitated, deep creases forming on his broad forehead. "You'll tell people you were on a special election committee that was focused on ways to reach out to minorities. But we'll talk more about that later," he said, waving a hand in front of his face like he was swatting a bug. "Until then, I want you concentrating on the task."

"Yes, sir."

Bennett glanced at his watch. "What about the research?"

"I've begun compiling biographies on the five individuals in quest—"

"The *jewels,* dammit! I don't want to hear you say *individuals* or *subjects* one more goddamn time. I want to hear you say *jewels.*"

Lucas nodded anxiously. He'd made the same mistake at each of their first two meetings. "Sorry, sir." He had to get used to the cloak-and-dagger crap. It seemed to be vitally important to the ex-military types. "I've begun my research on the *jewels.*"

"And?"

"Nothing yet, but I'll begin ramping up that effort as soon as you give me the order. I've made arrangements to get some help."

"Good." Bennett hesitated. "But nothing so far? Nothing that could be used against us, right?"

"That's right."

"Very good."

"But there is still a tremendous amount of information to go through, sir. I don't want you thinking I've reached any concrete conclusions. I'm not even close to that point yet."

"Uh huh. One more thing. I'm going to ask another man to join the operation. I've known him for some time."

"Who?"

"You'll know him only by his code name."

More mindless military bullshit. "What is that code name, sir?"

"Cheetah."

"Cheetah?"

"Yes. He has talents that will prove important to us as we move forward. Strong investigative skills. As well as a lot of strong contacts in both the public and private sectors. We'll pay him well, but he'll be worth every penny."

"If you say so, sir."

"I do say so."

"How exactly will we pay him?" Lucas asked. "If you want this cell to be transparent, I wouldn't think you'd want any money trails."

"I'll give you those details later," Bennett answered, checking his watch again. "Okay, that's it," he said sliding along the seat to the door. "Keep at it, Lucas."

"Yes, sir."

"Good-bye."

"Good-bye, sir."

When Bennett was gone, Lucas relaxed onto the seat. His body was damp with perspiration, his shirt and pants sticking to his skin. He let out a relieved breath when the driver began to turn around in the loading area. Being in Bennett's presence scared the hell out of him. Just once he wanted to do that to somebody else.

As the driver accelerated onto the main road in front of the strip mall, Lucas reached beneath the seat and pulled out a marble notebook, opening it to the last entry. He recorded everything of importance in this book: a critical move he'd made in a chess match; a particularly interesting baseball statistic; Brenda Miller's new telephone number at the law firm in D.C.

As well as details of each of his meetings with Franklin Bennett.

These were the minutes of his life.

CHAPTER 4

Conner hesitated for a moment on the darkened porch, then pressed the doorbell. It wasn't his fault if he was waking people up. Gavin had *ordered* him to come out here.

Gavin's second call had come while Conner was staring at Liz's engagement ring. He'd barely said hello, and the old man was barking at him to get his ass down to Penn Station to catch a late train to East Hampton, a wealthy Long Island town where Gavin owned a mansion. They had a great deal of work to do on the Pharmaco presentation before Friday's meeting, Gavin kept saying. He seemed angry, but wouldn't say what was wrong.

If it had been a normal working relationship, Conner would have made up an excuse so he could stay in the city. But Phenix Capital was a small firm, and he'd gotten close to Gavin since joining last year. The old man was the nearest thing to a father he'd had in a long time. Since his real father had died of a heart attack on the kitchen floor twenty years ago.

And Gavin was paying him $175,000 a year plus bonus. So when the late-night and weekend "jump" calls came, he didn't bother asking "how high." Besides, he wasn't going to stay in his apartment tonight. Not with the guy who'd murdered Liz — and shot him — still lurking.

The train ride across Long Island had seemed to last forever. He couldn't stop thinking about what had happened. How Liz's neck and chest had been covered with blood when he'd found her. How the place had looked as if nothing had happened when he got back there with the cops. And how he should have told them what had happened to her.

But he was caught in a twilight zone. He'd realized, as he stared into the suspicious eyes of the officers, that if he told them a woman had been murdered in his apartment, they would have taken him down to the precinct for questioning. And he would have become a suspect in the disappearance of every missing woman in New York.

"Hello there." Gavin's voice boomed into the darkness as the mansion's front door opened. "How you doing, pal?"

"Okay." Gavin didn't seem angry anymore.

"You sure? You look a little rattled."

The old man's speech still contained faint traces of a lisp he'd been born with. He'd worked all his life to eradicate it, and now it was undetectable to the untrained ear. But Conner had spent a lot of time around Gavin, and he heard it slip out once in a while.

"Just tired." Conner nodded over Gavin's shoulder. "I hope I didn't wake anyone up." Gavin's wife had died a year ago, just before Conner joined Phenix, and he knew the old man fought his loneliness with a constant stream of guests. There always seemed to be voices in the background when Gavin called late at night to talk business. "I know you entertain a lot."

"No worries. Everyone's still awake." Gavin hesitated. "Were the police any help?"

"Not really."

"I was afraid of that. Did the guy get anything valuable?"

Conner forced a smile. "There wasn't much to get." His smile faded quickly. The guy had gotten Liz.

"Well, don't stand there on my porch like a stranger, pal. Come in, come in," Gavin urged, pulling Conner inside. "Any problems catching a cab at the train station?"

Conner glanced around the two-story foyer, then at the ornate rooms beyond. He'd been to the mansion several times, but the place never failed to impress him. Chippendale furniture and Persian rugs filled the rooms, Renoirs and Monets decorated the walls, and the rich smell of leather permeated the interior. Wealth seemed to seep from every crevice. But Conner didn't begrudge Gavin his money the way he did those who'd inherited it. Gavin was from a working-class family. He'd earned every penny.

"No problem," Conner answered. "There were five of them waiting."

"Good, good. I've been riding the town council about that. A friend of mine came out from the city one night last month and there wasn't a taxi in sight. It was only eleven o'clock. Can you believe that? Not only does it show a total lack of leadership from those poor excuses for politicians, it's downright dangerous. I was pretty pissed off. I'm glad to hear the problem's been taken care of."

Conner's eyes flickered from the mansion's interior back down to Gavin. He was a little man — five seven and small-boned — who combed his thinning gray hair straight back. He had dark eyes and a deep tan after years of weekend sailing, his only passion outside of work. But what he lacked in physical stature, he more than made up for with brains and energy. Sometimes *too much* energy.

Gavin was a mercurial man with a fiery temper that had ultimately cost him his career at Harper Manning. Gavin had run Harper's high-profile mergers and acquisitions group, one of the firm's most profitable areas, for over a decade. But two years ago, he'd gotten into a shouting match with the head of the firm's equity research division over access to the confidential file of a large, publicly traded company. Gavin had demanded the file in front of several young analysts, yelling at the top of his lungs for someone to *"bring the goddamn thing"* to him immediately. Calling the other executive a moron. But the other man wouldn't turn the file over to Gavin, citing Chinese Wall concerns. Citing the fact that someone in Gavin's position — advising large companies on public acquisitions — shouldn't have access to an equity analyst's file that was full of confidential, nonpublic data because it might tempt him to illegally use that information to one of his clients' advantage.

Gavin had been fired that afternoon.

Given fifteen minutes to gather a few personal belongings from his office once the edict had been handed down. Escorted by security guards like some petty thief to Harper Manning's Water Street entrance. The emotional explosion and the appearance of impropriety the ammunition Harper's managing executives had been praying for. And they'd pounced on the opportunity. Conner had heard from a friend at Harper that Gavin had infuriated many coworkers during his career; however, his ability to generate hundreds of millions in fees had enabled him to stay in power. But the file incident had been the last straw.

Rather than try to catch on at another established New York investment bank, Gavin had founded his own firm and named it Phenix. Rise-from-the-ashes and all that, Conner knew, but Gavin had spelled it unconventionally as a reminder of his own inability to spell, a function of his dyslexia. As a reminder to himself — he'd told Conner once — that, even with all his money, there were things he couldn't conquer.

Conner gazed down at the old man. "I sure am glad you aren't a control freak," he muttered, smiling.

"What do you mean by that?"

"The taxi thing."

"Oh."

"*Riding* the town council. That's probably a massive understatement. What did you do, Gavin, follow them into stores and yell at them in front of registered voters?"

"Maybe."

"Or did you take a more subtle approach? Did you paint their cars yellow?"

"I would have if I'd thought of it."

Conner chuckled. "You're too much."

"It worked, didn't it?"

"Sure, but —"

"Listen," Gavin cut in, his voice rising, "if I were in charge, the world would be a better place. Guns *and* butter, pal. And plenty of both."

Conner grimaced. These were the first few words of Gavin's "beneficent dictator" speech. He'd heard it too many times in the last year. "Glad you dressed up for me," he said, changing the subject. Gavin wore a threadbare, blue Oxford shirt and a ragged pair of khakis that were almost worn through at the knees.

"Okay, okay," Gavin said, turning and walking away. "I can take a hint. You don't want to hear me pontificate. That's fine. But I'll remember."

Conner tossed his bag on a bench in the foyer and followed Gavin down the hall to the large living room. Paul Stone and his wife, Mandy, sat on a sofa in a far corner of the room, sipping drinks. Stone was a Phenix managing director who'd worked for Gavin in Harper Manning's M & A group, then followed the old man to the new firm. Conner had reported to Stone when he first joined Phenix, but a few months ago Gavin had done away with that reporting line. Now Conner worked directly with the old man on "special" projects. Which, he knew, irritated the hell out of Stone.

"Well, look what the cat dragged in," Stone said quietly. He was tall and thin with cherry blond hair and freckles covering his pale face. He wasn't physically intimidating, but he had a brooding demeanor exaggerated by a permanent scowl.

"Great to see you, too, Paul."

"Now, now, *boys*." Gavin gestured toward Stone's wife. "Conner, you remember Mandy. I believe you two met at the party I had out here last April."

The first time they met had actually been at a dinner Gavin had hosted at his Manhattan apartment back in January. Clearly, Gavin didn't remember that.

Which wasn't surprising. Gavin had an excellent memory when it came to business. Otherwise, it wasn't very good. "Uh huh." Conner noticed the distance between the couple as they sat on the couch. He nodded at her. "Hi."

Mandy smiled. She had short, light brown hair and a thin face. "Hi."

"Gavin, can we *please* finish our discussion?" Stone asked, rising off the couch and heading toward the hallway. "I'm exhausted."

"Be right there," Gavin agreed, turning toward Conner. "Paul and I are just wrapping up. We'll be only a few minutes. Then you and I can get started on Pharmaco. In the meantime, get yourself a drink. The bar's over there," he called, pointing as he followed Stone into the hallway. "Keep Mandy company, pal."

Conner watched Gavin until he disappeared. The old man never seemed to need sleep. He'd made a pile of money at Harper Manning. Conner had heard rumors that the figure went as high as thirty million, but he was still driven to make more.

Behind that drive, Conner knew, was Gavin's love of the game. The *mergers and acquisitions* game. Buying and selling billion-dollar businesses. Rubbing elbows with captains of industry while he instructed them on how to do the takeover tango. Constantly reading his name in the *Wall Street Journal* and the *New York Times*. Behind the drive was also Gavin's frustration that, after two years in business, Phenix Capital had yet to advise on an M & A transaction either of those newspapers deemed important enough to report on.

"How are you, surfer boy?"

Conner's eyes flashed to Mandy's. "Okay." He'd sat next to her during the dinner party at Gavin's apartment, and she'd quizzed him on his hobbies. So he'd told her about surfing. And, after several glasses of wine, she'd told him that she and Paul were having problems. Stone had been seated at the other end of the long table and hadn't heard their conversation.

"You know, you don't look like a surfer."

Conner eased into a chair facing the couch. It was all he could do to make himself concentrate. The brutal image of Liz sprawled on the floor kept flashing back to him. "What do you mean?"

"You've got dark hair," she explained, smiling over the lipstick-smudged rim of her glass. "Surfer boys are supposed to be blond."

"Sorry to disappoint you."

"Believe me, I'm not disappointed," she said, raising one eyebrow. "I never was." She motioned toward the bar. "Why don't you get a drink?"

Conner shifted uncomfortably in the chair. That night at dinner he'd caught Stone staring down the table at them several times. "Nah. I'm sure Gavin will keep me up for a while, and I'm beat. Booze would knock me out."

Mandy shrugged, disappointed. "Are you still dating that woman you brought out here to the party last spring?" she asked, taking another swallow of her gin and tonic. "What was her name?"

"Amy Richards." A few weeks later he'd met Liz. And broken it off with Amy. As he'd been reminded under the streetlight a few hours ago.

Mandy snapped her fingers. "That's right, Amy. Are you still seeing her?"

Conner shook his head. "No."

"Well, I'm glad to hear that."

He glanced up. "What's that supposed to mean?"

"To put it bluntly, I thought Amy was a wacko."

"Why do you say that?"

"She cornered me on the terrace during the party to make sure I understood that you and she were seeing *only* each other. She said she'd caught me watching you, and that I better not get any ideas."

"You're kidding."

"Ah, no."

Conner took a deep breath. Maybe he really did need that new address. "Sorry."

"It wasn't your fault." Mandy smiled. "Besides, I kind of liked it."

"I wish you'd told me about that. I might have ended it with her sooner."

"I figured the lightbulb would go on without my help." Mandy hesitated. "Are you seeing anyone now?"

"I was," he said quietly. "But it didn't work out."

"What happened?"

Conner grimaced. "I found out she was engaged."

"Really?"

"Yeah. To some guy at Morgan Sayers."

"Morgan Sayers?"

Conner looked up. "Uh huh. Why?"

"I work at Morgan Sayers."

"Really." He'd always figured she didn't work. That Stone had enough money to let her play. "What area?"

"Equity sales. I cover Midwest insurance companies and pension funds."

"Do you know anyone in corporate finance there?" Liz had never told him that Todd worked in this group. But if Todd really was one of the firm's top investment bankers, it would be a logical place to start looking.

"Is that where this woman's fiancé worked?"

Conner nodded.

"What's his name?"

"Todd."

Mandy rolled her eyes. "Morgan Sayers has a big corporate finance department. I know of at least four guys in that group named Todd. What's his last name?"

"I don't know," Conner admitted.

Mandy smiled. "So she didn't want you doing anything crazy, huh?"

"It's not like I would have."

"You never know. You might have —"

"I know he travels a lot internationally," Conner interrupted.

Mandy thought for a moment. "It could be Todd Bishop. He's in the worldwide group. Works mostly on European equity offerings to U.S. investors. If it's him you're talking about, he'd be in Europe a lot."

"Bishop," Conner repeated quietly, committing the name to memory. Wondering when the guy would start to suspect that something had happened to Liz.

"Yeah." Mandy nodded distractedly, gazing at her fingernails. "So, tell me something, surfer boy. Is there a woman named Rebecca at Phenix Capital?"

Conner's eyes moved slowly to Mandy's. In a way he hoped wouldn't arouse her suspicion. He was pretty sure Paul Stone and Rebecca, a recent hire, were having an affair. "I don't know."

"Oh, come on. There are only thirty people in the entire firm," she pointed out, standing up and walking to the bar. "Just thirty people and you don't know? That's hard to believe."

Conner watched her pick up the Tanqueray bottle. Last week he'd bumped into Paul and Rebecca in the lobby of the Marriott Marquis at Times Square on his way to a luncheon. Paul had mumbled something about both of them attending a tax seminar on an upper floor of the hotel. Which would have been believable except there was no tax seminar scheduled for that day — Conner had checked the daily event register in the lobby.

"Now that you mention it," he spoke up, "I think Gavin did hire a woman named Rebecca a few months ago."

"Is she pretty?"

"Not really." Rebecca had the face of an

angel and a body designed by the devil himself. "She's nice, but she's the matronly type. If it's the woman I'm thinking of, anyway."

"Uh huh." Mandy sat back down on the couch. "You know, my husband doesn't like you much."

As if that were a breaking news story. "Paul's entitled to his opinion," Conner said calmly.

"He says you try to come off as this hard-luck kid from a tough background. But he says the truth is you graduated from the University of Southern California, and that you're doing very well now. He says you use all of that poor-mouth stuff to make people underestimate you. Is that true?"

"Look, I —"

"He says Gavin pays you very well."

"I earn what I make."

"He also says you aren't as smart as you think you are. That you'll screw up in front of a client someday and Gavin will fire you."

Conner said nothing.

"And Paul says he'll do whatever he has to do to run you out of Phenix." She sighed. "But you know what I think?"

"What?"

"I think you scare my husband. I think

he hates the way Gavin has taken you under his wing. Hates hearing Gavin tell him how you're going to be a man of influence on Wall Street soon. I think what Paul's really worried about is that someday he'll be reporting to you. That's why he's trying to figure out how to get you fired." She hesitated. "*Now,* do you want to tell me about the woman at Phenix my husband has been seeing?"

Conner tapped the arm of the chair. Maybe Mandy ought to hear how Gavin had to warn Rebecca about her tight tops and short skirts. About Paul going from inhaling a sandwich at his desk to taking long lunches outside the firm. Lunches that coincided precisely with Rebecca's.

"You know, I —"

"Come on, pal!" Gavin's voice boomed into the living room. "You're up." He stood in the hallway, beckoning to Conner.

Conner rose from the chair and smiled politely. "It was nice seeing you again, Mandy. Maybe we'll have a chance to finish this conversation at some point," he said as Stone reached them.

"I'd like that."

"I'm going to bed," Paul announced, giving Conner a suspicious look. "Let's go, Mandy."

"But I just poured myself another drink."

"Too bad," Stone snapped, snatching her glass and putting it down on the coffee table. "Better get going, *pal*," he said quietly to Conner. "The old man's pretty pissed off. There were a ton of typos in your presentation." He smirked as he grabbed Mandy's wrist. "I wonder how they got there."

CHAPTER 5

Conner stretched as he relaxed into a comfortable chair in one corner of Gavin's den.

"What happened, pal?" Gavin sat in his USC-engraved captain's chair behind his rolltop desk.

"What do you mean?"

Gavin pointed. "Your arm. What happened to it?"

The gunshot wound had begun to bleed again in the cab on the way down Seventh Avenue to Penn Station. As he was waiting for the train to East Hampton, Conner had found an all-night convenience store in the station and bought a roll of cloth tape to wrap around the wound. As he'd raised his arms to stretch, the white tape had poked out from beneath the short sleeve of his shirt.

"You okay?"

"Fine." Conner saw in Gavin's expression that a one-word answer wasn't going to cut it. "I caught my arm on a hook in my bedroom closet as I was packing to come out here. I was rushing, you know. I wanted to get out of there. It's just a scratch." He shook his head. "I've been meaning to get rid of that hook, too. I did the same thing a couple of months ago."

"Doesn't look real *ship-sh*ape," Gavin said, grinning.

Sometimes Gavin consciously used words that challenged his lisp in front of people he trusted. It was his way of letting you know you were inside the fort, Conner knew.

"Yeah well, I —"

"You're off your game tonight."

Conner rolled his eyes. "What's that supposed to mean?"

Gavin shrugged. "Having your place broken into stinks. Believe me, I know. I've been robbed a couple of times, but it isn't the end of the world, pal. Cheer up."

"Gavin, I'm beat." It was almost four thirty. In a few minutes, sunlight would begin creeping through the bay window beside him. "Can we get on with this?" He was tempted to ask if they could put off the discussion until he'd had a chance to catch some sleep. But he knew what the answer would be.

On Gavin's rolltop desk were two copies of a presentation Conner had prepared for their meeting with Pharmaco, a drug company headquartered in Princeton, New Jersey. Last week, the company had been surprised by an unsolicited takeover offer from a European conglomerate. And the CEO and his board of directors needed advice. The CEO was a friend of Gavin's from the Harper Manning days, and suddenly Phenix Capital had an opportunity to get that first transaction the *Wall Street Journal* and the *New York Times* would report on. The competition was a young gun at Harper, and Conner knew that Gavin desperately wanted to win the mandate. He craved the long-lost personal publicity, but what he sought most was the chance to wave a victory flag in the faces of his expartners.

Gavin picked up the presentations, tossed one to Conner, then put on a pair of reading glasses. "Right off the bat there's a problem, pal," he said, tapping the page emphatically. "The goddamn company's name is misspelled. And there are lots more mistakes like this one throughout the presentation." He held the deck out toward Conner and rifled through the pages with his thumb to make his point. "I'm just glad I caught this stuff now. We would have looked like idiots in that boardroom tomorrow if I hadn't," he snapped. "This isn't like you. Usually you really pay attention to details."

Conner gazed at the page. The typo was right there. But that was impossible. He'd checked the whole thing three times before going home last night, and there hadn't been a mistake anywhere. "It wasn't like this when I left the office, Gavin."

The old man peered over his half-lens glasses. "Well, it is now."

"How did you get this?" Conner asked. "We were supposed to go over it yesterday afternoon, but after lunch you decided to come out here instead of staying in Manhattan. And I didn't e-mail it to you here."

Gavin owned a sprawling apartment in an Upper East Side high-rise where he usually stayed during the week. But occasionally he headed out to the mansion to get away. "You ended up taking off around three o'clock yesterday. You came by my office and we talked about how I hadn't finished yet, and how it didn't make sense for you to review it until I was done. We were going to go over it this morning when you got in, remember?"

"I changed my mind." Gavin gestured toward the living room. "I realized we didn't have much time. Paul printed out two copies and brought them out. He was coming here to East Hampton tonight to discuss another deal anyway. I talked to him at the office around eight. Apparently . . ." Gavin paused, silently communicating his displeasure at how early Conner had left, "you were already gone."

"How could he have done that?" Conner asked.

"Done what?"

"Printed out copies of this presentation."

"What do you mean?"

"The only place I have this file saved is on my hard drive, and I turned my computer off before I left."

"I guess he turned it on," Gavin replied, as though the answer ought to be obvious. "Where's the mystery?"

"He would have needed my password to get to my files."

"Really?" the old man asked innocently.

"Yes. And Paul doesn't have my password."

"Mmm."

"Does he, Gavin?"

"Well . . ."

"Gavin?"

The old man groaned. "Okay, I gave him your password. So what?"

"I can't believe you!"

"Relax, pal."

"Those are *my* files, Gavin."

"And Phenix is *my* firm!" Gavin shot back. "I keep a list of everyone's password. The network guy gives them to me. What's your problem? There shouldn't be anything on your hard drive you don't want me to see, right?"

"Paul changed this," Conner said firmly, holding up the deck. "He inputted the typos before he printed it out."

"Why would he do that?"

"To make me look bad."

"Oh, come on."

"I bet he pointed out all the errors when he was in here, didn't he? Probably told you he'd taken the liberty to review the presentation on his way out from Manhattan."

Gavin rolled his eyes.

Conner pointed at the old man. "You know what, I've got a hard copy draft of the presentation in my desk at Phenix. I printed it out before I left yesterday, and I guarantee you *it* isn't full of typos. I can prove Paul did this."

"You might be able to prove the presentation was changed," Gavin said calmly. "But you can't prove Paul did it."

"The guy's trying to get me fired," Conner said angrily. "It doesn't surprise me at all that he'd pull this kind of crap."

"Conner," Gavin said sternly, "you're being ridiculous. And more than a little paranoid."

"No, I'm not. And why are you protecting him?"

"I'm not. I just don't want to jump to any conclusions."

"Do you know about Paul cheating on Mandy?" The revelation had nothing to do with the conversation, but it had the desired effect. Conner saw Gavin's expression darken right away. "With that new secretary you hired," he continued, pressing his advantage. "Rebecca."

"I know."

"You *know?*"

"Of course."

"And you don't care?" Conner asked incredulously.

"I hired Rebecca specifically for Paul. He needed someone."

"You've gotta be kidding me."

Gavin tossed his presentation onto the desk. "I take care of people who take care of me, pal. Paul and Mandy are going through a rough time. She's a bitch."

"That doesn't mean you play pimp and go hire a whore."

Gavin glanced out the bay window, his right hand contracting into a tight fist. "Conner, I give you a lot of leeway in how you speak to me," he said, teeth clenched. "Don't make me regret that."

Conner looked down. He'd gotten ahead of himself. "Sorry."

"Paul's work and his attitude have improved dramatically since Rebecca joined," Gavin continued, still seething. "He's no longer talking about divorce."

Conner hesitated, giving Gavin a few minutes to cool down. "Maybe it'd be better for them if they did split up."

Gavin shook his head. "I can't let that happen."

The old man seemed to be calming down. That was one thing about him. His explosions never lasted long. "Why not?"

"Two reasons. First, I don't want another business partner."

"Another partner?"

"I gave Paul a piece of Phenix when he joined me," Gavin explained. "If they get divorced, Mandy would probably get half his shares. I don't want her showing up at my office looking for financial statements and telling me how to run my business."

So, Paul Stone owned a piece of Phenix. Conner hadn't known that.

"The second issue is image," Gavin continued. "Mandy's family is very connected on both coasts. I don't want Paul's name dragged through the mud. It wouldn't be good for business. Her family would be bitter if there was a divorce, particularly her father. I've met him, and his daughters are his most prized possessions. If you hurt them, you might as well hurt him. I understand he's a vindictive bastard." Gavin folded his hands in his lap. "Paul's been with me for ten years. He's a good man."

Conner held up the presentation. "Paul altered this and tried to make you think the mistakes were mine." His tone was respectful, but he wanted to make his point.

"Just fix it, okay?"

"Yeah, sure, but —"

"By the way, you're getting a twenty-five-thousand-dollar raise next month. Your salary will be two hundred grand beginning in September. Okay, pal?"

The discussion about Paul was clearly over. "Yes," Conner replied quietly. "Thanks."

"I told you, I take care of my people. You're one of those people. We'll be talking soon about you getting a share of the business too."

"That's very generous."

"Take some time to get to know Paul. Down deep, he's a good guy. And I want you two getting along."

There wasn't a snowball's chance in hell of them getting along. But it was time to appease the old man. "Okay."

Gavin removed his reading glasses and rubbed his eyes. "Tell me more about what happened at your apartment."

Conner hesitated, unsure of how much he wanted to say. "Like I told you, I went out for a few minutes around eleven thirty. When I got back, I surprised a guy who'd broken in. He had a gun, and he chased me down the stairs. But I lost him on the street. Then I found a couple of cops and they went back up to the apartment with me. But there was no sign of the guy."

"He didn't steal anything, right?"

"Right."

Gavin shook his head. "You aren't telling me everything."

Conner shrugged. "You're too smart for me. What do you mean?"

"A guy breaks into your apartment but doesn't take anything? You must have stereo equipment or a television or something he would want."

Conner gazed at Gavin, thinking about Liz sprawled dead in the corner of the bedroom. Maybe it made sense to tell him more. To get his reaction. "There was one thing that happened earlier that might have something to do with the break-in."

"Go on."

"A few minutes before I left the apartment I got an e-mail, but it wasn't meant for me."

"How do you know?"

"I didn't recognize the sender's address."

"So you were spammed."

"This wasn't an advertisement. It was a memo with information I'm sure the sender wouldn't want me to see."

Gavin leaned forward in his chair. "What did it say?"

"It talked about a publicly held company that's defrauding shareholders by manipulating its earnings," Conner explained. "It was written by someone who sounded like he had direct access to the books. Maybe someone at the company's accounting firm."

"What company was it?"

"The sender referred to the company only as Project Delphi. I'm not familiar with any large corporation named Delphi."

"It's probably a deal code."

"That's what I thought, too," Conner agreed. Accountants and investment bankers often referred to public companies they were working with by using code names in order to hide sensitive data in case it fell into the wrong hands. "So what do you think?"

"I think whoever sent the e-mail panicked when they realized it went to the wrong place."

Conner nodded. "When I got back to the apartment with the cops, it had been deleted from my computer."

"Given that, I'd say there's no doubt about what that guy was doing there." The old man shook his head. "But it amazes me he could figure out where the e-mail went so fast. Didn't you say it showed up on your computer a few minutes before you went out?"

"Yes."

"How long were you gone?"

"Ten minutes." Then Conner remembered his surprise encounter with Amy Richards. "Twenty at most."

"How could the guy figure out your address in the first place, let alone that fast?"

"Access to the service provider. In this case, AOL on both ends. I assume it's just like tracing a telephone number. The fact that we both use the same provider would make it easier, but it still seems awfully fast to me, too."

"No doubt."

"There was one more thing in the e-mail that might be important."

"What?"

"The person who sent it mentioned being in a Washington, D.C., office."

"Maybe Delphi is headquartered there," Gavin suggested. "And so is the office of the accounting firm that handles the audit."

"Maybe," Conner muttered. He was exhausted, but there was one more thing he needed to know. "The first time you called me tonight you mentioned a woman from Merrill Lynch. How do you know about her?"

"Like I've told you before, pal, you're an important person at Phenix. I need to know everything that's going on with you."

"And?" Conner pushed, his voice rising.

"And . . . I've had you followed a few times. What's the big deal?"

Gavin said it so casually. The same way he'd admitted giving Paul the password. Like Conner shouldn't be shocked or upset. Like it was his privilege to do whatever he wanted. "My God. I can't believe you would —"

"Look, I have a couple of ex-FBI boys help me out once in a while. They dug up information on the woman after one of them spotted you two having dinner earlier this summer at a very out-of-the-way place over on First Avenue," Gavin explained. "He followed you back to your apartment, then tailed her home in the morning. I believe her name is Liz Shaw." Gavin smiled smugly. "Hence your 'Lizzie' computer password."

"She's dead, Gavin." The words tumbled out. Almost against Conner's will. But he had to tell someone. He couldn't keep it to himself any longer.

"Dead?" the old man whispered.

Conner nodded. "She was at my place tonight. The reason I left the apartment was to get her a pack of smokes." He swallowed hard. "The guy who broke in killed her."

Lucas sat in his apartment, arms folded across his chest, staring at the virtual chess match on his computer screen. Two more moves to checkmate, and his opponent probably didn't even realize. Some of these people on the Internet were such rookies.

He leaned back and checked his watch. Quarter of eight. A few more minutes and he'd start his morning routine. Shower, shave, dress, then a twenty-minute walk to the White House. With a stop at Starbucks on the way.

Lucas watched with satisfaction as the opponent's rook moved exactly as he knew it would. He had a feeling this would be the last morning he followed his routine for quite a while.

CHAPTER 6

At noon, Conner was awakened by a well-groomed, silver-haired man. Lunch would be served on the terrace at twelve thirty, the butler informed him. Mr. Smith expected Conner to be there.

Thirty minutes later Conner emerged from the mansion and onto the terrace. It was a wide expanse of neatly manicured grass leading to the ocean, bordered on two sides by tall pine trees. Gavin sat at a round table in the middle of it, reading a newspaper. He was dressed in white, a sweater draped around his shoulders. The temperature had plunged overnight.

Conner walked across the freshly mowed lawn, admiring the setting. This was the life. This was why he worked seventy-hour weeks for a man who defined the word *driven*.

"Afternoon, pal." Gavin folded the newspaper as Conner sat down on the opposite side of the table. "You okay?"

"Fine." Conner assumed what Gavin really wanted to know was whether he felt like talking any more about Liz. After telling Gavin about her murder, he hadn't given the old man any details. He hadn't relayed the fact that the apartment looked as if nothing had ever happened when he'd returned with the cops. Or that Liz's body had disappeared. It had been enough just to tell someone that she was dead.

"You sleep all right?"

"Sure," Conner lied. The king-sized mattress had been soft and comfortable, but he hadn't slept well at all. "Where are Paul and Mandy?" There were only two place settings at the table.

"They left around ten," Gavin answered. "They had a nasty argument this morning."

"Sorry to hear that."

"Mandy's suspicious about Paul having that affair you and I talked about. At least, that's what I gathered from all the yelling." Gavin shook his head. "He accused her of doing the same thing. It sounded like World War Three."

It occurred to Conner that it would be better for him to volunteer information about his conversation with Mandy than to have Gavin find out about it from Paul. "Mandy asked me about Rebecca while you and Paul were in the study."

"Oh?"

"She wanted to know if Rebecca was pretty."

"What did you tell her?"

"I tried to make her sound plain." Over Gavin's shoulder Conner saw the butler and a maid emerge from the mansion carrying trays. "I don't think she believed me. It wouldn't surprise me if she showed up at Phenix to see for herself. She was pretty worked up."

"I don't think she's ever actually been to our offices. So I wonder how she'd know about Rebecca?"

"Beats me."

"Do you think Mandy is cheating on Paul, too?"

Conner looked down. He could feel Gavin's eyes boring into him. "I have no idea. I don't know her that well. I've met her only a few times."

Lunch was a seafood salad, and Conner dug into the healthy portions of shrimp and lobster. He hadn't eaten since midday yesterday, and he was famished. Liz had never gotten to order out for that Chinese food.

Conner paused, his fork in midair. Liz was gone.

"You okay?"

"Fine," Conner answered quietly. It was

93

the second time Gavin had asked a leading question.

"Salad all right?"

And the second time he'd followed with an innocuous question when Conner hadn't opened up. "Delicious. Thanks."

Gavin took a sip of iced tea. "Look, I'm sorry about Liz. It's a terrible thing." He paused. "And I also know you don't approve of what I did for Paul. Which bothers me."

Conner put his fork down and wiped his lips with the napkin. "Arrangements you make for Paul don't concern me."

"It's important that I have your respect."

"You do. You know that."

Gavin gazed toward the beach, watching the waves roll in beneath the gray sky. "Most men are weak when it comes to women, Conner. They can't control themselves. Some stupid instinct makes them risk family and career just to enjoy a beautiful female body for one night. It's something I can't relate to. I was married to my wife, God rest her soul, for thirty-four years, and I never cheated. I was never even *tempted* to cheat." He looked back at Conner. "Unfortunately, I think I'm in the minority. Based on what I hear, it goes on a lot. I don't know. Maybe it's just nature's way of ensuring the survival of the species. Don't think of Paul as a bad person. He simply has the same needs many other men have."

There was no point in talking about it anymore. "It's like you said before, Gavin. You have a firm to run, and Paul is a senior person at the firm. Someone you're counting on to generate income. If he's distracted, his performance suffers. You can't have that."

"But there's more to it than that, Conner. Like I told you, I'm loyal. Maybe *too* loyal. But that's how I've been throughout my career. How I've been throughout my life. I can't change who I am now. I'm too old. I have to decide who means more. A man who's been with me for over a decade, or a woman I barely know. A woman who isn't giving Paul what he needs."

The only thing Paul Stone needed was a hole to slither into at night. "I'm not going to endorse what you're doing, Gavin. It isn't right, and it's that simple."

"I'm helping a friend, pal. The way I may need to help you."

"What's that supposed to mean?"

"A woman was murdered in your apartment last night. I'm sure the police consider you a suspect. Don't kid yourself on that one. Oh, they consoled you while they were wheeling her body out the door on the gurney. But don't let yourself believe for a second that they aren't going to want to ask you more questions. They're paid to provide prosecutors with the most likely suspect." He pointed at Conner. "But I'll tell you this. If they come to the wrong conclusion, I'll do whatever I can to help you. I'll call in favors from people I know downtown. I'll run my own damn investigation if I have to. You're more than an employee to me at this point, Conner. You're a very good friend." He paused. "Almost a son."

Thunder rumbled in the distance. "You won't have to run an investigation," Conner assured the old man, glancing up at a wall of clouds scuttling in from the south. "The police won't be calling me in for questioning."

"Don't be naive," Gavin warned. "I have some experience in these matters."

"You don't understand." It was time to tell Gavin the whole story. After all, there was always a chance that the guy who'd broken in last night might show up at Phenix. It wouldn't be difficult for him to track Conner to the firm if he'd seen the

Phenix logo on the notebooks. It was un-
fair not to give Gavin an opportunity to
take precautions. Maybe even request a
resignation.

"I haven't told you everything, Gavin."

"Clearly."

Conner put his napkin down. "After
that e-mail comes last night, I go out to
pick up a pack of smokes for Liz. When I
get back, my place looks like a tornado
hit. I go into the bedroom and Liz is on
the floor, dead. There's blood everywhere.
Next thing I know, there's this guy in the
living room staring at me. He pulls out a
gun, and I end up hauling my ass out the
bedroom window and down the fire escape with him right behind me. He's
shooting, and he nails me once." Conner
pointed at the fresh tape he'd wrapped
around the wound. "I lose him in the
subway; then I find a couple of cops to go
back to the apartment with me and check
out what happened. I tell them the place
has been destroyed before we get there,
but I don't tell them about Liz. It's a
tricky situation."

"Why is it tricky?"

Conner rubbed his thumb across the
bottom of his front teeth, feeling the one
that was slightly chipped. The result of a

bad fall on the Pipeline. "She was engaged."

"*Engaged?*"

"Yeah, to some prick at Morgan Sayers. I'm surprised that guy who tailed Liz and me for you didn't dig that up."

"Me, too. Usually he's very thorough."

The mental alarm went off again. As it had last night in the squad car when Gavin had mentioned leaving a message on the apartment answering machine. "Here's the thing. When I get back to the apartment with the cops, the place looks like nothing ever happened."

Gavin's jaw went slack. "Oh, come on. Maybe you were just —"

"And Liz's body is gone."

"*Gone?*"

"Gone. Like I told you, there's a lot of blood on the floor when I find her, but there isn't a trace of it when I get back there with the cops. I get down on my hands and knees after they leave and I search the floor, but I can't find anything. It's as if she had never been there," he said, his voice hushed. Except for her engagement ring in the sugar bowl.

Gavin raised both eyebrows. "That's hard to believe."

"So you don't?"

Gavin put his hands up. "It's just an incredible story."

Thunder rumbled again. Louder this time. "The question is, what do I do now?"

"Don't go to the cops," Gavin advised quickly. "If you walk into a precinct babbling about some woman being murdered in your apartment, they'll suspect you immediately. I'm telling you, pal. Even if there isn't a body."

"But I have to find out what happened to her."

Gavin folded his arms. "No you don't."

"Excuse me?"

"Let her go."

"*What?*"

"You'll find someone else. A guy like you always does. You need to stay as far away from this as possible."

Conner had heard stories of how cold Gavin could be. But he hadn't experienced it until now. "This coming from a man who was devoted to one woman for thirty-four years? I can't believe you'd say that."

"You're talking about my *wife*, pal."

The tops of the tall pines swayed against a sudden gust of wind. "Liz and I were close," Conner said quietly.

"She was engaged. Isn't that what you said?"

Conner nodded.

"If you were so close, why didn't she break off the engagement?"

Typical Gavin. Straight to the heart. "You don't understand. There were extenuating circumstances."

Gavin smirked. "There are *always* extenuating circumstances. No offense, pal, but I don't like what I hear about this woman." He paused. "Are you absolutely sure she was dead?"

Conner's eyes raced to the old man's. "What's that supposed to mean?"

"Just a question."

"She was dead," he said firmly. "I'm sure."

Gavin glanced up at the threatening sky. "Walk with me, Conner."

They moved across the grass, side by side, toward one of the tallest pines. Its lower branches had been cut away, forming a small archway. Beneath the branches was a marble gravestone with the name HELEN inscribed on it.

"My wife," Gavin murmured, stopping a few feet away. "I didn't want her in a graveyard beside someone she never knew. I wanted her here with me. I loved her so much."

"I know," Conner said.

The rain began to fall, rustling the trees.

"Have you ever wanted to kill someone?" Gavin asked, staring at the tombstone.

Conner glanced up from the brown needles covering the grave. "What?"

"Have you ever been so angry, you thought you could actually take another person's life?"

Thunder rumbled again. The storm was coming in off the ocean, and it was close. The gentle shower would soon turn into a downpour. "Yes," Conner admitted.

"Frank Turner?"

Conner shut his eyes. Nine years ago a man named Frank Turner was driving his SUV home from his country club. Blind drunk after nine beers. He'd run a red light at forty miles an hour and broadsided Conner's mother, shearing her tiny Toyota in half and killing her instantly. Making her almost unrecognizable at the morgue.

Turner came away from the crash with a few stitches in his forehead and a manslaughter charge. Seven months later the judge sentenced him to nothing but probation and community service. There was no justice from the system for the poor. Things hadn't changed in a thousand years, and Conner was convinced they never would.

A few minutes after the trial Conner had found Turner chuckling with his slick-haired attorney in a parking garage connected to the courthouse. Laughing about how smoothly the whole thing had gone. It had taken four troopers on their way to traffic court to keep Conner from tearing Turner apart.

A week later Conner found the upscale neighborhood where Turner lived, and the office building he owned a few miles away. A month after that a small article appeared in a local newspaper describing how Turner had slipped down a stairway outside that office building late one rainy night. And how he'd died several days later from complications brought on by the severe head injuries suffered in the fall.

"Yes," Conner said tersely. "Frank Turner." He looked the old man straight in the eyes. "You don't miss anything, do you, Gavin?"

"No."

"You investigated me before you hired me."

"Extensively. I keep tabs on everyone and everything that's important to me. I know exactly what's going on in Paul Stone's life, too. I am as prepared as any man on earth. Preparation has been the key to my success, so I won't apologize for it." The old man hesitated. "I understand Turner died when he fell down a stairway one night after he was given nothing but a slap on the wrists for killing your mother."

Conner swallowed hard. "Why did you ask me the question about wanting to kill someone?"

"How did it feel when you read the article about Turner? Was it sweet?"

"Why did you ask me?"

The old man nodded at the gravestone. "One Saturday morning a year ago, Helen and I were sailing out of the Shelter Island Yacht Club."

Shelter Island lay in what was known as the alligator's mouth at the east end of Long Island. The large bay between the north and south shores.

"I was tacking in the main channel and Helen slipped off the boat," Gavin continued. "This young kid zipped by in a speedboat just as she went overboard. He was too close, and he hit her when she came up the first time. It was nine o'clock in the morning and the kid had a blood alcohol content of almost point twelve. He was fifteen years old. *Fifteen* and he was so drunk he could barely tell the coast guard his name when they caught up with him."

"I'm sorry."

"I wanted to kill him. Some days I still do." The old man glanced at the tombstone, his eyes growing misty. "I turned around just as the kid ran her down. It was the most horrible thing I've ever seen. Some nights I wake up in a cold sweat, thinking I can —"

"Thinking you can stop it," Conner finished the sentence. "Thinking you can save her." He hadn't witnessed his mother's death, but for years afterward he would wake up in the middle of the night from a horrible dream in which he saw it happen in slow motion. Saw that it was *about to happen,* but there was nothing he could do.

"Yes."

Conner nodded. "I know."

Gavin stared at him for a long time, then patted his shoulder. "I appreciate being able to tell you that. Paul wouldn't understand."

"What do you mean?"

"Paul's a shallow man," Gavin explained with a sigh. "Not a man given to deep thought. I don't respect him the way I respect you, Conner. Maybe the answer to Paul's insensitivity is that he's never had to work for anything. He's always had money. Not like you and me. Perhaps that's why he has no tolerance for people unlike himself. He doesn't understand how hard they've had to fight to survive. But I still find his lack of sensitivity distasteful. Sometimes downright offensive." Gavin nodded at the gravestone. The rain was falling harder now. "You cared for Liz, didn't you?"

"Yes."

"And you want to find out what happened to her."

"I *have* to find out what happened to her. I have to find her killer." Conner paused. "And I have to protect myself. They might come after me again. It might be better for me to take the fight to them first."

Gavin nodded. "All right, I'll help you. But you have to promise me something."

"What?"

"If you find out anything important, and it looks like things are going to get rough, you'll let me know so I can bring in law enforcement. You must keep me up to speed on what you're doing. Do we have a deal?"

Conner hesitated. "Yes."

The woman sat behind the dressing room table, admiring herself in the mirror. The sash of the red silk robe had come undone and her chest was partially visible. She reached up and pushed her hair off her shoulders, then pulled the robe down so her breasts were exposed. They were full and firm and she smiled, thinking about how many men had admired them.

She wasn't ashamed of the path she'd chosen. She'd simply made the most of a bad situation — and what God had given her. Done what was necessary to escape a dusty, west Texas trailer park. Left her mother and two sisters behind at sixteen with $107 in her purse and a few clothes in an old Samsonite suitcase. Uncertain of where she was going or how she was getting there. Now she had almost a hundred grand in a Miami bank. She'd come a long way from west Texas.

But she wasn't satisfied. A hundred grand wasn't nearly enough. She wanted more. *Deserved* more, dammit. The plan had to work. Failure wasn't an option.

The knock on the door was barely audible over the grinding music in the background. "Hey!"

"What do you want?" she snapped.

"Five minutes."

She didn't bother answering. They could wait. It was time for her to start taking control over every facet of her life.

Which was how the whole thing had started.

CHAPTER 7

"Good afternoon. Morgan Sayers investment banking group. How may I direct your call?"

The woman's greeting was practiced and professional. "Is Todd Bishop there?"

"Mr. Bishop is in Europe. May I put you into his voice mail?"

"Do you know when he'll be back?"

"Not until next week. Let me trans—"

"This is his brother-in-law," Conner interrupted. He wasn't going to wait until next week to start digging.

There was a brief pause at the other end of the line. *"Brother-in-law?"*

"Well, brother-in-law to be. He's marrying my sister, which is why I'm calling," Conner continued. "It's very important that I talk to him as soon as possible. He and I need to make some arrangements."

"Todd is getting *married?* My God, I had no idea."

"I doubt he's told anyone yet," Conner said. "He and my sister are trying to keep it quiet." Which wasn't true. Not according to Liz, anyway. She'd told him there was a huge engagement party at a Connecticut country club one weekend last month. And that formal announcements had been mailed out back in June. "They aren't planning to actually tie the knot for a year."

"Oh."

The woman at the other end of the line sounded confused. "What's wrong?" he asked.

"I don't understand."

"Don't understand what?"

"I . . . I don't want to say anything wrong," she said hesitantly. "Maybe Todd and Martha got back together before he left for Europe Sunday evening."

"Martha?"

"I'm going to put you into Todd's voice mail," said the woman quickly. "I don't think I better say any more."

"No, wait —" But she clicked off the line, and the voice mail greeting started.

Conner listened to the voice briefly but ended the call without leaving a message.

Martha. Maybe that was Todd's pet name for Liz. He shook his head. Doubtful. Besides, the woman who'd answered the phone thought Todd and whoever Martha was were separated. Liz hadn't mentioned anything about a breakup. She would have told him.

Then again, maybe she wouldn't.

So there were two possibilities. Todd Bishop was the wrong man, or Liz had been lying about the engagement. If she'd been lying about the engagement, maybe she'd been lying about a lot of other things, too.

Conner called Jackie Rivera's office next.

"This is Jackie Rivera."

"Jo, it's Conner."

"Hey there," she said, her voice coming to life when she realized who it was. "Isn't this a surprise? Conner Ashby actually calling me back when he said he would."

He felt a quick twinge of guilt. He needed something from her. That was why he'd been so prompt.

"Unless of course you're calling because you need something."

"Uh . . . maybe."

"I hate you," she said, laughing. "Well, I should. But I don't."

In every pound of sarcasm there was at least an ounce of truth. One of Jackie's favorite sayings. "Jo, I need to ask you some accounting questions."

Jackie had been an accountant for thirteen years, and she was as good as they came. Conner had met her through a business associate shortly after joining Phenix, and had retained her several times since to work on transactions with him. To make certain the big boys were doing their jobs. So often these days they weren't.

"Is it a couple of quick questions?" she wanted to know. "If it is, that's fine. We can do it now. But if you've got a lot of material you want to cover, we'll have to talk later. I've got a big client coming by in a few minutes."

"Yeah, this may take a while. It's probably better if we do it in person."

"How about tomorrow at two?"

"Great. See you then." He was about to say good-bye when he realized he hadn't asked the question. "Hey, how about my thought for the — ?"

"When you think you should keep going, stop," she said. "And when you think you should stop, that's when you *really* need to keep going."

Conner chuckled. "Thanks, Jo. See you tomorrow."

"Bye."

He slid the cell phone into his pocket.

"Would you like me to try Mr. Davenport again?"

Conner glanced up at the receptionist.

He'd been waiting in the lobby outside Merrill Lynch's high net worth individual group for twenty minutes. This group took special care of Merrill's very wealthy clients. A half-million-dollar net worth was chump change to these people.

"It's no problem," the young woman added.

He was waiting to see Ted Davenport, the group's senior executive. A man Gavin knew and had called this afternoon from the limousine while they were coming back into the city. That was one thing about Gavin: When he promised to help, he followed up right away.

"Thanks."

"Sure."

He watched the young woman place the call. She was pretty, which didn't surprise him. Most high rollers, especially the international types, were men. And they wanted eye candy walking around when they visited the States to check on their money. The Merrill executives knew this, so the group behind the lobby door was probably staffed with a bevy of attractive young women. Women like this receptionist. And like Liz. Probably Ginger, too, though he'd never met her. It was the same all over Wall Street. Savvy investment bankers understood the deal just as well as film producers and cola executives. Sex sold everything.

"Mr. Davenport says he'll be right out. He apologizes for keeping you waiting."

"Thanks."

Davenport didn't care about making him wait. What he cared about was Gavin hearing about it. Despite being fired from Harper Manning, the old man still cast a long shadow on Wall Street. People expected him to make it back to the top. Both *Forbes* and *Fortune* had run articles in the last several months predicting that, despite Gavin's advancing age, he had at least one more run left. In *Forbes*'s case, Gavin had made the cover, a copy of which he'd framed and placed prominently in the Phenix Capital reception area.

The lobby door opened and a trim man wearing round, tortoiseshell glasses appeared. "Conner?"

"Yes." Conner stood up and they shook hands in front of the receptionist.

"Ted Davenport. Nice to meet you. Come on back to my office."

Conner followed Davenport through the tastefully decorated floor to a spacious office overlooking New York harbor. As he'd anticipated, he'd seen several attractive young women along the way.

"Please." Davenport gestured at a comfortable-looking couch as he sat down in an easy chair.

"Thanks."

"Would you care for anything to drink, Conner? How about an Evian?"

"No, thanks."

People in this group didn't actually manage money. They didn't pick specific stocks or determine portfolio allocations. They simply collected cash and entertained. The better they entertained, the more they collected. So everything here focused on creature comforts and etiquette.

"How's my old friend Gavin Smith?" Davenport wanted to know.

"Fine."

"You work for him, right? I think that's what he told me when we spoke earlier."

"That's right."

"And the new firm? What's the name again?"

"Phenix Capital."

"That's right, Phenix. How many people has Gavin hired so far? He always was one of those guys who needed an empire."

"Thirty."

"*Thirty!* Jesus. That's a lot even for Gavin. At least, so quickly. You guys must be cranking out the deals."

"We're doing all right."

Phenix had closed just four transactions since Conner had joined — and none before that. A tiny number of deals for any mergers and acquisitions group. And none of them were more than $50 million in size, so the fees were small, too. Phenix's revenue was less than a million dollars for the year.

"Where are the offices?"

"On Park Avenue between Fifty-second and Fifty-third."

Davenport whistled. "High-rent district. But then our business is all about image, right?" he asked.

Not like he was really looking for an answer, Conner realized. So he didn't give him one.

"Thirty people and a Park Avenue address." Davenport laughed. "That's one hell of an overhead nut. Must be close to ten million a year, all-in."

It wasn't quite that high, but it was close. And the continuing losses concerned Conner. Thirty employees and four deals didn't add up to positive cash flow on anybody's books, so he'd asked Gavin about the situation. Twice. Both times he'd gotten angry responses, so he hadn't pushed. Besides, everything had to be fine if Gavin was doling out $25,000 raises and maintaining a Long Island mansion and a Manhattan penthouse.

"How did you meet Gavin?" Davenport asked.

"We both graduated from the University of Southern California."

Davenport chuckled. "A few years apart, I assume."

Conner smiled. "*Quite* a few. We were introduced at an alumni function two years ago," he explained. "Before the UCLA game. At the time, I was with a West Coast investment banking firm, and he was just starting up Phenix. We hit it off right away. We talked for almost an hour before the game and had to hustle to the stadium to catch the opening kickoff. After that he'd stop by to see me when he was traveling out West, and take me to lunch when I was in New York. I was pretty impressed that a guy as big on Wall Street as Gavin would take an interest in me. Last summer, he offered me a job, and I accepted on the spot. The idea of working at a small firm directly with a man like Gavin was an opportunity I couldn't turn down. He was pretty nice about the whole thing, too. He even paid for me to move to New York."

"That's Gavin. A good man." Davenport

shook his head sadly. "What happened to Helen last year was so terrible. She was a wonderful woman. I always enjoyed seeing her when she came in. Just a terrible shame," he murmured. "She was an active woman, too. Goes to show you what can happen when you don't wear a life jacket. The currents around Shelter Island are tricky. They'll drag you to the bottom and never give your body back."

"She drowned?"

Davenport looked up. "You didn't know that?"

Conner hesitated. "I knew she fell overboard. I just . . . I thought there was another boat involved. I thought she'd been hit and killed."

"Hit?"

"Yeah, run down by a drunk kid in a speedboat."

Davenport looked out the window at the harbor. "My understanding was that Helen drowned and they never recovered her body." He paused. "I never heard about another boat."

"I must have misunderstood."

"Maybe I'm wrong." Davenport sat up in his chair. "Gavin said you wanted to ask me some questions."

"Yes."

"All right, but I don't have much time. I've got a meeting in a few minutes."

"What can you tell me about a woman named Liz Shaw?"

Davenport's eyes flashed to Conner's.

"I believe she worked here," Conner continued.

"She did," Davenport confirmed, "until two weeks ago."

"What happened?"

"I fired her." Davenport held up one hand. "Let me clarify that. Technically, she resigned. But I would have fired her if she hadn't quit."

So Liz had kept at least one major event in her life a secret. She'd never said anything about being fired, and he would never have known, because she'd told him never to call her at work. "Did she come in late and leave early a lot?" That would make sense. It would fit with the trust fund story.

"No, Liz was always on time. She didn't know much about finance. But for her job that didn't really matter."

"So, *what happened?*"

Davenport hesitated. "Why are you so interested?"

"She applied for a job at Phenix and Gavin asked me to check her out," Conner

117

answered quickly. He'd been ready for the question.

"Uh huh. Well, let's just say I don't think it would be wise to hire her."

"Why not?"

"I can't say any more. It would be against our policy." Davenport stood up. "I'm sorry, but I've got to get to this meeting. You'll have to excuse me."

"Could I see Ginger?" Conner asked.

"Ginger who?"

"I don't know her last name," Conner admitted.

"There's no one in my group named Ginger."

"What?"

Davenport shook his head. "Sorry."

No one named Ginger here. Liz fired two weeks ago. Todd Bishop not Liz's fiancé.

"Conner, I really do need to —"

"One more question," Conner interrupted, standing up, too.

"Yes?"

"How do you know Gavin?"

Davenport opened the office door. "I used to take care of his considerable wealth," he explained. "Gavin didn't like his partners at Harper Manning knowing how much he had. So he kept it here instead."

"You said you 'used to' manage it."

"That's right."

"Why don't you manage it anymore?"

"To keep money in my group, you have to maintain a minimum net worth. Gavin fell below that minimum some time ago."

Conner emerged from the Merrill Lynch building into the long shadows of early evening. Men and women were hurrying toward subways and buses. Manhattan's rush hour was in full swing.

As he crossed the street, Conner glanced over his shoulder, startled by the sound of a vehicle backfiring. Through the crowd he spotted a striking woman standing on the far corner, gazing in his direction. She wore reflective sunglasses beneath the brim of a dark blue baseball cap with a red insignia.

Conner stared at the woman as commuters streamed past her. Sunlight blazed about her slim frame, making it difficult for him to see much. Just long blond hair flowing from beneath the cap down onto her shoulders. Then she faded into the crowd. As if into a mist.

Conner headed back across the street toward her, just as the light changed and a pickup barreled into the intersection. He jumped back on the curb, barely avoiding the right front fender of the truck. The driver slammed on his brakes and shouted through the open passenger window at him. Conner ignored him and bolted to the back of the truck, then across the street toward a huddle of people milling around on the corner waiting for the light to change. Through the crowd he caught a glimpse of the baseball cap and the blond hair moving away. The woman looked so familiar. So damn familiar. He raced after her.

Then a door opened and Conner veered right, directly at an elderly woman pulling a shopping cart. He tumbled to the sidewalk to avoid her, but was back up on his feet quickly. His eyes darted around, searching for the baseball cap and the blond hair, but they were gone. He sprinted ahead. She couldn't have gone far.

The woman lay on the backseat of a taxi, chest heaving, staring up into the brown eyes of the driver. He was looking down at her through the Plexiglas as if she were insane. She'd hurled open the cab's door without any warning, then tumbled inside and slammed the door shut, flattening herself on the seat.

"What the hell are you doing?" he demanded, one hand holding a steaming cup of coffee, the other on the steering wheel.

"This weirdo was stalking me." Her heart was racing — and she loved it. "I'm just lucky you were here." It had gone so perfectly. Conner had seen her and chased her, but she'd gotten away. They would be very satisfied when she reported back to them. "You're my savior."

"What I am is off duty," the man replied angrily. "Get out of my cab."

She propped herself up on one elbow and slowly removed the baseball cap and sunglasses. Then ran her fingers seductively through her long blond hair. "Really? I'm sorry to hear that. I was hoping you would help me."

The cabdriver's irritation faded as he got a better look at her. "Well, I guess I could take one more fare this evening. Where are you going?"

The elevator doors opened onto the seventh floor, and Conner headed quickly down the hall toward his apartment. Gavin had warned him in the limousine not to come back here. That it could be very dangerous. That whoever had broken in might be watching, hoping he'd show up. Gavin was probably right, too. It probably was dangerous. But he had to search the apartment one more time for anything that might help him figure out what had happened to Liz.

As he hurried along the corridor, Conner spotted a few scuffs on the tiles in front of several doors. And a couple of black marks on the walls. The guy next door had moved out recently and probably hadn't put down mats like he was supposed to. But that wasn't surprising. For the Upper East Side it was a cheap building, and the place wasn't maintained very well. So people didn't care if they damaged things here.

He noticed that the bulb above his door was burned out, and he had to squint as he slid the key in the lock. He shook his head as he moved into the apartment and locked the door behind him. If he and Gavin won the Pharmaco deal tomorrow, he was going to move into a better building. It was time.

The place was in perfect order. Like it had been when he'd left for Penn Station at one o'clock this morning. The bookcase was back against the wall — his Phenix binders replaced on the shelves — and the television was intact. His clothes were back in the dresser drawers, and the computer was on his desk. He glanced toward the corner of the bedroom. And no sign of Liz's body.

Over lunch Gavin had asked a question that now haunted him: Was he absolutely certain Liz was dead? Conner knelt down beside the spot where Liz's body had been and ran his fingers slowly across the smooth wooden floor. No remnants of blood. He leaned down and peered carefully at the tiny cracks between the boards, searching for residue. Nothing. He took a deep breath. He thought he was certain, but now —

The sound of a key sliding into the apartment door. Maintenance? He wasn't going to chance it. He glanced at the window over the fire escape. No time. He hurried to the bathroom, slipping behind the door so he could see into the bedroom. Just as the hall door opened and closed.

A moment later a man Conner recognized moved into the bedroom. The man who'd shot him last night.

The intruder moved to the far side of the bed and past the desk, then knelt down, disappearing from view for a moment. Conner could hear his loud breathing, then a groan as he stood up. The man retraced his steps past the desk and around the bed and headed for the bathroom.

As the man entered the bathroom, Conner slammed the heavy wooden door into him, catching him on the left side of his head. He tumbled backward into the bed, then crumpled to the floor. Conner raced out of the bathroom, grabbed the man by his collar, and landed a swift blow to his chin, then another to his stomach. The intruder clutched his belly, and Conner pulled back the man's sport jacket and reached for a revolver jutting from his shoulder holster. But, as Conner's fingers closed around the gun, the intruder coiled his leg and kicked.

Conner stumbled back and his head slammed into the wall beside the dresser. For a split second he was out on his feet, images blurring before him. He was vaguely aware of the revolver slipping from his fingers and the room spinning.

He shook his head, and his vision cleared just as the intruder came at him. In one smooth motion, Conner grabbed a dresser drawer and swung it, clipping the attacker on the head just as the huge man's hands closed around his neck. The man tumbled to the floor and Conner delivered another blow to the back of his head. The man's left hand trembled for a moment, then went still.

Conner shook his head again, still trying to clear the cobwebs. Then reached down and rolled the man onto his back. His eyes were open but glassy. Blood was dripping down his face. And he was mumbling incoherently. He tried to sit up but fell on his side after lifting his upper body just a few inches off the floor.

Conner glanced around and spotted the revolver lying beside the dresser. He hustled to it, then sprinted for the apartment door, thinking that the intruder might have an accomplice in the hallway. He slid the door's dead bolt into place, then raced back to the bedroom and, from the doorway, leveled the gun at the intruder, who had managed to pull himself to a sitting position.

"Who are you?" Conner demanded. The guy was coming around. "Talk to me!"

"Screw you," the guy mumbled, reaching unsteadily for the bed and trying to pull himself to his feet.

Conner took three quick strides forward and kicked him in the ribs.

The man collapsed to the floor again and curled into a fetal position.

"Come on!" Conner yelled. "Tell me everything. What happened to the woman who was here last night?"

No reply.

Conner grabbed the man by his hair and pressed the black barrel to his bleeding temple. "I'll kill you!" he yelled. A fury he'd felt only once before grabbing him. "I swear to Christ." The fury he'd felt watching Frank Turner and his slick-haired attorney laugh in the parking garage. *"What happened to her?"*

"Fuck off."

Conner slammed the man's head to the floor and stood up, adrenaline coursing through him. He opened the revolver, then pointed the barrel toward the ceiling and shook the gun, causing all six bullets to fall out. The shells clattered loudly on the floor around the man. Conner reached down quickly and retrieved one of them, then closed the gun, and spun the chambers. Holding the gun down beside the man's ear so he could hear them rotate.

"Five empty chambers," Conner hissed, pulling the intruder to a sitting position against the side of the bed. "One loaded." He placed the barrel of the gun firmly against the man's upper lip just beneath his nose. "Now, what happened to her?"

The man stared down the black barrel at Conner's finger curled around the trigger. "You don't understand, kid," he mumbled. "It's not what you think."

"How do you know what I think?"

"Don't be a hero. Stay out of this."

"What is *this?*"

"I can't, I can't."

"What happened to her?" Conner yelled, cocking the gun.

"I don't know. I swear. I wasn't responsible for that."

Conner pulled the trigger, and the hammer descended.

"Jesus!" The man wrenched his head to one side.

Metal clicked against metal — but there was no explosion.

Conner wrestled the man's face back into position, then forced the gun into his mouth and pulled the trigger. The chambers rotated once more — but again, no explosion. "Four chambers left!" Conner shouted. "Start talking."

"Stop, please stop!" the man begged frantically, his words garbled by the barrel.

"What happened to the woman?" Conner demanded. "Tell me!"

"She didn't have a choice." The intruder gasped, gagging on the barrel. "She was just a pawn."

Conner's grip on the gun relaxed for a moment and the barrel slipped from the man's mouth. "What do you mean, 'a pawn'?"

"I can't tell you any more than that."

This time Conner pressed the barrel flush against the side of the man's head. "Come on, you bastard!"

"You're making a big mistake, kid. You shoot me and you're in a lot of trouble. I'm a federal agent."

Conner's finger slipped from the trigger. Federal agent?

In that second the man brought both of his huge arms straight up, catching Conner beneath the chin with a powerful blow. Conner tumbled backward and the gun flew from his grip, clattering across the floor toward a corner of the room.

But the intruder didn't go for it. Instead, he pulled himself to his feet, raced to the bedroom window, threw it open, and scrambled out onto the fire escape.

Conner struggled to stand, then stumbled groggily to the window. Just in time to see the man trip as he reached the sixth floor landing and tumble over the thin black railing. Arms and legs flailing desperately as he plummeted headfirst to the alley.

Conner stopped on the corner of Lexington and Seventy-second Street and leaned against a mailbox. The image of the man falling over the railing was still vivid. He was dead on impact. No doubt.

"Sir?"

Conner's head snapped toward the voice. Standing beside him was a short, stout man with a round face and small eyes. "What?"

"You Conner Ashby?"

Conner's eyes narrowed. "Who wants to know?"

"Oh, sorry," the man apologized, holding out his hand. "Didn't mean to be rude. My name's Art Meeks. I work for a man named Charles Shaw."

Meeks's face blurred in front of Conner as they shook hands. Charles Shaw.

"I believe you know Mr. Shaw's daughter," Meeks continued. "Her name's Elizabeth."

"I know her," Conner said quietly, trying to keep his voice steady. "So, what?"

Meeks shrugged. "I just want to ask you a few questions. That okay?"

Blood pounded in Conner's brain. "I suppose," he agreed hesitantly. Meeks seemed friendly enough. And Conner didn't want to arouse his suspicion.

"Good. Thanks." Meeks removed a small notepad from his pocket and flipped through it. "The thing is, Mr. Shaw was supposed to meet with Elizabeth at ten o'clock this morning. At his attorney's office to go through several issues related to her upcoming marriage. The prenup, I think it was," Meeks explained, checking his notes. "But she didn't show. And she hasn't answered calls to her apartment or her cell phone. Mr. Shaw is very worried. As is her fiancé, who cut short a business trip to Europe to fly back to the States. I've been hired to find her. I thought you might know something."

Conner had begun to believe that Liz might still be alive. That Gavin was right. That the lies he'd uncovered this afternoon might mean she was somehow involved in what had happened last night. As he'd thought back on their first encounter at the West Side bar last May, he remembered that Liz had approached him right after they'd made eye contact. That she had suggested they leave together after half a drink. That in the weeks following that first encounter she'd been the one to make certain their relationship intensified. That having a fiancé made it seem reasonable for her not to want him to call her at work or be seen in public with her. Now this little man standing in front of him was blowing all that out of the water. Maybe she'd been honest with him after all.

"Why would I know anything?" Conner asked, glancing around the intersection warily.

"Because your name shows up in a datebook I found in her apartment. A couple of times recently, too," Meeks added.

That was odd, Conner thought to himself. Why would she write his name down somewhere if she was so worried about their affair being discovered? "How do I know you're who you say you are, Mr. Meeks?"

"Look, I —"

"What's the address of Liz's apartment?" Conner cut in.

Meeks checked his notepad. "Four-forty-seven East Fifty-first Street," he answered. "Apartment K-Five."

Conner made a quick mental note of the address. He had no idea if it was right, because Liz had never told him where she lived. He'd asked a couple of times, but she wouldn't say. She was too afraid he'd come by when Todd was there.

"Satisfied?" Meeks asked with a friendly smile.

"I suppose," Conner agreed, reaching into his pants pocket. Feeling the bullet the intruder had thought was in the revolver.

"Were you having an affair with Elizabeth, Mr. Ashby?" Meeks asked hesitantly.

"*What?*"

The investigator held his hands up. "Look, I'm not here to judge anybody. Me, I don't care what you and Elizabeth might have done. And I don't intend to tell anybody either. I just want to find her. That's all I've been hired to do."

Conner gazed down at the little man, wondering what in the hell was going on. Wondering how this guy had found him.

"When did you last see Elizabeth, Mr. Ashby?"

"Last night," Conner confessed.

"Where?"

"She was at my apartment."

"Did she stay the night?"

"No."

"What time did she leave?"

"Around eleven thirty. That was the last time I saw or spoke to her."

"Uh huh. Anything else you want to tell me about last night?"

"No."

Meeks scribbled a few notes, then closed his pad and glanced up. "All right, that's all for now. Thanks. I'll be in touch if I need to talk to you again."

Conner watched the investigator walk away down Lexington Avenue. If Meeks went to the cops with what he knew, Gavin's warning about Conner becoming a suspect in Liz's death would come true. The police would be all over him.

Conner strained his neck as the small man disappeared around the corner. Now he *had* to find out what had happened to Liz.

It hadn't been long. Not even twenty-four hours. Lucas and Bennett were back in the limousine, this time somewhere in northern Virginia.

"All right," Bennett said, his tone grave. "This is it. We're going live."

A wave of emotion rushed through Lucas. Going live. Just the sound of it made his pulse pop.

"Are you ready?"

"Yes, sir."

Bennett nodded. "Yes, I'm confident you are, Lucas. Which is why I'm putting you in charge of this thing." He hesitated. "You can spend tonight in your apartment and take care of any final arrangements. But tomorrow you'll move to Georgetown. I don't want you coming home tomorrow either. Understand?"

"Yes."

"When all this is over, after the election, your office on the second floor will be waiting. Got it?"

"Absolutely." It was strange. Suddenly he wasn't nervous at all. The jitters of only a few moments ago were gone. He was calm, completely confident.

"We need to move quickly," Bennett continued.

"Of course."

"Things have happened."

"What things?"

"Things," Bennett snapped.

"Yes, sir." Bennett was clearly on edge. Lucas had never seen him like this.

"One more thing. The man we spoke about yesterday will be coming to see you in Georgetown tomorrow afternoon. Expect him a little after three."

"You mean Cheetah."

"Yes." Bennett glanced out the limousine's window. "Now, there are some things I need to tell you about the monetary arrangements. Things that involve a man named Sam Macarthur."

Chapter 8

Jackie Rivera had grown up in a Bronx housing project, the daughter of a white mother and a Dominican father. Shortly after Jackie turned seventeen, both of her parents were killed in a car crash on the FDR. And she was left to raise her three younger siblings on her own.

It was a huge responsibility for a teenager, but she'd met the challenge head-on. The way she always did. Her brothers and sisters had all graduated from high school on time, and none of them were ever in trouble with the law. Not for so much as jaywalking.

Despite the demands on her time, Jackie attended City College, graduating with honors in business. After college, she accepted an entry-level audit position in the Manhattan offices of a national accounting firm, earning $18,000 a year. Seven years later she made partner. And, three years after that, resigned from the big firm to found her own consulting practice. Aware that she'd reached a ceiling as strong as steel and clear as glass. She'd come a long way for a woman from the Bronx who didn't have an Ivy League background, but she'd come as far as she could. She wasn't bitter about it, just pragmatic. The way she always was.

"Hello, Conner." She met him at the door of her understated fifth-floor office in the Empire State Building. Now thirty-five, she'd quietly accumulated a million-dollar net worth with twelve-hour work-days and savvy stock market investing. She could have had the big showroom office downtown with a panoramic view of the harbor, but she didn't see the need. More important, she believed that kind of opu-lence would turn off clients who wouldn't want to pay a high hourly rate just so she could watch ships sail beneath the Verrazano Bridge. "Nice to see you."

"Nice to see you, too, Jo."

"Come in," Jackie said, motioning as she moved back to her desk. "Close the door."

He grinned, watching her walk away in that confident stride of hers. Quick steps, shoulders back, chin pushed out defiantly. A small woman — just five two and not much over a hundred pounds — Jackie had dark brown eyes, a thin face with high cheekbones, full lips, shoulder-length straight black hair, and a trim figure, high-lighted by her chalk-stripe pantsuit.

"Do you ever wear dresses or skirts?" he asked. It occurred to him that he'd never seen her in anything but a jacket and pants.

She stood behind her platform desk, stacks of papers neatly arranged in a line across it. "Rarely," she answered in her Spanish accent. She was a vivacious woman who gestured constantly with her hands when she spoke. "If I did, how would men see my best asset?" she asked, turning and patting one hip provocatively.

Conner chuckled as they sat down. "You're a tease, Jo." It was a forward thing to say, but they were close friends.

"Excuse me?"

"You lure men into your web with that body, then drop them cold once they're caught." She rarely dated a man for more than a few weeks. When they got together for dinner or drinks, Conner always got an update on her love life. "Once you get bored, you cut them loose," he said, imitating a pair of scissors with his fingers.

"I cut them loose because they're losers. Like the last one." She grimaced. "Why do I have such bad luck with men, Conner?"

"What was so terrible about the last one?"

"He was a serial liar. Get this, he tells me he's a lawyer at a big Wall Street firm. Then I find out he's a clerk at the department of motor vehicles. Which would have been fine," she added quickly. "I don't care what a man does for a living. I just can't handle being lied to."

"What you can't *handle* is commitment."

"Can, too."

"I bet you don't even want to get married."

"Wrong."

Conner smiled. "Then marry me, Jo."

"*Ay Dios mío!*" She brought her hands to her face. "Oh, no."

"Why not?"

"Talk about a tease. I've seen the way you flirt with women."

"Oh, you're just —"

"And the way they flirt back," she continued. "I couldn't take all that. No, no. I like our relationship the way it is. Friendly."

Last February — shortly before he met Amy Richards — Conner and Jackie had had dinner at a place on the West Side near her apartment. Promising each other as they sat down that it would be a quick meal because both of them had commitments early the next morning. Three hours and two bottles of wine later he walked her home. Halfway to her apartment he'd caught her fingers in his. And, at her door, as they murmured good night, they almost kissed. Slowly leaning closer until Jackie turned away at the last moment.

They'd never talked about what had happened that night, but it was still there. Hanging between them every time they saw each other. Conner had caught her gazing at him several times since then in a way he'd seen other women look at him. The same way she'd caught him looking at her.

"All right, all right," he mumbled, trying to sound hurt. "I can take a hint."

"It's no hint," Jackie said firmly. "You stay away from me." She made a cross with her fingers. "You hear me?"

Conner laughed loudly. "I hear you already."

She smiled and stuck her tongue out. "Wipe that pout off your face. It's all an act with you anyway. You'd never marry me."

"You don't know that."

"You like blondes with big bosoms," she said pushing her chest out. "Not little brunettes like me who barely fill a B cup."

"How do you know what I like?"

"You told me once."

"I did not."

"You just don't remember."

"Maybe I was trying to make you jealous, Jo."

"Don't do this to me, Conner," she pleaded, waving her hands. "I can't take it."

"Okay, okay." He paused. "So what's the thought of the day?"

Jackie put a finger to her lips and looked at the ceiling. "When you lose, don't lose the lesson."

He'd heard that one before, but he liked it. "Good one."

"Would you expect anything less?" She gazed at him intently for a few moments, then looked down. "So, why did you need to see me?" she asked quietly. "What questions do you have?"

Conner rubbed his eyes. He'd spent last night at Gavin's sprawling Upper East Side apartment. He felt safe there, but didn't sleep well because of the images still haunting him. The intruder falling, arms and legs flailing. The blonde in the dark blue baseball cap. Art Meeks, notepad in hand. And the most vivid of all — Liz's neck and chest covered with blood.

And he was haunted by what the intruder had said. That Liz was just a pawn, and all those words implied. And that he was a federal agent.

Conner hadn't said anything to Gavin about what had happened — nothing about his second encounter with the intruder — and he felt guilty. He was even more of a target now. And so was everyone around him.

He finally fell asleep around three thirty, but Gavin's sharp knock on the bedroom door woke him an hour later. They had to be in New Jersey at eight for the Pharmaco presentation, and Gavin wanted to run through the deck one more time before they climbed in the limousine and headed into the Lincoln Tunnel. Gavin never read anything in a car. It made him sick.

The presentation to Pharmaco's board of directors had lasted three hours, and Gavin had been magnificent. Leading the CEO and the board members through a maze of possible outcomes of the European conglomerate's offer. And the effects and intricacies of each. The likelihood of shareholder suits if the board accepted the offer immediately without at least *attempting* to negotiate a higher price. The difficulty of identifying a white knight on short notice should the European firm launch a hostile tender offer if they were rebuffed. The possibility that other domestic drug companies would appear on the scene. The need for the board to entrench senior management by quickly approving bailout packages — golden parachutes and massive retirement benefits — because acquirers usually cut costs at a newly acquired company by firing highly paid executives if packages hadn't been adopted. Gavin's willingness to contact a close friend and partner at one of Wall Street's most prominent leveraged buyout firms to determine if a going-private transaction could be arranged.

Gavin's advice was delivered free of charge because fledgling investment banking firms like Phenix, even ones with Gavin Smith as their founding partner, still had to give away services to hook big clients. When the presentation ended, the CEO politely thanked Gavin for the information, but gave no indication that Phenix would be selected over Harper Manning to advise the company. Gavin hadn't said a word during the ride back into New York. He'd simply stared out the window, watching the rural scenery turn urban.

"I need you to explain how a public

company can manipulate its earnings," Conner explained. Jackie could smell fraud a mile away, and dissect financial statements like a surgeon. Her contact list was broad and deep, too: investment bankers, commercial bankers, lawyers, other accountants, corporate executives, and regulatory people at both the federal and state level. She was the perfect person to ask about all this. "How it can make the financial statements look better than they are without raising any suspicions, at least not in the short term."

She nodded. "You want to know how a company like Enron, with billions of dollars in revenues, can be worth eighty bucks a share one day and declare bankruptcy a few weeks later. How nobody — Wall Street's best equity analysts, the country's most prominent bankers, the rating agencies, a major accounting firm — nobody saw it coming. Right?"

Conner relaxed into his chair and chuckled. "I adore you, Jo."

"But why?" she asked quietly.

He'd said it almost without thinking. "Because . . . because you're such a wonderful person." He winked. "With a nice figure and a —"

"No, no. Why do you want to know how

a company could manipulate its earnings?"

"Oh. Oh, right. Well, I'm just doing some research."

Jackie picked up a wrist exerciser from her desk and squeezed the handles. She'd broken her arm last fall skydiving and her doctor had recommended the exercise. "How's Phenix Capital doing?" she asked.

"Fine. Why do you ask?"

"Starting an investment bank is tough. Even for a man like Gavin Smith."

"So?"

"I've been a CPA for thirteen years, and I'm not surprised by much anymore. But one thing that still amazes me is how crazy people act when they get squeezed financially. Especially people who've never been in that situation."

"What are you saying?" Conner asked evenly.

"I'm just asking a question."

"Spin it out for me."

Jackie hesitated, as if she wanted to say more. "No, let's get started."

"Come on."

She shook her head.

"All right," he agreed. He'd pulled on the door hard enough. He'd try pushing later.

"What you have to remember about ac-

countants is that they're just people,"
Jackie began. "They aren't computers."

"Jo, I don't need to hear a defense-of-
the-profession speech. I'm not here to
make a value judgment about —"

"They're corruptible," Jackie interrupted, folding her hands tightly in front of
her. "Corruptible as any politician, banker,
lawyer, or cop. And that's the problem.
That's how a company can be worth billions one day and nothing the next. There
has to be complicity." She sighed. "Everyone
gets those beautiful, glossy annual reports
in the mail and never questions what's between the covers. They get all warm and
fuzzy when they see that color picture of
the board of directors in the back. You
know, the socially responsible country club
ad. The one with the woman in a conserva-
tive dress and the respectable-looking
black guy, all surrounded by twelve silver-
haired Saxons."

Conner held back a smile.

"And the board members all have sterling résumés. They're CEOs of other *Fortune* 500 companies, professors emeritus of
top business schools and ex-politicos.
They're so credible, investors can't wait to
snap up company shares. Those steely ex-
pressions tell us they're tough and sophisti-

cated and nothing bad is going to happen while they're around." Jackie flexed the wrist exerciser. "Problem is, most of them can't balance their own checkbooks.

"And at the front of the annual report," she continued, "there's this letter from a big CPA firm because big companies can't hire anything but big CPA firms. It wouldn't look good if they didn't. As if the big firms are so much better than little ones like mine. Anyway, the letter from the big firm brags about how they've burned the midnight oil to make certain the company's numbers are fairly presented, and the name of the accounting firm is signed at the bottom. Not the name of the lead partner who's responsible for the audit, mind you, but the name of the firm itself. Like we're supposed to believe Mr. Arthur or Mr. Andersen actually got finger blisters themselves punching the old adding machines."

"I appreciate what you're saying, Jo," Conner spoke up. "But I'm looking for specifics. I need to know —"

"I'll get to all that, Conner. But it's so important that you *really* understand what I'm saying here. Most people don't. It's the key to everything bad that's going on in the business world right now — the lack of confidence in company numbers, the suspicions people have about corporate executives and Wall Street investment bankers and public accountants. Most investors think accounting is black-and-white. But there's a lot of room for interpretation when it comes to keeping company books. Anytime there's room for interpretation, there's room for fraud. Like I said before, accountants can be bribed, manipulated, and intimidated just like anyone else."

"Give me an example."

Jackie drummed her fingers on the desk, thinking. "Accounting Firm X's young storm troopers complete their annual audit of *Fortune* 500 Company Y, and one of them determines that Company Y's internal accountants have been booking something incorrectly during the year. Nothing that's going to start a major SEC investigation if it's uncovered, mind you. Just something that doesn't quite conform to generally accepted accounting principles. The young person at Accounting Firm X who finds the —" Jackie paused. "— *inconsistency*, as we'll call it." She smiled grimly, as though recalling this from personal experience. "The young person who finds the inconsistency brings it to the attention of the accounting firm's lead partner, the individual who is ultimately responsible for approving the audit. The lead partner then meets privately with Company Y's CFO at corporate headquarters and explains the problem. Lets the CFO know that when the glossy annual report with the picture of the woman, the black guy, and the twelve Saxons is released to the public, the earnings per share figure isn't going to be quite as good as he told Wall Street it would be.

"This is bad news, Conner. *Very* bad because Company Y's stock price has been going up over the last few months in anticipation of a great year. The great year the CFO has been bragging about to Wall Street analysts for months during those 'off the record' conversations CFOs aren't supposed to have with the Street anymore. According to the lead partner, the downward revision of the earnings-per-share figure won't be big, just a minor adjustment. But the CFO knows that these days analysts and investors are looking for any excuse to pound a company's shares. Once one analyst puts out a 'sell' recommendation, they all jump on the bad news bandwagon and that'll be that. The stock price will tank. So he's got to do something fast."

Jackie gazed at an old black-and-white picture of her mother and father on the credenza beside the desk. "Here's the rub," she said quietly. "Here's how everything gets sideways. The CFO and the CEO of *Fortune* 500 Company Y have been granted tons of free stock options. Call options the twelve Saxons have been doling out for the past few years like Italian lire. A million here and a million there and nobody notices because the details of the option grants are buried in the back of a proxy statement you'd have to pop a whole box of Nō-Dōz to get through. And because the stock price has been reaching new highs over the last few months, those call options are way in the money. Worth gazillions. But the CFO knows that when the officially announced earnings-per-share figure is suddenly below forecast, the stock market will punish Company Y. Even if the EPS figure is off a little," Jackie said, holding her thumb and forefinger barely apart. "And when the stock price dives, so does the value of the CFO's options. Maybe to zero depending on the option strike prices. But the CFO is building a ten-million-dollar beach house in Boca Raton that he's planning to pay for by exercising the options. And the CEO is doing the same thing in West Palm. Except that his new pad is costing *thirty* million. Without the option money, both of them are out of luck and the construction on their dream homes will come to a grinding halt. They'll be facing personal bankruptcy and the Saxons will have no choice but to boot them out of the company. Because the perception in the market is that a corporate executive who can't run his own life profitably shouldn't be in charge of a multibillion-dollar company.

"Our CFO is in a sticky situation. His Boca beach house is on the line. So are his career and his reputation. His whole way of life, for crying out loud. His ability to keep up the ten-thousand-dollar monthly mortgage payment on his primary residence in Greenwich or Brentwood. His ability to keep his kids in the best private schools. His country club memberships. Everything he's worked so hard for is about to go up in flames. He's got to do something.

"He folds his arms across his chest and doesn't say anything for a while, staring the accountant straight in the eye after getting the bad news. When the guy can't take the heat anymore and finally looks away, our CFO starts talking. He tells the guy he's *very* disappointed. That his internal accountants swore to him that the way they were doing the numbers all year was technically correct. That they had actually been relying on information from the accounting firm. When the accountant mumbles something into his hundred-and-fifty-dollar silk tie about how they were wrong, our CFO tells him that the board of directors was thinking about switching accounting firms last year. But that he personally recommended to the board to stay with this firm because of the solid personal relationship they had developed.

"Now it's the lead partner's turn to sweat. Accounting firms make tens of millions of dollars off just *one Fortune* 500 audit, and Company Y is by far this partner's biggest grossing client. If Company Y switches its audit to another accounting firm, his personal compensation will drop like an airliner with engine failure and suddenly he won't be able to make *his* monthly mortgage payment. Now both men have a problem. When the EPS figure is released, the CFO will be out of a job. And with the CFO out of a job, the lead partner won't have his internal advocate at Company Y, and the accounting engagement will go to another firm.

"A shiver runs up our lead partner's spine. He thinks back to college and how his ethics professor warned him that sooner or later this day would come. The moment of truth. His life is flashing before his eyes, and he's sweating like he's running a marathon in the Sahara because now we're edging toward criminal issues. He tells the CFO that he'll think about things for a few days and get back to him. That's code for, 'I'll look the other way this time, but don't put me in this situation again.' Problem is, now the accountant has complied with something that doesn't conform to generally accepted accounting principles — and the CFO knows it. The chink in the armor is tiny, but that's enough these days.

"They shake hands and the lead partner leaves, bouncing off walls on his way out of Company Y's headquarters. Wondering all the way home how in the hell he got sucked into the fraud vortex so quickly.

"The CFO pats himself on the back, chuckling as he watches the accountant stumble away. He's played it perfectly, he thinks to himself as he sits back down at his desk. He calls the builder down in Boca and tells the guy to get started on that wine cellar the wife wants. He'd been holding off on that extra because it's going to cost another hundred grand and, somehow, it didn't feel right. But now he's confident about his personal financial situation again. The accounting firm has been corrupted. Life is beautiful."

Jackie put the wrist exerciser down. "Next year, there's a whole different issue with Company Y's books and once again a junior person on the audit raises the issue with the lead partner. The lead partner politely thanks the junior guy, then tells him to keep his goddamned mouth shut. The web is expanding. And, this year, the issue isn't up for interpretation. It *is* black-and-white this time, and it'll have a *huge* downward impact on Company Y's earnings-per-share figure if the books are revised. Fifteen to twenty percent negative. But the young guy doesn't say anything either, because he's got school loans he's still paying off, and his first child is on the way — all of which the lead partner knows. This past weekend, the junior guy realized it's going to take ten grand he doesn't have to set up the nursery the way his wife wants it. Now he's in the vortex, too.

"For a while, the junior guy doesn't sleep well. His wife asks him what's wrong, but, before he can answer, she puts his hand on her tummy because the baby is moving. He's totally screwed now, and he's thinking he's headed straight for Leavenworth without passing 'Go.' He's just waiting for the SEC to show up on his doorstep and lead him away in shackles like those poor bastards he's seen on the evening news.

"But Company Y's annual report comes out and nobody blinks an eye. The stock price keeps going up and nobody questions the numbers. Our junior guy starts doing better. He isn't up at three in the morning watching Nick at Nite reruns. He's in bed by eleven again, just like he used to be. Nestled beneath the covers next to his lovely wife who only has a month to go before she delivers. The nursery is even nicer than what she wanted thanks to the twenty-five-thousand-dollar 'special' bonus the lead partner surprised our young guy with.

"The only major change to our young guy's routine is that he's started to drink when he gets home. One or two glasses of red wine at first. Sometimes three. Suddenly, he's draining an entire bottle every night. Suddenly, he understands those three scotches his father guzzled."

Jackie glanced out the window at the

building across Thirty-third Street. "The lead partner never even bothers to raise the big issue with Company Y's CFO this year. He's been sucked way down into the vortex, and now he's just as guilty as the CFO. They're clearly defrauding the shareholders, but making a mint at it. The CFO has exercised truckloads of options at stratospheric prices, and he's loving his vacations to Boca. The house turned out great and the wine cellar is stocked with vintage bottles. The lead partner got a year-end bonus that's twice what it was last year — over half a million — from which he personally gave the junior guy the twenty-five-thousand-dollar cut.

"And why is that, you ask? Why was the lead partner's bonus so big this year? Because Company Y's CFO handed the lead partner a big Christmas present. He retained Accounting Firm X's consulting group to recommend strategic acquisitions, and he agreed to pay them five million dollars for a six-month engagement. The CFO has no intention of listening to mergers and acquisitions advice from Accounting Firm X's consulting group — he has New York investment bankers for that and no savvy CFO would ever listen to a bunch of accountants about merger and aquisition advice. But it sounds good. And it isn't as if the board is going to question him. The CFO roped *them* in, too. A few months ago, he proposed to the CEO that the Saxons and the two poster kids start getting options, too. The board took a vote on it, and what do you know? It's unanimous. They think it's a great idea. It's like Congress considering a raise for themselves. Think that vote would ever fail?

"The pattern is established. You scratch my back, I'll scratch yours. The CFO and the lead partner get even chummier. The wives become friends and the couples take vacations together at the Boca beach house."

Conner stopped scrawling notes for a moment. The e-mail was starting to make perfect sense. Rusty was the junior person and Victor was the lead partner. "You haven't painted a pretty picture of the accounting profession," he commented.

"Understand," Jackie replied, "I've described the exception, not the rule. But it happens. Enron and WorldCom are excellent examples. And I guarantee you there are more big companies out there with problems. Some will be exposed and some won't. But you better believe those problems usually involve complicity between the company and its outside auditors. I don't like throwing stones at my profession, but you asked me how it could happen. That's how."

"Why wouldn't accounting firms do something to address these problems?" Conner asked. "Like rotate lead partners? If that lead partner you described automatically had to transfer to another client every two years, the scenario would be less likely. Don't you think? He wouldn't want the next partner to discover what he'd been doing."

"Some firms do implement that kind of rotation. But what you have to appreciate is that it takes a great deal of time to fully understand a *Fortune* 500 Company. They're so huge. So many divisions, products, and locations. At the point a lead partner on an audit is just getting his hands around the company, and is best prepared to identify problems like fraud — if he's honest — he'd be moved on. If you believe your people are ethical, it's better to keep them in place. You can't assume your people are dishonest. That creates a terrible culture."

"What's the answer?"

"Accounting firms have to do their best

to hire ethical employees. Then have checks and balances that aren't overly invasive. Two lead partners on every client. An audit department within the accounting firm constantly doing internal spot checks on their people just like the IRS performs random audits on taxpayers. So that it's expected, not unusual."

"Which would add costs," Conner observed. "A great deal of overhead burden."

"Exactly. And that's the last thing a professional services firm wants. So if one firm doesn't do it, then the others can't either because they won't be able to compete on price. It's a very difficult problem," she acknowledged.

Conner held up one hand. "Okay, I understand your point on the big picture. But now I want specifics. How does that CFO who's building the vacation home in Boca actually manipulate the company's EPS number so he can keep paying the construction crew to build the wine cellar? Where's the sleight of hand?"

"The easiest thing to do in the short run is book fraudulent revenues," Jackie answered without hesitation. "Just claim you sold more products than you actually did. It sounds simple, but, executed the right way, it can be very effective."

"Explain," Conner said, beginning to take notes again.

"Let's use a one-product company for this discussion. It'll make things easier to explain. And to understand. Let's say we're talking about a T-shirt company. They have to buy machines to knit the T-shirts, and yarn to feed into the knitting machines. They have to pay people to service the machines, a sales department to sell the T-shirts, and they have overhead. Executives, a finance staff, human resources people, et cetera. Let's say they sell each shirt to the retail stores for a dollar, and, after all their costs, the company makes ten cents a shirt. If they sell thirty million shirts a year, their annual revenue is thirty million dollars, and their net income is three million. That three million is what's left over for shareholders after everything else is paid. As I'm sure you can appreciate, there's a lot of hard work and risk involved in making that three million dollars, too."

Conner shrugged. "Yeah, so?"

"If the T-shirt company's CFO wants to turn three million dollars of net income into six million real quick, to double it, the easiest way is just report that the company sold another three million shirts. That would add another three million dollars to the bottom line at a dollar a shirt because there haven't been any costs associated with those fraudulent revenues. It's pure profit at a dollar a shirt. The CFO would be more than happy to open the books and dare anybody to find those additional expenses, because he knows nobody could. They really aren't there, because they weren't incurred. The only thing the CFO would have to worry about is that someone finds out that the revenues aren't real. That those extra three million shirts weren't really shipped to stores."

"Exactly," Conner agreed. "Which is a big risk."

"Not as big as you might think," Jackie cautioned. "Not in the short term anyway."

"Why not?"

"How can anybody figure out how many T-shirts the company actually sold?" Jackie asked.

Conner considered the question. "You could contact the retail stores and get a person in the purchasing department there to confirm how many shirts they bought from you that year. Retailers have to keep track of that information."

"They do, but they aren't going to go out of their way to volunteer it to anyone.

And the retailer doesn't have any idea how many shirts the company sells to other accounts. So they aren't going to think anything's unusual if someone there picks up the company's annual report and sees thirty-three million dollars of revenue as opposed to thirty. The point is, you'd have to really be looking for the problem. And you'd have to be inside the company because the retailers aren't going to hand that sales data out to just anybody. That kind of information is closely guarded. The executives at the T-shirt company who are in on the scam certainly aren't going to tell anyone. And, if the accounting firm is in on the scam, they aren't going to tell anyone, either."

"But the cash won't be collected because the retailers have never been billed for those extra three million shirts," Conner protested. "That's the problem."

"True, but big companies don't report their financial statements on a cash basis. They book revenues when they ship the T-shirts, not when they get the cash. In a lot of industries, corporate customers may not pay invoices for sixty or ninety days. Sometimes even longer. So the CFO would record the extra three million dollars of revenue when he claimed his company shipped the T-shirts to the retailers, making the company's net income go up by three million, and doubling the earnings per share. When the CFO recorded the revenue on the income statement, he would also record a receivable on the balance sheet. An IOU from the retail store that he records on the T-shirt company's balance sheet to reflect the fact that the retailers supposedly owe the company another three million dollars. Just as he would do when real shipments occurred. And nobody suspects a thing."

"But those bad receivables will be on the balance sheet forever," Conner pointed out. "The T-shirt company will never collect the cash, because the CFO never actually sent a bill to the retailers. The retailers don't really owe the company anything."

"So what?" Jackie asked. "When the company prepares their financial statements for the public at year end, the receivable amount on the balance sheet is an aggregate number. There are plenty of real receivables in that line item. Only a few people have access to the details of the receivable ledger. Only they would know that some of the receivables are no good. *But they're all in on the scam.*"

Conner nodded, understanding now why Jackie had spent time explaining why complicity with the independent accountants was so important.

"Maybe next year the T-shirt company's sales really take off," Jackie continued. "The company sells *sixty* million shirts, so revenues would be sixty million dollars. But the CFO wants to make certain his fraud isn't uncovered, so he claims the company only sold fifty-seven million shirts. And he applies the extra three million dollars of cash that comes in from the three million T-shirts he says they didn't sell to that fake three-million-dollar receivable he booked last year. Again, nothing comes to light because only a few people know what happened. Everything's fine and they've all gotten stock options anyway, so why are they going to blow the whistle?"

Conner nodded. "The company records fake revenue on the income statement and fake receivables on the balance sheet and everything looks great. The books are inflated, but how would Joe Investor ever figure out that anything was wrong?"

"He never would," Jackie agreed. "Especially if it's a *Fortune* 500 company with multiple divisions and thousands of products."

"Right," Conner agreed.

"Maybe that's the dirty little secret our junior guy detected at Company Y," Jackie said. "Maybe he did a spot confirmation at one of Company Y's divisions and the receivables ledger didn't jibe with what the customers told him. In fact, it wasn't even close. But he and his wife needed that nursery and, besides, the lead partner promised him that the CFO would reverse those fraudulent entries over the next year as business improves. So our junior guy complies and Mr. Merlot becomes his best buddy.

"Now let's determine what effect the accounting magic has on the stock price," Jackie suggested. "Let's say Company Y's price-earnings multiple is pretty constant at around twenty times. So, if the earnings per share is one dollar, the share price should be about twenty dollars. But suddenly, net income doubles because they do the same thing the T-shirt company did. They book false revenues and rope the board and the accountants into the scam with financial incentives. So earnings per share doubles. Now it's two bucks a share and the share price quoted on the New York Stock Exchange quickly climbs to forty bucks because the world is accustomed to this company having a price earnings ratio of twenty times. Now *everybody's* building houses in Boca and West Palm. 'Live large' becomes the company motto. There's champagne and caviar at the board meetings, and private planes for the senior executives. The banks and the bond markets lend the company a ton more money to expand, because *they* believe every number and every word in the glossy annual report, too. How could they not? The so-called independent accountants have signed off on everything.

"The senior executives use the bank and bond money not only to expand but also to pay themselves exorbitant salaries and bonuses. To build an even bigger headquarters with all the latest high-tech gadgets, and maybe even give the worker bees a little extra cash. Everybody loves these guys, and Wall Street is throwing more money at them.

"Back to the CFO," Jackie said, switching gears. "He really had intended to reverse the fraudulent revenue entry over the next year because, down deep, it makes him nervous. But he can't. In fact, instead of reversing the entry, he's got to make another fraudulent revenue entry the following year because the recession has gotten worse. An even bigger fraudulent entry this time because earnings per share needs to go up again so the party can rock on. The CEO has given him the directive. He doesn't care what the CFO has to do, but the party has to keep going." Jackie shook her head. "But now it's too much. Almost all the receivables are bad and one day somebody starts sniffing something in the company's accounting department. Somebody who isn't in on the scam. Somebody who hasn't been given a ton of options and a big bonus. He notices that it's taking the company longer and longer to collect cash from customers. So, late one night he digs into the details of the receivable ledger when everybody else is out gulping down champagne. The next day, he makes a few calls to customers, finds out that the company never really shipped the goods. And suddenly, the party's over.

"Maria Bartiromo breaks the story on CNN a few mornings later and by that afternoon the banks and the bondholders are accelerating their loans because of multiple covenant defaults in the loan agreements and the indentures. They demand to be repaid immediately, but the company can't possibly repay all the loans and the notes at the same time. So the business seeks bankruptcy protection, and the executives are escorted single file out of the glittering new headquarters building in cuffs. The next thing you know, those same executives are up in front of Congress trying to explain their actions. One or two try, but the rest of them plead the Fifth because they see it's all happening just so the congressmen can look like hard-asses to their constituents. So the president can pound the lectern during his State of the Union Address and tell the nation how he's going to propose massive changes in the accounting profession and the cozy way things are done on Wall Street. The executives wait for their trials while the lawyers and the regulators sift through the ashes.

"The Saxons shrug their shoulders and slink off into the night, while the poster children on the board whine about how they thought something was up, but the Saxons wouldn't listen. Congress and the president end up proposing regulations my five-year-old niece could circumvent — which are never passed anyway — and our executives spend a year or two in a minimum security prison somewhere in Pennsylvania playing round-robin tennis tournaments." Jackie sat back in her chair. "And that's how it goes, Conner. The really sick thing is that when the executives get out of prison, they've still got millions of dollars in their bank accounts. Millions of dollars they've stolen from Joe and Jane Investor."

The office was silent for a few moments.

"What happened at WorldCom?" Conner finally asked, glancing at the picture of Jackie's parents.

"WorldCom happened because the accountants were *understating* expenses, as opposed to *overstating* revenues like I just described. They were recording expenses on the balance sheet that should have gone directly to the income statement. But it had the effect everybody wanted. It made the EPS number higher. *Billions* higher. You can understand why the stock price crashed when people found out that expenses were really billions and billions of dollars higher than what had been reported."

"Sure," Conner agreed, checking his shirt pocket to make certain the cargo was still there. "When we first sat down, you wanted to know why I was interested in all this," he reminded her, now trying to push gently on the door instead of pulling harder. "Why?"

Jackie looked up from her desk. "Companies in trouble sometimes turn for help to small financial firms that are struggling, too. They know that small financial firms trying to make a name for themselves might be willing to overlook certain irregularities just to get a deal done." She hesitated. "Be careful of the transactions Gavin Smith wants you to get involved in, Conner. I'm not accusing anyone of anything. Just be careful."

Conner nodded. Jackie's instincts were so good. Maybe he needed to take an audit of his own. "I will."

"Did you know that Gavin Smith was supposed to have used investigators when he was at Harper Manning?"

Conner looked up. "What do you mean?"

"He'd dig up nasty nuggets on potential clients to influence them. At least, that was the rumor."

Jackie wasn't a gossip, and her network was very reliable. Besides, if Gavin was willing to spy on people inside his own firm, he probably wouldn't hesitate to do the same thing to clients. "Tell me more."

"Let's say Gavin was competing with another investment bank for a big mergers and acquisitions assignment from a *Fortune* 500 company. The eight-figure kind that could earn him a personal million-dollar bonus by itself. He'd hire his people to go sniff around for nasty information about the company's senior executives, and use it to influence them to select him. The 'If you choose me, no one will ever know what I found' kind of thing. A lot of people are convinced that he was successful with his investment banking practice at Harper Manning because of that. A lot of people *say* they'll go to any length to do a deal. He actually did."

"What kind of information would his people dig up?"

Jackie shrugged. "Affairs, drugs, sketchy financial dealings. The standard stuff."

"How do you know?"

"I have friends, Conner. Lots of friends all over the Street. So I hear things. You know?"

"Why are you telling me this?"

"You need to watch out for yourself. If for nothing more than guilt by association."

"Who did Gavin use to get that information?"

"I heard it was some ex-FBI guys he was close to, but I'm not sure."

Conner took a deep breath. That sounded all too familiar. "One more question."

"Yes?"

"Does the name Delphi mean anything to you? As in the name of a company or a division of a company based in Washington."

Jackie's eyes narrowed. "Maybe."

After leaving Jackie's office, Conner walked fifteen blocks north to Manhattan's Diamond District, a concentration of jewelry stores located in the upper Forties between Fifth and Sixth Avenues.

He entered one of the stores and carefully removed a bundled-up tissue from his shirt pocket. Placing it on the glass counter in front of an elderly man dressed in a white shirt, black tie, and black pants. He peeled backed the thin paper. Inside was Liz's engagement ring. "I want to know what this is worth."

The elderly man leaned down and his long, curly earlocks fell about his face. He eyed the ring for a few moments, then removed his spectacles and picked up a jeweler's loupe, scrutinizing the huge stone under a bright bulb. "A thousand dollars," he finally announced, replacing the spectacles on his nose.

"*A thousand dollars?* You must be joking. That stone is three carats."

"Yes. Three carats of *sheet*."

Conner walked out of the jewelry store, diamond ring rewrapped inside the tissue and the tissue restowed in his shirt pocket. Art Meeks, the man who had appeared out of nowhere on Lexington Avenue yesterday, mentioned that Liz Shaw's fiancé had cut short a business trip to get back to the States. Confirming the existence of an engagement Conner had started to doubt. But the ring was paste. Worth just a thousand bucks. Why would a star investment banker at Morgan Sayers give Liz a three-carat diamond worth a thousand dollars? And how could that investigative firm Gavin used have missed the fact that she was engaged?

As Conner headed west on Forty-seventh, he caught a glimpse of a familiar head of blond hair shimmering in the afternoon sunlight. The woman was on the sidewalk across the street, moving quickly in the opposite direction.

He took off, slicing between two taxis and past a delivery truck to get to the other side of the street, craning his neck as he ran. He raced down the crowded sidewalk, dodging pedestrians. Almost bowling over a man in a suit, but catching him, steadying him, and then racing ahead again.

She was almost to Sixth Avenue, but he could still see her. Barely. Long blond hair not covered by a baseball cap this time. She was crossing the wide avenue in the middle of a group of people. It had to be the same woman.

Conner made it to the corner just as the light changed. Just as the blonde made it to the other side and red turned to green. But he sprinted across the intersection anyway. Cars skidded around him, but he made it safely to the other side. Only a few more feet.

As he came up behind the woman, she stopped and turned to face him.

"Hello, Conner," she said calmly.

It was Amy Richards. The woman who had stopped him outside the deli on Second Avenue two nights ago.

"Why are you in such a hurry?" she asked, smiling.

"I thought you were . . ." Conner's voice trailed off.

"Thought I was . . . someone else?"

Conner took a couple of deep breaths. "No, no."

Amy's expression hardened. "You couldn't have thought I was Mandy Stone."

"What?"

"We don't even have the same color hair."

"Mandy Stone? Why would I think you were Mandy Stone?"

Amy shook her head. "I'm sorry about the other night, Conner," she murmured. "I was such a bitch."

"Don't worry about it."

"I had a bad day, but that's no excuse. I hope you can forgive me. But I wouldn't blame you if you never called me."

"I told you I would."

Amy leaned forward and kissed him on the cheek. "I'd really like that." She glanced at her watch and sighed. "I wish I could stick around, but I'm late to meet a friend. Bye."

Conner watched Amy walk away, still breathing hard. Then his cell phone rang and he pulled it out of his pocket, checking the number on the LCD. "Hello, Gavin."

"Hello, pal."

"What's up?"

"Great news."

"Really? What?"

"The presentation we made to Pharmaco this morning must have gone over pretty well. The CEO just called to let me know that Phenix Capital has a new client. Congratulations, pal. You're gonna be rich."

CHAPTER 9

During the last twenty-four hours, Washington, D.C., had enjoyed clear skies and unseasonably dry air. Heat and humidity were more typical for the nation's capital in late August, but a cold front that had blown through the East yesterday had been replaced by an autumnlike high.

Lucas didn't notice the weather as he walked down Wisconsin Avenue toward the center of Georgetown. He was thinking about how it would have been nice to spend tomorrow — Saturday — camped on the grass in the shadow of the Washington Monument, studying the copy of John Watson's *Secrets of Modern Chess Strategy* his uncle had sent him last Christmas. Or poring through baseball statistics in *USA Today* as the pennant races heated up. But there wasn't time. He had to push forward with his research on the jewels.

In all, there were forty-three potential smoking guns. Five individuals who had held from five to fifteen corporate board positions before becoming high-ranking officials in the administration. Just one rung below the president on a very important ladder. Five people who could destroy the president as he pressed his agenda of boardroom and Wall Street reforms during the last ninety days of what had turned into a dogfight of a campaign against a pit bull challenger. It was three months to the election and the president trailed the pit bull by five points in the polls. Two weeks ago it had been four.

The president had decided that his new agenda, aimed at slamming the rich and helping everyone else, would resonate with the masses during the stretch run to November. Grabbing headlines and airtime when he needed them. At the same time interrupting the momentum his opponent had gained over the summer by constantly banging a drum of criticism about the president's historically close ties to big business and Wall Street. If he played his cards right, the president believed, he could drown out his opponent's message with the headlines and the airtime and seize a healthy enough slug of the undecided vote to snatch victory from the jaws of defeat.

But pushing the reform agenda was a double-edged sword. The jewels — the vice president and the secretaries of treasury, state, defense, and energy — were all former corporate and investment banking senior executives. All men the president had known for years. Men the masses suspected had probably profited in some way at the expense of shareholders during their high-level corporate careers. But if someone could *prove* that any of the jewels had engaged in the same kind of appalling corporate governance behavior that had come to light at Enron, WorldCom, or Tyco, it would destroy the president's bid for a second term. At the very least making him seem blatantly hypocritical. At worst, guilty, too.

According to Franklin Bennett, party leaders were panic-stricken. Afraid that after the president announced his agenda the other side would unearth something terrible about one of the jewels.

That *couldn't* happen. Which was why Lucas had this assignment.

He hesitated in front of the gold-domed Riggs Bank building at the corner of Wisconsin Avenue and M Street, doing his best to blend in with the crowd waiting for the light. Blending in would be vitally important for the next three months. Not once during his twelve years in the nation's capital had his name ever appeared in the *Washington Post*. If he could say that at Thanksgiving dinner back in Illinois, the operation would have been a success.

Crossing M Street, Lucas spotted Harry Kaplan, a speechwriter who worked in the West Wing and reported directly to the deputy chief of staff, Roscoe Burns. Kaplan stood beside a mailbox, looking lost and disheveled, as usual. His wavy gray hair a rat's nest. His bulky black spectacles sitting crookedly on his nose as he squinted at a piece of paper.

Their friendship had hatched more out of necessity than anything. Neither of them really liked anyone else in the West Wing. But they'd found that they had a mutual interest in chess, and that bond had cemented their relationship. Kaplan hadn't turned out to be much of a challenge for Lucas on the chessboard, but he provided an opportunity to test new strategies without being a pushover. Still, the record between them was thirty-six wins and seven losses in favor of Lucas, documented in fastidious detail in Lucas's marble notebook. It would have been forty-three to nothing if Lucas hadn't let Kaplan win those seven games — he didn't want Kaplan getting so discouraged, he refused to play. And the beauty of it was that Kaplan didn't even know what was going on.

For a moment Lucas thought about turning around. Being so close to the apartment, he didn't want to see anyone he knew. Then Kaplan spotted him.

"Hello," Kaplan called, his expression brightening as he limped past the mailbox and Lucas stepped up onto the curb. Kaplan had been the victim of a nasty automobile accident a few years ago. A head-on collision with a pickup truck that shattered his right leg. After three operations, there was still a pin in it. "How are you, Mr. Avery?"

"Fine, Harry. And you?"

"All right. Still working on that same speech."

"You mean the new one you can't tell me about?"

"Yep." Kaplan pushed his glasses higher on the bridge of his nose again. "Hey, I didn't see you today. Where were you?"

"Around."

"How about some chess tomorrow?" Kaplan suggested. "I've been working on this new opening against the computer."

An opening I probably mastered years ago, Lucas thought to himself. "Love to, but I've got friends coming in from out of town. Got to do the tourist thing."

Kaplan nodded compassionately. "I hear you. At least the weather's supposed to be nice."

"Right."

"Maybe next week then."

"Yeah . . . maybe."

"Hey, do you know where this place is?" Kaplan asked, holding up a crumpled piece of paper. "J. Paul's. I'm supposed to meet some people from Senator Lord's office there."

Lucas grabbed Kaplan's shoulder and spun him around. "It's up that way not too far," he said, pointing.

"You wanna come?"

"Thanks, but I *really* have to get going."

"Why?" Kaplan asked. "What's up?"

He had to be so careful about everything for the next ninety days, Lucas suddenly realized. Even the tone of his voice. "I need to get ready for my friends. They're flying in tonight."

"What are you doing in Georgetown? I thought you lived over by the Capitol."

"Ah, picking up a present for one of them. It was her birthday last month, and I didn't send her anything." Lucas nodded up the street. "You better get going, Harry. You're late." Safe bet to say that — Kaplan was always late.

Kaplan glanced at his watch. "Oh, God, you're right. See you."

Lucas watched Kaplan limp away. Harry was a tremendous speechwriter, but ordinary in every other way. And extremely gullible.

When Kaplan was gone, Lucas continued on M past Nathan's restaurant and down the hill toward the Potomac River. Until he reached a plain-looking, four-story redbrick building on the left. The building's basement apartment would serve as the operation's headquarters for the next three months. It was close to the West Wing, but not within its walls. Which was vitally important. If word of the operation ever leaked out, the West Wing would be able to distance itself from him.

Lucas was under no illusions. If that happened, there would be no prospect of a further political career. Perhaps of *any* career. Bennett had warned him that this thing was risky. If Lucas discovered something nasty about one of the jewels, said nothing, and the fact that he had covered it up was revealed later, he might become the central figure in the biggest political scandal since Watergate. But he'd made his choice. This was his chance to be somebody.

The apartment was comfortably furnished and equipped with a secure phone, a wide-screen television, and a personal computer linked to the Internet by a T-1 line. It had no windows. By design, the only access was a lone door constructed of reinforced steel and equipped with two code locks. Not only would the apartment serve as the operation's headquarters until November, but it would also be his home. He wasn't to go back to his apartment until this was over.

Lucas removed his coat and tie and slung them over a chair in the living room. Then moved quickly to the bedroom and retrieved a computer disk from a wall safe; he'd been instructed not to store anything on the computer's hard drive. When he returned to the living room, he sat down at the desk beside the television and flipped on the computer. No more suits and ties for a while, he thought, glancing over at his jacket lying on the chair. Just jeans and casual shirts. He wouldn't see the inside of the White House again until after the election.

If he needed to communicate with the West Wing, he was to leave a playing card — an eight or ten of diamonds on even-numbered days, a three or five of spades on odd ones — inside a blank envelope in a mail box at an Office Express location on the eastern edge of Georgetown. Someone at home also had a key to that Office Express mailbox, and would check it once a day late in the afternoon. The following morning someone would meet him on the Washington Mall, near the Vietnam Memorial. He was to leave a card in the box only if a meeting was *absolutely* necessary.

While the computer warmed up, Lucas moved to his jacket. From an inside pocket he removed the photograph of Brenda that had been taped to his desk drawer at the West Wing. He gazed at her face for a few moments, then turned the photograph over and scanned the faded blue, looping script on the back. "I'm so glad we found each other, Lucas," the inscription read. "This is real."

Two weeks after giving him the photograph, she'd dropped him cold. Never bothering to give him an explanation. They'd never made love, because she told him she wanted to save herself for marriage. And he hadn't pushed because he respected her. He'd found out several years later that a few days after leaving him, she'd spent the night with a Northwestern University football player.

Lucas placed the photograph in one of the desk drawers — careful to put it back inside its cellophane bag, then inside a manila folder — then sat down and began tapping on the computer keyboard. Bringing up a file from the disk. The disk contained reams of information on the jewels. Information he'd compiled over the last week in anticipation of today's "going live" order.

The first file was a biography of Bill Parker, vice president of the United States. Head of a huge private foundation prior to the election, Parker was a former chairman and CEO of one of the country's largest car companies, as well as an ex-director of IBM and five other publicly held companies. Parker and the president had met thirty years ago playing golf at Pine Valley, an exclusive country club in southern New Jersey where business was never supposed to be discussed. In truth, more deals had probably been struck in Pine Valley's clubhouse than in any Wall Street conference room. Both the president and vice president were hard-core golfers despite their twenty-something handicaps, and they still played together as much as possible. These days at the Congressional Club west of Washington.

The next file covered Alan Bryson, secretary of treasury. A former managing partner of the investment bank Morgan Sayers, he had served on the board of IBM with Vice President Parker and the current secretary of state, Sheldon Gray. Bryson had also served on the boards of six other publicly traded companies. He had prepped with the president and the current secretary of energy, Milton Brand, at Exeter, and they had all stayed close through the years. When the president won the election, his first call had been to Alan Bryson.

Lucas smirked as he scanned the third biography, a profile of Sheldon Gray, secretary of state. A tough talker, his penchant for intimidation rivaled Franklin Bennett's. In fact, Bennett and Sheldon Gray were close friends. Though it was kept very quiet, the Bennetts and the Grays frequently jetted to the Grays' compound on Bermuda for long weekends. Gray had been CEO of one of the country's largest data processing companies, Enterprise Information Systems, and a member of seven other corporate boards, including Microsoft and Morgan Sayers, Alan Bryson's investment bank.

Fourth was Walter Deagan, secretary of

defense. Prior to his appointment by the president, he had run one of the nation's largest defense contractors. He'd also been a member of fourteen other boards in the decade before coming to the Pentagon, including Bill Parker's automobile manufacturer and Sheldon Gray's Enterprise Information Systems. Deagan had been on enough boards to make a good living on that income alone. And to be harshly criticized by shareholder rights groups who believed he couldn't possibly add value to one particular company when he was associated with so many. Walter Deagan and Franklin Bennett had also known each other for years. Ever since basic training at Parris Island.

The fifth and final jewel was Milton Brand, secretary of energy. Prior to the election, Brand had been CEO of a California utility with interests in electric power generation and distribution, natural gas pipelines, and commodities trading in one of the company's unregulated subsidiaries. In addition to running the utility, he had served on four other public company boards. Of all the jewels, Brand was the only one who had encountered significant legal troubles during his business career. The commodities unit of the utility had been accused of questionable trading activities. And there was circumstantial evidence that Brand had known about and encouraged the shady practices. But nothing had ever been proved and his old friend, the president of the United States, had called him to Washington to help stabilize an aging national power grid. He and Walter Deagan had known each other since childhood, growing up on the same street in Santa Monica.

Lucas rested his chin on his hand and reviewed each of the biographies once more. Bill Parker, Alan Bryson, Sheldon Gray, Walter Deagan, Milton Brand. "The Beltway Boys," as they'd been labeled early on by the Washington press corps. The incest running through the five files was amazing — and fascinating. They'd known each other, and the president, for years. They'd been powerful forces in corporate America and on Wall Street. Then, four years ago, after conquering the business world, they'd ridden into town like a gang from the Old West to see what they could rustle up in the political arena.

The president-elect had been roundly criticized on Sunday morning talk shows and by members of the other party after appointing the jewels. Reporters had painstakingly documented the incest. There had been loud predictions of insider deals and pork barrel parties for an expanding circle of Beltway Boy cronies. But, so far, nothing had been proved. The economy was staggering and unemployment had reached 6.5 percent, leaving the president vulnerable as the election approached. But nothing untoward had come to the surface.

In all, the jewels had held forty-three board seats before coming to Washington. Forty-three potential smoking guns the president, the party, Franklin Bennett, and Lucas needed to be worried about as November approached.

If there was a bad apple in the bunch, it was probably Milton Brand, Lucas thought to himself. Clearly the guy had been briefed about what was going on in the trading unit of the utility. *Once a thief always a thief,* as Lucas's grandfather often said. But then there was Sheldon Gray. He was the kind of prick who wouldn't have thought twice about screwing shareholders to line his own pockets. He had that arrogant air of entitlement about him. A big *E* tatooed on his forehead. Of course, Alan Bryson had run one of the most prominent investment banking firms on Wall Street. He would have known about every major deal going on in the world *before* it was announced to the public. Talk about temptation.

Which was what made this so difficult. It could be any of them, more than one of them, or none of them.

The doorbell rang and Lucas glanced at his watch. Right on time. "Who is it?" he asked into the intercom beside the door.

"Roger Maris."

"How many home runs did you hit the season you broke the record?"

"Seventy-one," came the response from outside. Giving Lucas the password he and Bennett had agreed on yesterday. The wrong answer as far as history went, but a number an impostor wouldn't guess.

Lucas pressed the button on the intercom panel and waited for the knock. Two raps, a beat, three more raps, another beat, and finally two more raps. The way the World Series and the league championships were played if they went the full seven games. Two games in one city, an off day, three games in the opposing team's city, another off day, then two more games in the original city. Lucas opened the heavy door.

The man on the other side wasn't what Lucas expected. He was an inch or two shy of six feet, red-haired, and pudgy. The extra pounds obvious beneath his loose, untucked rugby shirt. Lucas had been anticipating a physical specimen. One of those lean, hungry-wolf types who constantly swirled around the president.

"Come in."

The man breezed past Lucas and sat down on the couch, snatching the television remote off the coffee table and flipping on ESPN.

"Make yourself at home," Lucas muttered.

"Don't fall in love with baseball," the other man advised, ignoring Lucas's comment. "Or anything else, for that matter."

"What are you talking about?" Lucas demanded, sitting down in a chair beside the couch.

"I'm talking about Roger Maris and that two-three-two crap. Never show a pattern. People will pick up on that in a heartbeat, kid."

This guy didn't look that much older than him. Not old enough to be calling him *kid* anyway. "Look, I —"

"Where are you from?" the other man asked, racing through channels as *Sports Center* went to commercial. "The West Wing or State? Bennett works with people

190

from State, too. The Bureau and the Company, too, but I say you're from State."

"It doesn't matter where I'm from."

"Don't sweat it, kid. No need to be hush-hush. I'll forget ten times what you'll ever know about classified work. I may be in the private sector now, but I used to be where you are. I've already partnered on a couple of things with Bennett on the profit side, and let me tell you a little secret. He isn't as tough as he thinks he is." The other man's eyes flashed from the television to Lucas. "But he's still pretty damn tough." He chuckled as he landed on a *Cheers* rerun. "You ever see this one?" he asked, gesturing at the screen. "It's the one where the therapist hooks Cliffy up to an electric shock device with a remote clicker. I love it."

"Hey, I —"

"Call me Cheetah," the man interrupted. "That's what I go by. Nothing else, just Cheetah."

"I know, but I don't care if —"

"Which means I'm either fast as hell or a con man from Brooklyn," Cheetah interrupted again, smiling smugly.

"Listen to me," Lucas said forcefully. "Bennett gave me full authority to run this operation any way I want. I'm in total control of this thing, and right now I'm not seeing you in the picture."

"No need to threaten me, kid," Cheetah answered smoothly. "I'm —"

"Which is too bad for you." It was Lucas's turn to interrupt. "My budget for this operation is a million bucks. Two hundred fifty thousand of which I've reserved for you." Franklin Bennett had dictated to Lucas what the amount for Cheetah was to be, but Lucas wanted Cheetah to think he was the decision maker.

Cheetah clicked off the television and replaced the remote on the table. *Two hundred and fifty?*"

Lucas nodded, spotting the frayed cuffs of the other man's shirt. A spook's way of being inconspicuous, or a symptom of a paycheck-to-paycheck life? "Yeah. With the ability to give you more if it makes sense. So let's be damn clear on who's in charge here."

Cheetah nodded. "We're clear."

"Good." It was the first time in his life Lucas had ever been curt with someone he'd just met. The first time he'd ever really been confrontational. A moment he'd been dreading his entire life, and now he had no idea why. It felt great.

"Where's the money coming from?"

Cheetah wanted to know.

"For the next six months, you'll be an employee of Macarthur and Company."

Macarthur & Company was a large management consulting firm based in New York. Its CEO and sole owner, Sam Macarthur, was a staunch party loyalist. A man the president had considered bringing into his cabinet. However, the party had turned down that request because Macarthur was more valuable where he was. Able to fund "special projects" through his privately held company without any risk of a link to the West Wing. "Transparent financing" as Bennett had termed it. Macarthur was paying the rent on this apartment.

Cheetah whistled. "This must be some serious shit. I've never been paid by Macarthur before. Sam's one of the party big dogs, you know. Lots of money there." Cheetah grinned broadly. "Enough to pay me two hundred and fifty grand. That's all I care about."

A quarter of a million dollars, Lucas thought to himself disgustedly. For ninety days' work. And here he was earning $53,000 to take a lot more risk than Cheetah. If some reporter broke the story, Cheetah would slip into the palm tree shadows of a distant Pacific island with his money. Lucas, on the other hand, would face the Washington music: Congressional hearings and a criminal jury, probably doing time for obstruction. The party would try to minimize the sentence from behind the scenes, but there could be no assurances that they could help. Lucas had asked Bennett why the amount for Cheetah was so much, but Bennett wouldn't say.

"I'll only need you until early November," Lucas explained. "But, as I mentioned, you'll actually be paid out over six months. I don't want your W-2 matching up exactly with your engagement in case somebody starts nosing around." This was another of Bennett's directives.

Cheetah's eyes narrowed. "So what you're saying is that you really only need me through the election."

Lucas could see the wheels turning in the other man's head. "Let's talk about the operation," he suggested.

"Okay."

"We will be focused on five men," Lucas began. "The vice president and the secretaries of treasury, state, defense, and energy. From now on, we'll refer to them as the jewels. Got it?"

Cheetah smiled. "The Beltway Boys."

"No, the *jewels*."

"Yeah, sure."

"I'll be scrubbing their pasts looking for anything bad," Lucas continued. "Anything they might have done that could embarrass the president."

"White collar crime stuff."

"Exactly."

"Ah. Now it all makes sense."

"What does?"

"Why I'm involved."

"What do you mean?"

"One of my specialties is forensic accounting," Cheetah explained. "Among other things."

Now it made sense to Lucas, too. Cheetah wasn't muscle, he was brains. What Lucas and Bennett needed was right up Cheetah's alley.

"Why now?" Cheetah asked.

"What do you mean?"

"Why the intense focus on these guys —"

"The *jewels*," Lucas interrupted.

"Right, right. The *jewels*. Why the emphasis now?"

Lucas hesitated. He didn't want to give away too much, but Cheetah needed to know at least the basics. "In the next few weeks the president will announce a series of initiatives aimed at bringing much stricter regulation and oversight to corporate America and Wall Street. We need to make certain the jewels aren't carrying around any baggage themselves. Understand?"

"Of course. Because if they are, they undermine the president. So exactly what kind of reforms is the president going to announce? What's he gonna do to the blue bloods?"

"I can't tell you at this time."

"Because if you did, you'd have to kill me, right?" Cheetah snickered.

"Right," Lucas said, stone-faced. Truth was, Lucas didn't know what the specifics were. But he didn't want Cheetah knowing that.

"Lighten up with the spook talk, Lucas. I can play nice for two hundred fifty grand." Cheetah raised both eyebrows. "Bennett must have a lot of confidence in you."

"He does."

"I can see why," Cheetah said quietly.

Lucas blinked several times, taken off guard by the compliment. He was beginning to like the other man. He had a competent air about him, and he wasn't saying *kid* anymore. Plus he seemed to know his baseball, so he couldn't be all bad. Of course, he was probably a Yankee fan, and

Lucas hated Yankee fans. It was so easy to be one. Not gut-wrenching, like cheering for the Cubs.

"What's so funny?" Lucas wanted to know, checking the television. Cheetah was chuckling to himself, but the music video didn't seem funny.

"It just kills me," Cheetah said, his expression slowly turning serious.

"What does?"

"That you and Bennett have to go through this. Worse, that you're justified doing so."

"What do you mean?"

"Look, these cabinet guys go through extensive screening before they become secretary of treasury or state or whatever it is the president asks them to be. Including a lie detector test near the end of the process that would intimidate anyone. Lots of scary looking guys standing around in a dim room and a single bare bulb hanging from a cord. It's called 'Come to Jesus Hour,' and it's right out of Hollywood. But it works, and I know it works because I've administered those tests. Another of my specialties," Cheetah added. "As the interrogator, you're allowed to ask anything you want, no matter who the subject is. No holds barred. And the subject can't have a representative present. He's on his own. It's the price of admission to the big time."

"Like what?" Lucas asked, fascinated. "What do you ask?"

"Have you ever bounced a personal or company check? Ever forged an expense reimbursement? Ever traded securities based on what you suspected might have been inside information? Ever covered up materially damaging information as a board member or senior executive in exchange for any kind of consideration? Ever had a homosexual experience? Has your wife or husband ever had a homosexual experience that you know of? Have you ever had an affair? Has your wife or husband ever had an affair with your knowledge or approval? Have you ever even considered raping a woman?"

"Jesus," Lucas murmured.

"Yeah, it's pretty extreme. Mental X Games for business bigwigs. I've seen some high-profile people reduced to tears in those rooms. People whose names you'd recognize. Pillars of the community who walked into that room full of confidence, and crawled out pleading with us not to tell anyone what we found out."

"So why are you laughing?"

"Wouldn't you think the president could

trust people who'd made it through all that?"

Lucas had heard about "Come to Jesus Hour" before from people on the Hill, though not in the detail Cheetah had just provided. But that thought had never occurred to him. "Yes," he replied hesitantly. "I suppose." He anticipated the other man's next point. "Of course, if that's true, why should Bennett go through this? Why should he need to set up this operation?"

"Exactly."

"What's the answer?" Lucas asked hesitantly, torn between his curiosity and not wanting Cheetah to realize how much he didn't know.

Cheetah shrugged. "The answer is that there are some pretty crafty critters out there. People with ice water in their veins who want to be secretary of something so bad they can lie their way through it, and even the most sensitive polygraph machines won't pick it up."

"How do they do it?" Lucas asked.

"For that hour, they make themselves believe their own lies. They pop two aspirin, wash 'em down with a Coke and they can tell you anything with a straight face and a steady heart rate. It's amazing. Something we try to teach our counterintelligence types at the FBI and Langley. It's the thing the president has to worry about most right now. That his closest friends and business associates, the men he's asked to help him run the highest levels of government, are serial liars."

CHAPTER 10

The interior of Gavin Smith's sprawling Upper East Side apartment was a carbon copy of his Long Island mansion — huge rooms, tasteful furniture, expensive decor. And it was twice as big as the *house* Conner had grown up in.

Conner slipped the key Gavin had given him back into his pocket and closed the apartment door. It was eight thirty. Gavin had promised to be here no later than eight, but you never knew with Gavin. He was a "best offer" guy who often accepted what he thought was a better invitation at the last minute.

"Gavin."

No answer.

"Gavin!"

Still no answer.

Conner headed for the kitchen, humming "Don't Be Cruel," his favorite Elvis tune. Humming helped him process information, like all that had happened in the last forty-eight hours.

The intruder saying Liz was *just* a pawn.

And claiming that he was a federal agent. Truth — or lies designed to throw someone off track?

Amy Richards showing up out of nowhere twice in the last forty-eight hours, maybe three times if that had been her outside Merrill Lynch yesterday. Once might have been coincidence — not twice.

Gavin using investigators to follow Liz, and him. And not identifying Liz as being engaged.

Liz leaving Merrill Lynch two weeks ago under circumstances Ted Davenport wouldn't discuss.

And no Ginger at all. At least not at Merrill.

But, unlike Todd, Conner was sure Ginger existed. Somewhere, anyway. He'd talked to her on the phone when she called the apartment looking for Liz. Briefly, but he'd heard the voice.

Conner pulled a Heineken from the refrigerator, then rummaged through several drawers, searching for a bottle opener. Stopping short as he was about to close the third drawer. A stack of open envelopes inside had caught his eye.

He put the beer down and removed the stack, placing it on the counter beside the bottle. Bills. He glanced over his shoulder at the kitchen doorway, then picked up the top one and pulled out the folded paper from inside. It was a monthly mortgage statement covering a property in Miami. "How many places do you own?" Conner muttered to himself. Gavin had never mentioned a Florida residence.

Conner spotted the amount. Over ten grand. Must be a big place, he thought to himself, checking the address at the top of the page. He was about to slide the invoice back into the envelope when he noticed that the amount due covered the last four months. So, that was why the amount was so large. Gavin was behind on the loan.

Conner picked up the next envelope. This bill covered the monthly lease on Phenix's computer equipment, and, once again, Gavin was delinquent. According to the information on the invoice, the bill hadn't been paid in five months.

It was the same with the rest of the envelopes — past due monthly invoices. In total, over fifty thousand dollars' worth.

When Conner had been through all of them, he replaced the stack carefully in the drawer, making certain the mortgage invoice for the place in Miami was on top.

He was about to close the drawer, just as a woman wearing nothing but a pinstriped suit jacket breezed into the kitchen. She was brushing at something on the lapel and didn't see him standing there.

"Hello."

Rebecca let out a shriek and backed up against a pantry door. As she did, the jacket fell open, giving Conner a quick glimpse. No wonder Paul Stone had been distracted lately. Conner shook his head as he thought about how he'd described Rebecca to Mandy as matronly. Maybe in some parallel universe where shimmering auburn hair and a body out of *Playboy* were things men didn't want.

"How are you, Rebecca?"

"Conner!"

He grinned. "You know, that jacket looks good on Paul. But it looks *great* on you. You should think about wearing it at the office. Just like that."

"What are you doing here?" she demanded angrily, pulling the jacket tightly together.

"Listening to the sounds of the jungle. Damn, you two could have sold tickets." Stone must have brought her back here because he felt it was safer than going to a hotel. Mandy wouldn't have been able to get past the doorman.

"Why didn't you tell us you were here?" she asked.

The apartment was so large, they hadn't heard him call Gavin's name. "What exactly did you want me to do? Stick my head in the door?"

"Oh, God." Rebecca put one hand over her face and looked down, her cheeks burning.

"I'm only kidding."

She looked up. "What?"

"I just walked in."

"Why you —"

"What's going on?" Stone snapped, appearing in the kitchen doorway. Shirttail hanging out of his pants, his feet bare.

"I was just telling Rebecca how much I liked this jacket-only look," Conner explained.

"Go back to the bedroom," Stone ordered quietly. "I'll get the wine."

"Quite a girl," Conner spoke up when she was gone. "I don't think I fully appreciated her until just —"

"What are you doing here?"

"In case you hadn't heard, Paul, we won the Pharmaco mandate this afternoon." Conner wasn't going to tell Stone he was staying at the apartment. That would spark more questions. "Typical Gavin. He wanted to get going on it right away. He told me to come over tonight so we could start mapping out strategy."

"Did I hear you say, *we* won the Pharmaco mandate?" Stone asked sarcastically. "What you meant to say was that *Gavin* won it. Don't kid yourself, Conner. You didn't have anything to do with that mandate."

Conner shrugged. "Whatever you say, Paul."

"Why are you poking around in here?" Stone asked, nodding at the open drawer.

"I was looking for a bottle opener."

Stone moved slowly toward Conner. "I understand you and my wife had quite a conversation in East Hampton the other night. About Rebecca mostly," he added, stopping a few feet away.

"Look, I told your wife —"

"In the future keep those nasty little comments to yourself. Or I'll sue your white-trash ass off for libel."

"Mandy started the conversation. She brought up Rebecca. Not me. I was just trying to help."

"Sure you were."

"I told her Rebecca wasn't very attractive."

"That's not my wife's story."

"Well, it's the truth."

Stone took another step toward Conner.

"Mandy showed up at Phenix today and introduced herself to Rebecca."

Conner grimaced. That couldn't have been pretty.

"You're probably happy about that."

"Why would I be happy?" Conner asked.

"Because you figured out what happened to the presentation I brought out to the old man's mansion Wednesday night, didn't you?"

"I sure as hell did," Conner snapped. "And I didn't appreciate it."

"Too damn bad."

"Why don't you get off my back, Paul?"

"Why don't you leave Phenix, Conner?"

Conner moved directly in front of Stone. "Not a chance."

"It won't matter anyway." Stone smirked, stepping back. "You'll screw up on your own at some point."

"And you'll do everything possible to make that happen, won't you?"

"Of course." Stone sneered. "Welcome to the big leagues."

"You might screw up first, Paul."

"Not a chance," Stone shot back confidently. "I've been in the business for fifteen years."

Conner hesitated. It was time to get into the other man's grill. "Maybe not under normal circumstances, but when people are under pressure, things slip. Little things at first, then big ones."

"What are you talking about?"

"I hear Mandy's father could make it pretty tough on you if he found out about you and Rebecca."

Stone glared at Conner, but said nothing.

"Now, if her father was to get a few anonymous tips on those extracurricular activities, I bet he'd —"

Stone lunged forward and swung, but Conner blocked the punch easily and tossed the other man to the floor. He reached down and grabbed Stone by the neck, yanking him roughly to his feet.

"Get off me," Stone gasped, trying desperately to pry Conner's hand from his throat.

"Listen to me and listen to me good, you prick," Conner seethed, jacking Stone against the wall. "I'm not a guy who rats on people. But you screw with my career one more time, and so help me, I'll do whatever it takes to get you out of my life."

"Let me go!"

"You understand me, Paul?"

"You stay away from my wife, you bastard!" Stone shouted. "You see her again, and I'll have both your knees broken."

"What the hell are you — ?"

"What's going on!" Gavin roared, rushing into the room.

Conner released his grip and backed off. He hadn't heard the old man enter the apartment.

"He's trying to kill me, Gavin!" Stone pointed a trembling finger at Conner. "You saw him just now. He's crazy. I told you there was something wrong with him."

"He swung at me first," Conner said calmly. "I was just making sure he didn't hurt himself."

Gavin glanced back and forth between them, finally focusing on Stone. "What's your problem, Paul?" he growled, furious.

The color drained from Stone's face. "What?"

"You've got to stop this," Gavin snapped. "It's getting ridiculous."

"Gavin, I —"

"Go in the living room, Paul," Gavin ordered, turning toward Conner as Stone walked away, shoulders slumped. "I'm sorry about all this, pal. I really am."

Conner watched Gavin's eyes flicker down to the open drawer. "It's all right.

Like you said, Paul's going through a tough time."

"That's no excuse for what just happened." Gavin shook his head. "Be back in a minute. Stay where you are."

Conner nodded, watching Gavin stalk out. That had been an important moment. The old man wasn't going to put up with Stone's pettiness any more. His cell phone rang as he was sliding the drawer shut. "Hello."

"Conner?"

"Yes?" CALLER ID UNAVAILABLE had flashed on the tiny screen.

"It's Jackie."

"Hey, Jo. What's up?"

"Remember asking me when you were here at the office today if the name Delphi meant anything?"

"Sure."

"Well, I did some research."

"And?"

"And I think I've got an answer."

"Fantastic." This was incredible news. He'd been counting on Gavin to come up with an answer to this question. But, so far, the old man hadn't found anything. "What's the deal?"

"Delphi was an ancient town in central Greece. It was built on a hill called Mount Parnassus."

"I'll have to take your word, Jo. Ancient history and I never got along too well."

"Which probably had a lot to do with some blonde sitting next to you in class," Jackie observed dryly. "But the point is, there's a Parnassus Road in Fairfax County, Virginia. Fairfax is just west of Washington, D.C. At 2000 Parnassus Road is the worldwide headquarters of Global Components Incorporated."

"Global Components," Conner repeated. "They're big, right?"

"Huge," Jackie confirmed. "Twenty-first on last year's *Fortune* 500. Sixty billion in revenue and four billion in net income. They make all kinds of component parts for everything from automobiles to oil rigs to airplanes. They've got plants all over the world."

It seemed to fit. A simple two-step code. Delphi to Parnassus Road, then Parnassus Road to Global Components. But he would have felt more confident if there had been something more.

"And," Jackie continued, "according to the company's annual report, they have operations in Birmingham, Dallas, and Seattle. Just like you told me Delphi does."

"What about Minneapolis?"

"No. No mention of Minneapolis in Global's annual report."

That was strange. Still, three of four were the same and maybe Minneapolis was too small to be mentioned in the annual. And it seemed unlikely another company based near Washington would have manufacturing operations in exactly those three same locations. Especially Birmingham. "Thanks, Jo." Now that he had a solid lead on Delphi's identity, there was another way to confirm her suggestion. He'd follow up on that as soon as they finished talking.

"And I didn't stop there," Jackie said.

"What else you got?"

"I also checked the annual report to see who the company's auditors were. I figured it would be one of the big firms, and I was right. Global's accounting firm is Baker Mahaffey."

"That's one of the *really* big firms." Conner remembered reading somewhere that Baker Mahaffey audited one of every three *Fortune* 500 companies. "Right?"

"Yes. I called a woman I know in Baker's Washington office to find out who the partner on the Global account is in case you want to talk to him. I wasn't sure exactly what you were looking for, so I didn't say anything specific. I didn't mention your name either."

"What's the partner's name?" Conner asked.

"Vic Hammond. He's been with Baker awhile. He's a big wheel in the D.C. office."

Conner caught his breath. Vic. Short for Victor. The name of the individual who was supposed to have received the e-mail that ended up on the apartment computer two nights ago. "That's great, Jo. You're the best." He didn't want to raise her antenna, but it would be critical for her to find out one more thing as quickly as possible. "Could you call your contact at Baker Mahaffey again and ask her if there's a junior guy on the Global audit account named Rusty?" There was dead air at the other end of the line. "Jo?"

"What's all this about?" she asked suspiciously.

"I can't say right now," Conner answered, lowering his voice. "I'll come to your office and fill you in, but I really need you to call that person back and find out about the junior guy. Can you do that for me, Jo?"

"I suppose."

"Can you do it for me tonight?"

"*What?*"

"Yeah, like right now."

"It's after eight on a Friday night," Jackie protested. "She's probably gone home."

"Then call her at home."

"Conner!"

"I need you to do this, Jo. I need the answer ASAP."

"Conner, I deserve more of an ex—"

"Just do it, Jo. Please." Conner heard Gavin's footsteps heading toward the kitchen. "Got to go." He slipped the phone into his pocket just as Gavin appeared in the doorway.

"Sorry again about all that," Gavin apologized. "I know I told you I'd be here at eight, but I got caught at a meeting downtown. If I'd been here on time, none of that would have happened."

Conner noticed Gavin's glance at the drawer containing the stack of bills. "Don't worry about it."

Their eyes met for a moment.

"Mandy showed up at the office this afternoon to get a look at Rebecca for herself," said Gavin. "As you suspected she might. I got to Mandy before she was at Rebecca's desk for too long. I took her to my office and had a long talk with her, and I think I got her calmed down. But it's going to be touch and go for a while."

Gavin had been calming Mandy down at the same time her husband was with another woman, Conner realized. Stone was such a slime bucket.

"Mandy wanted to talk to you," Gavin continued, "but you were over seeing Davenport."

"She wanted to talk to me?"

"She seems to like you for some reason."

Conner grinned. "She just doesn't know me very well."

"Yeah well, I can't have Paul distracted by divorce right now," Gavin muttered. The old man's expression brightened. "Hey, we've finally got ourselves an A-list client, pal. The world's going to be pretty impressed when it hears about us winning the Pharmaco mandate."

"*You* got the client," Conner pointed out. Stone was right about this. It had been Gavin's reputation that had made the difference. "You figure it'll be announced in Monday's newspaper?"

"No, no. I asked the CEO to keep the mandate quiet. If there's one thing I've learned in my years on Wall Street, it's that you do your best work when you fly below the radar. Once the deal is done, we'll let everybody know what our role was."

Gavin was the consummate professional.

He wanted his name in the *Journal* so badly so he could let the financial community know he was back. Despite that, he was going to do what was best for his client. It was a good lesson. Keeping the ego in check, no matter how hard it is to do, pays dividends down the line.

Gavin rubbed his hands together. "We've got a lot of work to do, pal. First thing Monday morning I want you cranking on the Pharmaco valuation. I've asked the CEO to get his assistants to send over all the internal numbers by messenger. We need to figure out very quickly if the European bid is fair." He winked. "I have a feeling it isn't."

"I won't be in the office Monday," Conner spoke up quickly. He was going to Washington. He was certain the answer to what had happened to Liz somehow involved Global Components and their accounting firm, Baker Mahaffey. Conner saw the old man's temperature flare. "I'll be ready to go first thing Tuesday morning," he promised. "And I can do a lot of prep work this weekend."

"Pal, I need you to be in Monday morning. As soon as the numbers get to our offices, I —"

"I can't, Gavin."

"Can't? Why not? What in God's name could be more important than this mandate?"

"Personal business."

"Personal business?"

Conner stared back at Gavin, not flinching. "Yes." Despite the deal they had struck yesterday at Helen's grave, he would say no more. Not yet.

Lucas relaxed onto the couch of the Georgetown apartment and flipped on the television. Cheetah had left an hour ago, and Lucas had used the time to continue researching the five jewels. It was going to be tough going. Forty-three possibilities and so much information to cull.

He glanced at his watch. 9:04. The network anchor was just handing off coverage to a White House reporter. Moments later, the president of the United States appeared behind his desk in the Oval Office, flags on either side.

Lucas smiled as the president looked directly into the camera. The man looked the part with that straight silver hair, strong jaw, and reassuring smile. And he had that NPR voice laced with the hint of a southern drawl.

The president was originally from Massachusetts, but party leaders had determined that a southern drawl would hold more national appeal than the New England hard *a* accent. So they'd arranged for him to hone it for a few years prior to the election. Lucas had seen tapes of the man speaking twenty years ago, and the difference between then and now was remarkable. But that was America. All about packaging.

"Good evening, my fellow Americans," the president began. "I speak to you tonight from the Oval Office on a matter of grave importance. Trust. A simple word but a vital concept that somehow seems to have been forgotten by corporate America and Wall Street. Forgotten by a financial system that has been one of our country's greatest assets. A system the entire world depends on every minute of every day. As it has ever since a few men began to trade securities beneath a small tree in lower Manhattan many years ago. On ground that is now the New York Stock Exchange. A system that touches every man, woman, and child in our country through IRAs, 401Ks, savings accounts, insurance policies, and mutual funds. A system under fire but a system that *must* endure. A system I will not allow to be compromised by a few evil people.

"At its core, this great financial system of multiple capital markets depends on a fundamental trust in numbers. This may sound obvious, but it is so vitally important. We must be able to trust those who compile, audit, and analyze those numbers for us. The system depends on the public's ability to open a company's financial statements and believe that the data between the covers is absolutely accurate. It depends on the public's ability to believe that the figures presented on the pages are 'fair and accurate,' to borrow a phrase from my friends in the accounting world."

The president paused for a confident smile, conveying to millions on the other side of the lens that even with all the demands on his time, he understood the nuances of financial accounting. That they had chosen well in the last election, and would be wise to make the same choice again in November.

"Without that fair and accurate presentation of a company's income statement and balance sheet our system is no more dependable than that of a third-world country run by a dictator who could nationalize assets at any moment. Because without that accuracy, a strong company may turn weak overnight, and a man or woman's life savings may disappear in the blink of an eye. Which is an abomination. Something we simply cannot let occur ever again in our great country.

"I will keep my remarks brief tonight. At this time, I only want to assure you that in the coming days I will propose a series of regulatory reforms aimed at preventing the kind of irresponsible and unforgivable examples of corporate largesse we have all witnessed — or worse, been directly affected by — in recent times. Unforgivable actions committed by corporate executives and Wall Street investment bankers, with help from their accounting partners, that have been driven by unbridled greed.

"I will call this initiative Project Trust. A contract between you and me. A promise to clean up corporate America, Wall Street, and the accounting profession. I will be working directly with senior members of my administration, including Secretary of the Treasury Alan Bryson, who will personally direct Project Trust. Secretary Bryson is a man who came to Washington three and a half years ago with great experience in these matters. He is the man who ran Morgan Sayers, one of the largest and most respected investment banks in our great nation and the first major Wall Street house to shun the questionable practice of promoting price targets on the stocks of companies they do business with. Alan Bryson is a man of unquestioned integrity. Together, he and I will make certain that your retirement investments and stock portfolios will no longer be threatened by the vagaries of a few individuals acting purely out of self-interest.

"I will make my specific reform proposals associated with Project Trust clearer in the coming days in another speech, but have faith that I will not allow what has happened in the boardrooms and on the trading floors of our country to continue any longer. And that those few who have caused irreparable damage to so many, will pay a heavy price. Our country has been and will continue to be strong at home and abroad. Good night and God bless the United States of America."

A shiver ran up Lucas's spine as the network anchor reappeared on the screen. Not because the last sentence of the president's speech had affected him deeply. The reaction had come because the pressure on him had just been ratcheted up several terrifying notches. The president had thrown down the gauntlet in front of the entire nation, making Alan Bryson his finance czar in the war against corporate and Wall Street fraud. In the war against absurd salaries and bonuses, hidden loans, massive option grants, and out-and-out stealing. Suddenly the need for the operation he was running to succeed had just become infinitely more essential. The party was depending on him. An election lay in the balance.

"You okay?"

The young girl was looking down at the floor of the narrow hallway leading to the stage. Looking down at the four-inch red heels she was wobbling on. Partly because she wasn't accustomed to heels this high, and partly because she was more nervous and scared than she'd ever been in her life.

The woman reached out and lifted the young girl's trembling chin. "You okay?" she repeated.

The girl nodded hesitantly, her arms crossed over her barely covered breasts, her eyes fixed in a stare of resignation, as though she knew she had no choice. There were bills to pay and this was quickest and most lucrative way of satisfying those debts.

"It'll be all right," the woman murmured.

"Will it?" the girl whispered.

"Just don't look at their faces."

Then the girl was gone. Whisked away by a security guard to the edge of the stage. It was her time.

The woman heard a voice announcing that it was the girl's first time on stage, then a roar of approval.

"Bastards," she muttered, hurrying back to the dressing room. She hated seeing that petrified expression of a first-timer. Hated hearing that roar of approval from the animals. Hated knowing that the girl she had just spoken to had now headed down a path from which there was no return. Could she have stopped her? Maybe not, but she hadn't even tried.

For the first time in her life, the woman wanted out. Not because she was ashamed. For her, this had been the right choice because she was strong and able to disregard the terrible influences that were all around. But it was time to get out. Only a little while longer, she reminded herself, slamming the door of the dressing room behind her. Then she'd be able to leave this behind forever.

As long as the man she'd chosen to depend on came through. It was all in his hands now, and she hated having to rely on anyone but herself.

"Conner?"

"Yes?"

"It's me again."

Jackie seemed on edge this time. "What's the matter, Jo?"

"I reached my friend at Baker Mahaffey a few minutes ago."

"What did she say?"

"She said there *is* a young person named Rusty on the Global Components account."

Bingo. And a minute ago he'd talked to an Ameritrade broker on their twenty-four-hour help line. The broker had confirmed that Global Components' stock price had closed at sixty-two dollars a share Wednesday afternoon — just as the e-mail from Rusty had indicated. Conner had no doubt now that Global Components was Project Delphi's real identity.

"Thanks, Jo."

"Yeah, sure."

"One more thing."

There was a frustrated moan at the other end of the line. "What is it *now*, Conner?"

"I want to meet Monday in Washington with that lead partner from Baker Mahaffey."

"*What?*"

"You said his name was Victor Hammond. I want you to call right away and set up the meeting."

"You have some nerve."

"Please, Jo. You've got to do this for me."

"And you've got to tell me exactly what this is all about if you expect any more help from me, Conner," she said angrily. "Everything. I'm not dialing one more number until that happens, and I'm not promising anything either. If I don't like what I hear, I'm washing my hands of it."

"I'll tell you whatever you want to know."

"Okay, go right ahead."

"I can't now."

"Conner!"

"You have to believe me that this is not a good time. But that I will tell you everything."

"When?"

"Are you working this weekend?" he asked.

"I'll be here Sunday to finish up some tax work."

Conner smiled. Jackie was acting irritated so she could wedge herself into the loop. By nature, she was extremely curious. "I'll come by your office around four on

Sunday. But you've got to get me that meeting with Hammond."

There was a long pause.

"What is this meeting supposed to be about?" Jackie finally asked.

"Starting a relationship with Phenix Capital. Let Victor know that Gavin Smith is Phenix Capital's founder. He may not recognize the name of the firm, but he'll recognize Gavin. And tell Victor I have a transaction I want to show him. An opportunity for immediate income. He'll like that."

Another long pause. "All right."

"Thanks, Jo." He was about to end the call when she spoke up.

"Conner?"

"Yes?"

"Do you ever try crossword puzzles?"

"No."

"Start."

"Why?"

"It'll give you a new perspective."

CHAPTER 11

Lucas had always been dedicated to structure. He took five shirts to the cleaners every Saturday morning. On the first Monday of every month, he cleaned the keyboard of his computer and the touch pad of his telephone in his tiny West Wing office with a Q-tip dipped in rubbing alcohol. And every New Year's Day he went through his perfectly ordered closet and bureau and threw out any article of clothing he hadn't worn in the last twelve months. Structure gave Lucas comfort.

Just as risk gave him heartburn. He didn't try to be the center of attention in West Wing meetings. He didn't play the stock market. And he didn't enjoy games of chance involving dice and cards, because there were too many factors he couldn't control. Chess allowed him to plan far in advance without having to worry about luck playing a role. It allowed him to methodically put himself in position to win, while tempting his opponent to take chances born of impatience.

Patiently putting himself in the best position to win while letting others take risk. That was how Lucas had lived his life.

His father had been a dreamer. A small-time attorney who accepted cases based on how much they interested him, not on the potential payoff. As a result, the family had constantly teetered on the brink of bankruptcy. It was Lucas's mother who'd instilled in him the need for structure — and practicality. She detested living in a drafty split-level home on a quarter-acre lot. Which was why it had always surprised Lucas that she'd allowed him to choose politics as a career after scrimping and saving to put him through Northwestern. She'd made it clear early on that she wanted him to be wealthy, and most of the time you didn't get wealthy in politics. Not unless you made it to that club Lucas had heard whispers about.

From the office doorway Lucas watched the sixteen analysts as they sat quietly behind metal desks arranged in two neat rows. Poring through annual reports, proxy statements, and SEC documents covering the forty-three companies. Those critical forty-three companies the jewels had been involved with as board members and senior executives. The analysts were scouring the data for anything that was inconsistent with control guidelines Lucas had provided. Reading and rereading blizzards of reports and jotting down copious notes on legal pads when something caught their attention. Pausing only long enough for a sip of coffee or a bite of bagel, courtesy of the United States government.

The analysts were Georgetown University business school students earning twenty dollars an hour for as many hours as they could log. They thought they were working for a nonprofit shareholder rights group funded by an anonymous benefactor who was tired of watching corporate executives and board members use public companies as personal playgrounds. Lucas suppressed a smile as he leaned against the doorway, arms crossed over his thin chest. They would have been surprised to learn that the anonymous benefactor was actually Franklin Bennett, the president's chief of staff. With a little help from Sam Macarthur, of course. A man who currently sat on the boards of ten companies and had probably used one or two of them as his personal playground along the way.

Lucas had understood immediately that, by himself, he couldn't accomplish what Bennett wanted. Not in the compressed period of time Bennett had laid out. There was simply too much information. He needed help and quickly formulated his plan to use the Georgetown business students. They would be familiar with the documents that had to be scoured, but wouldn't ask too many questions. They'd buy the story about the anonymous benefactor because all they cared about was twenty bucks an hour.

Lucas was proud of how quickly Bennett had embraced the plan. Of how Bennett had praised him for the way it involved well-trained resources who would do as they were told without suspecting anything. Of how the plan minimized risk.

He grimaced. It minimized risk, but didn't remove it. If one of the analysts found something, then there would be a problem. He just prayed to God none of them ever knocked on the office door.

A familiar figure appeared at the front of the room and ambled confidently past the unoccupied receptionist desk.

"Good morning, Mr. Reed," Cheetah called, using the alias Lucas had given the analysts. Only two of the analysts even bothered to look up.

"Good morning." Cheetah seemed subdued. Not loose like he'd been yesterday afternoon at the apartment. "Come in." He stepped aside, allowing Cheetah to enter the office first, then dropped a towel down on the floor to cover the small crack at the bottom of the door. He didn't want the analysts overhearing what was said.

Cheetah nodded approvingly, easing into a chair in front of Lucas's rented metal desk. "Glad to see you're being careful."

"I'm always careful."

"Good. You *need* to be. It's pretty grim in here," Cheetah observed, checking out the office's gray, bare walls.

Lucas had set up the operation on the third floor of an inconspicuous five-story building in Rockville, Maryland, northwest of downtown Washington by fifteen miles. He'd rented the space and recruited the analysts a week ago, but hadn't brought them in until he'd received the "go live" order in the limousine yesterday. This was their first morning.

"What did you mean about needing to be so careful?" Lucas asked.

Cheetah picked up a copy of the *Washington Post* from Lucas's desk and held it up, pointing at the front-page picture of the president sitting behind his Oval Office desk. "Did you see that speech last night?"

"Of course."

"And?"

Lucas shrugged. "And what?"

"And the president is *really* going for it with Project Trust. I mean, he's going after everybody. Corporate execs. The Street. Accountants."

"Which is *exactly* what I told you he was going to do yesterday. Why are you surprised?"

Cheetah dropped the newspaper back on the desk. "You didn't make it clear how far he was going."

"He didn't say anything earth-shattering in the speech," Lucas said, frowning. "Just the standard crap. There were no specifics." Lucas had recognized Harry Kaplan's fingerprints all over the speech. It had probably taken him less than five minutes to draft it.

"I'm not talking about the speech," Cheetah said, his voice low. "I'm talking about what's going on behind the scenes. I spoke to a couple of my sources last night after the speech. People who matter in the party are very uncomfortable about this. They're getting the impression that the president is serious this time. So the pressure is squarely on those narrow shoulders of yours to keep this administration in the clear."

Lucas's eyes shot to Cheetah's. He hated

it when people said anything about his size. "Everything's under control," he said evenly. Pressure was an understatement. He'd gotten only a few hours' sleep last night.

"Don't try to fool me with the casual act," Cheetah said. "You're so damn nervous about the next ninety days, you probably can't hit the can when you piss."

"Why did you want to see me?" Lucas asked quickly, irritated because Cheetah was right. "What was so damn important that you had to see me right away?" Cheetah was going to New York City this morning. He'd called the apartment at the crack of dawn to see if he could stop by on his way to the train station.

"I wanted to see the operation," Cheetah explained, gesturing toward the door. "And see if anyone had found anything. Anything I need to check out?"

"No, they just got started. Besides, there won't be anything to check out. You'll earn your two hundred and fifty grand without lifting a finger."

"I hope so," Cheetah said. "Okay, then I'll keep checking out the five subjects through my —"

"The jewels," Lucas snapped. "The jewels."

"Right, the jewels."

"Is that really all you wanted? Just to see the operation. Is that why you came all the way out here to Rockville?"

Cheetah didn't answer for a few moments, then slowly shook his head. "No. There's something else."

Lucas had heard a different tone in Cheetah's voice. "What?"

"I found out that you're West Wing."

"Congratulations. I'm sure that was tough. So?"

"How much contact do you have with Franklin Bennett at home?" Cheetah asked.

"Not much," Lucas admitted.

"Did you know him before you came home?"

"No."

Cheetah hesitated.

Lucas sighed. "Look, I've got a lot of work —"

"I've been suspicious of Franklin Bennett for a long time." Cheetah glanced at the towel running along the bottom of the door. "I've got a bad feeling."

"What about?"

"This operation."

"Why?"

"I know a lot of people inside the party. Deep inside it."

"Yeah, and?"

"And there are those who question Bennett's motivation for setting up this thing."

"*You told people about this operation?* I ordered you not to discuss it with *anyone*."

"Easy, Lucas. Give me a little credit. The people I spoke to don't even realize what I told them. Or what they told me."

"Uh huh. So why do these people question Bennett's motivation?" Lucas's mind was racing through the possibilities. He'd been in politics for twelve years, but all that time had been spent in midlevel positions. Suddenly he was in the big leagues, and there were smiling assassins everywhere. "I don't understand."

"Maybe this operation is really just cover," Cheetah suggested mysteriously.

"Cover?"

Cheetah ran his hands through his red hair. "You have to understand how Franklin Bennett operates. Bennett spent twenty years in special forces before cycling out into a corporate career. The first six he was boots on the ground in hostile countries. The last fourteen he was involved with top secret projects. He's a master manipulator."

Lucas frowned. "His résumé doesn't indicate that. It just says he was a regular Marine."

"He wasn't a regular Marine, I assure you."

"How do you know?"

"I can also assure you he didn't say good-bye to the intelligence community after he entered the private sector," Cheetah continued, ignoring the question. "Just like he didn't say good-bye to the private sector when he became the president's chief of staff."

"What do you mean?"

"When he left the military, he took a post as a senior vice president for a communications equipment manufacturer named International Telephone and Wireless Corporation."

"I've heard of ITW. So?"

"In addition to manufacturing, ITW operates a services division responsible for all telecommunications wiring and installations at every important foreign embassy in Washington, D.C. And another division that does the same thing for embassies of countries deemed unfriendly to the west in Ottawa, London, Paris, Madrid, Bonn, and Tokyo. You'd never know it, because those two ITW divisions aren't identified in any corporate information or in any SEC reports."

"Why are you telling me this?"

"Like I said, you have to understand how Bennett thinks if you're going to be in business with him — and survive. He's always operating with several agendas. You can never be certain which one is real and which ones are decoys, simply providing cover for the primary mission."

"Are you saying that this operation might be cover for another agenda?" The words seemed to stick to Lucas's tongue.

"Maybe. Or maybe your operation involves the real agenda. It's just that the real agenda isn't what he's told you."

"Spell it out."

Cheetah leaned back and contemplated the ceiling. "If you're trying to get elected, what's the only platform you *never* run on?"

"Raising taxes," Lucas replied automatically. During his years in Washington Lucas had been involved in two campaigns. He knew the answer to that one cold.

"Right. And why?"

"Because people always vote with their wallets," Lucas answered. Like he was reading from a campaign textbook.

"Exactly. When it comes down to it, human beings care more about money than any social issue. Because they care

237

more about themselves than anyone else. It's human nature," Cheetah said matter-of-factly. "Everybody in this country, rich or poor, believes he or she ought to be paying less taxes."

"Agreed. But what does that have to do with me?"

Cheetah nodded at the newspaper lying on the desk. "The president launched the opening salvo of a very ambitious plan last night. Project Trust. My contacts tell me the president's planning things behind the scenes that will drastically change the lives of a lot of important and influential people. People who want the system to stay the way it is. Executives who like running billion-dollar companies any way they want, granting themselves stock options, bonuses, perks, and loans whenever they want to. Wall Streeters who would look at increased government regulation with about as much enthusiasm as they would a rectal exam. Accountants who've been able to pry their way into some pretty lucrative consulting work over the last decade and who are now going to be frozen out of it just as the getting is getting good. Ordered by the government to go back to the basement, put on the green eyeshades, and be satisfied making six figures, not seven."

Cheetah paused. "The president is going to radically change the corporate landscape. Gold mines are going to turn to salt mines. Easy street's going to turn into panhandle alley. He's going to take these people who consider getting paid five million bucks a year their birthright, and make it a challenge for them to earn a hundred grand. Which still sounds like a lot to you and me, but wouldn't support their lifestyles for more than a few weeks. *Now* do you understand what I'm saying?"

"You think the president of the United States has become an enemy of his own party?" Lucas said deliberately, his voice hollow.

"Exactly. I think the president is out there on his own as far as Project Trust goes. He doesn't have any behind-the-scenes support from the party leaders. In fact, I think they're against him. That's what my contacts claim. I saw Alan Bryson being interviewed on CNN this morning about last night's speech. About his role as the main man in the president's new initiative against all the corporate crap that's been going on. Bryson was saying all the right things, but he looked like a man who owed the Mafia a lot of money. He looked scared."

"Why would the president defy the party?"

"To get elected. He's figured out that Americans have had it up to their eyeballs with these corporate bigwigs raiding 401K plans to build castles, buy personal jets, and keep wives and girlfriends in mink stoles. Had it up to their eyeballs hearing about how investment bankers play with a marked deck and how accountants will bless any number you ask them to as long as you throw them a bunch of options. How the whole thing is nothing but an insider's game where the rich get richer. A game people like you and me don't have a snowball's chance in hell of playing.

"And the president wants another four years more than he wants his next breath," Cheetah continued. "He lives for the power and the glory, and he can't stand the thought of losing all that before his time. His ego is too fragile. He'll do anything to make the history books read that he had two terms.

"The problem with Project Trust is that it's the last thing party leaders really want. The money men, men like Sam Macarthur, will switch parties quicker than you can say 'campaign contributions' if they think Project Trust has any teeth. The money men don't want to see the system change. Which means party leaders don't want to see it change. Oh, sure, they talk a great game about implementing regulatory reforms to help the little guy, but they don't really mean it. Change for them isn't good because the fallout can be disastrous. Lots of opportunity for redistribution of wealth before things get back to normal. If things ever do."

Lucas cleared his throat nervously. "You're implying that Franklin Bennett isn't using me to *protect* the president. That, in fact, he's using me to *bring down* the president."

"That's not what I'm implying, Lucas. That's what I'm *saying*. And you may not be the only one he's using. He may have set up other cells that are also searching for information to use against the president under the guise of getting their hands on it first to subvert it."

"The president's chief of staff turning traitor," Lucas murmured, as though he were trying the sound of it out on himself.

"The *entire party* turning traitor," Cheetah said, gazing at Lucas intently. "At least from the president's perspective. From their own perspective, they're simply doing what's best for the party. And themselves."

"That's too much for me to accept."

"Why?"

"Entire political parties don't turn against their leader." Lucas realized how naive he sounded even before he finished speaking.

"Does the name John F. Kennedy mean anything to you?" Cheetah asked.

"Here we go," Lucas said, rolling his eyes. Trying to seem unconcerned — even though he was starting to think what Cheetah was saying might not be far-fetched. "Who do you believe really killed JFK? The Cubans, the CIA, the FBI, the mob, or the military establishment?" he asked cynically. "Or was it really Oliver Stone himself?"

"I have no idea who killed JFK," Cheetah answered, taking no obvious exception to Lucas's sarcasm. "You see, it doesn't matter *who* killed him. What matters is what happened after he died. The country recommitted to the Vietnam War just as it was about to pull out of Southeast Asia. Bobby Kennedy's war against the Mafia stalled, and then he was executed. Civil rights were no longer a high priority in the West Wing. Things got back to normal at home. A drastic step was taken because there was no other choice. But in this situation, there may be an alternative."

Lucas shook his head wearily. "Why are you telling me all this? Bennett's the one who put the two of us together and gave you the opportunity to earn a quarter of a million dollars in the next ninety days."

"Because of exactly that," Cheetah said firmly. "I've never had the opportunity to earn anywhere near this kind of money in such a short time. And I've never been paid by Sam Macarthur. It makes no sense to pay me this much to keep something *hidden*. But it does if they want to find it fast and use it. And they involve Macarthur only on very important projects."

Which hadn't been lost on Lucas either. He gathered himself in his chair, wishing what Cheetah was saying didn't sound plausible. "Why do you care? Even in the one-in-a-million chance that what you're saying turns out to be true, why not just earn your two hundred and fifty grand and say nothing?"

"Because you and I would be finished."

"What do you mean?"

"Let me lay out a scenario for you," Cheetah suggested. "Let's say you find out something nasty about Sheldon Gray, that son of a bitch at the State Department who has enemies all over Washington because he's such a cocky A-hole and he's screwed so many people on his way up. Let's say that while he was CEO of Enterprise Information Systems he defrauded the company of twenty million dollars, then dumped the money into numbered accounts in financial black holes like Antigua, Switzerland, and Liechtenstein. Gray was clever about hiding the money, but somehow you pick up his trail. Maybe because you know a man like me who has a network of informants trained to find things like that. Because you can't ever really hide your financial tracks. Not from people like me.

"You go running back to Franklin Bennett with the information I've uncovered about Gray, and Bennett cracks the first real smile you've ever seen. Says he's proud of you and now that he knows about it, he can protect Gray and, by extension, the president. Tells you to lie low and keep doing what you're doing. You feel pretty damn good about yourself because even though you've found out that Sheldon Gray is a thief, you've helped the party and you've kept your eye on the bigger picture. The president will stay in power. He'll win a second term because of what you've done, and that's the most important thing. Yeah, you feel good about yourself until you pick up the *Washington Post* one morning a couple of weeks before the election and read about the whole thing right there on the front page. 'Sheldon Gray defrauds EIS of millions' the article reads. You can't believe it. 'What the hell is going on?' you demand. 'How can this be?' The answer is, you and I have been set up. Bennett's real agenda has just come to the surface — like a geyser.

"Sheldon Gray resigns immediately and the president starts backpedaling. The initiative against corporate America and Wall Street is completely undermined. Project Trust becomes Project Bust. You can already see the headlines, can't you? Suddenly the president is as guilty as everybody else because his secretary of state, one of the highest ranking administration officials and a man who knows all our national secrets, is one of the worst offenders of all times when it comes to defrauding the financial system. A man who stole twenty million can't be trusted. The press implies that other senior members of the administration have skeletons, too. The initiative that was going to push the president over the top suddenly becomes the anchor that drags him down. He loses the election.

"Now there's hell to pay. Party leaders claim they're furious. They launch an investigation, and they," Cheetah paused, making quotation marks with his fingers, " 'uncover' a rogue operation within the party. A couple of people who are expendable: i.e., you and me. That's why I asked earlier if you were close to Bennett. If you were, I'd feel a lot better because at the end of the day, he is a loyal man. He wouldn't set up someone he was close to. Anyway, when they call you in for the interrogation, you swear Franklin Bennett was behind the whole thing. But they don't listen. And the most maddening thing about it is that they don't even come up with an explanation for why you would have done this on your own. Done it at all, in fact. Somebody in the background mumbles something about you being a mole for the other party, but they don't even bother setting up a false money trail leading to the other party. It isn't necessary. The damage is done. The objective has been achieved. The president is out on his ass, and now the party can turn off the reforms. All the drastic initiatives against Corporate America and Wall Street die on the vine, and things get back to normal.

"They aren't worried about you saying

anything either, because they know that nobody's going to listen. You're nothing but a pawn and pawns don't get headlines without proof. Which you won't have. The only thing you *will* have is a black mark that will follow you until the day you die. You won't even be able to hold a job flipping burgers at McDonald's for more than a couple of weeks before the night manager taps you on the shoulder and tells you that you've been fired for some absurd reason. They'll follow you forever, Lucas. They do it to people all the time. They get off on it. I know. I used to be one of them."

"But Bennett would be finished, too," Lucas protested. "What would he do?"

Cheetah's eyes narrowed. "He slips back into the private sector, probably working for Macarthur. Earning twenty times what he's making as the president's chief of staff. Or he retires on some beautiful estate all paid for by someone else. By one of the money men. The party takes care of him because he's in the club, but I'm a black sheep in the intelligence business forever because Bennett puts the word out on me. And you're finished, too. Believe me, Bennett can and would do it. Without a second thought. And, Lucas, the intelligence business is the only business I've ever known."

"So you're telling me all of this out of self-interest."

"Absolutely," Cheetah agreed, standing up. "I don't do anything in this world for any other reason."

Which didn't make Lucas feel any better.

"All I ask is that you consider what I've just laid out," Cheetah said. "I know you don't put much stock in it right now. You can't. You just heard it. But I've been around too long, and too many things triangulate to what I've just described." He pointed at Lucas. "The moment you sniff anything that smells remotely like this, you must let me know so we can take immediate steps to protect ourselves. Do you understand?"

Lucas didn't react. He was thinking about what a Wall Street career would have been like. Lots more money without anywhere near this kind of pressure. But Wall Street wouldn't hire him. They didn't want a runt. They wanted a Phi Beta Kappa quarterback captain like the one who had stolen Brenda. Lucas hadn't told his mother about all the Wall Street rejection letters he'd gotten senior year, but perhaps somehow she'd known. Perhaps that was why she'd allowed him to enter politics without any complaints. She'd realized there was nothing else.

He sighed. Maybe it was time to go for a long drive, or buy a one-way ticket on a westbound plane. And end up at Wrigley Field on a clear sunny day and maybe catch a foul ball.

Cheetah hesitated at the door. "Lucas?"

"Yeah?"

"Are you a homosexual?"

"*What?*"

Cheetah held his hands out. "What a man does in private is no business of mine. But we're in this operation together, and I need to understand how you could be manipulated."

"I'm not gay," Lucas said firmly.

Cheetah nodded. "Call me when you need me." And he was gone.

Lucas stared after him. Worried that what Cheetah had suggested about Franklin Bennett might be true. He'd met Cheetah only yesterday. He couldn't trust him at all. In fact, the whole thing could be nothing more than a loyalty test, set up by Bennett to see how Lucas would react. Lucas shook his head. But Cheetah had that air of credibility about him. As did the theory, he hated to admit.

Slowly Lucas allowed his head to sink to

the desk. He was so damn tired.

There was a soft knock on the office door. "Mr. Reed?"

His alias. "Yes?" Lucas asked, raising his head quickly off the desk. Berating himself for not remembering instantly that he'd given the analysts the false name. Even the slightest hesitation in responding to the name Reed could give him away. "Yes?" he repeated, gazing at the young woman in the doorway. "What is it?"

"I think I found something."

Lucas gazed at the young woman. And it was just the first morning.

It was a beautiful Saturday afternoon in New York. The sky over Central Park was a deep, cloudless blue and the air was warm but not humid.

"This is fun."

"Hey, every once in a while I get a good idea." Conner handed Amy Richards the diet Coke he'd just bought from the street vendor. "You sure you don't want anything else?"

She shook her head. "No, thanks."

Conner pointed toward a softball game. "Want to go over there and watch for a while?"

"Sure."

He glanced over at Amy as they walked side by side. Her long blond hair was down about her shoulders, and she wore a loose cotton shirt and jeans. "You look nice."

She smiled up at him. "Thanks."

He'd called her this morning while he was eating breakfast at a diner near Gavin's apartment. Her mother had answered the phone and wasn't very friendly. But Amy had been her old self when she picked up, and they'd agreed to a casual day in the park.

"I was so happy this morning when it was you," she murmured as they reached a fence running down the left field line. "I was sure you wouldn't call. Especially after the way I acted on the street the other night. God, that was terrible. I'm sorry." She hesitated. "I've missed you so much."

Conner leaned on the fence, feeling guilty. He'd called Amy so he could try to figure out why she'd appeared again so suddenly. Just as everything else was exploding. Convinced there was more to what was going on with her than met the eye. Now he felt terrible. After spending an hour together, he'd come to the conclusion that there was nothing suspicious going on at all. That their two encounters over the past few days really had been coincidental

— and that it hadn't been her in front of the Merrill Lynch building. She'd explained that she worked a ten-hour lunch and dinner double shift Thursday that hadn't ended until eleven o'clock. She'd gone into great detail about one particularly irritating customer who'd sent his meal back three times, then refused to pay. So it couldn't have been her in front of Merrill. Just his imagination playing tricks on him.

"Conner?"

"Mmm?"

"Were you sleeping with Mandy Stone while we were going out?"

Conner's eyes flashed to hers. "*What?* Why would you ask me something like that?"

"It was the way she was watching you at that party on Long Island. Like a hawk. She never took her eyes off you."

"You're exaggerating."

"Oh, no I'm not."

"Amy, I —"

She shook her head. "I'm sorry. I don't know what's wrong with me. Here we are having a nice time, and I ruin it with a stupid question like that."

They were quiet for a long time, just watching the game.

"I think I will come by and see you sometime," Conner finally spoke up. "What did you say the name of that restaurant where you work now is?" Just as she answered, the batter hit a long fly ball and the crowd roared. He wasn't certain he'd heard her correctly. "What did you say?"

"Mr. Ashby."

Conner turned to his left, startled. "Jesus." It was Art Meeks again. Conner shot a glance at Amy, who was watching the game, then back at the private investigator. "What do you want?" he asked quietly.

"I need to ask you a few more questions."

"Everything all right?" Amy was leaning over the fence, looking at Meeks.

"Everything's fine," Conner assured her. "I'll be right back."

"Who is he?"

"A friend," Conner called over his shoulder, guiding Meeks away. "This has got to stop," he said angrily when they were out of earshot.

"Calm down, Mr. Ashby. There's no need to be upset."

"I'm not upset."

"Could have fooled me."

"Just ask me the questions," Conner demanded. "And make it quick."

Meeks pulled out his notepad. "Have you heard from Miss Shaw since we last spoke?"

"No." Conner glanced back at Amy, who was keeping one eye on the game and the other on him. He signaled to her that it wouldn't be long.

"Who's that?" Meeks wanted to know.

"A friend."

"Your girlfriend?"

"No."

"Uh huh." Meeks checked his notes. "You live on Ninety-fifth, right?"

"Yeah."

"Between Second and Third?"

"Yes," Conner snapped. "Why?"

"A man was found dead over there the other day. In an alley beside your building. In fact, I believe your apartment overlooks that alley."

"People die all the time."

"Not after falling from a fire escape. Or being pushed," Meeks added.

Conner said nothing.

"Did you hear about that incident?"

"No."

Meeks hesitated. "You sure you don't know anything about Miss Shaw's whereabouts? She's been gone for three days now, and I'm no closer to figuring out where she is than I was last time we talked. Pretty soon I'm going to have to recommend to her parents that they go to the police. And I'll have to tell them that the last place I can trace Miss Shaw to is your apartment. Sorry, but that's all I've got. It won't look good for you. If there's anything you can add to what you've told me, it would be wise to tell me now."

The ring was three carats, but it was a piece of junk. He could tell Meeks that and maybe get him to focus on Todd as a suspect. The thought had occurred to Conner several times after finding out yesterday the diamond was of such poor quality. But the guy was supposed to have been traveling in Europe Wednesday night. He had an airtight alibi. "No. I've got nothing to add."

Meeks nodded. "Hey, it's your funeral, not mine."

Conner watched the private investigator walk away, heart pounding.

"Hey!"

Conner whipped around. Amy had sneaked up behind him and grabbed his shoulders.

"What's wrong with you?" she asked, laughing.

"What do you mean?"

"You look like you just saw a ghost."

He was about to answer when Amy spotted two golden retriever puppies rolling around on the grass a few yards away.

"I love puppies," she said, scampering toward them. As she did, her backpack fell to the ground and spilled open.

Conner's eyes raced to the contents, now spread out on the grass. Makeup, a camera, a small pack of tissues — and a dark blue baseball cap with a red insignia.

Lucas stared at the young analyst standing in the doorway. "I think I may have found something." Words he'd hoped he would never hear. Even more so after his conversation with Cheetah.

"Can I come in?" the young woman asked.

"Yes, of course." He motioned for her to put the document she was holding down in front of him.

"It's right here," she explained, pointing at a chart on the page.

"What is?"

"Option grants. Pretty big ones, too."

"What are we looking at?" Lucas asked, squinting. He could barely make out the tiny black print.

"It's a proxy statement," she explained. "A communication to company share-holders describing the issues up for vote at the annual meeting."

"What did you find?"

"I've been going through this thing all morning. I just about had to use a magnifying glass to make out these tiny little numbers. Anyway, I finally found this thing way in the back."

"What thing?"

"I compared what was in this chart in the proxy statement to the guidelines you gave us," she said, placing a piece of paper down beside the statement.

The handwriting on the paper listed the company's board members, and next to each name that individual's reported share and option holdings. Lucas had listed every board member so she wouldn't suspect that he was investigating only government officials. He'd done the same thing for each of the other forty-two companies. In the case of government officials, Lucas had identified shareholdings as each official had reported them to the government accounting office.

"Look at this," the young woman said, pointing at a page in the proxy statement. "Four years ago a board member named

Alan Bryson received options to purchase up to fifty thousand shares. Which matched the information on the list you gave me," she said, now pointing to the paper Lucas had provided her. "And probably wouldn't be a big deal except that another entity, the AB Trust, listed in another section of the statement, was granted options to purchase *five hundred thousand shares*." She flipped forward in the statement a few pages and pointed again. "I'm going to call the company Monday morning and ask for more details on this AB Trust. I'll bet it's controlled by Alan Bryson."

Lucas squinted at the tiny black print, the pit in his stomach growing larger by the second. Until it felt like it was the size of a basketball. There was no need to call the company. He had no doubt that the initials *AB* stood for Alan Bryson. "So you think this guy got himself options to buy another five hundred thousand shares through this trust."

"Yes."

"What were the option prices?" Lucas asked, glancing at a loose-leaf pad on his desk.

"Three dollars and fifty cents a share," the young woman answered. "For both the fifty thousand options Alan Bryson got personally, and the five hundred thousand options the AB Trust got. That's another clue. They both got the same strike price. Both Bryson and the trust could buy shares of the company at three dollars and fifty cents apiece any time they wanted."

"It would be interesting to know where the price of this company's shares are trading."

"Sixty-four dollars."

"How do you know?" He hadn't yet had time to equip the office with Internet access.

"I called a friend of mine over at Georgetown University. She looked the price up on the Web for me a few minutes ago."

Sixty-four dollars a share. Alan Bryson could buy shares anytime he wanted from the company at three and a half bucks, then turn around and sell them right away at sixty-four. The gain would be 550,000 shares multiplied by $60.50 a share — the difference between the $3.50 strike price, where Bryson could buy the shares from the company, and the current trading price. It was almost thirty-five million dollars' worth of option value.

"You'll also need to find out where the

shares were trading when the company granted these options." Maybe there was still hope, Lucas thought. If the built-in gain wasn't that big at the time the options were granted, then the press would have a hard time making a major story out of this. But if the immediate gain was big, then there would be a problem.

"Thirty-three dollars a share," she said, her eyes dancing. "I got my friend to run a historic search and find that out, too."

Lucas glanced at the paper of the loose-leaf pad on his desk again, specifically at the lines listing Bryson's holdings. Bryson had reported to the government that the option strike price on those fifty thousand options was thirty-*five* dollars a share. He'd claimed to the government that the options were out-of-the-money at the time of the grant. That the price at which he could buy shares was *above* the then current trading price. In which case he wouldn't have had any immediate gain if the shares were trading at thirty-three when the options were granted. But he'd lied.

Lucas's expression turned grim. Four years ago, just before Alan Bryson had joined the president's administration, this company had handed him $20 million. The grant was worth nearly double that now because the share price had increased. But even back then, the grant had been huge. Now the question was, why? Why had Secretary Bryson received such a huge amount of money and why was there such a gross inaccuracy on his report to the government? Had it just been an oversight? Had he meant to put down $3.50 as the strike price and inadvertently omitted a decimal point? That was hard to believe. It was starting to look like Alan Bryson had something to hide.

"This is interesting," the analyst spoke up.

Distracting Lucas from thoughts about how he was going to handle what he had just learned. "What is?"

"The company's annual report indicates that Mr. Bryson was a member of the board's audit committee."

"What's an audit committee?" he asked.

"Corporate boards typically have subcommittees that are responsible for specific tasks that they report to the full board about on an annual basis. Sometimes more often. Executive compensation, for example. You don't want the senior executives of a company deciding what their own pay will be. So a subcommittee of the board reviews the performance of the five or six most senior executives. Then recommends salary increases and bonuses to the full board for their approval."

Lucas nodded. "I see."

"Another common subcommittee is the audit committee. Once a year several members of the board sit down with the company's outside auditors to discuss with them how they went about scrutinizing the company's books. To make certain that the auditors are doing what they're supposed to do." She pointed at the page again. "That year the three audit committee members received a lot of options. I'm going to check the following years to see if the pattern continued." She hesitated again. "It seems kind of suspicious. Maybe they got all these options in return for covering up some kind of inaccuracy in the way the accountants audited the company. Maybe we can nail these guys."

"Easy there, pardner," Lucas warned, trying not to seem overly concerned. "Let's not get ahead of ourselves."

"I don't know, Mr. Reed. Seems pretty suspicious."

"What company is this?" he asked, flipping the proxy statement closed so he could see the name on the front page.

"Global Components Incorporated." She

tapped him on the shoulder. "Hey, I recognize Alan Bryson's name. He's the treasury secretary."

"I had Art Meeks approach Conner Ashby again this afternoon."

"And?"

"He said Ashby's a cool customer."

"We already know that."

"But Meeks made it clear to Ashby today that he was gonna go to the cops soon."

"So there is extreme motivation. We should expect immediate action."

"Yes."

There was a short pause.

"There is one piece of challenging news."

"What?"

"The woman screwed up."

"The woman?"

"Amy Richards."

"How?"

"After all my warnings about being careful, she had an article in her backpack Ashby had seen when we had her appear outside the Merrill Lynch building Thursday. A baseball cap. The backpack spilled and he saw it. He picked it up and took a good hard look at it."

"That stupid bi—"

"I've already spoken to her about it."

"But the damage is done."

"That was a mistake. No doubt."

"Should we remove her?"

"No. We need her to stay close to him. We have to have as many people as possible feeding us information on him at this point."

Today was the twenty-eighth. Lucas was positive. But he checked the date on his watch to make certain. Then he opened the white, letter-sized envelope and checked its contents. Again, just to make absolutely certain. The ten of diamonds. An even-numbered card for an even-numbered day of the month. He glanced around the Office Express store to make certain no one was watching. Then he licked the back of the envelope, sealed it, and slid it into the mailbox.

CHAPTER 12

Conner donned wraparound sunglasses as he moved quickly down the stairs in front of Gavin's apartment building. It was another cloudless afternoon in Midtown Manhattan. He stepped to the curb and raised his hand. Moments later a cab swerved toward him.

"Eighty-ninth and Second," he ordered, easing into the back of the taxi.

"Yes, sir."

And they were off, squealing away from the sidewalk.

Gavin had gone out to East Hampton last night, leaving a few minutes after Conner returned to the apartment from his afternoon with Amy in Central Park. He'd asked Conner to come with him to the mansion, apparently no longer angry about Conner taking Monday off. But that was Gavin. Over things quickly.

Conner had turned down the invitation to go to East Hampton. He had things to do. Spotting that familiar dark blue cap fall out of Amy's backpack yesterday had set off the alarm again. He was going to check out the restaurant where she claimed to waitress to make sure she'd pulled that double shift last Thursday. Then he was going to see Jackie.

He gazed out the cab at the crowded sidewalks as the cab sped north on Third. He'd tried to check out the stack of bills in Gavin's kitchen drawer again last night after Gavin left, but it was gone.

The taxi pulled to a stop in front of the Wild Irish Rose. Conner thought this was the restaurant Amy had mentioned at the softball game yesterday just as the crowd had roared. Just as Art Meeks had appeared. But he wasn't certain. He should have asked her again after Meeks left, but he'd been too distracted by what the private investigator knew. And by what would happen if Meeks went to the cops.

Conner paid the cabbie and headed for the restaurant.

"Table for one?" asked a harried-looking waitress, grabbing a menu from a pile on top of the maître d' stand.

"No," he answered loudly. It was noisy inside the restaurant. "I just want to ask you a question."

"Make it quick. We're busy. Sunday brunch, you know."

"Is there a waitress here named Amy

Richards? She's tall and blond." He held one hand up to the top of his shoulder. "I think she started working here a couple of weeks ago."

"Not that I know of." The woman tossed the menu back on the stack. "Hey, Angela," she yelled at another waitress moving past, a heavily laden tray balanced on one shoulder. "Is there a girl here named Amy?"

"No," came the terse reply from behind the tray.

The waitress shrugged. "Sorry."

Amy had claimed that the restaurant where she had taken her new job was only a few blocks from Ninety-first Street and Second Avenue — where Conner had run into her Wednesday night. So he spent the next two hours systematically checking as many places as possible in an area bounded on the east and west by First and Third Avenues, and on the north and south by Eighty-eighth and Ninety-third Streets. But no one had hired a waitress named Amy Richards.

A few minutes before four he caught another cab and headed down to the Empire State Building.

He knocked on Jackie's office door, and it swung open right away. She'd been alerted by the security people in the lobby that he had arrived.

"Four o'clock straight up," she said approvingly. "Right on time. I like that about you. Sometimes you don't return my calls for days, but you're usually on time when we get together."

Conner hadn't heard her. He was gazing at her and smiling. He'd expected her to be wearing something casual, this being the weekend. Dressed in a T-shirt and jeans, maybe, as Amy had been yesterday. Instead, Jackie was wearing a sundress that exposed her smooth brown shoulders and shapely legs. "Wow."

"What?" she asked innocently.

He nodded at the dress. "You look great." The faint scent of a pleasing perfume drifted to his nostrils.

"Oh," she said, twirling quickly left and right so the dress flared high on her legs. "Well, you told me I never wore dresses, so I figured I'd surprise you."

"Very nice," he complimented, his gaze moving back up her body. His smile faded. "You okay?" He'd seen sadness in her eyes.

"I'm fine," she said brusquely, turning and heading for her desk.

He'd known her long enough to recognize that something was wrong. "Jo, come on."

"I'm fine," she repeated firmly, sitting down. "Now what's all the mystery about? Why do you need to meet with this Vic Hammond guy about Global Components so badly? And why do you need to know if there's a junior person on the audit named Rusty?"

"I've been thinking a lot about this," he said, sitting down, "and it might be better if you don't know."

Jackie shut her eyes tightly. "That's not fair, Conner. You want favors from me but you don't want to tell me what's going on. No way."

He stared at her, unsure of what to do. It could be so dangerous for her to know anything. "First things first. What's the thought of the day?"

"Don't be afraid to say the word *problem*," she answered immediately, ready for the question. "So many people say the word *challenge* in conversation when what they really mean to say is the word *problem*. It's so irritating."

She was right, Conner realized. Especially in the business world.

"Don't fall into that habit," Jackie advised. "*Challenge* doesn't have the same meaning as *problem*. Never hesitate to say the word. Admitting you have a problem is the first step in solving it. Without making the admission, you'll never reach a resolution, because you'll never have conviction." She pointed at him. "Now. Tell me what the *problem* is."

"Well —"

"And before I forget," she interrupted, "you have an appointment tomorrow morning in Washington with Vic Hammond at eleven o'clock. Remind me to give you the Baker Mahaffey address down there before you leave."

"Thanks, Jo," Conner said gratefully. He was still bothered by the sadness in her eyes. "You sure you're okay?"

"Just tell me what in the hell is going on."

He glanced down. It was the first time he could ever remember hearing her curse. "Wednesday evening I got an e-mail on my home computer that wasn't meant for me," he began. The same way he had with Gavin Thursday morning at the mansion. "It was sent by someone named Rusty to someone named Victor and it described a public corporation, code-named Project Delphi, that was playing games with its earnings per share. Basically committing fraud."

"Which was why you wanted me to explain how companies can manipulate their earnings."

"Yes."

"Did you save the e-mail?"

"I would have."

"What do you mean, 'would have'?"

"I left my apartment a few minutes after the e-mail arrived. When I got back, I surprised this guy who'd broken in."

"My God, what did you do?"

"He had a gun, so I took off down the stairs."

"Conner!" Jackie gasped.

"He chased me, but I got away. Then I found two cops and we went back to the apartment. When I checked my computer, that e-mail had been erased."

Jackie's eyes were wide open, and she had one hand over her mouth. "The guy came to your apartment to erase the e-mail?"

"And make sure I hadn't made a record of it," he added, remembering how the place had been ripped up.

"How long were you gone?"

"Twenty minutes."

"How could the guy have found where you lived so fast?"

"Good question. One I've thought a lot about. But I can't come up with a reasonable answer."

"It's too bad you didn't print out the e-mail or take down the sender's address."

"I did the next best thing," Conner said. "I memorized it and wrote it down later. It was an AOL address."

"Do you have it with you?"

"Yeah."

"Read it to me," she said, picking up a pen.

"Why?"

"I know someone at Time Warner. I'm sure he could get an AOL person to find out who the address is registered to. After all, they are the same company."

Conner pulled the small piece of paper from his wallet and read off the characters, looking up when he finished the string the second time.

"I'll call my contact in the morning," she promised. "Have you had any more trouble? Anyone else tried to break in?"

Conner thought about the man who'd fallen from the fire escape. "I don't know." He didn't want to alarm her. "I've been staying at Gavin Smith's place over on Park."

"That's probably smart. I can't believe you didn't tell me any of this the other day."

"Like I said, I'm not sure it's good for

you to know about it. For *anybody* else to know about it."

"Are you worried that somebody might come after you again?"

"Absolutely." He could see that he'd scared her.

"You should go to the authorities and tell them what happened," she suggested, a worried look on her face. "Let them handle it. If Project Delphi and Global Components turn out to be the same entity and you go down to Washington asking a lot of questions, you might end up in trouble again. Why not let people who are trained to deal with this kind of stuff follow up on it? I've got a friend at the Securities and Exchange Commission who could help."

Conner grinned. "You sure have a lot of friends."

"It's good to have friends," she murmured, looking down into her lap.

He tilted his head to one side. Usually she had so much energy. "Jo, what is it?"

Jackie hesitated. "Let me put a call in to him tomorrow," she said, ignoring the question. "And please don't go to Washington. This thing sounds very dangerous. I'm going to call Baker Mahaffey and cancel your meeting with Vic Hammond."

"Don't do that," Conner said firmly. He had to find out what had happened to Liz before Meeks went to the cops. "I have to go down there. And don't call that person at the SEC either," he warned.

"Why not?"

"I've got to take care of this myself."

"But why?"

"I just do."

"Don't be stubborn."

"Remember what you said about moving forward when you think you should stop," he reminded her, standing up. "I'm just taking your advice."

"I'm calling my contact at the SEC," she said loudly as Conner reached the door.

He spun around. "What?"

"I'm calling the SEC whether you like it or not," she snapped.

"What's your problem?" He'd never heard talk like that before. "Look, if you don't want to help, I understand. It could be dangerous. But don't get in my way."

"You think you're bulletproof or something? You think nothing bad is ever going to happen to you because you're Conner Ashby and nothing bad ever happens to Conner Ashby." Her lower lip was trembling. "Let me tell you something, bad things happen to good people all the time."

"I've never seen you like this before, Jo. What the hell is wrong?"

She didn't answer.

"Jo?"

Still no answer.

He hesitated a moment longer, then stalked out of the office and slammed the door.

Amy stood on Thirty-third Street across from the Empire State Building, watching the entrance Conner had disappeared into twenty minutes ago. They'd been all over her last night about the cap falling out of the backpack. Which meant they were watching her. If not all the time, most of it. Maybe even while she was watching Conner. Maybe right now.

The hell with them. She didn't care if they were watching. The only reason she'd agreed to help them was to get back into Conner's life. But it didn't seem to be working. Yesterday in the Park had been nice, but now he was cheating on her with Jackie Rivera up in that office. The way he had when they were dating back in the spring.

She'd watched Conner have dinner with Jackie several times before he'd dumped her for Liz Shaw in May. And he hadn't stopped seeing Jackie while he was dating Liz.

Amy knew everything about Conner Ashby. She'd been following him for months. She loved him.

Amy gritted her teeth. Jackie Rivera had bought herself a lot of trouble.

Conner waited outside the office door for five minutes, listening to Jackie sob quietly, feeling awful. Finally he turned the doorknob and pushed. She was sitting in her chair, elbows on her desk, face in her hands, shoulders heaving.

"I forgot to remind you to give me the address of Baker Mahaffey's Washington office," he mumbled.

She glanced up, startled. She hadn't heard him come back in. "Just leave," she pleaded, wiping mascara from her tearstained cheeks. "Please."

"Nope," he said, moving into the office. "Not until you tell me what's wrong."

"I'll call security," she warned, reaching.

But Conner grabbed the phone before she could. "No you won't."

She tried to dart past him, but he caught her by the arm. "Why are you crying?"

"Let me go." She struggled to break free, but he was much too strong.

"Talk to me, Jo. Come on. We've known each other too long for this crap."

"I'll scream."

"Jo, don't. You know I just want to help."

She gazed up into his eyes for a few moments, then leaned against him, tears beginning to stream down her face.

"Jo," he whispered. "What is it?"

"My sister has cancer," she sobbed. "I found out yesterday afternoon."

Conner hugged her tightly. *No wonder.* "I'm so sorry."

"Maria's such a good person. So nice to everyone. So generous. Everybody loves her. How can this happen?"

"You can't think like that, Jo. It'll drive you crazy. What's happened to your sister has nothing to do with being good or bad. It just has to do with being."

"Why not take me? She's a better person than me."

"Nobody's better than you," he said, caressing her damp cheek. "Why didn't you tell me before?"

"I didn't want to bother you. It's my problem, not yours. I have to deal with it myself."

Jackie had been the matriarch of her family for so long. The one who was always strong for everyone else. She didn't know how to be weak. Conner kissed her gently on top of her head. "It'll be all right."

"Now *you're* involved in something dangerous," she continued. "I don't want to lose you, too."

"You aren't going to lose me."

"You don't know that." She reached up and ran her fingers through his hair. A powerful sob racked her body.

"Yes, I do. Nobody's going to get me."

"I hate you," she said softly.

"Thanks a lot."

"You know I don't mean that. I just . . . I just don't want to lose another person I care about."

The words hung in the stillness of the office. "You're going through a difficult time, Jo. This doesn't have anything to do with me."

"Conner, you must know I have feelings for you," she whispered.

"You're upset about Maria."

"That night you walked me home from dinner, last winter. When we almost kissed. Do you remember?"

Conner nodded. "Of course."

"Would you have kissed me if I hadn't turned away?"

"Jo, I don't think now is a good time for us to talk about —"

"Tell me," she demanded, staring deeply into his eyes. He looked away, but she put her hands to his face and made him look at her. "Tell me."

Several of the analysts were still at work, and Lucas didn't want them seeing Cheetah again, so they couldn't meet in Rockville. In fact, he wasn't going to allow anyone other than the analysts into the Rockville facility from now on. He'd decided that at six this morning while he was driving his rusting '95 Accord around the Capital Beltway toward the I-270 spur. A few of the analysts wanted to get started early this morning, so he'd had to go in and unlock the space at the crack of dawn. Easy money was a strong incentive.

Which was the thing that bothered Lucas about Cheetah's reaction yesterday. The man stood to make a quarter of a million dollars if he just kept his mouth shut and played along. Instead, he'd suggested an incredible explanation for Franklin Bennett's true motivation in setting up the operation. But why? The only answer seemed to be that these men really did have the power to permanently ruin someone's life — or worse. A shiver raced through his body. It was August, but for a moment it had felt like February standing out here.

They were meeting in the Union Station parking garage; Cheetah had come back from New York City by train. On the top deck of the structure. Lucas was in the southwest corner of it, gazing up at the stars. The Sunday night sky over Washington was crystal clear and the light show above him was spectacular. His eyes flickered down to another spectacular sight — the lighted dome of the Capitol.

"Hello, Mr. Reed."

Lucas's eyes raced toward the sound of the voice. Cheetah stood a few feet away. He'd never heard the man coming. "How was your trip?"

"More fuel for the fire."

"What do you mean?"

"People are definitely worried about what the president is doing. Project Trust is getting a lot of attention behind the scenes. But nobody can get specifics on what he's going to announce. He's got it covered up very well."

"Well, we've got our own problems."

"What do you mean?" asked Cheetah.

"One of the analysts found something yesterday."

"What?"

Lucas hesitated. "It appears that Secretary Bryson may have an issue. I want you to check into a company board seat he held before joining the administration."

"What company?"

"Global Components Incorporated."

"Global Components?" Cheetah whispered. "You're kidding."

Even through the gloom Lucas could see the shock on the other man's face. "No, I'm not," he said. "Why? What is it?"

Cheetah glanced at the Capitol, then back at Lucas. "I was with a contact of mine today in New York. A man I've known for a long time who used to be in the FBI. He's in the private sector now, but he has just one client. Seems that client is also very interested in Global Components."

CHAPTER 13

Conner hoisted the briefcase strap to his shoulder as the elevator doors parted, then stepped into the deserted lobby of Gavin's building, the clicking of his hard-soled shoes on the black-and-white tiles echoing loudly. The ceiling was fifteen feet high, bordered by intricate moldings, and the walls were covered with beautiful paintings. Classic statues, nice furniture, and large plants decorated the area, too. There was even a small waterfall in one corner, bubbling soothingly. The monthly maintenance on this building had to be more than the entire rent on Conner's apartment. He'd always assumed Gavin could easily afford this lifestyle — the apartment, the mansion in East Hampton, and, now that he knew about it, the place in Miami. But the red ink on that stack of bills in the kitchen drawer was making him wonder.

"Have a nice trip, sir." The uniformed doorman held the door open.

Conner pressed a five-dollar bill into his white-gloved hand and moved down the steps to Park Avenue. "Thanks for getting the cab."

"My pleasure."

Conner hesitated at the bottom step, checking up and down the darkened avenue, then hurried toward a waiting taxi. "Port Authority," he ordered, dropping onto the backseat and slamming the door. "And step on it."

"Easy on the hardware, buddy," the cabbie said gruffly, flicking on his blinker and moving slowly out toward the middle lanes.

Conner pivoted in the seat, peering through the rear window. Even at four in the morning there was traffic in Manhattan. "Come on," he urged. "Let's go."

"Relax, kid. We'll get there when we get there. If you're late, you should have left more time. As I always tell my daughter: Leave early. But, of course, she's like you. Constantly rush-rush. That's what's wrong with your generation. You're all trying to jam too many activities into too little time. You've got to stop and smell the roses . . ."

Conner wasn't listening. He was studying a pair of headlights that had pulled away from the curb up the street from Gavin's building along with the cab. He'd noticed the sedan before getting into the taxi, but figured there wasn't anyone in it.

"You got to appreciate life, kid," the cabbie continued. "You only go around once."

"Right."

"Because the thing is . . . you never know."

Conner turned halfway around, taking his eyes off the headlights for a moment. "What did you say?"

"You never know, kid. If there's one thing I've learned in sixty-two years on earth, it's that very sobering fact. You just never know."

Conner sank down onto the seat. Jackie had said the same thing to him last night while they were standing at her apartment door. He'd taken her to dinner after leaving her office, then walked her home. She invited him in, but he politely refused. They had shared a bottle of wine during dinner, and he'd almost accepted the invitation, tempted to explore his feelings for her. He was certain he'd done the right thing by leaving, but now he was having second thoughts. He realized how much he cared for her, and, realistically, *you never did know.* There might never be a second chance.

"You think you know," the cabbie muttered. "You think you can anticipate everything, or at least be ready for it." He frowned. "But you can't. And it's exactly when you think you're ready for anything that you get shocked. It always happens that way."

Conner nodded. That was true.

"Listen to what I'm telling you, kid."

Conner pictured Jackie's face, regretting for a moment what he hadn't done. Then he shook his head. No. That had been the right decision. The timing was all wrong.

He took a deep breath, pulling himself back into the present, then checked for the headlights again. Still there. "Pull over here," he directed, making a snap decision. The traffic light ahead had just turned red. "Right now," he said, shoving a wad of ones into the slot.

"All right, all right."

They were still several blocks from the Port Authority, but this was his opportunity. The red light would block the sedan for a few seconds. If whoever was inside wanted to keep up, they'd have to get out and follow on foot. He'd know in a few seconds what the deal was.

Conner darted from the cab and ran down Eighth, checking over his shoulder every few steps until he reached the Port Authority, hurrying inside and hustling up two long flights of steps. This early in the morning the place was deserted. When he stopped at the top of the second flight to see if he'd been followed, there wasn't anyone in sight.

Conner headed toward the door leading to the bus bays. Most of which were empty, still awaiting the inbound rush from the suburbs. But there were a few buses in the lot, engines idling, running lights on. He coughed and waved his hand in front of his face. There weren't that many buses, but the carbon monoxide was still thick. He glanced around, then headed toward the ramp to the street.

"Hey!"

Conner looked back as he reached the top of the ramp. A Port Authority police officer was loping after him.

"You can't go down there! It's *way* too dangerous. That's only for bus traffic. Stop!"

Conner ignored the man and sprinted onto the spiraling ramp. Halfway to the street he heard the roar of an engine and was momentarily blinded by powerful high beams as a large bus swung into view. He rushed to the side of the ramp, a waist-high retaining wall, and pressed his legs against it. Holding his breath and gazing over the side at the street, twenty-five dizzying feet below. He shut his eyes as the shiny silver bus roared alongside, just inches away.

Then the bus was past him in a burst of wind, and he was still in one piece. He sprinted the rest of the way down to the street, reaching Ninth Avenue just as another bus roared onto the ramp. He leaned over to catch his breath for a few seconds, then took off. Running past delis and shops just opening up.

At Thirty-seventh Street he turned right and slowed to a jog. A friend from Merrill Lynch — the same guy he'd asked to help him find out more about Liz's resignation — was to have left him a rented white Taurus on the north side of the street between Ninth and Tenth. Keys hidden beneath the left front fender. Conner spotted a white Taurus at the far end of the block, sprinted to it, knelt down, and ran his hand along the underside of the fender. There. He grabbed the keys. Moments later he was behind the steering wheel and headed toward the Lincoln Tunnel and New Jersey, his eyes flashing back and forth between the road ahead and the rearview mirror. Thinking about Amy Richards and what had happened Saturday in the park.

He was certain the dark blue baseball cap with the red emblem that had fallen out of her backpack in Central Park was the same hat he'd seen the blond woman wearing outside Merrill Lynch. Which meant that the woman he had seen was Amy. Too much of a stretch to think that another tall blonde wearing the exact same cap had appeared out of nowhere. Plus, he'd run into Amy on Wednesday night, then again Friday afternoon in the Diamond District.

Three times in less than a week. Way too often to be coincidence.

Saturday afternoon, when they'd said good-bye at Grand Central Station where she'd caught the Number 7 train back to Queens, he made another date with her. For tomorrow night, Tuesday night. He was going to try to figure out what she was doing. Just like he was going to try to figure out what had happened to Liz by going to D.C. today. He had to beat Art Meeks to the cops, or at least have an explanation when they confronted him.

Conner's eyes narrowed as he guided the car into the tunnel entrance. It was all too slick, he kept thinking. Remove all traces of the e-mail. Then all traces of the break-in. But why?

"Dammit!" There was something here he was missing. Something staring him in the face. He gripped the steering wheel tightly with both hands. He could feel it.

The sun was beginning to break through broken clouds when the Taurus emerged from the New Jersey side of the Lincoln Tunnel. It was beginning to warm up, too. As the weathermen had predicted, heat and humidity had returned to the East Coast during the night. Conner flipped on the air conditioner. As he did, he glanced into the rearview mirror and noticed a black sedan with tinted windows coming out of the tunnel behind him. As he sped around the wide, sweeping U-turn in front of the entrance, the sedan seemed to be pacing him. The same way the car in Manhattan had paced him from Gavin's apartment to the Port Authority. Maybe it was the same car. He'd never gotten a good look at that vehicle. It had been too dark.

"Let's see what this guy wants to do," Conner muttered, punching the Taurus's accelerator and speeding west, the panoramic view of Manhattan's skyline sinking below the horizon.

The black sedan stayed with him, several hundred yards back, moving out of the lane he was traveling in only to pass through a different gate at the tollbooth to the New Jersey Turnpike. When Conner had made it through the toll, the sedan fell in behind him again.

A few miles down the Turnpike, he turned off at the Newark Airport exit, quickly paying the toll, then heading for the airport entrance and daily parking. The lot was packed, but he finally found an open spot well away from the three terminals. When he'd swung the car into the spot, he reached into the backseat, grabbed his briefcase, and headed toward Terminal B, the middle terminal. Jogging along a narrow sidewalk leading to the massive building.

Halfway to it Conner spotted a man on his left. Thirty yards away, not carrying a bag. Trying too hard to seem inconspicuous. As he picked up the pace, so did the man.

Conner sprinted across several access lanes and into the airport. He walked quickly past idle baggage carousels, then up a set of steps to the terminal's main level. Most of the ticket counters were still dark, and he moved past them to the far end of the terminal. Then back downstairs, racing out the door to the first taxi stand.

"Where you headed?" the taxi master

wanted to know, opening the back door of the first cab.

"Terminal C," Conner replied, breathing hard. "I screwed up. Came to the wrong one."

"Happens all the time," the man said, scribbling something on a yellow ticket and handing it to the driver through the passenger window of the front seat. "No problem."

Conner ducked into the cab, then held a hundred-dollar bill out the window. "There's going to be a guy here in a few seconds. He's going to ask you where I'm going. Tell him exactly what I just told you, but hold his cab here for thirty seconds. Just thirty seconds. Will you do that for me?"

The smile disappeared from the taxi master's face, but he snatched the money and nodded. "Yeah."

"Thanks." Conner leaned over the front seat as the cab driver pulled slowly away. "We're not going to Terminal C," he said. "We're going to Amtrak's Penn Station in Newark. And we're going there fast."

"I can't do that," the cabbie protested. "That's against policy. You told the man you were going to Terminal C, and now I got to go there."

Conner pulled another hundred-dollar bill from his pocket and held it up so the driver could see it. "What did you say?"

The driver's eyes widened. "I said I can get you to Newark in about seven minutes." He gunned the cab's engine. "I hope that'll be fast enough."

Conner looked back at the taxi stand. "That'll be fine." He smiled as he watched the man who'd been chasing him duck into the next cab in line, then saw the taxi master amble slowly around in front of the cab to the driver side, squat down, and begin talking. Then Conner was past Terminal C on his way to Newark. "Just fine," he murmured, settling into the seat.

Thirty minutes later, Conner was on a train headed for Washington and his eleven o'clock appointment with Victor Hammond. He glanced at his watch. It was a few minutes after six. He thought about calling Jackie, but it was still too early. He didn't want to wake her up.

He picked up the *USA Today* he'd purchased at the Newark train station, going straight to the Sports section. Then he chuckled, put it down, and picked up the Life section, taking a pen from his shirt pocket and turning to the crossword puzzle. It was the first time he had ever tried one.

All right, Jo, he thought to himself, humming "Blue Suede Shoes." Let's see about this new perspective.

"They lost him at Newark Airport."

"*Newark* Airport?"

"Yeah."

"He should have been leaving from *LaGuardia*. The shuttle to Washington leaves from LaGuardia Airport. Are there any flights from Newark to Washington?"

"Not many. Besides, they lost him on his way to Terminal C. There aren't *any* flights from Terminal C to Washington."

"How could they have lost him?"

"He ran. He must have realized he was being followed."

"Christ!"

"Which means he suspects something."

"Thanks, Einstein." There was a long pause. "Where's he going?"

"No idea."

Another pause. "Are there any flights to Minneapolis from that terminal?"

"I don't know. I'll check."

"Lucas?"

"Yes."

"It's Cheetah. I got news."

Lucas glanced at the towel on the floor.

He hadn't bothered to cover the crack at the bottom of the door. "Hold on." He moved quickly to the door, and put the towel in place. "What did you find out?" he asked, picking up the telephone again.

"The AB Trust is definitely controlled by Alan Bryson. The financial tracks run through a bunch of offshore corporations and several limited partnerships. Accounts at fourteen financial institutions in all, but Bryson is sitting squarely at the end of the trail."

Lucas winced. He'd been praying all night that Cheetah would tell him something different. But he'd had a bad feeling about the AB Trust ever since the young woman had found it Saturday morning. "Anything else?"

"Yes, and this is important. The year Bryson and the AB Trust got all those options, Global Components switched accounting firms. They fired Deloitte and Touche and hired another firm named Baker Mahaffey."

Lucas hesitated. "Why is that important?"

"Whenever a company switches accounting firms, you need to find out why. There's always a possibility that the new accountants won the assignment by agreeing to be more aggressive about pumping up the company's EPS. You know, using a little sleight of hand. What makes this situation even more suspicious is that a man on Global Component's audit committee got all these options the same year they switched accountants. By the way, Alan Bryson wasn't just a member of the three-person audit committee, he was the chairman of it."

"You're telling me he was bought off."

"I wouldn't stake my life on it yet. I'm just telling you it's a good bet. But I'll keep digging."

Lucas glanced at the phone's dial pad. The white buttons were dirty, and he made a mental note to buy Q-tips and rubbing alcohol at lunch. "You've been busy this morning. Is that all, or is there more?" Perhaps there was an opportunity here.

"There's more."

"I'm listening."

"Last night, when we met in the parking lot, I told you I'd talked to a friend of mine in New York who works for one specific client."

"Yes," Lucas said, playing the conversation back. "You said the client had an interest in Global Components, too." He couldn't believe what he was thinking.

"That's right."

"You know something more about that?"

"My friend has a few men who work for him. A couple of other ex-FBI guys who handle the day-to-day investigative stuff."

"And?"

"And he lost one of them a few days ago on the Upper East Side of Manhattan. My friend believes the guy was pushed off a fire escape."

"How does that tie in?"

"He's a loyal guy. Eye-for-an-eye and all that. But he hasn't gone after anyone yet. He's sure he knows who killed his guy, but he's been standing down."

"I still don't understand why this is so important," Lucas said.

"It means the mission is more important than the man. It means that there's something huge at stake."

Lucas closed his eyes, debating whether to tell Cheetah what he'd learned about Alan Bryson.

"Anything else on Bryson?"

"No," Lucas answered curtly. "Call me when you have more."

"Right."

Lucas hung up the phone and leaned forward, putting his face in his hands. Five years ago, Alan Bryson had quietly settled an incredibly ugly sexual harassment suit with a female subordinate at Morgan Sayers. A woman who had secretly taped Bryson promising her promotions in exchange for sexual favors. It had cost Bryson $12 million to keep the woman out of court and the story out of the papers.

But Lucas had a friend from Northwestern at Bryson's Manhattan law firm. And, an hour ago, he found out what had happened.

For Bryson to have forced Global Components to hand him 550,000 deep-in-the-money options, there had to be a good reason. As managing partner of Morgan Sayers, he would have been wealthy. But even Bryson wasn't wealthy enough to gin up $12 million without tipping off his wife.

So, like any good capitalist, he'd been opportunistic.

CHAPTER 14

"Thanks for meeting with me on such short notice, Mr. Hammond." Conner sat in front of the accountant's desk, gazing out the large window behind Hammond at the dome of the Capitol in the distance. It was Conner's first time in Washington, and he'd been impressed by the classic architecture on the short ride from Union Station to Baker Mahaffey's offices on Seventeenth Street. "It was good of you to do this."

"You were lucky to catch me," Hammond replied. "I'm on the road constantly. I'm *the* top earning partner in Washington, and top five in the entire firm. You don't achieve what I have by sitting around. Remember that as you go through your career, Mr. Ashby."

Hammond was completely self-absorbed. Conner had sensed that about the man right from the start. But, at this point, Hammond was his only connection to Liz. So he was willing to stroke a healthy portion of ego to get what he needed.

"Thanks for the advice."

Hammond had white hair, blue eyes, and a ruddy complexion. Despite the white hair, Conner guessed that Hammond was no older than forty-five. He had a sleekness about him that belied age. And he spoke with a deliberate precision that made it clear he knew exactly what he was talking about.

"How are you set up here?" Conner asked. "Do you have responsibility for all companies in this geographic area? Or do you — ?"

"At Baker Mahaffey we don't believe in being generalists," Hammond broke in. "One can't provide truly value-added advice when one is involved in many different business models. A bank versus a company that makes furniture, for instance. So we specialize. I run the firm's manufacturing practice for the entire East Coast. I'm responsible for manufacturing companies headquartered from Maine to Florida. Other people handle service companies and the financials."

Conner nodded respectfully. "Maine to Florida. That's impressive."

"Of course, I travel to quite a few cities outside the region to audit client facilities in other parts of the United States and the world."

Conner glanced at a bookcase beside the desk. On the top shelf, inside a small frame, was a photograph of Hammond and a woman Conner assumed was Hammond's wife. "Must keep you busy."

Hammond chuckled without smiling. "Let's put it this way. I'm on a first-name basis with a lot of flight attendants."

Conner glanced at Hammond's left hand. No wedding band. "Traveling gets old."

"It sure does," Hammond agreed with a sigh. "And the more I do it, the less I like it. Especially with terrorism in the back of your mind every time you get on a plane these days."

"I can understand that. I —"

"I was actually in the air on the morning of September eleventh," Hammond continued. "On my way down to Miami."

"Must have been nerve-wracking."

"More of an inconvenience really. The pilots put us down in Atlanta. I had to rent a car and drive the rest of the way to Florida."

"You're a dedicated man."

Hammond looked up, a curious expression on his face. "What do you mean?"

"You kept going," Conner said, glancing at the woman in the photograph. If she was

Hammond's wife, she hadn't aged grace-fully. Or there was a big age difference. Maybe there was another reason Hammond wanted to get to Miami so much that day. "You didn't come back to D.C."

"Oh, right."

"Most people would have turned right around and come home. What you did shows a lot of dedication to your client."

"My wife and I don't have children," Hammond explained, understanding the inference, "and her family lives in the area. She went to her mother's after that plane went into the Pentagon. Hell, she was fine."

Conner gestured at the photograph. "Is that her?"

"Huh? Yeah." Hammond glanced at the photograph, then quickly away. "You know, if I'd been on any of those planes that went into the Trade Center or the Pentagon, I'd have made damn sure they didn't reach their targets. At a minimum we would have ended up in a field like the plane in Penn-sylvania."

Conner shifted in his chair. "I think it's tough to understand what it was like to be on those planes. It was a terrible tragedy, and that's probably all we'll ever really —"

"Look, I only have a few minutes,"

Hammond broke in impatiently, checking his Rolex. "In fact, I've got to catch a flight this afternoon. So why are you here, anyway?"

Before Conner could answer, the office door opened and an attractive brunette walked to where Hammond sat. She handed him a note, turning her back to Conner as she leaned against the arm of Hammond's chair. Conner noticed Hammond nod subtly up at her, then watched her fingers graze the accountant's shoulder when she turned to walk back out.

"There's another good reason not to travel," Conner observed, nodding at the door when the woman was gone. It was a risky thing to say. Hammond might be offended. But Conner had only a few minutes with the man, so he had to build a bridge quickly.

Hammond's eyes flashed to the door. "Yup."

Conner saw a slight smile crease Hammond's face.

"A man who works as hard as I do deserves a few perks."

Conner smiled back. "The founder of our firm has the same attitude."

"That's Gavin Smith, correct?"

"Yes."

"The same Gavin Smith who ran Harper Manning's mergers and acquisitions group for so many years?"

"That's right."

"The son of a bitch," Hammond said good-naturedly. "He isn't just a legend on Wall Street. We know him in the accounting world, too." He chuckled. "I've lost a few clients thanks to him. Companies he bagged for his clients who were audited by the acquirer's accounting firm the next year. Of course, he helped some of my other clients get bigger by acquiring companies for them. And we earned bigger audit fees because there were more divisions to examine. I guess after it's all said and done, everything turned out even."

"He's been a force on the Street for years."

"Didn't I see an article about him in *Forbes* or *Fortune* a few months ago?" Hammond asked.

"Both actually, but he was on the cover of *Forbes*."

Hammond snapped his fingers. "I remember those articles. They described how he was starting his own firm."

"Yes. It's called Phenix Capital. Which is why I came down today, Mr. Hammond."

"Call me Vic," Hammond offered.

"Everyone here does. I hate formality. Gets in the way of business."

Conner's mind flickered back to Wednesday night's e-mail. It had been addressed to "Victor."

"Conner."

Conner glanced up. "Sorry. As I was saying, I came down to Washington today to introduce you to Phenix Capital. We want to find ways to work together."

"Why did Gavin leave Harper Manning?" Hammond wanted to know. "The articles weren't clear."

Conner was ready for the question. "There were differences over management styles. Gavin felt that after making Harper Manning so much money for so many years, he didn't need the kind of day-to-day oversight he was getting." That sounded plausible. Not the whole story, but enough.

"I can understand that. Fortunately, my managing partners in New York give me a lot of leeway."

"You make them a lot of money. Anyway, Gavin decided to start his own firm specializing in merger and acquisition advisory work."

"When was that?"

"Two years ago. I joined Phenix last August. We now have thirty people at the firm."

Hammond sniffed. "I think it would have been appropriate for Gavin to come to this meeting. Baker Mahaffey is one of the biggest accounting firms in the country, and, as I told you, I'm one of the top earning partners. I'm sure there's plenty we could do together, but I'll need to meet the man in charge. No offense, Conner."

"None taken," Conner answered calmly. "Gavin was hoping you would come to lunch with us next time you're in New York City. Our treat, of course."

"I'm not up there very often. I don't like New York. I make my New York clients come here. They seem to like it that way."

"Or we can come back down here," Conner continued.

"Fine. Well, I've got to get going," Hammond said, standing up. "You can arrange that lunch with my assistant on your way out. Get her to give you one of my business cards, too."

"I was hoping we could talk about a specific transaction we're working on at Phenix before we finished," Conner said, staying seated. "One that could be very profitable for both of us, Vic."

"I really am running late."

"We've been retained by a large, precision manufacturer of equipment components."

"Oh?" Hammond sank slowly back down. "What's the name?"

"As I'm sure you can understand, I'd need you to sign a confidentiality agreement before I could tell you."

"Give me the agreement," Hammond said, picking up a pen and motioning at Conner's briefcase sitting in an empty chair beside Conner. "I'll sign it right now."

"I don't have it with me," Conner said quickly. "I'll fax it down tomorrow when I get back to New York."

Hammond put down the pen. "What exactly have you been retained to do for this company?"

"Explore strategic alternatives," Conner explained. Which anyone even remotely connected to the financial world knew was code for one thing: Sell it. "I noticed on your Web site that one of Washington's big clients is Global Components."

"That's right. In fact, Global is *my* client."

"Really?" Conner asked innocently.

"I personally brought Global in-house

five years ago," Hammond bragged. "I took it away from Deloitte and Touche. Global is the most profitable client in the Washington office."

"Congratulations." Conner paused. "I also noticed on your Web site that Baker Mahaffey has started a consulting practice. Like a lot of big accounting firms."

"The managing partners want us to get our share of that business. It's tough, though."

"I couldn't find much information about that side of the business on the site. What kind of assignments is your consulting practice looking for?"

"Typical stuff. Business practice. Industry studies. Strategic initiative directives."

"What about investment banking work?" Conner asked.

Hammond shook his head, frustrated. "We've tried to get those kinds of deals and we've had some limited success with smaller companies. But the big companies, *Fortune* 25 companies like Global Components, still want to deal with firms like Harper Manning and Morgan Sayers."

Morgan Sayers. The name rattled around in Conner's head, reminding him of why he was sitting in Hammond's office.

Liz Shaw. "Does Baker Mahaffey have a mergers and acquisitions practice?"

"Yes, but it's tiny."

Conner needed to take a chance if he was going to get anywhere. "Just between us, the company that retained Phenix would be a perfect fit with Global Components. Any chance you could arrange for me to meet with someone in your mergers and acquisitions group while I'm here? Or are those people all in New York?"

"No, we have M and A people here. But I thought you said I had to sign a confidentiality agreement before you could tell me the name of the company you're representing. Given that, what could you say to them?"

"I could give them a couple of quick sound bites to see if there might be any initial interest."

"Why don't you give them to me?"

"Well, I . . ."

Hammond's expression turned steely. "Look, if this deal makes sense, I can get you in front of someone at Global Components this afternoon. The company is just a thirty-minute cab ride from here."

Anticipation surged through Conner. He'd been hoping to see someone at Global by the end of the week, but

Hammond was going to get him in right away. He had no idea what he'd find when he got there — he didn't really even know what to *look* for. But just having a connection to someone at Global Component's headquarters might be all he needed. "It's just that —"

"There's no reason to involve our consulting people," Hammond said confidently. "Especially the M and A guys. I hate to say it, but they're not very good. If they were, they'd be at an investment bank, like you, earning a lot more money. I'm the senior person on the Global account. You should feel comfortable discussing the opportunity with me. Like I said, I'm more than happy to call someone at the company. But you've got to give me some details first."

Conner nodded. "Okay." Phenix hadn't really been retained by a precision manufacturer of machine components, so he had to play this carefully.

"Is your client public or private?" Hammond asked.

"Private."

"How big is it?"

"I can't say exactly. That would violate the confidentiality agreement we've signed with them."

"Is it over five hundred million in sales? If it isn't, the guys at Global Components won't be interested. Buying companies smaller than that doesn't make sense for them because they're already so big."

"It's over five hundred million," Conner assured Hammond.

"U.S.-based?"

"Yes."

"Why do the owners want to sell?"

"Estate planning issues."

"And Phenix has an exclusive mandate to sell this company?"

The risk here was that Hammond might call Gavin to confirm the mandate. It would be a convenient way for him to initiate a direct relationship with a legend. Then there'd be a problem because Gavin wouldn't know what in the hell Hammond was talking about. Hammond would find out this was a sham, and Gavin would find out where Conner had been. Which, for some reason, Conner didn't want yet.

"Yes, we have an exclusive."

Hammond reached for the phone and punched out a number. His call was answered immediately. "Jenny, this is Vic. Right, right. Where's Jim?" A pause. "At the Miami facility today?" A chuckle. "Third time this month, isn't it?"

Conner glanced up. Miami again.

"Terry down there, too?" Another chuckle. "Of course he is. Why wouldn't he be? What about Glen? He ought to be in the office. He doesn't get into all that." Hammond nodded at Conner. "Good. Let me talk to him."

A few moments of silence.

"Glen? Yes, it's Vic. I've got a guy in my office from an investment bank in New York who has a mandate to sell a company you guys might be interested in. Yeah, it's a precision parts manufacturer. Uh huh, sales are over five hundred million. Sounds like a good fit. What? Phenix Capital. No, it's not bulge bracket. It's a boutique shop run by a guy named Gavin Smith. Yeah, that Gavin Smith." An irritated expression twisted Hammond's face. "*What?* Because I *want* you to see him. Jim would, too." Hammond nodded. "Conner Ashby. He'll be out there within the hour. Okay? *Good.*"

Hammond hung up. "You're all set, Conner. You're seeing Glen Frolling. Glen's the treasurer of Global Components. He can take a first look at what you've got, then report to the senior guys."

"Thanks, Vic. I really appreciate you setting this up."

"Don't forget that I did," Hammond

warned. "When the guys on our consulting side try to get their hands on this thing, you tell them to pound salt, you hear me? You keep dealing with me. I want the fee for my group."

"Of course. By the way, who were the other people you were trying to hook me up with?"

"Jim Hatcher is Global Component's chief financial officer. He's the person I really wanted you to see because he's the ultimate decision maker. The other one is Terry Adams. He's head of corporate development. But don't worry, Glen will be helpful. He reports directly to Jim." Hammond laughed. "Glen doesn't have much personality, but don't be put off. It's nothing personal, just the way he is." Hammond stood up once more. "Now, I really do have to get out of here."

"Where are you going today?" Conner asked, standing up, too.

Hammond reached across the desk to shake hands. "Minneapolis."

Minneapolis. Again, Conner thought back to the e-mail. Suddenly he needed an excuse to come back. His eyes drifted to his briefcase. "Well, thanks for everything, Vic, and have a safe trip," he called over his shoulder, heading quickly for the door.

An hour later, Conner signed the Global Components visitor register at the front desk and was escorted to the third floor. Then down a long hall to the lobby of the senior executive offices.

"Wait here," the woman instructed, pointing at a comfortable looking couch. "Someone will be with you in a few minutes."

"Thanks."

Conner sat down and glanced over at a woman sitting outside a door marked JIM HATCHER in bold black letters. She was young and extremely attractive. On her desk was a nameplate, JENNIFER HUGHES inscribed on it. She was on the phone, giggling as she squeezed the receiver between her ear and shoulder while she filed her nails. She didn't seem busy. And, from what Conner could see, she was provocatively dressed. Her chest was all but spilling out of her top.

Conner's eyes shifted left. Beside Jenny was Terry Adams's assistant, and it was the same story here. Young, beautiful, and not busy.

He glanced around the large lobby. It was filled with artwork, and the furniture was all leather. On the wall to his right were three flat-screen televisions — turned to CNN, ESPN, and the Weather Channel. The volumes were off, but words scrolled across the bottom of the screens. On a table to the right he spotted a Bloomberg terminal, so he got up and checked Global Component's share price while he waited. It was up to sixty-seven.

"Mr. Ashby?"

Conner looked up from the terminal. This woman was older. In her fifties, Conner guessed. "That's me."

"I'm Mr. Frolling's assistant. He'll see you now."

"That's quite a crew back there," Conner said quietly, following Frolling's assistant into a hallway that led out of the senior executive lobby.

"Yes, we call that the 'stable,'" the woman replied icily. "All full of fillies." She took an exasperated breath. "Some of us wonder exactly what it is they do all day. We end up doing most of their work."

The hallway opened up to another lobby, but this one wasn't as plush as the one they had just left. Decorations here were scant and the office doors around the perimeter were much closer together. These guys were subordinate to the alpha dogs. No doubt about it.

"Go on in," the woman said, stopping at

one of the doors and gesturing. "Would you like anything to drink?"

"No thanks," said Conner. A stout man with gray hair and glasses sat at a small table in one corner of the office, studying a report. "Mr. Frolling?"

"Yes," the man responded, not taking his eyes off the report. He nodded at a chair on the other side of the table. "Have a seat," he said gruffly. "Close the door, Alice."

"Yes, sir."

As Vic Hammond had warned, Frolling wasn't going to win any congeniality contests.

"I'm Conner Ashby."

"Yeah, sure." Frolling stared at the report a few more moments, then turned it over. "What do you want?" he asked, finally looking up. He had the alcoholic look. Blue spider veins ran through his red cheeks and his large nose.

"As Vic explained on the phone, I'm with Phenix Capital," Conner began. "We're a mergers and acquisitions advisory firm based in New York City. We're representing a company for sale that manufactures precision machine components for a wide variety of industries," Conner explained. "It would make a nice fit for

Global. Vic thought that, since I happened to be in the area, it would make sense for me to sit down with someone at Global to start a dialogue. That turned out to be you."

"My lucky day." Frolling rubbed his wide forehead. Acting as if this was the last thing he wanted to do right now. "I know most of the companies in the industry. Which one is it?"

"I can't say. We'd need you to execute a confidentiality agreement first."

"Then why are you wasting my — ?"

"I'd just like to ask you a few questions. That'll help me determine whether or not the company I'm representing really would fit into Global as well as I believe it would."

Frolling shrugged, obviously irritated. "We're publicly held. There's lots of information available about us from lots of different sources."

"I've been through all the public stuff," Conner assured him. "Your annual reports for the last few years and the SEC docs."

"I'll answer what I can," Frolling said. "But there are rules about what I can and can't say."

"I know," Conner agreed. "Okay. Global

316

has a facility in Miami, correct?"

"Yeah."

"What kind of facility? I couldn't tell from the 10-K."

"An import office. We have several plants in Central and South America and we bring a lot of that stuff in through Miami. Mostly work-in-process inventory. But some finished goods, too. It helps to have a local office, if you know what I mean. It's good to have people on the ground if there are paperwork problems at the docks."

"How many people in that office?"

"Twenty."

"How many employees total at Global Components?"

Frolling thought for a moment. "Two hundred and fifty thousand."

A small import office staffed by twenty people and the company's chief financial officer had visited the facility three times this month when he had almost a quarter of a million other people to worry about. That didn't make sense.

"Why do you want to know about Miami?" Frolling asked.

"The company we're representing has a facility down there, too, but it's a manufacturing plant. I was thinking that if you acquired our company, you might be able to save money folding that operation into yours. But I guess not."

"No."

"How long has Jim Hatcher been the CFO?"

"Seven years, and that information is definitely in the 10-K."

"Right." Now for the money question. "I understand from a friend that Global Components has an operation in Minneapolis. But I couldn't find any mention of it anywhere. Not in the company's annual report, the 10-K, or any news articles I pulled up. I was hoping you could tell me what that Minneapolis operation does. The company I'm representing also has a plant in the Twin Cities, and again I was thinking that there might be some synergy opportunities available if Global made the acquisition."

Frolling stared intently at Conner for several moments before answering. "Global Components has *no* operations in Minneapolis," he finally said. "Whoever told you that we do has no idea what he's talking about. You got that?"

Conner stared back. "Sure," he said slowly.

"Now, you'll have to excuse me. I've got

work to do." Frolling snorted. "Somebody around here has to."

Conner stood up. Frolling wasn't going to be as helpful as Vic Hammond had promised, but maybe that didn't matter. Maybe he'd already gotten what he needed. "One more question, Mr. Frolling," Conner said when he reached the doorway.

"What is it?" snapped the other man.

"I believe one of the SEC reports lists you as secretary of Global Component's board of directors."

"That's right, I am."

"Do you attend all board meetings?"

"Yes."

"But you aren't actually a *member* of the board."

"No."

"How long have you been the board's secretary?"

"Eleven years."

"And in that capacity, are you responsible for taking and keeping the minutes of the meetings?"

"I am."

"Do you take extensive minutes when you're in those board meetings, Mr. Frolling?"

"*Very* extensive."

Conner nodded. "Yes, I'll bet you do."

Frolling's eyes narrowed. "Why do you ask?"

"Here you go." Vic Hammond's executive assistant handed Conner the briefcase.

"Thanks," he said, trying to laugh self-consciously. "I'm such an idiot." He was on his way back to Union Station. "I was almost to the train station when I realized I'd forgotten this thing." He'd mussed up his hair and pulled his tie way down, trying to look as pitiful as possible. "I apologize for the inconvenience."

"No problem." She smiled, as if she felt sorry for him.

"Well, see you later," Conner said, heading for the elevators. He'd seen the compassionate smile. "My cab is waiting."

"Have a safe trip," she called.

Conner snapped his fingers. "Oh, one more thing."

"What?"

She seemed eager to help. He wasn't getting the cold shoulder he'd gotten this morning. Perhaps because Hammond was gone, or because the pitiful routine was working. "Vic mentioned that he works with a young person here at Baker Mahaffey named Rusty. Vic said that if I had any questions about what we're working on, I could call him. But I spoke to someone at the front desk, and they don't have a record of anyone named Rusty."

She laughed. "That's because Rusty is his nickname. He's got kind of a squeaky voice. Like it needs to be oiled or something. So Vic started calling him Rusty a while back. It caught on pretty fast around the office. His real name is Phil Reeves."

"Is Phil here today?"

"No. He went to Minneapolis with Vic."

Patiently putting himself in the best position to win while letting others take risks.

Lucas sat in the Rockville office, staring at the bare, gray walls around him, thinking about the mantra that had guided his life. But other than chess matches, what had he ever really won? He felt his face flush with the answer. Nothing. So what good was the damn mantra?

He swallowed hard. Perhaps this was the opportunity he'd been waiting for. The chance to finally make his mark on the world. He shuddered. But it would take so much courage and conviction. Two assets he'd never been long on.

CHAPTER 15

It was a few minutes before eight as the Metroliner pulled into New York, creeping the last few hundred yards as it screeched, scraped, and swayed across a maze of switches at the throat of Penn Station's yard. The train was an hour and a half late. It had broken down between Wilmington and Philadelphia on its way from Washington, giving Conner more time to work on the crossword puzzle he'd started early this morning on his way south from Newark. He pursed his lips, frustrated. He'd done all right for a first try, but there were still a lot of empty squares.

He reread twenty-seven down's clue for what seemed like the hundredth time. *Egyptian goddess of fertility.* Put that one in the "not happening" category, he thought to himself, dropping the newspaper onto the empty seat next to him as the train finally eased to a stop. He grabbed his briefcase and headed up the aisle toward the door. Jackie was right. He *had* gotten a new perspective. A humbling one. Of course, that had been her intention, he realized, managing a grin.

He pressed his arm to his side, feeling for the cell phone in his jacket pocket. He'd tried calling several times today but hadn't reached her. They hadn't spoken since last night, since he'd walked her home, and he missed her. There was that gnawing anxiety, too. The sense that anyone he came into contact with at this point might come under scrutiny — or worse.

And he was finally starting to figure out why. Fortunately, he hadn't seen any more of the guy who had chased him at the airport this morning. He was constantly looking over his shoulder now.

"Fifty-second and Park," Conner ordered, climbing into a cab in front of Madison Square Garden.

"Yes, sir."

Conner removed the phone from his jacket as the cab pulled away from the curb, and tried to reach Jackie. First at her office. Then at her apartment. Then he called her cell number. But there was no answer anywhere. "Dammit!"

"Whatsa matta?" the cabbie asked.

Conner shoved the cell phone back in his pocket. "Ah, I'm having a tough time with a crossword puzzle."

"Oh yeah? Give me a clue."

This ought to be interesting. "Egyptian goddess of fertility."

"Isis."

"Huh?"

"Yeah, Isis. That's easy. Give me another one."

Conner glanced at a bar as the cab barreled past. Suddenly he wanted a drink. A good stiff shot of scotch. "Tell me you do a lot of crosswords."

"Not really."

The perspective was becoming even clearer.

Ten minutes later Conner walked into Phenix Capital, dropping his briefcase on a credenza next to his cluttered desk. He was dead tired, but he needed to get started on the Pharmaco valuation. Gavin had pinged him several times today on his BlackBerry, demanding to know where he was. Reiterating the importance of getting started on the transaction immediately. Conner hadn't responded to any of the messages. Including the last one explaining the old man's plan to leave the office early this evening to go to East Hampton. But to be back in the office tomorrow morning no later than nine. Which was why Conner needed to get started on the analysis tonight. Showing Gavin some progress in the morning would go a long way toward calming him down.

There was a huge accordion file sitting in the desk chair. It was the file Gavin had asked Pharmaco's CEO to send over, Conner realized, peering inside. He picked it up, dropped it on the floor, then collapsed into the leather chair. He leaned back and closed his eyes. He needed to relax for a moment.

"So, where'd you go today, pal?"

Conner's eyes flew open. Gavin stood in the doorway, scowling. He hadn't gone to East Hampton — not yet, anyway. "I told you. I had personal business."

Gavin moved into the room and closed the door. "Personal business," he repeated, like he hated the sound of it.

"Yes."

"In a suit and tie?"

"Yes, so?"

"You sure you want to stick with that story?"

Gavin felt he was one-up in some important way. Conner recognized the tone. "Why the inquisition?"

"A man named Victor Hammond called me today. He's a partner at the accounting firm of Baker Mahaffey. Works in their Washington office."

Conner's fingers curled around the arms of the chair as Gavin said the words. "What did he want?"

"He called because he wanted to talk about a company named Global Components."

"Global Components?"

"Come on, Conner!"

"All right, all right. So I went to see him."

"How is that 'personal business'?" Gavin demanded. "Are you interviewing for a job with Global? Can Victor somehow help you with that? Or are you going to Baker Mahaffey?"

"It's nothing like that."

"Is this about Paul? Are you that pissed off about what he did to your presentation? Are you thinking about leaving Phenix? After all I've done for you? I told you, there's nothing to worry about. Paul's just going through a tough time. I told you I'm going to give you *a piece of the firm,* for God's sake. Just give me a few weeks to work out the details, pal."

"Going to D.C. had nothing to do with taking a new job," Conner said flatly. "I'm fine here at Phenix. You know that."

"I *thought* I did."

"Well, I am."

"Then why did you go? What's so interesting about Victor Hammond and Global Components?"

Gavin was going to dig until he got to the truth. "It has to do with Liz Shaw."

The old man's eyes widened. "Really? How?"

"Remember I told you about that e-mail I got the night she was murdered."

"The e-mail that wasn't meant for you."

"Right."

"So?" Gavin asked impatiently.

"Whoever sent it identified a company that is fraudulently pumping up earnings per share. The company was code-named Project Delphi."

Gavin nodded. "I remember."

"I think Project Delphi is code for Global Components," Conner said quietly.

The old man's mouth fell open slowly. "You've got to be kidding me, pal. Global Components is one of the biggest companies in this country. It has a sterling reputation in the financial markets. Right up there with Procter and Gamble and Coca-Cola."

"I know."

"Global is high profile," Gavin continued. "Consistent earnings with an A-list of very prominent directors. In fact, I think

Alan Bryson was on that board at one time. Bryson used to run Morgan Sayers."

"And now he's treasury secretary." Conner had seen Bryson's name in several SEC reports he'd studied on the way down to Washington this morning. After his first several passes at the crossword puzzle. "A lot of other prominent people have been members of the Global Components board, too."

"Global must be worth fifty billion dollars."

"Almost a hundred." Conner had checked that figure on the Bloomberg terminal in the "stable" while he was waiting for Glen Frolling.

"I can't believe it," Gavin muttered.

Conner explained the Parnassus and Delphi connection, and the fact that Global's headquarters were located on a road by that name very close to Washington. The fact that the e-mail had identified Delphi as having operations in Dallas, Birmingham, and Seattle, and that Global had operations there as well. "The e-mail I got the other night was sent to a person named Victor from someone named Rusty," he added. "There's a young guy at Baker Mahaffey whose nickname is Rusty. He works with Vic Hammond."

"Holy shit," Gavin whispered.

Conner nodded grimly. "That's exactly what the stock market will say if what Rusty wrote in his e-mail is true and the company is baking the books in the fraud oven," he said, recalling the line in the e-mail. "And someone breaks the story."

"How did you make the connection?"

"Ah, I kind of stumbled onto it." Conner could tell by Gavin's expression that he wanted a better answer. But the old man didn't push.

"I don't know if what you've found is proof positive that Global is the company in the e-mail," Gavin said. "But the coincidences are compelling, I have to admit."

Conner had no doubt that what he'd found was proof positive. Especially with the mystery surrounding Minneapolis — the mention of it in the e-mail the other night, Hammond and Rusty flying out there this morning, and Frolling's adamant denial that Global had *any* operations in the Twin Cities.

"How did you approach Victor Hammond?" the old man asked.

"What do you mean?"

"You didn't just tell him you'd intercepted a confidential e-mail outlining the fact that Global was defrauding its shareholders, did you, pal?"

"Sure," Conner said with a half-smile. "It's always better to hit them right between the eyes with the two-by-four. Isn't that what you've always told me?"

"Come on," Gavin said angrily. "What was your story?"

Conner glanced down at the Pharmaco file. "Didn't Hammond tell you?" he asked casually. The old man kept calling the Baker accountant "Victor."

Gavin blinked. "No. He just told me that you were down there today asking questions about Global Components. He wasn't specific."

Conner hesitated, giving Gavin time to say more. Hoping that Gavin's first instinct — like most people's — would be to fill the dead air. But the old man stayed silent. "I told Hammond we were representing a company for sale that would be a good strategic fit with Global Components," Conner explained. "He didn't seem suspicious, and I didn't give him a name of the company we were supposedly representing. I told him we were under strict instructions to handle the assignment secretly, and that I couldn't release the name of the company until he'd signed a confidentiality agreement. He understood. In fact, while I was in his office he got me an appointment to meet with one of Global Components' senior executives. Because I didn't give him the name of the company, there's nothing he can check to figure out that we aren't really representing anybody in the industry." Conner looked up as a thought crossed his mind. "Unless you told him we weren't."

"I didn't say anything. I wanted to talk to you first." Gavin paused. "I'll tell you something, pal, I'm not happy about you lying to this guy," he said sternly. "Hammond sounds like a pretty senior guy at Baker Mahaffey. We might be able to do a lot of business with him. If he finds out we go around lying about companies we aren't representing, we won't have a second chance with him."

"I'm sorry. I just couldn't think of any other way to —"

Gavin held up one hand. "Did I hear you say that Hammond arranged for you to meet with someone at Global Components?"

"Yes."

"Then you didn't actually meet with anyone at Global today."

"No, just with Hammond." Conner was going to play things close to the vest. "I couldn't. The people Hammond wanted me to see were all down in Miami. So I'm set up to go back down there next week. It's killing me to wait, but what I can do?"

"Who did Hammond arrange for you to meet with?"

"I forget his name."

"What's his title?"

"I really don't remember. Hammond's assistant is going to send me an e-mail with all that information."

"Check and see if she sent it."

"She didn't. I already looked."

"You just sat down. How could you have already looked?"

Why the hell was Gavin was pushing so hard? "I checked my BlackBerry on the way up here in the cab from Penn Station. *It hasn't come yet.* I told her this morning I wouldn't be back in the office until tomorrow, so she'll probably send it then."

"Oh."

"Let me follow up on this thing, Gavin. Don't stop me."

"What exactly are you going to ask this person from Global when you meet with him?"

Conner shrugged. "I'll make it up as I go. Like I told you, I don't know where else to go to figure out what happened to

Liz." Except for his friend at Merrill Lynch who was still checking into why Liz had left the firm so suddenly. But he wasn't going to tell Gavin about that either.

"I'm disappointed you didn't feel you could tell me this *before* you went to Washington," Gavin said, moving to the door. "I told you I'd help as much as I could."

"This was just something I needed to take care of myself."

"What you thought was that I might not let you go."

"Well, maybe," Conner admitted.

"We had a deal."

"I know."

Gavin hesitated at the door. "Keep me informed, pal. I want to know who Victor Hammond is having you meet with at Global as soon as you get that e-mail from his assistant. I'll have my people check him out. If there's something fraudulent going on at Global Components, you have no idea how far the execs there might go if they think someone's closing in on them."

"I understand." It was the same warning Jackie had given him.

The old man pointed at the stack of Pharmaco files. "Get to work, pal. I told the CEO we'd be back to him by the end of the week, but I don't want to wait that long. I want to know by tomorrow after-noon what you believe Pharmaco's value is so we can assess the European company's offer." He chuckled. "And, Conner, I think it would be a good thing if your valuation is a lot higher than the European offer. Don't come back and tell me that their offer is fair. I'd hate to have to put some-body else on the transaction. Remember, we get paid on a percentage of the deal. The bigger the better."

"Of course, Gavin." He'd heard that so many times.

Gavin expression brightened. "By the way, I'm discussing a second engagement with another old CEO friend of mine. This time it's a buy-side deal. His company is considering a major acquisition. The target is worth several billion dollars, which would mean another fat fee for us. I want you to be my lieutenant on that deal, too, pal."

"Thanks."

Gavin smiled. "Looks like it's going to be a damn good year after all. I can feel it." He waved and was gone.

Conner stared into the hallway until he heard Gavin go out the front door. Two multibillion-dollar transactions closing be-fore year end, which would translate into at least $30 to $40 million in fees for Phenix Capital. Conner reached for the Pharmaco file. That would take care of the stack of bills he'd seen in Gavin's kitchen drawer — and leave plenty for seven-figure bonuses.

Amy Richards picked up the napkin and placed it in her lap as Paul Stone sat down on the other side of the table. Stone was nice enough to her when they met, but something told her it was all just an act. That if he didn't want anything from her, he wouldn't have given her the time of day.

"How have you been, Amy?" Stone began.

"All right."

"How's your son?"

"His birthday is next week."

"Really? And how old will he be?"

"Six," Amy answered, "and I want to get him something nice. Something *very* nice."

"I'm sure you —"

"But I don't have any cash, because you haven't paid me, Paul." The most important thing about all this for Amy was to get herself back into Conner's life. But, after all, a deal was a deal. Stone had promised her $25,000, and he hadn't delivered a cent of it. She'd given up her waitressing job to do this, and her meager savings were gone. "I want my money."

Stone's expression turned grim. "Have you gotten me anything yet? Any proof?"

"That wasn't the arrangement. You never said that payment was contingent on me finding —"

"Conner Ashby is screwing my wife," Stone blurted out, teeth gritted. "I know it. You have to get me evidence."

Amy glanced around, aware that people at the tables close to them had stopped talking. "Look," she said quietly, leaning forward, "I've been following Conner and your wife for a while now, and they haven't met once."

"You can't be sure of that," he hissed. "And how do I know you've really been following them? Why should I trust you?"

Amy tossed her napkin on the table. "I don't need this," she said, starting to stand up.

But he caught her hand. "I'm sorry, I'm sorry. I'm just upset. Mandy took today off and I couldn't reach her. I'm sure she was with —"

"She was with a couple of her girl-friends," Amy explained, easing back into the chair. "I watched her all day. I'm telling you, she didn't see Conner."

Stone caressed Amy's hand, nodding. "Good. I'm so glad," he murmured, sounding relieved. He shook his head, gazing into her eyes. "You're so beautiful, Amy. Sooner or later, Conner's going to wake up and realize what a fool he's been."

She watched his thumb move back and forth on her skin. "I hope so," she said quietly.

Stone squeezed her fingers. "From now on, stay with Conner. There's no need to follow Mandy anymore. Okay?"

"Okay."

"One more thing," Stone said, releasing her hand.

"What?"

"Be careful with Conner."

Amy glanced up. "What do you mean by that?"

Stone picked up a roll and began buttering it. "Gavin is having friends of his check Conner out very thoroughly."

"Why?"

"We have questions."

"What kind of questions?" she asked.

Stone shook his head. "I can't say any more right now. Just be careful."

For the last three hours Conner had been going through the Pharmaco file: financial statements, SEC documents, and news articles about the company. Now he was ready to get to the valuation. With a couple of quick taps on the keyboard, he called up a spreadsheet. With it, he could project Pharmaco's earnings and cash flow, then discount the cash flows back to the present to see what the company was worth. To see if the European company was offering a fair price, or trying to steal it.

Conner heard the Phenix front door open and close, and he glanced up from the computer. He'd assumed he was the only person left in the office. Someone must have come *in*. He leaned forward in the chair, straining to hear anything.

Suddenly, there was a loud crash followed by several bangs. He rose quickly from the seat and raced to the hallway, hesitating at the door. He heard a female voice scream; then there was the sound of smashing glass. The commotion was coming from Paul Stone's office, three doors down. He sprinted the short distance to Stone's door and peered inside. Rebecca was about to hurl a file against the wall.

"Hey!" Conner charged into the office as papers flew everywhere. "What are you doing?"

Rebecca was sobbing, tears streaming down her face. She ignored him and reached for a banker's lamp on Stone's desk.

Conner grabbed her wrist before she could get it. "What's the problem?" he demanded.

"Let me go!" she shouted, twisting to break free.

But Conner held on tightly until she finally stopped struggling.

"Please let me go," she begged, still sobbing.

"Not until you stop the wrecking ball imitation. If you break anything else, I'll call the cops. Promise me you'll calm down."

"Okay, okay," she murmured.

"Good. Now I'm going to let go. You better not do anything," he warned, releasing her arms.

Her shoulders sagged and she stared down at the floor.

"What's the matter?" Conner asked again.

"I can't believe it," she said, her lips quivering.

"Believe what?"

"I can't believe Paul could do this to me."

"Do *what*?"

Rebecca looked up slowly, her face streaked black by mascara. "I thought he loved me. I'm so stupid," she muttered.

"What happened!"

"He told me he was going to leave his wife. He swore he would. He said he loved me."

Conner grimaced. This was something he didn't want to get in the middle of. Somehow Rebecca had figured out what the real deal was. That she was nothing more than a physical distraction. "Yeah, well —"

"I'm so stupid," she repeated.

"No, you aren't," Conner said compassionately, pushing several strands of hair from her face. Stone was an arrogant prick, but he could turn on the charm when he wanted to. Conner had seen him in action. A snake of a salesman who could make even sophisticated business types believe he liked them. Believe they would all be friends whether there was a transaction or not, when all he really wanted was their money. If Stone could do that to people who were already jaded, it was no surprise he could reel in a young, naive woman like Rebecca. "You have to look hard to see the real Paul Stone."

"But I never thought he'd cheat on me, too."

Conner looked up. "What do you mean?"

Rebecca wiped her face. "I just saw him having dinner with some blonde. And I know it wasn't his wife, because she was in here the other day. So he's cheating on Mandy with me, and on *me* with some other woman!" she screamed, her emotions spiraling out of control again. She reached for the lamp.

"Oh, no you don't!" Conner caught her wrist before she could do any damage. "A blonde?" he asked.

"Yes," Rebecca said, seething. "And he told me he didn't even like blondes."

It made no sense for Stone to cheat with a woman other than Rebecca. Sooner or later Gavin would find out. Then there'd be hell to pay because the whole reason Gavin had arranged Rebecca for Paul was so he could carry on an affair without Mandy finding out. By going outside the firm, he'd be risking discovery, and Gavin would go ballistic, maybe even fire him.

"What did this woman look like?" Conner asked.

"I don't remember. I was so damned mad when I saw them."

"Did she have *long* blond hair?"

"I think so."

"Was she tall or short?"

"I don't know."

"You must have seen," he pushed.

"They were sitting down at a table. I couldn't tell." She glanced angrily at his hands, which were still gripping her wrist tightly. "You're hurting me."

Conner released his grip. "Sorry." A thought had flashed through his mind. Something that, if he could prove, would take everything that was happening to a new, almost unbelievable level. "Is there anything you can tell me about the woman? Any distinctive feature?"

Rebecca thought for a moment. "Not really. She was blond and kind of pretty. But not as pretty as me."

Then it hit him. The answer to that frustrating feeling that had been gnawing at him since Wednesday night. The feeling that he was missing something that should have been obvious.

"All right," he said quietly. "Go home and get some sleep. I'm sure there's a reasonable explanation for what you saw."

"I don't think so," she said angrily. "You should have seen how close they were. Leaning toward each other while they were talking. He was . . . He was stroking her hand."

"Paul's told me how much he cares about you, Rebecca," Conner said.

"He has?" she asked meekly.

"Several times. And to tell you the truth, I wasn't surprised. It's pretty obvious to everyone in the office how he feels about you. I mean, he's a changed man since you showed up." Conner smiled sadly. "It's not like anyone blames him either. For wanting to be with you, I mean. His wife is such a . . ."

"A bitch!" Rebecca finished the sentence.

"Well —"

"Yes, she is."

Conner snapped his fingers. This would convince Rebecca. "You know what I just remembered?"

"What?"

"Paul told me he was having dinner tonight with the granddaughter of a man we've been working with for quite some time. The old guy owns a big sports apparel company in California or something. Paul's been trying to convince him to sell the company because his family wants cash. The granddaughter has been representing the rest of the family in the whole thing. Paul was meeting with her tonight to update her. What you saw was business. Nothing more."

Rebecca suddenly looked as if the weight of the world had been lifted off her shoulders. "Really?"

"Yup. Paul and I talked about it last week. It slipped my mind."

She put her hands on her chest. "That makes me feel a little better."

Conner nodded, spotting an AT&T Wireless bill lying on top of the in-box on the corner of Stone's desk. "You should get going," he urged. "Call a car service to take you home."

"Are you sure that's all right?" she asked timidly. "I live all the way out on Staten Island. It's an expensive ride."

"No problem," Conner assured her. "You shouldn't be riding the ferry this late at night. Go call a car. And get a receipt. I'll sign it. Okay?"

"Thank you very much, Conner." She glanced around the office, surveying the damage. "What should I do about this?"

"Don't worry, I'll take care of it. You go call that car."

When she was gone, Conner moved to Stone's desk, picked up the cell phone bill, and slipped it in his pocket.

"A man named Conner Ashby was in Washington today."

"Should that mean anything to me?"

"Ashby met with someone named Victor Hammond at the accounting firm of Baker Mahaffey who then sent him out to see Glen Frolling. Frolling is the treasurer of Global Components."

"How do you know he saw Frolling?"

"That's how he signed the visitor register. To see Frolling. We checked the register an hour ago. You should know that Frolling is the corporate secretary of Global Components. The man who keeps minutes of the board meetings."

"So he would be in a position to know."

"Yes."

Cheetah paused. "Do you think he told Ashby anything?"

"Frolling is no idiot. He knows where his bread is buttered. But this guy Ashby turns out to be pretty resourceful. Frolling might not have had to say anything."

Cheetah looked out the window into the darkness. "What is Ashby's interest in Global Components?"

"I can't be specific. But I will tell you that it's ultimately the same as yours. Even though he doesn't know it yet."

"Hello, Eddie."

"Hey, Mista Ashby." The doorman glanced up from the sports section of his *New York Post*.

"Thanks for sticking around." Eddie's shift had finished at midnight and it was almost one o'clock.

"What do you need?" Eddie wanted to know.

Conner glanced at the on-duty doorman, then gestured for Eddie to follow him to a spot in the lobby where they wouldn't be overheard. "Are there any apartments on the seventh floor, my floor, that are rented but not occupied?"

"What do you mean?"

"An apartment that's leased, but you never see the tenant?"

Eddie scratched his head. "Now that you mention it, I can think of one place. I've never seen anybody from 7G."

7G was a few doors down from Conner's. One of the doors where the fresh scuff marks on the floor and walls were. Scuff marks he'd noticed the day he'd fought with the intruder.

"I just figured it was coincidence," the doorman continued. "Or that the people in that apartment were on a schedule that didn't square with mine. I've been doing the four-to-midnight shift for six months. They just rented 7G in June. At least, that's what the sheet says."

"The sheet?"

"Yeah, it's a list we keep at the front desk that lets us know about new tenants. This is a big building. There's lots of people moving in and out all the time. Without the sheet we'd never be able to keep track of everybody."

Conner glanced warily at the on-duty doorman. "Do you guys have master keys?"

"Yeah," Eddie confirmed hesitantly.

Almost suspiciously, Conner could tell. "Can we go up and take a look inside 7G?" he asked, his voice low.

"Huh?"

"I want to take a look at that apartment."

"No way. I could get fired for that, Mista Ashby."

"No one will ever know."

"The tenants in the apartment will know."

"You just said yourself you've never seen them. And that it's been three months since the place was rented. Don't you think you would have seen someone by now?"

Eddie shrugged. "Yeah, yeah. But like I

also said, that might be coincidence."

"No," Conner said confidently. "The place is empty."

"Then why do you want to look around?"

"I've got my reasons, Eddie. Please."

"I . . . I can't."

Conner checked over his shoulder, making certain there wasn't anyone outside the front door peering in through the glass. He'd been careful coming out of the Phenix building, scanning up and down Park Avenue several times before climbing in the cab.

"Tell you what," Conner said, "why don't you ask the guy who's on duty now if he's ever seen anyone from 7G. If he hasn't, then you'll know it's clear and we can check it out."

"I still don't want to —"

"I can get you and your dad those Yankee tickets." Gavin could get tickets to any major event in New York City with twenty-four hours' notice. And not for nosebleed seats. He got the best in the house. He was that connected. "The ones I got for you in the spring."

Eddie's eyes widened. "Right behind the dugout?"

"Yup. I might even be able to get you

into the clubhouse after the game."

The opportunity to rub elbows with the Yankees was too much for Eddie. "Let me talk to Charles," he said quickly, nodding at the other doorman.

"Okay."

"Go wait by the elevators," Eddie ordered, sauntering toward the other man. A few moments later he was back with a set of keys. "All right, let's go. Charles says he's never laid eyes on anybody in 7G either. He says it's weird."

The elevator rose quickly to seven. The doors parted, and they headed down the hallway, Eddie in the lead. When he reached 7G, he hesitated, glancing around, then knocked several times. When no one answered, Eddie slid the master key into the lock and pushed.

"Jesus," Conner whispered, flipping on the lights.

"Damn," Eddie murmured.

It was exactly as Conner had suspected. What had hit him as he'd stared into Rebecca's eyes. There was nothing in 7G but the broken remains of his original furniture. Whoever was responsible for what had happened in his apartment last Wednesday night had used 7G as a staging area. A place to keep the identical furniture that would be swapped out with the smashed articles in his apartment — and a place to store the broken goods until they could be removed without drawing any attention.

Conner spotted a bucket in one corner of the living room. A long mop handle rose from it, propped against the bare wall. He hustled across the parquet floor, freezing when he reached the corner. Paralyzed as he stared down at the liquid. It was bloodred.

Jackie Rivera handed the taxi driver a twenty-dollar bill, and he took off without even asking if she wanted change. When the taillights disappeared around the corner, she glanced up and down the deserted, tree-lined street, then up at the four-story West Side brownstone. It was two o'clock in the morning.

A dog barked somewhere in the distance and she hurried toward the basement entrance. It was beneath the steps leading up to the brownstone's main entrance on the second floor. She lived in the garden apartment, behind the thick black bars of a protective outer door.

She moaned as she moved carefully down the narrow slate path beside the front steps. The bulb outside the protective door was out and it was pitch black. She rooted through her purse, finally finding her keys. Glancing back over her shoulder when she heard something.

She tried to guide what she thought was the right key into the lock, but it wasn't going in. Her hands shook as she tried the next one, but now she couldn't find the keyhole.

Jackie screamed as a strong hand clamped down on her shoulder, dropping her purse as she turned to fight the attacker.

"Jo, it's me."

She brought her hands to her mouth, then threw her arms around Conner. "You scared me to death!"

"Sorry. I tried to call you a couple of times today, but I couldn't get through."

"I've been with my sister, and I turned my cell phone off," she explained, trying to calm down. Still shaking badly.

"How is she?"

Jackie was silent.

"Jo?"

"Not good," she said, her eyes tearing up. "Oh, Conner, it's just . . . It's just so hard."

Conner pulled her close. "I'm sorry, Jo. I'm so sorry."

CHAPTER 16

It was early Tuesday morning. So early, the sun's rays hadn't begun to filter down through the humidity that had drifted back over the mid Atlantic yesterday afternoon, enveloping Washington in a gray haze. But they soon would, and he needed to be long gone before they shed any real light on the matter.

Lucas stood in a grove of trees near the Lincoln Memorial, gazing at the faint images of stars rippling in the reflecting pool — a man-made pond that stretched out several hundred yards in front of the steps leading up to the massive statue of the sixteenth president sitting in his great chair. Lucas lifted a cigarette slowly to his lips and inhaled deeply. He smoked only when he was under pressure. It had been that way ever since the night at Northwestern when Brenda had left him. The night she'd figured out how much better she could do. But tobacco did the trick. Moments ago, his fingers had been shaking so hard, he'd barely been able to light the match. Now they were dead calm. He leaned around a tree and peered into the gloom, but there was still no sign.

He put his head back and exhaled, blowing smoke up into the low-hanging branches. Make the move or not? That question had dogged him for the last forty-eight hours like a far-off drumbeat, gradually growing louder and louder. The problem was that he didn't have all the information.

He had a lot of it. He knew for certain that Alan Bryson had received 550,000 in-the-money options from Global Components. While he was a member of the company's board of directors — specifically, chairman of the audit committee. Fifty thousand directly to him and five hundred thousand to him via the AB Trust. Cheetah had confirmed through forensic accounting and several well-placed calls to friends in financial institutions around the world that Bryson ultimately controlled the trust. Those options were now worth over $35 million. But the real issue was that they had been worth almost $20 million *the day Bryson had received them.* Lucas also knew that Bryson had received the options the same year Global Components had hired a new auditor — Baker

Mahaffey — which Cheetah believed was a huge red flag. And Bryson had motive for his fraud: paying off a huge sexual harassment suit.

Lucas had determined that Alan Bryson was not as close with the Beltway Boys as they were with each other. Bryson wasn't actually as much of an insider as the press portrayed. Bryson was close to the president, but not to the jewels. In fact, Franklin Bennett, with his close connections to Sheldon Gray and Walter Deagan, was actually more of a Beltway Boy than Bryson. Lucas had learned this Sunday from a woman he knew at the Pentagon. Sometimes it was an advantage to seem meek.

Finally, Lucas knew that the president had very publicly made Alan Bryson his second in command on Project Trust. And told the nation that he was a man of unquestionable character in a speech only a few nights ago.

But Lucas couldn't yet *prove* that Bryson had received all those options as the result of a quid pro quo. He couldn't prove Cheetah's theory about Bryson agreeing to look the other way while the new accountants from Baker Mahaffey performed black magic on Global's financial statements. If he could, Bryson had a problem. Then, so would the president.

Lucas couldn't prove the quid pro quo yet. But he had a pretty good idea of how and where to start.

Another thing Lucas needed more information about were the specifics of what the president had planned for corporate America, Wall Street, and the accounting world. There were rumors that what was coming was catastrophic, but that might just be a bunch of bullshit. The speech the president had promised — detailing his plans to stop the pirating of 401Ks and IRAs and restore trust to the financial system — might be a huge disappointment.

Make the move or not? *Be a man or not?* That was the real question. And he'd need to swallow a heavy dose of courage before he could answer in the affirmative.

He grimaced and looked down. He might need a dose of that courage before he had dinner tonight, too. He was meeting Brenda at a nice place downtown. She had suggested it on the voice mail she'd left at his apartment the other day — he was allowed to check his machine once a day. He'd finally called her back this afternoon to accept — after starting to call at least six times, then hanging up.

Lucas took a long drag from the cigarette. So many years and so much pain. He was proud of himself for calling her back. It was something he probably wouldn't have done a couple of weeks ago.

After placing that ten of diamonds in the mailbox, Lucas had met Sunday afternoon with one of Franklin Bennett's lieutenants at the Vietnam Memorial, after having lunch with his friend from the Pentagon. But he hadn't told the low-level West Winger anything important. All he'd communicated was that he needed to meet directly with Bennett.

Now that meeting was scheduled. It would be tomorrow. Adrenaline surged through Lucas at the thought of confronting the president's chief of staff, and he quickly brought the cigarette to his lips again. The plan could backfire so easily. Which was why he was standing in a grove of trees near the Lincoln Memorial at four in the morning. He had to gather as much data as possible before facing Bennett.

In the dim light, Lucas spotted someone walking alongside the reflecting pond. Though he could make out no specific physical features, he recognized Harry Kaplan's distinctive limp.

Lucas moved out of the trees, careful to avoid the exposed roots snaking across the ground. "Harry," he called softly as he broke the tree line and stepped onto the sidewalk beside the water.

Kaplan squinted into the darkness. "Oh, hello," he said, extending his arm as they came together.

Lucas flicked the butt of his cigarette into the reflecting pond, and they shook hands. Harry Kaplan wasn't just another speechwriter on the deputy chief's staff. Not one of the people who opened a can from a closet and touched up a few words here and there for an early November VFW rally. Roscoe Burns used Kaplan to draft original speeches that mattered. State of the Union and direct-from-the-Oval-Office communications to the entire country. Like the one last Friday night introducing Project Trust. Because of that, Kaplan had inside information. Information that could help Lucas find his courage.

"Thanks for coming, Harry."

Kaplan nodded. "How was your weekend? Did your friends from Illinois enjoy Washington?"

"Huh?"

"Your friends. The people that were coming to see you for the weekend."

"Oh, *oh right*." Lucas suddenly remembered what he'd told Kaplan in Georgetown on Friday afternoon. "Yes, they had a great time. Thanks for asking."

"Sure."

"Look, I know this may seem a little strange," Lucas said with a self-conscious grin. "Meeting out here at four in the morning and all."

"A little," Kaplan agreed warily, pushing his glasses higher on his nose.

But he'd come anyway, and Lucas was pleased with himself for knowing that the other man would do so without asking questions — at least beforehand. Kaplan loved mystery, manifested in the way he played chess. He was constantly trying to use deception to mask his true attack. He just wasn't very good at it.

Kaplan was a wizard with words, but that was all he was used for at the West Wing. He often complained that if the deputy chief of staff would just give him more information and give it to him sooner, he'd be able to write even better speeches. But Roscoe Burns didn't let him in on the most essential data until the very end. Which Kaplan resented. Another reason he'd agreed to meet under mysterious circumstances, Lucas knew. After two years in the West Wing, Kaplan wanted to feel he was more of an insider — as everyone in Washington wanted to feel. But he wasn't getting that from the deputy chief.

"It had to be this way," Lucas began ominously.

"Why?"

Lucas glanced back at the grove where he'd waited for Kaplan. Dawn was breaking over the trees. He needed to make this quick. "You have to promise me you won't say a word to anybody at home."

"I promise."

"I'm working on a project directly for Franklin Bennett," Lucas explained. "It's top secret."

Kaplan's eyes widened. "Really? I had no idea you were close to Bennett. You never told me that."

"I couldn't," Lucas answered, using a self-important tone to enforce the false perception. "Franklin doesn't want anyone to suspect something is going on. But he's given me permission to talk to you, and *only* you." Which was a complete lie. Bennett would have a heart attack if he knew this meeting was taking place. But the hell with him.

"Wow. What's going on?"

"The deputy chief might confront you at

some point to see if you have been approached. If he does, you cannot admit that our meeting took place. You must keep our communication to yourself."

"I swear to you, Lucas. I won't tell anybody."

Lucas suppressed a smile. It had been so easy to hook Kaplan. As easy as it was to beat him on the chessboard. "Here's the deal. Bennett's concerned that the deputy chief of staff, your boss, may not be giving him complete information on a certain issue. That Burns may be holding back on some very important data. Or worse, that Burns may be a loose cannon."

"It wouldn't surprise me," Kaplan agreed. "He's cocky, and he hates Bennett. But what kind of information are we talking about? What's the issue?"

"Project Trust," Lucas replied. "I need to know exactly what's going into the president's speech that will detail Project Trust. I need to know what the president is going to propose."

Kaplan didn't answer right away.

Lucas stared at the other man through the feeble light, trying to assess the hesitation. "Has the deputy chief conveyed these things to you yet?" That could be the problem. Kaplan might not know specifics yet. "Harry?"

"He's told me certain things," Kaplan confirmed quietly.

"Well?" Lucas prodded. "What?"

"This is strange."

"What is?"

"Roscoe Burns told me that all information concerning Project Trust is highly confidential. He told me I couldn't say anything to anyone." Kaplan paused. "Even to Franklin Bennett. He mentioned Bennett by name, and he's never done that before, Lucas."

A shiver charged up Lucas's spine. Roscoe Burns should never be telling *anyone* on his staff to keep *anything* from Franklin Bennett. The directive had to have come directly from the president himself. Suddenly Cheetah's speculation didn't seem so crazy.

"The president is really going to come down hard on these people," Kaplan spoke up. "*Really* hard."

Lucas nodded. "Specifics, Harry. Come on."

"Next week, the president is going to announce sweeping regulatory changes for Wall Street," Kaplan began. "And intense oversight of corporate boards and specific

requirements for the way public accounting firms conduct audits," he continued. "It's armageddon for corporate
America, and the president is completely
committed to it. According to Burns, the
president is willing to go nuclear on this.
And you know what? He's got the votes on
the Hill to do it."

It was exactly as Cheetah had specu-
lated. Or was it really speculation, Lucas
wondered. Maybe Cheetah knew more
than he was letting on. Maybe he and
Bennett had planned this. Lucas had to be
so careful. He was walking through a nest
of vipers, and the key to taking advantage
of the situation would be to anticipate the
strikes, just as he did in chess. Or maybe
he'd have to turn into a snake himself and
become the smartest viper in the pit. "Tell
me about the new Wall Street regulations."

Kaplan chuckled. "When the president
gets through with all this, and I'm quoting
Roscoe Burns now," Kaplan said, interrupting himself, "investment bankers will
be trading in their white collars for blue
ones because they'll be lucky to earn minimum wage."

"How's he going to make that happen?"

"The president is going to propose a
pricing grid for *everything* Wall Street does.

From mergers and acquisition deals to initial public offerings to selling shares to your grandmother. It's effectively going to chop fees the suspender-set can charge to a bare minimum. A government oversight board will be created to enforce the grid and will have the right to review any transaction it wants. If the oversight board finds that an investment bank charged more than what the grid allows, or if the institution can't provide the information concerning a transaction the board has requested details on immediately — probably within twenty-four hours of the board's request — heavy fines and sanctions will be levied. It's going to be worse than a public utility commission, for Christ's sake. Of course, the real reason to implement this whole thing is so that the government can look at everything Wall Street does. To make transparent an industry that's operated in the shadows for a hundred years. In the process, the president will slash investment banking compensation to the bone. The days of kids just out of business school making millions are over, and it will be even worse for the top guys." Kaplan smiled. "Personally, I love it. I'm tired of hearing about these big shots making ten to twenty million dollars a year to press a few palms and play eighteen holes three times a week." He pushed his glasses higher on his nose. "But listen to this. This is the kicker. The president is going to propose raising the top marginal income tax rate for individuals to *seventy-five percent.*"

Lucas caught his breath. "Seventy-five percent?"

"Seventy-five percent," Kaplan confirmed excitedly. "Most people don't remember, but it was that high before. Back when Nixon was in office. But yeah — seventy-five percent. That rate will apply to all income over a million dollars. Plus he's going to wipe out deductions for those people. No exceptions. At the same time, he's going to lower rates on the middle and lower class. And like I said, he's got the votes to do it."

Before Kaplan had finished the sentence, Lucas was off, sprinting down the sidewalk beside the reflecting pool.

"Hey!" Kaplan called. "Where are you going?"

Lucas didn't answer. There wasn't much time.

CHAPTER 17

Conner sipped coffee from a porcelain mug as he reviewed the Pharmaco valuation analysis he'd printed out before leaving last night. The mug had been a gift from Liz a few weeks after they met. It had ELVIS on one side in bold black letters, surrounded by musical notes. The memory of her giving it to him was bittersweet. She had surprised him with it one night, and he'd wanted to go out afterward to eat at an Italian place around the corner. But she'd refused to leave the apartment with him — as usual, her need for secrecy dictating their relationship.

He had an appointment with his contact at Merrill Lynch in a few hours to find out why Liz had quit the firm so suddenly. Maybe the answer would clear up the question of why she never wanted to be seen with him, too.

It was six thirty — early even for Conner. But he wanted to be ready when Gavin got in from Long Island. If there were suddenly going to be tens of millions of dollars in the Phenix bonus pool at the end of the year because of the two huge transactions on the horizon, he wanted his share.

He stretched, leaning back in the chair and reaching for the ceiling. His body was stiff. He'd stayed at Jackie's apartment last night, holding her until she fell asleep. Stroking her hair until her breathing had finally turned slow and regular. She'd hugged him at the door two hours ago as he was leaving for Gavin's apartment to shower and change, whispering how wonderful it had felt to be wrapped in his strong arms all night.

A slight smile creased Conner's face as he thought about it. It had been nice to hear that.

He stretched one more time, then scanned the cluttered desk and credenza. Searching for his copy of the presentation he and Gavin had delivered to Pharmaco's board of directors last Friday. He wanted to check a number they'd put in there, but he couldn't remember where he'd put the damn thing. And he couldn't pull up an electronic copy, because the office network was temporarily down, according to a message flashing on his screen. "I'll never find it in here," he muttered, standing up and heading for the doorway.

He chuckled as he passed Paul Stone's office. It was way past cluttered. It was a wreck — thanks to Rebecca. And it was going to be fun watching Stone's reaction.

Conner moved into Gavin's office. The old man's copy of the Pharmaco presentation ought to be in here. They'd come straight back to the office on Friday after the meeting in Princeton. And it seemed unlikely that he'd taken it to Long Island.

Conner searched the desktop, then the credenza beside the desk, picking up a stack of magazines when he spotted something that looked like the presentation. As he picked up the magazines, a plain white envelope fluttered to the floor. Conner replaced the magazines on the credenza, then leaned down and retrieved the envelope, staring at the return address as he slowly straightened up. Pharmaco International. Princeton, New Jersey. Postmarked last Friday. The day he and Gavin had made the presentation.

The envelope was open.

He slid the letter out and began to read.

Dear Gavin,

Thank you for coming to Princeton today. The board wholeheartedly agrees with me that you made a strong case for hiring Phenix Capital to represent Pharmaco.

Unfortunately, the board has come to the conclusion that we must hire Harper Manning to represent us instead. Harper Manning has the resources and the reputation the board believes Pharmaco requires for such a challenging and important assignment. It would be too great a risk for us as directors to hire your firm. In these times of activist shareholder rights groups, we would be second-guessed for the rest of our corporate careers if we hired you and something went wrong. I know that at some point Phenix Capital will be ready for this kind of assignment, but you aren't there quite yet. At least, not for us.

I hope you understand our position. Perhaps there will be other things you can work on for us. I'll keep you in mind. Please feel free to call me to discuss this matter. Once again, I'm sorry, but there is nothing I can do.

All best.

Kenneth (Kenny) R. Johnson
Chief Executive Officer
Pharmaco International

The letter shook in Conner's hand. There was no transaction — at least, not for Phenix. Pharmaco's board of directors had selected Harper Manning to represent the company. The old man had lied. The huge file sitting in Conner's desk chair the other night had been a forgery. Not sent over by Pharmaco. Probably put together by Gavin himself. "Jesus Christ," he whispered.

He slid the letter back inside the envelope and replaced it in one of the magazines, then glanced at the doorway. He hadn't seen anyone else in the office when he'd arrived. He had to be the only one here.

He started going through Gavin's desk, beginning with the top drawer. The hell with privacy. Gavin had investigated his life, and had him followed. Gavin had shown no respect for privacy, and lied about Pharmaco. It was time to find out what other secrets the old man had.

In the bottom right-hand drawer was a small box. Conner knelt down and removed it, then placed it down on the carpeted floor. He lifted the lid off and peered inside. Envelopes. He picked up the top one — just the word *Gav* scrawled on the front of it — and pulled the folded page from inside. It was from Helen. Signed by her at the bottom.

He leaned around the desk and glanced at the office doorway once more. Prying into the intimacies of a man's marriage wasn't something he wanted to do, but he needed information anywhere he could get it right now.

Gav, what's going on? Why are you away from me so much these days? Is it really business? Please tell me. I'm beginning to think it isn't. And if it isn't, I swear I'll call the lawyer. I can't have you do this to me. I'm not going to keep playing the fool. We've been married for thirty-four years. I love you so much. But I'm going crazy thinking that you're —

"What are you doing?"

Conner's eyes flashed to the doorway. Lynn Jacobs, Gavin's assistant, stood there staring at him. "I was looking for Gavin's copy of that presentation we made to Pharmaco last Friday," he explained, sliding Helen's note back inside the envelope, the envelope back inside the box and the box back inside the drawer. She couldn't see what he was doing because the desk blocked her view. He closed the drawer, stood up, and grabbed the presentation off the credenza. "Here it is," he said, holding it up as he headed toward her.

As she stepped aside to allow him out of the office, he could see the suspicion all over her face.

The woman pulled back the pastel yellow comforter and rose slowly from the king-sized bed, then moved out onto the balcony of the fifth-floor apartment overlooking the glistening turquoise waters off south Florida. She put her head back and closed her eyes as she leaned against the railing, enjoying the warm morning breeze coming in off the ocean. It blew gently over her body, causing her to shiver even in the heat as her long hair fluttered in the breeze, tickling her shoulders.

She grinned smugly when she spotted two men in bathing suits standing beside a palm tree on the beach below, holding surfboards as they ogled her. She loved to manipulate men. Had since she was a teenager. Starting with her uncle, the pervert. He lived three trailers down. Until he'd drowned in his bathtub one night after drinking half a bottle of Jack Daniel's.

After coming on to her that morning.

Men thought they were so strong, but they weren't. Men were weak. So vulnerable to what a woman could offer.

Most men, anyway. But not her benefactor. He was different. Cold to the core — which she admired.

She gazed at a ship on the horizon. She loved the ocean, but she hated water. She couldn't swim and she was terrified of boats. She loved the ocean because it was so different from the dusty part of west Texas she'd abandoned ten years ago. And there couldn't be a more important reason than that.

She glanced back down at the two young men and waved, watching with satisfaction as they elbowed each other like schoolboys when they realized she'd noticed them. Then she turned and moved back into the apartment, collapsing onto the bed. She'd worked late last night, earning almost eight hundred dollars. But she was sore from climbing up and sliding down that damn pole so many times. From manipulating her body in ways she knew turned them on.

Eight hundred dollars in one night. A few years ago that would have been big money, but not now. Now it paled in comparison to what she was about to earn. And they were so close. It was all about to happen. He'd called last night to tell her that, and she'd heard the excitement in his voice. A tone she'd never heard before. She closed her eyes again as she thought of what it would be like to have tens of millions of dollars — the way she'd thought about it every day of her life since she'd understood the difference between poverty and prosperity.

So many people had tried to tell her money wasn't everything. That never having to worry about it simply meant there would be other problems that could turn out to be worse. She pulled the yellow comforter over her body, her eyelids growing heavy. Those people had never had the pleasure of rooting through a restaurant Dumpster for breakfast.

Conner checked his watch as page after page of the Pharmaco valuation analysis emerged from the printer. Eight forty-five. The office network had come back up at seven, and he'd completed the valuation as though he hadn't seen the letter from Pharmaco's CEO. Completing the analysis was an exercise in futility at this point, but he couldn't let on that he knew the real deal. He needed to keep playing the game.

When all fifteen pages had printed out, Conner scrawled a quick note asking Gavin to review the data, then paper-clipped the note to the printout and hustled down the corridor to the old man's office. He dropped the analysis on Gavin's chair and hurried back to his office. Gavin still wasn't in. But it wouldn't be long before he got here, and Conner didn't want to give the old man a chance to call him in for questions. Things Conner needed to follow up on had suddenly taken on incredible urgency. He grabbed his wallet and cell phone and headed for the elevators, leaving his jacket hanging from a hook on the back of the office door. He wanted Gavin to think he was around.

As the elevator doors opened, Conner hurried toward the car — and almost ran into Paul Stone coming out of it. "Excuse me," he muttered, stepping back.

"Where are you going?" Stone demanded.

"Downstairs to get something to eat. Want anything?"

"Nah, I already ate. Hey, how are you coming on the Pharmaco analysis? This is going to be a huge fee for us. You should be turning that thing fast. Chop, chop."

The elevator doors closed behind Stone.

Gavin would be arriving at any moment. He rarely got in later than nine, even when he'd spent the night in East Hampton. "I am, Paul," Conner assured Stone, moving around him and pushing the "down" button. The numbers above the doors indicated that several cars were approaching.

"What's wrong?" Stone asked.

"Huh?"

"You seem a little edgy. You all right?"

"I'm fine." Another elevator opened and Conner held his breath. Several people filed off, but Gavin wasn't among them. Conner bolted toward the car, slipping his arm between the doors just as they closed. Prying them open as the next car reached the floor. "See you in a few minutes," he called over his shoulder as he made it inside.

"Conner, that car is going . . ."

Conner didn't hear the rest. He leaned against the back of the car and let out a long breath as it began to move. He'd spotted Gavin getting off the other elevator.

He glanced around at the other people in the car. They were all staring at him wide-eyed. "Sorry folks," he apologized. "Guess I shouldn't have had that third espresso."

★ ★ ★

"Was that Conner?" Gavin asked, gesturing at the elevator doors that had just closed.

Stone nodded. "Yeah."

"Thought so. Where's he going in such a hurry?"

"Downstairs to get something to eat. At least, that's what he claimed." Stone nodded at the still illuminated "down" button. "But the elevator he got on was going up." Stone looked over at Gavin. "You think it's anything to worry about?"

"Nah," Gavin said, shaking his head as he walked toward the Phenix front door. "I'll talk to him when he gets back."

Conner had been standing in a doorway across from the apartment building on Fifty-first for thirty minutes. Waiting for an opportunity to get past the doorman. But the guy hadn't left his post once. He just kept standing on the sidewalk with his white-gloved hands clasped behind his back, not even reading a newspaper as he waited to open the door for people. Conner pulled a piece of paper from his pocket and checked the address again, then glanced at the numbers over the building's entrance. This was definitely the address Art Meeks had mentioned. Liz Shaw's address.

Watching the doorman reminded Conner that he needed to call Eddie this afternoon. Eddie had promised to check the name on the lease of the apartment they had entered last night. Conner had spent fifteen minutes in there, going through the broken furniture. Looking for any clue that might help him figure out what had really happened last Wednesday night. But he'd found nothing and finally given in to Eddie's urgent pleas to get the hell out.

Why had Gavin lied about Pharmaco? That question kept racing through Conner's mind. Maybe he was just trying to be reassuring about Phenix's financial situation. Conner had pushed the old man hard about that twice, and the last time Gavin had gotten angry. Not just a run-of-the-mill temper tantrum, either. There had been something else in the steely expression and curt words, and it looked a lot like desperation. But Gavin had to realize that the Pharmaco deception wouldn't have much of a shelf life. That Conner would figure out what had happened quickly. Which meant the Pharmaco lie was a delaying tactic for something else.

His cell phone rang. It was Gavin calling from the office. The third time in the last forty-five minutes the old man had tried to reach him. Conner waited for the call to go to voice mail, then dialed another number, glancing up and down the sidewalk as he waited for an answer. Scanning the area for anyone who looked like they were watching him.

"Good morning, Vic Hammond's office."

"Patricia?"

"Yes, this is Patricia."

Patricia was Hammond's assistant. The young woman who had handed him his "lost" briefcase yesterday morning. And confirmed that a young person named Phil Reeves, nicknamed Rusty, worked at Baker Mahaffey for Vic.

"Hi, it's Conner Ashby. I was down there yesterday seeing Vic. You were very helpful finding my briefcase." Leaving the briefcase in Hammond's office had worked perfectly. Giving him an excuse to return to Baker Mahaffey and speak to Patricia without Vic there.

"Oh, hello, Conner."

"Vic's out today, right?"

"Yes, he's out the rest of the week."

"Could you give me his cell number?" Conner wanted to confirm Hammond's call to Gavin about Global Components. "It's important that I speak to him as soon as possible about a transaction we discussed yesterday."

"I'm sorry, Conner. Vic doesn't let me give out that number."

"Well, could you tell him I called? And have him call me on my cell phone?"

"Of course. What's your number?"

Conner reeled off the digits. "One more thing."

"Yes?"

"Is Rusty in?"

"No, he's with Vic."

"Is he out all week, too?"

"I don't know. If you can wait a sec, I'll check with his assistant."

"Thanks."

Conner glanced up and down the sidewalk again, then across the street at the doorman. He was still there, hands clasped behind his back.

Patricia came back on the line. "Conner?"

"Yes."

"Rusty should be in the office tomorrow afternoon."

"So he's flying back from Minneapolis in the morning."

"Yes. He and Vic have a business dinner scheduled out there tonight."

"But I thought you said Vic was going to be out all week."

"That's right."

"So he's going down to Miami from Minneapolis." It was a shot in the dark. Conner had no idea where Hammond was going. "I think he mentioned that to me yesterday during our meeting."

"That's right," Patricia confirmed. "Miami."

"Thanks for your help, and please ask Vic to call me."

"I will."

"Oh, one more thing," he spoke up quickly.

"Yes?"

"The woman you just spoke to. Rusty's assistant."

"Uh huh."

"What's her name?"

"Theresa."

"And her extension?"

Conner jotted the number down. "Thanks a lot."

His next call was to Jackie.

"Hello."

"Jo."

"Hi, Conner."

He smiled as he heard her voice perk up. "You okay?"

"I'm all right," Jackie said with a sigh. I'd be doing better if you were here. By the way, I have a couple of things to tell you."

"Oh?"

She started to explain, but Conner cut her off. "Sorry, but I've gotta go. Something just came up." The doorman was ambling down the street toward a news-stand on the corner. "Tell you what, let's meet at that coffee shop over on Thirty-sixth in an hour," he suggested, moving out of the doorway. "The place where we had breakfast last month. Remember?"

"Why don't you come by my office?"

"Just meet me at the coffee shop in an hour." They could be everywhere now, he realized. Watching everyone he knew.

"Conner, I —"

Conner stepped up onto the curb in front of the apartment building and shut the cell phone, cutting off the call. He had to at least get to the mailboxes. Liz used AT&T Wireless for her cell phone service, just like Paul Stone. Stone's monthly bill had come yesterday. Maybe Liz's had, too.

Conner had studied Stone's bill on the way to the office this morning, checking the list of calls made in July. He hadn't found anything suspicious. Most of the calls had been to or from Gavin's many numbers. As well as to Stone's extension at Phenix — Stone checking voice mail. But there were several numbers Conner didn't recognize. Now he wanted to check Liz's bill.

He moved into the building and hurried toward the back of the lobby, spotting the mailboxes past the elevator banks. Rows and rows of small silver doors. He found K-5 quickly and reached into his pocket for a flathead screwdriver he'd bought on the way over. The locks on the mailboxes would be easy to snap if they were like the ones in his building.

"Hey! What are you doing?" The doorman rushed toward him, a folded newspaper clutched in one hand.

Conner squeezed his right hand into a fist. The doorman was small, no more than five five. He'd fall like a bag of potatoes with one good shot to the chin.

But then a maintenance man appeared at a side door, poking his head out to see what was going on. "What's wrong, Andy?" he called.

Conner slowly unclenched his fist.

"This guy snuck past me when I went to the corner to buy a *Post*," Andy explained, pointing at Conner.

"I didn't *sneak* past anybody," Conner

said. "I'm here to see a friend, and there wasn't anyone at the front desk when I came in. It isn't my fault you weren't here."

"Who you here to see?"

"Liz Shaw. She lives in K-5."

"There's no one in K-5 named Liz Shaw," Andy said suspiciously. "The woman in K-5 is named Tori, and she's away on vacation right now."

Conner's eyes narrowed. *"Tori?"*

"Yeah."

That was a curveball. "When will she be back?"

"She didn't say."

"When did she leave?"

Andy thought for a moment. "Wednesday. She gave me the heads up that morning. Not that it's any of your business."

"What does she look like?"

"Who wants to know?" Andy asked defiantly.

"You okay, Andy?" the maintenance guy called down the lobby.

"Yeah, fine. I'll yell if I need you."

The other man ducked back inside the doorway.

Conner reached for his wallet and took out a twenty. "This is important," he said, pressing the money into the other man's palm.

"Must not be *that* important."

Conner handed him another twenty. "*Now,* what does Tori look like?"

"In a word, gorgeous," Andy said, slipping the cash into his shirt pocket. "Makes my day every time I see her."

"How tall is she?"

"About five eight."

"Hair color?"

"Blond." Andy smiled lewdly. "She's got a hell of a set of jugs on her, too," he said. "Face out of *Cosmo* and a body out of *Hustler.* The kind of woman that makes nations go to war, if you know what I mean."

"Yes," Conner agreed in a low voice, "I do."

Andy had just described Liz Shaw.

Conner pointed to the rows of mailboxes. "What's happening to Tori's mail while she's away? Is it just piling up in her box?"

"Nope. I'm taking care of it."

"Gavin."

The old man looked up from his *New York Times.* Paul Stone stood in the office doorway. "What?"

384

"Have you gotten your July cell phone bill?"

Gavin nodded. "Lynn gave it to me yesterday. It's in my briefcase. Why?"

"I'm pretty sure Rebecca put mine in my in-box yesterday, too. But it's not there now." He turned to go, but Gavin called him back.

"What happened to your office, Paul? It looked like a tornado hit."

Stone shrugged. "I have no idea."

Lynn appeared in the doorway behind Stone. "Gavin?"

"Yes?"

"Well . . ." She hesitated.

"What is it?" he pushed, putting down the newspaper.

"I feel like a real snitch, but I think you should know."

"Know what?"

"Conner was in here early this morning. He was going through your desk."

Conner called Jackie on her cell phone as he crouched beside a tire.

"Hello."

"Jo?" he whispered.

"Hello? Hello?"

"Jo."

"Conner?"

385

"Yeah, it's me."

"I can barely hear you. This connection is terrible."

The fact that she could barely hear him had nothing to do with the connection, and everything to do with the fact that he didn't want to give away his hiding place. He was keeping his voice very low.

He raised up from behind a Volvo sedan and checked the dimly lit area. He was on the sixth level of a parking garage near Grand Central Station. A few blocks from the apartment building on Fifty-first, he spotted the guy who chased him at Newark Airport yesterday morning. Recognized him on the sidewalk and ran like hell. Making a snap decision to enter the parking garage as he rounded a street corner. Running all the way up the stairwell from the ground level. His heart was still pounding.

"I'm at the coffee shop," Jackie said. "You were supposed to be here thirty minutes ago."

"I know. I'm sorry."

"What did you say? I can't —"

"I'm not going to be able to get there," Conner said, raising his voice so she could hear. His words echoed loudly around the garage. "Something's come up." He thought he heard a door close in the distance. He was supposed to be at Merrill by noon to find out why Liz Shaw — or Tori — had left the firm.

"Is everything all right?"

"Everything's fine," he assured her, easing back down behind the Volvo. "What information do you have for me?"

"Two things. Remember I told you about that person at Time Warner?"

"Yes."

"He tracked down the AOL e-mail address."

"And?"

"You want it now?"

"Yes. Hold on." Conner pulled out a pen and the piece of paper Liz's address was written on. "Okay, go ahead."

"The Internet service is billed to an address in Queens."

Queens. Here was confirmation that Rusty hadn't sent the e-mail on Wednesday night. At least, not the Rusty from Baker Mahaffey. Conner had started wondering about that as soon as Hammond had insisted on being called Vic. The e-mail had been addressed to Victor. Someone like Rusty, who worked with Hammond all the time, would have used Vic.

"Queens?"

"Yes. The street address is 662 Greenport Avenue."

Conner almost dropped his pen. "Really?"

"Does that address mean something to you?"

"Maybe." Not maybe, definitely.

"What, Conner?" she pressed. "What does it mean?"

"I'll tell you later. What was the other piece of information?"

"Conner!"

"Please, Jo!"

She paused. "I called my contact at the SEC."

"Jo, you swore you wouldn't do that! I told you I needed to take care of this myself. I can't have the authorities involved."

"I didn't tell him anything about you," Jackie snapped. "I told you I wouldn't do that, Conner. I keep my promises."

"I'm sorry," he said soothingly, taking a deep breath. The pressure was starting to get to him.

She was silent for a few moments.

"Come on, Jo," Conner pleaded. "I don't have much time. What else were you going to tell me?"

"I shouldn't tell you now," she said, pouting.

"Please. I'm sorry. I've got a lot on my

mind, but that's no excuse. It's nothing compared to what you're dealing with."

She sighed. "All right, all right. Earlier this year, Paul Stone was under investigation for insider trading."

Conner pressed the cell phone tightly to his ear.

"It seems Stone found out something negative about a public company from an insider," she continued. "From a senior executive at the company. Something the market wasn't aware of. So he bought a bunch of put options on the company's stock, knowing the price would dive once the market heard the bad news. Then he released what he knew on the company's chat board. It had to do with a product liability lawsuit that was only days away from being filed. Stone thought he was doing everything anonymously, but the Feds tracked down the information release on the chat board to his computer. Then they studied Stone's trading activity and figured out what had happened." Jackie hesitated. "It didn't involve a whole lot of money, but here's the wild part. My contact said that suddenly the investigation was kicked upstairs, and he never heard anything more about it."

Conner eased back against the garage

wall. "Why did your contact at the SEC *happen* to tell you this?" he asked suspiciously.

"I swear I didn't mention your name, Conner. I asked him to check out the senior people at Phenix for me. Smith and Stone. I want to help you, Conner. I don't want anything bad to happen to you. Why did you use that tone of voice? *Happen* to tell me. How can you possibly think I would do anything to hurt you?"

Because I can't trust anyone at this point, he wanted to say.

"You need to leave Phenix immediately," Jackie said. "Please, Conner. Gavin Smith and Paul Stone are bad people."

Conner took a deep breath. "What's the good word for today, Jo?"

Jackie was silent for a few moments. "Figure out who your friends are, Conner. It could save your life."

He could hear the emotion in her voice. "Jo."

"Yes?"

"I love you, sweetheart." It was the first time he'd ever said those words to anyone. He could almost hear her smile.

"You better," she murmured.

CHAPTER 18

Jerry Mitchell was a Merrill Lynch bond trader Conner had met through a friend of a friend at a bar one night. He was light-haired and big-boned, chronically disheveled, and constantly stuffing his face with something fatty. Conner saw Jerry every few weeks for a beer, and they'd become good friends.

"Hey, man," Jerry called as he barged into the lobby from the trading floor. Jerry said *man* as much as Gavin said *pal*.

"Hi." Conner heard people yelling and shouting behind the door Mitchell had just come through.

"Sorry to make you hoof it all the way down here from Midtown," Jerry said apologetically, guiding Conner to a far corner of the room, "but I couldn't tell you this stuff over the phone. They tape all calls on the trading floor. And I don't want to get sideways with Human Resources for telling you all this juice, you know?"

"Sure. By the way, thanks for getting me that rental car."

"No problem." Jerry winked. "Maybe

next time we get a beer you'll tell me why you wanted it parked over by the Port Authority."

"Oh, it was just that I —"

"So, why do you want to know what happened with this chick?" Jerry interrupted impatiently. "You dating her or something?"

"No, it's nothing like that."

"Well, what is it?"

"She applied for a job at Phenix," Conner explained, using the same story he had with Ted Davenport.

Jerry's grin widened. "I'd definitely hire her then."

"Why? What's the deal?"

"She's a stripper."

"You're kidding." Conner saw the receptionist glance over at them.

"She must be hot, right?"

A stripper. Liz Shaw was a stripper. He couldn't believe it. "How do you — ?"

"Here's what the HR guy told me," Jerry said, "and this is strictly on the QT, man."

"Sure, sure," Conner agreed, still stunned.

"Last year a couple guys in our mergers and acquisitions group were doing a deal for a company in Miami."

Conner felt his heart skip a beat. Miami again.

"It was a nice deal," Mitchell continued. "When it was done and the checks cleared, our guys hosted a big closing dinner for everybody at some five-star joint on the waterfront downtown. Merrill made a ton of money selling this business to a *Fortune* 500 company, and our guys wanted to show their appreciation for being picked to do the job over Morgan Sayers and Harper Manning."

Which was typical. Investment banks always hosted swanky dinners after closing a big deal. "And?"

"There was a lot of booze. By the time dinner was over, people were up for anything. A couple of the guys suggested going to a strip club, so they all piled in a limousine and headed to a place called the Executive Suite. I talked to a trader at a brokerage firm down in Miami yesterday, and I found out it's a pretty exclusive spot. Like five hundred bucks a head just to get in the door. But the chicks are supposed to be awesome and pretty much anything goes once you're inside. One of the selling shareholders at the closing dinner knew about the place, and it was his idea to go over there." Jerry chuckled. "I guess there were some pretty interesting stories that came out of that evening."

Conner bit his lip. Probably involving Liz. Which was why Jerry had asked if he was dating her. And why she would *never* have wanted to be on the street. Someone might have recognized her because you never knew who you were going to run into in Manhattan. Then she'd have had a hell of a lot of explaining to do.

"Did one of the Merrill M and A guys identify Liz Shaw?" Conner asked, his voice shaking. He'd been played the whole time.

"Not exactly," Jerry answered. "After the transaction, the selling shareholders had a pile of cash to invest and our high net worth people convinced them to stick a bunch of it with us here in New York. In Ted Davenport's group. A couple of weeks ago one of the sellers was up here from Miami to check on his money, and he saw Liz Shaw walk past Ted's office. Turns out she was one of the strippers from the night of the closing dinner. I guess he had one of those interesting stories and Liz Shaw was involved. Anyway, the guy jumps out of his chair and goes after her. He can't believe what he's seeing. She recognizes him right away and takes off. They can't find her for a few hours, but when she finally shows up again, the HR people call her in. They'd contacted the club in Miami and confirmed everything after the guy ratted her out. He told Davenport how he knew her. He'd divorced his wife after selling the company and getting all the money, so he didn't care." Jerry laughed as he finished the explanation. "It's the old six degrees of separation."

"What?" Conner was barely listening. He was thinking of Liz. How everything she'd told him had been a lie.

"You know, how we're all separated by six degrees, at most. How you can connect yourself to everyone else through six other people. Six at most. It's usually three or four."

Conner glanced up. "It seems strange to me that Liz Shaw would use the same name in New York as she did as a stripper in Miami."

"She didn't," Jerry replied. "Her stage name at the Executive Suite was Tori. But the physical description fit, and she had this tiny little tattoo of a lady bug right here," he said, pointing at his hip. He laughed harshly. "The guy who was visiting Davenport knew all about that tattoo. I guess he'd gotten a close-up look at it that night after the closing dinner."

Liz had a scar in that spot about the size

of a dime, Conner remembered. She'd claimed it was the result of an injury as a teenager, but that had been just another lie. Just like her name. Just like everything.

Lucas almost stopped breathing when Brenda Miller stepped through the restaurant door. He felt himself getting dizzy, and he had to consciously inhale and exhale for a few moments to get his breath back as he watched her approach the maître d' stand. As he watched the maître d' nod and lead her down the aisle toward the table where he was sitting. He'd gazed at that old picture of her at least once a day for the last twelve years, and suddenly here she was. Back in his life.

Lucas had craved a cigarette on the walk over from his apartment to J. Paul's — the restaurant Harry Kaplan had been looking for Friday afternoon — but he'd forced himself not to pull the pack out. He'd spent a lot of money on cologne, and he didn't want the smell of tobacco smoke ruining it.

He shoved his hands in his pockets as he stood up. They were shaking like saplings in a thunderstorm. She was fifteen minutes late, and he'd convinced himself that she had decided at the last minute to abandon him. Like she had at Northwestern.

"Lucas!" she cried, spotting him.

A smile Lucas couldn't help ran across his face. He'd wanted to stay calm during their first few moments, almost aloof. To make her believe he hadn't missed her so much. But, as she pushed past the maître d' and ran toward him, he couldn't control his emotions.

"It's wonderful to see you," she gushed, throwing her arms around his neck and hugging him tightly. "I was so glad you called."

Lucas saw the maître d' give Brenda a snobby look at her public display of affection, but he couldn't have cared less. "It's nice to see you, too," he murmured. Was his voice calm? He couldn't tell.

"You smell good." She kissed his cheek, then ran her nose lightly along his neck.

The sensation brought goose bumps to his skin.

Brenda reached down and pulled her chair close to his, then sat, taking his arm and pulling him down beside her. "Wow."

"What?" he asked, another grin tugging at the corners of his mouth. As he eased into the chair, she placed her hand on the inside of his thigh, and it had an electric effect.

"I get the feeling you're a very different person from the one I knew in Chicago."

"I am," Lucas said firmly. "What's wrong?" he asked, wiping away the tear that had suddenly appeared on her cheek. "What is it, Brenda?"

She shut her eyes tightly. "I treated you so badly, Lucas," she whispered. "Can you ever forgive me?"

"Good evening, ma'am."

Amy Richards's mother stood in the doorway of the Queens row house, scowling at Conner. "Hello," she finally said in a scratchy voice. "Come in. Amy's almost ready."

"Thank you." Conner followed her into the living room of the modest home at 662 Greenport Avenue.

"Stay here. I'll tell her you're waiting."

"Thank you."

Conner wanted to search the house and find the computer the e-mail had come from. The one from Rusty to Victor. He wanted to go through the "Sent Items" file and see it for himself. He slipped into the living room as Amy's mother walked slowly toward the kitchen. But Amy had probably deleted the e-mail completely from her computer moments after sending it. She would have been instructed to do so.

When Jackie had told him the billing address this morning, Conner couldn't believe it. The address was Amy's. He recalled it right away from the night he'd taken a cab out here to pick her up on their first date — she'd made a big deal out of the fact that he hadn't made her get herself into Manhattan like other guys did. And she'd confirmed her address this afternoon when he'd called to make arrangements for the date they'd agreed to last Saturday in Central Park. She'd offered to meet him in the city, but he'd refused, reminding her how she'd been so impressed with his chivalry on their first date. But this time he didn't really care if she was impressed.

When Amy's mother disappeared into the kitchen, Conner moved quickly to the small fireplace and began checking each of the family photographs lining the mantel. He was searching for one in particular. A picture of Amy holding her son he remembered from one of the times he'd come to pick her up. Amy's mother had shown him the photographs while Amy was still upstairs, getting ready.

He moved along the mantel, scanning each picture. He could hear Amy's mother calling, then Amy's footsteps on the stairs. He came to the end of the line, but couldn't find the photo he was looking for. The one that looked most like her now.

As he heard Amy reach the bottom of the steps, he glanced over at a table beside a chair in a corner of the room. Bingo. There it was. He hustled to the table, picked up the picture, and slipped it into his jacket pocket — just as Amy came around the corner.

"Hello, there." She moved to where he was and leaned forward to slip her arms around him and give him a kiss.

But he caught her hands as their lips met. He didn't want her feeling the picture in his pocket. That would be tough to explain.

"What is it, Lucas?"

Cheetah smiled as they stood in the same corner of the Union Station parking garage they had last Sunday night. The dome of the Capitol so close it seemed to Lucas he could reach out and touch it. "What are you talking about?" he snapped.

"You got a little shit-eating grin on your face. And, if I'm not mistaken, I smell cologne. What's that all about?"

"It's not about anything."

Thirty minutes ago, he'd said good-bye to Brenda after a three-hour dinner. She'd been so impressed with everything about him. The fact that he worked in the West Wing of the *White House*. The fact that he knew the president's chief of staff so well. And how he was working on a highly confidential project directly for Franklin Bennett. He'd probably told her more than he should have, but nothing too sensitive. Nothing that would get him in trouble.

It was as if it had been only twelve days since he'd seen her, not twelve years. She'd apologized several times during dinner for how immature she'd been in college, and given him a nice kiss just before getting in the cab. They'd made another date for Saturday night, and suddenly he remembered what it was like as a child to anticipate Christmas. How the minutes seemed to pass like hours.

"Come on, Lucas," Cheetah urged. "What are you wearing?"

"Why did you want to see me tonight?" Lucas demanded, tempted to tell Cheetah about Brenda and what he was anticipating on Saturday. To let Cheetah know exactly what kind of man Lucas Avery was.

"Okay, okay." Cheetah's expression

turned serious. "There's weird shit going on."

"What do you mean?"

"I spoke to another person in New York today."

"Not the friend with the special client?"

"No. Someone in the Justice Department up there."

Lucas looked up from the cigarette he was lighting. *"Justice?"*

"Yes."

"Why were you talking to somebody at Justice?"

"Because a couple of people there have an interest in Global Components, too."

"You're kidding me."

"No."

"What's their interest?"

"Do you recognize the name Gavin Smith?"

Lucas took a puff from the cigarette. "Vaguely. Not sure exactly —"

"Smith was a big wheel on Wall Street a couple of years ago. Now he's started his own little investment banking firm in Manhattan. It's called Phenix Capital."

"So?"

"So somebody at Justice has a hard-on for him."

"Why?"

"Seems this somebody use to work at Harper Manning, one of the big investment banks in Manhattan. Before he went to the Justice Department. The same place Gavin Smith worked before he started Phenix."

"And?" Lucas asked impatiently.

"The reason the guy went to Justice was because Gavin Smith fired him," Cheetah explained. "It was real bullshit, too. Smith had made some big mistake, so he fired this guy to cover himself. Now the guy wants to stick it to Smith real bad. He's trying to hang an insider trading charge on Smith's neck. And using some kid named Conner Ashby to do it. Ashby has no idea what's really going on, but he did visit a man named Glen Frolling yesterday."

"The treasurer of Global Components?" Over the last several days Lucas had reviewed everything he could get his hands on concerning Global Components.

"And the secretary to Global's board of directors."

"Why did Ashby go down there?" Lucas asked excitedly, taking a long puff from the cigarette. "What does that have to do with an insider trading charge?"

"I couldn't find out much, but my friend told me Ashby's ultimate objective may have a great deal in common with yours."

"What does that mean?" Lucas pushed. "What the hell did you tell this guy?"

"Calm down. I didn't tell him anything about Bryson."

"You shouldn't have told him anything."

"To get you have to give," Cheetah retorted. "That's how it works, little man."

"Who is this Conner Ashby?" Lucas asked, bristling at Cheetah's remark.

"An investment banker from New York. He works for Gavin Smith. I'm doing some background work on him. I'll let you know when I have something definitive."

"You do that."

Lucas gazed over Cheetah's shoulder at the Capitol, thinking about how he'd wanted that bike for Christmas when he was thirteen. How he'd been sure he was going to get it because it was all he asked for and how it had taken *forever* for Christmas to come. How on Christmas morning there hadn't been a bike in front of the tree or in the garage. In fact, there hadn't been much at all. It was the first time he'd understood how poor a provider his father was. The first time he'd been disappointed in his father.

Brenda better not disappoint him. He was counting on her. Counting on his ability to recognize someone he could depend on.

He glanced back at Cheetah, searching the man's expression. Did they think he was that stupid?

Amy smiled at Conner from across the table. He was being so nice tonight. Like she wanted him to be all the time. She glanced down. She wasn't going to help Paul Stone anymore. The hell with the money. She'd pick up another waitressing job and live with her mother until she could get back on her feet financially. The point of all of this had been to get back into Conner's life, and, based on tonight, she was going to get what she wanted.

"You look really nice tonight, Amy."

"Thanks." Suddenly she felt so guilty for spying on him.

"I'll be right back," he said, standing up. "Gotta make a quick pit stop."

She reached out as he went by, and he leaned down and kissed her on the cheek. "Don't be long," she murmured.

"I won't."

Amy watched until he disappeared at the back of the place. As she turned around, a waiter passed the table, accidentally knocking Conner's jacket from the back of the chair. The man didn't notice what he'd done, so she got up and picked the jacket up, draping the shoulders around the chair again. As she did, the framed picture Conner had taken from the mantel fell from the inside pocket to the floor. Amy knelt down slowly and retrieved it, gazing at herself and her son. Stone's words of warning echoing in her ears.

She stared at the photograph a few moments longer, then slipped it back into Conner's jacket and sat back down. Tonight was an act and nothing more. Stone had been exactly right. Conner was using her. Why or how, she didn't know. But suddenly, those things didn't matter.

Amy glanced up as Conner returned.

"Ready to order?" he asked cheerfully, sitting down.

She wanted to tell him what she'd just found. Wanted to confront him with the evidence and understand what he was doing and why he was using her. But she didn't. That wouldn't be the best way get back at him. "Yeah," she said, smiling at him sweetly. "I'm very ready."

Conner helped Amy into the cab and waved to her as it headed out into traffic. When they'd hugged good night a few moments ago, he'd had to make certain she didn't feel the frame in his pocket. He smiled to himself. He had what he needed. Now to confirm the connection.

Amy pulled the cell phone from her purse after waving to Conner. He was the enemy now.

CHAPTER 19

Conner tapped on the keyboard, scouring the Internet for more information on Global Components. It was eight thirty Wednesday morning. Gavin and Stone weren't in the office yet. He'd never called Gavin back yesterday, and he'd stayed at the Hilton Hotel in Midtown last night. So he had no idea if the old man had made the trip out to East Hampton again last night or stayed at his apartment in the city. He hadn't gone back to Gavin's place, because he didn't trust anyone at this point. It was that simple.

Conner hadn't returned any of the five messages Jackie had left on his cell phone, either. She was probably angry and hurt, but it couldn't be helped at this point. There was too much on the line. She'd said it herself. The one thing that still amazed her after thirteen years in the financial world was how far people would go when the walls started collapsing in on them.

Conner buzzed Rebecca's desk on the intercom for the third time in the last ten minutes, but there was still no answer. She didn't usually get in until a little before nine because her important duties didn't start until lunch. But he was praying that she'd change her routine this morning so he could leave before Gavin or Paul arrived.

A color picture of the Global Components board of directors flashed onto his computer screen — twelve Saxons and two poster children. Conner focused in on Jim Hatcher, the CFO. One of three Global executives on the board. He enlarged the man's face as much as possible without distorting the image. Hatcher had made three trips to Miami in a month. The odds were long, but it was worth a shot. Conner sent the image to a color printer, and clicked. Maybe the odds weren't really that long after all. There were too many arrows pointing in the same direction.

Conner clicked out of Global Components' current annual report and went back a few years, whistling softly as the list of directors appeared. Most of the same names appeared, but there were some impressive new ones, too. Like Alan Bryson. Conner peered at the treasury secretary's name. Gavin really was incredible when it came to business. He'd remembered that Bryson was on this board without any prompting.

Conner zipped around the annual, looking for any mention of a Minneapolis operation in the older report. But there was nothing. It was just as Jackie had said. He let out a frustrated breath. He'd been scanning reports for days looking for this needle in the Global Components haystack. Maybe Frolling wasn't kidding. Maybe Global really didn't have anything out there.

He picked up the phone and dialed the 202 area code number. There was one person who almost certainly knew if Global had an operation in the Twin Cities.

"Good morning, Phil Reeves's office."

"Theresa?"

"Yes."

"My name is John Bellamy," Conner said loudly. Trying to sound brusque, older than he was, and important.

"Yes, Mr. Bellamy."

"I'm working on a deal with my old friend Vic Hammond, and Vic tells me there's a young guy named Rusty who works for him. That's Phil's nickname, right?"

"Yes, sir."

"His voice is squeaky or something," Conner said, adding a detail for credibility. "Whatever."

Theresa laughed. "That's right."

"Well, I spoke to Vic a few minutes ago. He's about to get on a plane in Minneapolis on his way to Miami."

"Yes, and Rusty is coming back to the office this —"

"And what I need is Rusty's *home* address," Conner continued, not allowing Theresa to interrupt. "I've got a package I need to get out right away. Vic told me to send it to Rusty at his home since Vic won't be back to Washington for a few days. I'm in the Washington area, and once my people have everything put together, why, I'll have one of them drive the package over to him." Even if Theresa had Caller ID, there'd be no way for her to tell the call was coming from a 212 area code. Gavin had made certain to get the blocking feature. As much as he coveted the ability to watch other people, he hated the thought of people watching him.

"Rusty is coming into the office this afternoon after he lands at Reagan Airport," Theresa explained. "Why don't you send the information here?"

"Because I won't have it completed until this evening," Conner snapped. "And I want to make certain it gets to Rusty *tonight*. What if Rusty gets delayed on the

Detroit to D.C. leg?" He had checked Rusty's flight schedule by talking to a helpful customer service representative at Northwest Airlines. Most flights going in and out of Minneapolis were Northwest, so it didn't surprise him when the woman found the booking immediately. Rusty was going Minneapolis to Detroit, then Detroit to Reagan. "What if Rusty decides to go straight home when he lands?" Conner asked angrily. "Then where will I be? More important, where will *Vic* be?" He could sense that the young woman was struggling about what to do. She was probably under strict orders not to give out this kind of information. "Vic is going to be damn angry if this package doesn't get to —"

"Rusty lives in Reston, Virginia, Mr. Bellamy."

Thirty seconds later Conner had Rusty's home address and his home telephone number.

After hanging up with Theresa, he went to get Jim Hatcher's picture from the color printer. He nodded as he held it up. "Not bad." Anybody who knew Hatcher would recognize him from this.

Out of the corner of his eye, Conner saw Rebecca sit down at her desk. "Thank God," he whispered, hurrying back to his office. He reached into a desk drawer and grabbed the photograph of Amy and her son he'd lifted from the mantel of her mother's place last night.

"What you got there, Conner?"

Conner stopped short. Paul Stone stood in the corridor, briefcase in hand. Conner pressed the photograph to his body so Stone couldn't see. "Nothing."

"Come on," Stone said, smirking, "show me."

"It's nothing. Just an old family picture I was going to show Gavin."

"Gavin isn't in yet."

"Oh."

Stone stepped toward Conner. "Gavin was wondering where you were last night. He couldn't find you."

"I stayed with a friend."

"What about yesterday?" Stone demanded. "Where were you?"

"I had a personal emergency."

"We tried to reach you several times. We have comments on your Pharmaco valuation analysis. Things we want to adjust. We lost a lot of time getting back to the company."

Conner wondered if Stone knew about the letter from Pharmaco's CEO. "Well, I'm here now. Why don't you get settled," he suggested, making certain to keep the photograph of Amy and her son pressed to his leg as he stepped around the other man, "and I'll be right in." He glanced over his shoulder as he reached the end of the corridor, but Stone hadn't followed him.

Conner hurried to Rebecca's desk. She was just taking the lid off a large cup of coffee. "Morning," he said.

"Hello."

He looked back toward the corridor once more. Still no sign of Stone. "You remember that conversation we had Monday night about Paul."

Rebecca put her hand to her face. "I'm so embarrassed about that."

"Don't worry about it," he urged, holding Amy's photograph out so Rebecca could see. "Is this the woman you saw with Paul?" His heart was racing. Depending on the response, he might be able to confirm the first link in the chain.

She gazed at it for a few moments, then glanced up. "Yes," she said firmly. "That's her."

A chill coursed through Conner's body. Rebecca had seen Paul Stone and Amy Richards together and now things were falling into place. Amy had appeared out of nowhere on Second Avenue after he'd bought the cigarettes Wednesday night so someone could buy time while his apartment was being destroyed. That was why she'd grabbed his arm twice as he'd tried to get past her. It also explained her persistent questions last night at dinner about what he'd been doing in Washington on Monday. She was keeping tabs on him — for Paul Stone.

Maybe for Gavin Smith, too. That was really the million-dollar question. Did all of this involve Gavin as well?

"You sure this is her?" Conner asked.

"Absolutely."

He nodded. "Thanks."

"How did you get that?" she asked suspiciously.

Conner searched for an answer — but there wasn't one. "I'll see you later."

Thirty minutes later, Conner stood at the front desk of the apartment building on Fifty-first Street. "So?"

"I got what you want," Andy assured him.

"Show me."

The doorman hesitated, then reached beneath the desk and pulled out two AT&T Wireless bills. "Show me the money. Five hundred bucks. Like we agreed."

"All I need is the most recent one," Conner said, eying the two envelopes. "Just the one for July."

"They're both for July. At least, they're both postmarked the same day."

Conner handed Andy the cash and took both envelopes. It was just as he had said. Both were postmarked the same day. AT&T Wireless must have inadvertently sent a duplicate. "It would really help if you'd let me go up to Tori's apartment for a few minutes."

Andy shook his head. "No way. Giving you those things could get me in enough trouble as it is," he said, nodding at the envelopes.

"You can come up with me. I'll give you more money."

"Nope. And nobody better find out I did this," Andy called, shoving the cash in his pocket.

Conner was already headed toward the front door. He hesitated in the foyer, spotting a dark sedan parked down the street. It had followed the cab up here. He turned around. "You got a back door to this place?"

The doorman smiled smugly. "Sure. But it costs a hundred bucks to use."

Two hours later, Conner was on a Continental flight headed for Miami. When the plane reached cruising altitude and he had a scotch in front of him, Conner put his seat all the way back and pulled the two cell phone bills out of his briefcase. The first one covered the cell number he was familiar with. The number Liz had given him the night they'd first met. It confirmed that the apartment on Fifty-first Street was hers. That Tori Hayes — the name on the invoice — and Liz Shaw were the same person. That if he could somehow get into her apartment when he got back from Miami, he might find something interesting. Or nothing at all, as he thought about it. They'd probably cleared it out by now.

Conner scanned the invoice, searching for numbers he recognized. But the only numbers on this invoice were his. His cell number, his office number, and his apartment number.

He took a quick swallow of scotch, then ripped open the second bill. He pulled out the folded pages and instantly recognized Paul Stone's office number. Just the last digit of the string different from his own extension. Conner checked the top of the page. This bill was for a different number. Liz had two cell phones. One she had used to communicate solely with Conner, and another she used for all other calls.

He scanned the pages of the bill. There were at least three calls a day to Paul Stone.

CHAPTER 20

Middleburg, Virginia, is a tiny, colonial-era town tucked into the eastern foothills of the Blue Ridge Mountains forty miles west of Washington. Although it's one of the prettiest and most desirable dots on the commonwealth map, real estate brokers here don't usually earn the standard 6 percent. They don't have to. Few properties trade hands for less than a million dollars, and brokers make an excellent living by being reasonable. Technology executives, prominent political figures, movie stars, and venture capitalists mingle at the pricey shops and restaurants of the quaint village — as well as on the private polo fields, steeplechase courses, and foxhunting trails of the sprawling estates outside of town.

It was in the middle of this Norman Rockwell painting Lucas now found himself.

No blue-collar strip mall this time. This time the venue was a stately, three-story stone home overlooking the seemingly endless white-wooden fences of a thoroughbred horse farm. Perhaps the change of venue could be explained by Lucas's unwillingness to relay anything to the low-level West Winger who'd met him at the Vietnam Memorial. Or perhaps it was simply more convenient for Franklin Bennett on this day. Bottom line: Lucas didn't care *why* the venue had changed, only that it had. Because the existence of the estate and the fact that he and Bennett were meeting here confirmed for him that there was some kind of secret society within the party. There was no way Bennett could afford all of this. Somebody inside had to be making it available to him.

Which was fine with Lucas. At heart, he was more utilitarian than possessive. He cared more about using assets than he did owning them.

"Something to drink, sir?"

A maid held a tray in front of Lucas as he sat in a wicker chair on the wide covered porch. On it were tall glasses of lemonade and iced tea, perspiring in the heavy humidity of the August afternoon.

"Thank you." Lucas chose lemonade and took a long drink, ice cubes pressed to his upper lip. It was so damn hot and the cold liquid was refreshing. He wiped his lips with the back of his hand as the maid placed the tray on a small glass-top table beside his chair, then disappeared inside the house.

He'd been waiting for an hour, and he'd happily wait another. Another *several,* in fact. He was nervous. Hands-shaking nervous. This was it. High noon. He thought about smoking but didn't. He didn't want Bennett knowing that he needed a crutch.

From the porch Lucas could see the long driveway leading down to the main road, and he checked it constantly to see if Bennett was coming. He despised himself for it, but he could feel the indecision seeping back. He took another long guzzle of lemonade. As confident as he'd been an hour ago on the way out here, he was reconsidering the consequences. Maybe it was wiser to stay quiet and hold on to the life he'd grown accustomed to. Minutes passed like hours more days than he cared to admit, but it was an uncomplicated life. Perhaps most important, it was a safe life, fraught with no critical responsibilities. With increased responsibilities came increased risk. With increased risk came the potential for disaster. He'd lived his entire life trying to avoid disaster. It was terrifying to suddenly fly in the face of it.

He placed the glass of lemonade down

on the table, leaned forward on the edge of the chair, and rubbed his eyes. Be the man Brenda would want, he told himself. Not the coward she'd discarded at Northwestern.

"Hello, Lucas."

His head snapped around. Franklin Bennett stood there, glaring at him.

"What do you want?" Bennett asked gruffly, easing into the chair on the other side of the table. "This better be important."

Lucas's mouth went dry. Franklin Bennett was chief of staff to the president of the United States of America. Who the hell did he think he was, taking on this kind of power? Bennett could call in favors from people like the ones Cheetah had talked about. People who could easily cause those disasters Lucas had been running from his entire life.

He thought about Brenda again. Of how impressed she'd been by his career — and how disappointed she'd be by the truth. The hell with it. No risk, no reward.

"Have something to drink, Franklin."

"No. I don't care for anything."

Lucas had seen Bennett's posture stiffen at the sound of his given name. No one in the West Wing ever called him that. Not even the president. "Hot out here, isn't it, Franklin?" At least he'd gotten the bastard's attention.

"Yes," Bennett answered deliberately. "But peaceful, too."

"What do you want, Lucas?"

"I have a matter of grave importance to report."

"Yes?"

Lucas took a deep breath. Conviction. Keep your conviction. "Before I discuss it, I have questions."

"You what?"

"I have questions." When was the last time anyone had done anything like this to Bennett? he wondered. "Questions," Lucas repeated firmly.

"What questions?" Bennett demanded.

The moment of truth had arrived. Would he or wouldn't he? He could still back off. He hadn't yet passed the point of no return. "Why did you really want me to research the jewels?" Lucas asked. And there it was. Just that quickly he was in as deep as he could get. "What was your real motivation?"

"Motivation?" Bennett raised both eyebrows so they arched halfway up his forehead.

Bennett probably knew about Lucas's

genius level intelligence quotient, and the summa cum laude graduation from Northwestern. It might even have crossed his mind that there was a remote possibility Lucas could have suspicions about the operation's real objective. But Bennett never would have guessed that a 140-pound weakling who would have failed the first day of basic training at Parris Island would actually confront him.

"Yes." Now that Lucas was committed, he was thinking with surprising clarity. The cotton balls that had stuffed his mouth moments ago had dissolved like cotton candy. "Why did you have me research the jewels?"

Bennett folded his arms tightly across his chest. "We've been through all of this many times. I need to know if the men closest to the president have any skeletons so I can keep the bones locked in the closet until after the election. I don't understand why we're going through this again, Lucas. If you didn't fully understand the order when we started, you should have told me."

"I understood," Lucas assured Bennett, "but I believe you have another agenda." He was proud of himself. The words had come out calmly, even laced with a hint of his own irritation.

"What in the hell are you talking about?" Veins in Bennett's forehead rose to the surface, creating a roadmap stretching from one temple to the other. "What's going on here? I tasked you with a mission of vital importance to the party. I trusted you. Now, what have you found, my little friend?"

Lucas had prepared himself for the onslaught. It was just like those chess matches. Bennett was trying to end the conflict quickly with a massive frontal assault, but he was leaving his flank open. It was so predictable. "I've uncovered several important pieces of information, Franklin. One of those pieces of information would be very damaging to the president if it ever got out. It's that serious. But I want to know the truth before I tell you more." Lucas paused. "So, what is your real agenda?"

Bennett smiled defiantly. "What do you think it is? What's your little conspiracy fantasy?"

"I think you're more interested in using what I've found *against* the president," Lucas answered, closely watching the other man's expression as he dropped the bomb, "than suppressing it."

"You're out of your mind."

"Am I?"

"Lucas, I order you to turn over everything you have on the jewels," Bennett demanded. "Members of my team will escort you back to Georgetown, and you *will* give it to them. Do you understand?"

This was going to be easier than Lucas had anticipated. Despite his position of power, Bennett wasn't all that intelligent. He was nothing but a bully, and Lucas had lots of experience dealing with bullies.

"Wipe that smirk off your face, boy," Bennett snapped, standing up. "I'll have my associates meet you at the Beltway and Route 50, then go with you to Georgetown."

"Why don't you just have them go to Georgetown without me?" Lucas asked. "You have the combinations to the apartment's door and wall safe. You don't need me around." He paused, watching horses graze in the lush green fields. "What you need to understand, Franklin, is that I'm not here to make trouble."

"You could have fooled me," Bennett snapped.

"I'm here because I'm loyal to the party," Lucas continued, making certain his voice was strong. "Not necessarily to the president." He hesitated. "I'll give you what you want, but I want things in return."

Bennett sank slowly back onto the wicker chair.

"I know the details of Project Trust, Franklin," Lucas continued. "I know what the president will propose. I also know that you're in the dark about it. That you've been kept out of the loop. On purpose." Lucas saw that he'd struck a chord. Bennett was transfixed. "I'll give you some broad strokes, Franklin. But that's all I'm willing to tell you right now."

Bennett nodded, lips pursed.

Thank God for Harry Kaplan.

"The president will create a commission from hell to oversee Wall Street and cut investment banking compensation to the bone. They'll have a license to kill, and they'll be paid extremely well. So they won't be vulnerable to blue-blood bribery." Kaplan had relayed additional details concerning Project Trust during another clandestine meeting in the woods near the Iwo Jima Memorial late last night. "The president is going to shove accounting regulations so far up corporate asses that CEOs won't be able to take five dollars from petty cash without getting written permission from the SEC. But here's the real red hot poker. The president is going to propose raising the federal tax rate on all earnings over a million dollars to *seventy-five percent.*"

Bennett's mouth fell slowly open.

"He's going to propose a wealth tax, too," Lucas continued. This was another piece of new information Kaplan had relayed last night. "Anyone with a net worth over ten million dollars will have to pay the federal government five percent of the amount over ten million every year."

Bennett gazed at Lucas, as though he were hypnotized. "How do you know all this?" he finally whispered.

Bennett was ready to fall. One more volley and this thing would be over. "The president is dealing only with the deputy chief of staff on Project Trust. And Roscoe Burns has ordered the few people on his staff who know what's going on to tell you nothing. I have a connection on Burns's staff who's on the inside." Lucas had just put Harry Kaplan in terrible danger because Bennett might figure out the connection. But this was the big leagues and this was the play. Kaplan knew the risks involved by relaying this kind of information. "I can only infer from the gag order that the president doesn't trust you, Franklin. That the president is working solely with the deputy chief on Project Trust because he doesn't think you would support him. In fact, he fears that *many* people inside his party wouldn't support him. That even though he's the leader of the party, the money men behind the scenes would turn against him if they knew what he was planning. He knows you have close ties to the money, but that Burns is completely removed from that. That's why he's working with Burns on this, and he's shut you out. More than anything he wants to be reelected. He'll sacrifice all else to have that happen.

"He's keeping his plans quiet so you can't anticipate," Lucas continued. "So you can't throw up roadblocks and put together coalitions on the Hill to block him. So once he makes the details of Project Trust public, it's a done deal. So that when he ends his speech with 'God bless the United States of America,' the Project Trust train will have already left the station and there won't be any stopping it. The press will jump all over his proposals, and he'll be a hero to the masses. No one will be able to get in his way at that point.

"The president believes most people in this country want to see investment bankers, corporate executives, and the rest of the rich get screwed. He thinks he'll get the undecided vote with his proposals, and he's adding a little extra incentive to make sure. He's *cutting* tax rates for the middle and lower classes.

"He thinks the election may ultimately turn into a landslide, and he's probably right. People vote with their wallets. We all know that. He'll have to follow through on Project Trust, but so what? He'll win four more years in the Oval Office and that's all he cares about. He'll worry about the implications of his actions later.

"So what do you do, Franklin? You haven't been able to uncover the details of Project Trust, but you and a few other senior level officials inside the party anticipate that this thing is going to be bad. Very bad. The president is going to make his speech soon, and then he's in the driver's seat." Lucas smiled. "But there's one thing the president hasn't anticipated. The *extent* to which you and the other higher-ups in the party will go. The president figures once he's made his speech, he's in. All he's got to do is keep the train on the tracks. But you and the others see the window of opportunity as ninety days. Until the election. Like Yogi said, 'It ain't over till it's over.' You're not going to give up until the election is actually in the books. You see a way to use Project Trust *against* the president. How? Simple. Dig up something nasty on one of his handpicked boys and show the country he's guilty of exactly what Project Trust is trying to fight. Make it look like the president's promises are empty. Which will be a cakewalk if you can show that one of his boys is a thief. That would prove to the American people he isn't going to follow up on what he's proposed because he and his guys have benefited from exactly the kind of old boy network, backroom dealings Project Trust is supposed to stop." Lucas took a breath. "Which is where I come in. I have what you need."

Lucas's hands were shaking. But not with fear. With elation. He'd finally figured out the key to life. Confidence. Belief in self.

"What have you found?" Bennett asked, his voice barely audible.

Lucas thought about the marble notebook. He hadn't brought it with him today, but it was in a safe place. It was the first time in as long as he could remember, not having the book physically within his reach, and, he missed it like it was an old friend. But he couldn't risk losing his leverage if Bennett were able to physically take it from him.

On the blue-lined pages between the marble covers Lucas had recorded everything in copious detail. Cheetah's suggestions about the operation's true objective; Harry Kaplan's information about Project Trust; specifics related to the 550,000 in-the-money Global Component options granted to Secretary Bryson and the AB Trust; the indisputable connection between Bryson and the AB Trust that involved fourteen financial institutions on four continents; a description of Secretary Bryson's sexual harassment lawsuit; party financing particulars — including specific bank account and wire transfer numbers — related to Sam Macarthur and his private consulting firm; Franklin Bennett's involvement in the operation; and much more.

There was still the matter of verifying Bryson's quid pro quo for receiving the options, but Bennett didn't know that. Besides, Lucas knew exactly where to go to get that verification. But he wasn't going to do it until the deal was set.

"What do you have, Lucas?" Bennett repeated.

Bennett's tone wasn't one of anger, Lucas realized. It was more one of resignation. "Wait a minute." His hands were still shaking. He was close, but now he had to be so careful. He removed the pack of cigarettes from his pocket and turned away so Bennett wouldn't see how difficult it was for him to light up. He didn't care if Bennett knew he needed a crutch at this point. He'd found his conviction. But he didn't want the man to see his hands shake. He inhaled deeply, then turned back toward the chief of staff. "What intrigued me about the assignment was that I knew how close you are to Sheldon Gray and Walter Deagan," he said, already settling down, thanks to the tobacco. "If I had found something on either of them, you would definitely have kept the information hidden, if at all possible." Another puff of the cigarette. "Let me assure you what I found has nothing to do with Gray or Deagan."

Lucas saw relief in Bennett's expression. Which told him the bastard might even have sold his friends down the river if there were no other choice.

"Who does it involve?" Bennett asked, barely able to keep his temper under control.

"That's all I'll tell you at this point."

"Lucas, I swear to you I will —"

"And I want to make you aware that I've

put together an information book detailing everything." He stopped and pointed at Bennett with the cigarette. "Including information about how the party uses Sam Macarthur as a financing source for its 'special' projects. I'm sure there are those in the Justice Department sympathetic to the other party who would have a great deal of interest in that kind of information. You understand what I'm saying, don't you, Franklin?"

"You'll never work again!" Bennett shouted. "You'll never get a loan or a credit card. You won't be able to open a checking account. I swear to God!"

"I told you," Lucas said calmly, "I'm not here to cause trouble. I'm here to get something. It's horse trading, plain and simple."

"What, what? *What do you want?*" Bennett stammered, clenching his fists, his eyes bulging.

"See? That wasn't so bad."

"Out with it, Lucas!"

Lucas nodded. "Okay, here goes. I want to be a member of the club, or whatever it is you 'haves' call it."

"What are you talking about?"

"The usual stuff. After we take the president down, I want use of the private jets and the vacation homes. I want money wired to me in financial black holes like Antigua. Just a couple hundred grand now and then. It's a rounding error for a guy like Macarthur, but it's the world for me. And, if I can engineer what you want, it's a bargain." He looked around. "I want access to places like this." The sweeping gesture Lucas made with his hand left a smoke trail from the tip of his cigarette. "You can do that for me, Franklin, can't you?"

Bennett remained quiet for a long time. "Yes," he finally admitted, "I can."

Lucas took another puff off the cigarette. "I was right, wasn't I?" he asked. "You wanted information on one of the jewels to *destroy* the president, not to help him." He watched, careful not to blink. Careful not to miss the reaction.

Bennett nodded.

Almost imperceptibly, Lucas thought to himself. Now things were going to get interesting. "All right, Franklin, let's talk about next steps."

When Lucas was gone Bennett put his head back and closed his eyes. He was getting too old for this. He'd fought off cancer twice, but he had no confidence in his ability to win a third war. Maybe it was time to enjoy what the party could do for him. Time to retire to the ranch one of the party's money men owned in southwestern Montana and live out his days fly-fishing for trout in the Beaverhead and Big Hole rivers.

They'd played Lucas in chess anonymously on the Internet several times prior to initiating the operation to help them develop a profile. He was a brilliant strategist with a deliberate temperament who would wait out the thawing of an ice age if that was what it took to win. A man who would find something if there was something to find, but was unlikely to *ever* question orders. Particularly in situations where he was not intimately familiar with the rules of the game, and situations involving high-level superiors he did not know well. That was the report's profile.

It had turned out to be nothing but psychobabble bullshit. At least, that was Bennett's analysis. Lucas had turned out to be as cunning a political operative as Bennett had ever run into. A man who was willing to make up his own rules.

Bennett's eyes narrowed. Financial black hole. One of Cheetah's favorite phrases. Perhaps Lucas had gotten help being so cunning.

He heard footsteps coming down the main stairs. He straightened up and opened his eyes.

"Hello, Franklin."

Bennett watched as the other man eased into the chair Lucas had occupied. "Hello, Sam," he said quietly.

Sam Macarthur was the blond-haired, blue-eyed, forty-two-year-old son of a Kansas wheat farmer. He'd hit it big in the late nineties with a string of dot-coms. During that time he'd pocketed over a billion dollars founding three Internet retail companies selling everything from groceries to used cars, then taking them public. All three had ultimately gone bankrupt, but that hadn't mattered to Macarthur. Wall Street had gotten him his money and he was long gone by the time the companies collapsed.

Three years ago, Macarthur had come knocking on the party's door, explaining to Bennett that he simply wanted to get involved now that he had money and could do good things.

Bennett's analysis of Macarthur's motive was very different. Bennett believed Macarthur's real agenda was to learn the political game from the inside because he wanted to run for office. Bennett believed that once Macarthur had learned the game and made high-level contacts in Washington, the young man would campaign for Congress or the Senate. As long as he threw money at a couple of hospitals and schools, people would forget how he'd taken the public markets to the cleaners three times. Bennett also believed that Macarthur's ultimate goal was to be president. He'd known enough megalomaniacs to recognize the signs. The thing was, Macarthur could probably do it. He had Kennedy-like charisma, and everyone saw it.

Bennett had been brutally candid with Macarthur. There would be a price to learning the game and having access to party members who mattered. People who could pave his way to the Capitol, then the White House. Macarthur would set up a legitimate consulting business in New York, then funnel dollars out of the company to fund special projects for the party. And he'd make all of his toys available to certain nonelected senior party officials. His planes, boats, and homes.

A month later, Macarthur had purchased this Middleburg estate, then invited Bennett to meet him on this porch in this chair to inform the president's chief of staff that he had leased five floors of a Manhattan skyscraper on Fifth Avenue and hired a hundred professionals from McKinsey, Bain, the Boston Consulting Group, and other top consulting firms. To inform Bennett that Macarthur & Company was fully operational, and he was prepared to make those special funds available. One thing about Macarthur, Bennett thought to himself, he did things in a hurry.

"What did Lucas tell you?" Macarthur asked, picking up a glass of lemonade off the serving tray.

Bennett shook his head. "He told me that in the next Project Trust speech the president will announce a committee from hell to rule Wall Street with an iron hand. That the suspender set can anticipate having their multimillion-dollar annual compensation packages disappear."

Macarthur shrugged. "I don't give a flying fuck about those Wall Street pricks."

"No?"

"They're nothing but leeches. Skimmed seven percent of everything I got when they took my companies public. They deserved no more than one," Macarthur continued. "*Maybe.* I mean, how hard is it to sell stock, for Christ's sake?" He took a quick sip of lemonade. "What else did Lucas tell you?"

"That, as part of Project Trust, the president is going to propose a seventy-five percent income tax on annual earnings over a million dollars."

"Fucking Christ!" Macarthur shouted, hurling his glass against an oak tree in the front yard, shattering it into a hundred pieces.

"And a wealth tax of five percent a year on net worths over ten million dollars."

"*Holy shit!* He can't do that."

"The president can *propose* anything he wants to."

"He'd never get either of those fucking things passed."

Bennett raised an eyebrow. "Don't be so sure, Sam. We're in the middle of a recession, and the ninety-nine percent of America that's struggling right now doesn't give a rat's ass about a man who drinks lemonade served on a silver tray by his personal maid on the porch of his thousand-acre thoroughbred horse farm. And he's giving the have-nots a tax break. Just as insurance."

Macarthur pulled at his blond hair with both hands. "Has the little fucker found anything that can help us?"

"Yes, but he wouldn't tell me what it is."

"Why didn't you have some of your boys beat the snot out of him until he told you, then throw his body in the Potomac?"

"Because he's covered himself."

"What do you mean?"

Bennett turned toward Macarthur. "Lucas has recorded what he knows and stored that information in a safe place. Remember, what he knows involves Macarthur and Company."

"The little shit's bluffing."

"A man like Lucas doesn't bluff. He doesn't have the courage."

Macarthur rose from his chair and stalked to the porch railing. "So what the hell do we do?"

"Lucas is smart enough to have figured out that men like you take care of political appointees who don't have a chance to make fortunes in the private sector. He wants in on that."

"So?"

"We let him in."

"We let him in?"

Bennett smirked. "We let him *think* we're letting him in."

Macarthur smiled for the first time since coming out onto the porch.

"We let him think he's inside," Bennett repeated quietly, "until we've recovered those notes."

"How are you going to do that?"

"Don't worry," Bennett replied. "I have that angle covered." He glanced out at the horses dotting the fields. When this was over, he was definitely going to the ranch in Montana. "Did you speak with your contacts at the Justice Department this morning?"

Macarthur nodded. "Yes."

As chief of staff, Bennett had to be careful about being linked to certain federal agencies and departments on a regular basis. So he was using Macarthur as his go-between on this one. As a test. And as something the party could use against the young man in the future if they ever needed to. Macarthur didn't even realize what was going on. He'd jumped at the chance to get to know these people because Bennett had told him they were important. "And?"

"Several of the other operations are making significant progress, including the one involving Conner Ashby. We may not even need whatever Lucas has uncovered." Macarthur hesitated. "What would happen to someone like Ashby if he finds what we're looking for and we have to forcibly take it from him?"

Bennett chuckled. "He'd take that swim in the Potomac you recommended for Lucas."

CHAPTER 21

Conner hustled up the jet-way, quickly switching hands with his cell phone as he peeled off his suit jacket. Miami's heat and humidity were terrible. You could sweat while you were swimming down here.

"Hello."

"Is this the Executive Suite?" he asked, darting past slower passengers carrying bags.

"Yeah."

"Do you have a dancer named Tori there?" No one had answered when he called the club a few hours ago from New York.

"Why you wanna know?"

The air turned cooler as Conner reached the top of the jet-way and moved into the terminal. "I was here in Miami one night last March on business, and she was working. I bought her a drink and we talked a little. She was nice. But she wasn't at the club when I came back in June, and I was . . . well, I was disappointed. I . . . I thought she was . . . real pretty," he stammered, trying to sound embarrassed. "I was just hoping she'd be there tonight."

"You liked her, huh?" the man at the end of the line asked, laughing.

"Yeah," Conner admitted, lowering his voice. The man had no idea how much.

"You and a thousand other guys."

"Look, I —"

"Tori was away for a few months," the man cut in, "but she got back last week. I'm checking tonight's schedule and . . ." His voice faded momentarily. ". . . and you got lucky. She's gonna be here."

Conner had been worried that he might have to stay in Miami for a few days to run everything to ground, but maybe that wouldn't be necessary after all. Maybe he'd be able to catch that nine o'clock flight back out of here. "What time does she go on?"

There was another pause. "Six."

"Is she there yet?"

"No. She won't get here until right before she goes on. She never does."

Conner glanced at his watch. It was just before five. He might still have time to get to the Executive Suite before she did. He didn't want to have to wait around until the club closed, because then he'd miss that flight. And that would give the people trying to track him down more time to figure out where he was.

They must be going crazy right now, Conner thought to himself. One of them in particular.

He rented a car and followed the directions the man behind the counter gave him, glancing in the rearview mirror every few moments. Looking for anything suspicious.

The Executive Suite was located beside a strip mall on the edge of an upscale neighborhood north of downtown. He swung the car into an open parking spot in front of a jewelry store. From here he could see anyone who drove onto the club's lot.

Conner watched a palm tree sway in the warm breeze as he sat in the car, engine idling, air-conditioning turned on high. It had been a long time since he'd been back in Florida. It would have been nice if the homecoming could have been under different circumstances.

He shook his head. There'd been no engagement to a Morgan Sayers investment banker named Todd. Which was why the three-carat diamond was so cheap. Why spend a lot of money on a ring that was meaningless? The story about a trust fund left to her by a grandfather was a lie, too.

Just like Art Meeks's claim about being a private investigator. Amy Richards's story about taking a new waitressing job at an Upper East Side restaurant. Everything was smoke and mirrors. The e-mail, the break-in, and the murder. A complete sham.

A sham, but an intricately crafted one with a very specific goal, Conner realized. To get him to investigate Global Components, specifically what was happening in Minneapolis. So the person behind the sham — without risking his own neck — could confirm that Global Component's senior executives were committing fraud on an enormous scale. Overstating Global's earnings to keep the stock price going up — it had closed today's trading at sixty-seven, according to a broker at Ameritrade. To keep it moving north so the executives could keep cashing in the massive amount of call options the board had granted them.

Conner was convinced he had figured out the ultimate objective of this thing: To confirm the fraud baked into Global's EPS numbers so that once there was definitive proof of what was happening in Minneapolis, the person behind the sham could release the information to the financial markets and make millions as Global's share price crashed in the face of panic selling. Selling Global's stock short or buying tons of put options before he released the information. Global's share price would likely hit single digits in the hours immediately after the information was released, and the perpetrator of the sham would stand to make sixty bucks on every share he shorted and every put option he bought. Global was so big and had so many shares outstanding that by the time investigators sifted through the ashes and discovered any unusual trading activity — if they ever actually did discover it — the perpetrator would be long gone.

Liz's "murder" had put the sham in motion. It had forced Conner to act on the e-mail from Rusty. At first, because he wanted to bring the murderer to justice. Then to protect himself as Art Meeks turned the screws tighter and tighter. Because, as Meeks — and Gavin — had pointed out several times, the police would ultimately focus on Conner as the prime suspect in Liz's murder. He was in love with a beautiful woman who was engaged to another man. Conner had motive — jealousy — and opportunity. And he showed up in her diary so many times.

Which was all crap, of course. But he hadn't known that there was no diary when Art Meeks had confronted him the first time on Lexington Avenue. Then the second time in Central Park. It wasn't until he discovered that the errant e-mail had actually come from Amy Richards's computer — not from the computer of some accountant named Rusty at Baker Mahaffey — that he had begun to understand what was really going on. It was an e-mail that had turned out not to be errant at all. Liz's "murder" had been the explosion that had put the sham into motion, but the e-mail had been the fuse that had ignited the explosion. And ultimately led him to the truth — thanks to Jackie.

The truth was that Paul Stone was the one behind this thing. Rebecca had seen Stone with Amy Richards. Eddie had confirmed Stone as the name on the lease of the apartment down the hall from Conner's where he and Eddie had discovered his old furniture and the bucket of red liquid — just dye intended to look like blood. Stone was on the lease at Liz's Fifty-first Street apartment, too. And, according to the cell phone bills, Stone and Liz had talked at least three or four times a day during July.

Conner had also discovered that Stone

was in a world of hurt financially. Stone's mortgage was three months past due, his credit cards were maxed out, and his country club membership had been revoked — it always helped to have a friend at a background check company. That same friend had run a trace on Mandy Stone's family and informed Conner that her family was leading a middle-class life in Omaha, Nebraska. They weren't influential, as Gavin had suggested. Apparently, Stone had fooled Gavin, too. About a lot of things.

Paul Stone had been caught committing insider trading once before, and he was at it again. But this time it was on a huge scale.

Conner still hadn't confirmed exactly what was going on at Global's Minneapolis operation. Or how Stone knew that Global had a problem in Minneapolis, but didn't have possession of the kind of conclusive evidence that would influence the markets. Which would be the key to a short selling strategy involving the kind of money Stone would want to clear out of this. Having a knockout punch. Having enough credible information in hand to instantly and completely convince the markets that Global Components was going down because of the accounting fraud. With the same lightning-quick speed Enron had imploded. So Stone could get in and out fast. His plan wouldn't work if the information was unspecific and dribbled out. And, if he put out information that didn't contain the knockout punch, the massive company might have time to somehow hide what was going on.

The image of Liz sprawled on his bedroom floor flashed through Conner's mind. The sham had been choreographed so perfectly. He'd seen her body for only a split second before hearing the intruder in the living room. Only a moment to see the blood covering her throat and chest.

He lifted his arm, rolled up his sleeve, and glanced at the bullet wound. Being shot had convinced him that what was going on was very real, too. The guy chasing him down the fire escape must have been a hell of a marksman. A few inches to the right and —

A red Mustang zipped into the Executive Suite parking lot and pulled into a spot well away from the club's entrance. Conner cut the rental car's engine and grabbed the door handle as a young woman emerged from the Mustang. But he eased back into the seat as she shut her door. It wasn't Liz. He watched as the woman trotted toward the club's entrance.

When the woman had disappeared inside, he looked up at the Executive Suite sign over the entrance. Liz Shaw was a stripper. No wonder she'd been so comfortable being nude in front of him. He chuckled wryly. He'd wanted that sapphire belly piercing to be the rebel side of a society girl. Instead, it had been the sound business judgment of a woman trying to earn a living. An ornament intended to titillate. And, damn. How it had.

A rusting, light-blue Honda rolled into the parking lot. Conner caught a glimpse of long blond hair and a beautiful face. He held his breath as the Honda pulled to a stop alongside the Mustang.

Then a pair of long legs emerged from the driver's side. He'd recognize those legs anywhere — even from a distance. He'd found Liz Shaw. She wasn't dead after all. She was alive and well in Miami.

On the flight down Conner asked himself over and over how he could have fallen for the con. He prided himself on seeing things for what they were. Then Liz emerged from the Honda. She was wearing three-inch heels and a tiny dress that covered very little. Suddenly he realized exactly how he'd fallen for it. She was one of the most stunning women he'd ever seen.

Liz lifted a bag to her shoulder, locked the car, and began walking across the parking lot toward the club.

When she was halfway to the entrance, Conner broke from the rental car and headed toward her. She'd turn an ankle if she tried to run far in those heels.

Liz spotted him as he hurdled a divider separating the jewelry store and the club parking lots. She froze, glued to the asphalt for a split second. She made a move for the club, then stumbled and stopped short, realizing she wouldn't make it. She dropped the bag, kicked off her heels and dashed back toward the Honda.

It was exactly what Conner had hoped for. If he'd been forced to drag her to the rental car screaming her lungs out, someone would have heard her and called the cops. But there were woods out beyond Liz's Honda. A thick grove of pine trees separating the Executive Suite parking lot from a neighborhood, and that was what he needed — an isolated spot where he could interrogate her without being seen.

It was going to be close. She was faster than he'd anticipated. Covering a lot of ground quickly. If she made it to the

Honda and managed to lock the doors before he got there, he'd lose her. She'd go squealing away, and he'd lose his chance to solve this thing. She'd call Stone, and then Conner would suddenly become the rabbit.

Conner heard a high-pitched beep and saw the Honda's parking lights blink when Liz popped the locks with the remote button. He raced the last few yards as she grabbed the driver side handle and yanked the door open. He jammed his arm into the car just as she slammed the door shut — right on his elbow. Searing pain shot up to his shoulder and down to his fingers, but he kept the door from closing. He wedged his knee into the crack, forced the door open and grabbed Liz as she tried frantically to scramble into the passenger seat.

"Get off me!" she screamed, clutching the steering wheel in a death grip. "Get the hell off me!"

But he grabbed a fistful of her hair and wrenched her from the car, hustling her roughly into the grove of pines. Twenty yards into the woods he hurled her onto a bed of needles in a small clearing, then dropped on top of her, pinning her arms to the ground with his knees and pressing one

hand to her mouth. She was still screaming.

"Shut up!" he hissed, leaning down so
his face was only inches from hers. He
slipped his fingers to her throat and
squeezed. "Shut up or so help me I'll break
your goddamn neck!"

Liz turned her head to the side and
cringed. "All right, all right."

Conner's eyes flashed around. The cover
was dense in here. No one could see them.
But someone might have heard her
screams. "Tell me everything," he demanded. "Everything!"

"Don't kill me," she begged. "*Please*
don't kill me."

"Is it Paul Stone? Is that who you're
working with?"

"I don't know what you're talking about.
I don't know any Paul Stone."

"I've got phone records, Liz. Multiple
cell phone conversations between you and
Stone every day in July. Don't lie to me."

"Okay, okay. I'm working with him."

"Why did he approach you?"

Liz hesitated, her eyes flickering wildly
from side to side. "He . . . he didn't."

"What do you mean?"

She swallowed hard. "Ginger was the
one. Ginger approached me."

"The woman you worked with at Merrill Lynch?"

"Yes."

Conner gritted his teeth. "Ginger never worked at Merrill," he snarled, aware of a siren in the distance. "I talked to Ted Davenport. You lied to me about that. That and everything else."

Liz moaned as his dug his knees deep into her arms. "I'm sorry."

"Stop apologizing. Give me answers. How do you know Ginger?"

"She works at the club," Liz said, nodding back toward the parking lot. "She's my roommate here in Miami. We've known each other for a while."

"Is she working tonight?"

"No. She's back at the apartment."

The siren was growing louder. Someone must have called the cops. "Let's go," he said, pulling her up off the ground roughly.

"Where?"

"Your apartment. You, Ginger, and I are going to figure this thing out."

Twenty minutes later Conner pulled to a stop in front of the entrance to the Ocean View Condominiums. "This it?"

"Yes," she said quietly.

Conner glanced at the address on the

side of the building. It was the same as the one on the mortgage invoice in Gavin's kitchen drawer. This was Gavin's place. "You're going to answer a few more questions before we go upstairs."

"Okay," she agreed meekly.

There was no fight left in her. Conner could see that. "So Ginger had you seduce me? *She's* the one working with Paul Stone."

"Yes," Liz confirmed. "Ginger met Paul when he was here in Miami on a business trip about a year and a half ago. Paul's the one who arranged for us to move into this building. It's nice. It's a two-bedroom on the fifth floor. We were living in a rat's nest before on the south side, and Paul got us out of there." She hesitated. "I think your boss is the one who actually owns this place. What's his name? You mentioned him to me a couple of times."

"Gavin Smith."

"Yeah, that's it. I think this is Gavin Smith's place." She rolled her eyes. "Paul told us Gavin wouldn't mind if we stayed here, but I think he was lying. We had to clear out one weekend a few months after we moved in and make it look like we'd never been here. That happened a couple of times, so all I can think of is that Gavin doesn't really know we're here. But it's worked out all right. And, like I said, it's a lot nicer than the place we were in."

Conner's eyes narrowed. "It was Ginger who had you come on to me at that bar back in May."

Liz looked down. "A few months after they met, Ginger and Paul hatched some kind of crazy get-rich-quick scheme. I don't know any details. They didn't tell me anything, and I didn't really want to know. But part of it involved me being your girlfriend. It was creepy, but I did it because they paid me." She slipped her hand to his. "I'm sorry about this, *Conner*. I just —"

"How much?" he asked, picking her hand up and placing it back in her lap. It was the first time she'd ever called him by his first name. "How much did they pay you?"

"A hundred grand," she answered. "But they've given me only five so far." A tear rolled down her cheek. "I was down to my last dime. That's the only reason I did all this. I didn't mean to hurt you. I almost told you so many times, but I was scared. You don't screw with Ginger. She can go psycho sometimes." Liz paused. "I think Paul might be capable of some pretty whacked out stuff, too."

"So Ginger never told you anything about what was really going on?"

"No. Like I said, all I knew was that I was supposed to be your girlfriend. But I wasn't supposed to let you get too close. That's why Ginger cooked up the story about me being engaged. She said that would keep you at a distance. I wasn't supposed to go out in public with you at all."

"But we did go out a few times," Conner reminded her. As a result, the man working for Gavin had seen them over at that place on First.

"Ginger was afraid you were going to say the hell with it and screw up the whole thing, so she said I needed to go out with you a couple of times. But they were always out-of-the-way joints."

Conner nodded. "And I could never come to the place they had for you over on Fifty-first. Where the doormen know you by the name Tori."

Liz's eyes widened. "You know —"

"Just keep talking," he ordered.

"That was really it," she mumbled. "I had to report to Stone constantly. He called me all the time. I had no idea we were going to stage my murder until the day before it happened."

"Who was the guy that chased me down the fire escape?"

Liz shrugged. "I don't know. After you and he went out the bedroom window, I took a shower real fast to clean up. To get the dye off me. Then I went down the fire escape, too. It was all prearranged. Another guy was waiting for me in the alley and he helped me get down there at the bottom. You know, where the ladder was pulled up off the alley. Then he drove me to the airport and handed me a ticket to Miami. That was it. I swear to you. I still don't know why Paul and Ginger did what they did to you."

Conner was silent for a few moments, thinking. "All right, let's go upstairs. I want to talk to Ginger."

Liz glanced at the building fearfully. "Can I just stay down here? She's crazy. I promise I won't go anywhere."

Conner shook his head. "No way."

Lucas and Brenda sat on a bench near the Washington Monument. It was early evening and the sun was casting long shadows.

She'd called him this afternoon as he was returning from Middleburg. She wanted to see him, she said. She couldn't wait until the weekend. He'd agreed to get together with her immediately, making a quick stop in Georgetown before hurrying over here.

"It was just that I had such a good time at dinner, Lucas," she murmured. "And I feel so guilty about what I did to you at Northwestern. It was such an awful thing. I want to make certain you know how much I regret all that. Just telling you on the phone didn't seem like the right way to do it. I had to see you."

Lucas patted her hand gently. Her skin was so soft. "That's very nice," he said quietly. He took a deep breath and raised both eyebrows. "I can't say that it doesn't still hurt. What you did crushed me. I was a basket case for months. I . . . I still have that picture of you. Do you remember giving it to me?"

"Of course."

"I've looked at it every day since you left."

Brenda leaned forward and kissed him. "I'm sorry." She sighed. "Maybe I should go. Maybe this was wrong. I don't deserve another chance," she said, rising from the bench.

But he pulled her back down onto the bench. Closer this time. "Another chance? What do you mean?"

Brenda moaned. "I've had enough of the macho types. I want a man who's caring and considerate." She paused. "Like you." She turned away. "But I know you could never trust me . . ." Her voice trailed off. "Never."

Lucas took her gently by the chin and turned her face back toward his. "You don't know that."

She smiled sadly. "How could you after what I did?"

He glanced around, then clasped her hand tightly. "There's something I need to tell you. And something I need you to do."

She gazed into the intensity of his expression. "Of course, Lucas. Anything. Are you in trouble?" she asked, her voice rising. "My God, what is it?"

Lucas reached into his jacket and pulled out the marble notebook he'd carried with him from Georgetown. "Take this and keep it safe. If I haven't contacted you within forty-eight hours, you need to open the sealed envelope that's taped to the inside of the back cover and follow the instructions printed on the page inside the envelope. Do you understand?"

"Lucas, I —"

"Do you understand?"

She searched his expression again, then nodded. "Yes."

"You better be careful," Liz whispered, removing the key from her purse. "I'm telling you, Ginger can go off in a heartbeat. She does crazy things sometimes. And I'm not sure, but I think she has a gun in her bedroom closet."

Conner leaned close to the door, listening for any sound from inside. But there was nothing.

"She's probably asleep," Liz whispered. "She worked real late last night."

"Give me the layout of the place," Conner ordered, taking the key from Liz's trembling fingers.

"When you go in, her bedroom is ahead and to the left."

Conner nodded. "All right. You go first, then I'll follow." He pointed at her. "So help me, if you try anything, I'll —"

"I just want to get this over with."

"Good answer." He slid the key into the lock and turned the knob, then slowly pushed the door open and followed Liz into the condominium.

Liz pointed toward a closed door to the left. "That's her bedroom."

He motioned for Liz to stay where she

was, then stepped noiselessly to Ginger's door. He was about to turn the knob when he looked back one more time. He wanted to know where the bed was in the room. As he glanced over his shoulder, he noticed that Liz had edged farther away. Close to another door, also shut.

"It's to the right," she said quietly, anticipating his question.

He gazed at her, adrenaline pumping through his body. Then his eyes fell to the coffee table. On it was a handwritten note.

"Have a great week, T," it read. "See you Friday. Love, G."

As Conner scanned the note a second time, it hit him. There was no one behind this door. Ginger was gone.

He glanced up into the mirror above the couch. Liz was staring back at him.

As he turned, Liz bolted for her bedroom, hurling open the door and vanishing inside.

"Christ!" Conner tore after her, leaping over the couch and bursting through the door she'd slammed shut behind her. He caught a glimpse of her disappearing into a walk-in closet, and raced toward it. As he rounded the corner, she was pulling a gun from a shoe box. He lunged at her, grabbing her hand before she could point the weapon. Ripping the pistol from her fingers.

"Let me go!" she screamed. "Let me go!"

Conner clenched her wrist, pulling her out of the closet even as she dropped to her knees and tried to grab the door. He dragged her to the bathroom and slammed the door shut, shoving her ahead of him. Then he leaned down, jammed the plug into the tub's drain and turned on the hot water.

Liz's eyes grew wide as the tub began to fill. "What are you doing?" she asked, her voice trembling as steam begin to rise.

"Answer my questions and you won't have to find out," he answered, standing up. "Now get on your knees," he ordered sharply, pointing at a spot beside the tub.

"No, please, I —"

"Get on your knees!"

Liz sank down. "Please," she begged. "Please don't hurt me."

"How did it start?" he asked above the sound of water rushing from the faucet. "Start talking," he ordered, gripping a fistful of her hair.

"They came into the Executive Club last December," she said quickly, turning her head to the side as steam rushed past her face. "Right before Christmas."

"*Who* came in?"

"These two corporate types." The words were tumbling out now. She was terrified. "It was almost midnight, and they were already pretty drunk when they got there. They wanted company so I sat down. I recognized them. They'd been in before."

Conner released his grip on her and allowed her to sit up. Then he pulled the picture he had run off the color printer this morning at Phenix from his pocket, then unfolded it and held it. Jim Hatcher, Global Components's CFO. "Is this one of the men who came in that night?"

Liz nodded, wiping tiny droplets from her face. "Yes. How did you know?"

"Lucky guess. So, what happened?"

"They kept getting drunker and drunker. They could barely stay in their chairs they were so wasted, but they were tipping me good, so I put up with it. I mean, they were tipping *really* good. Two hundred bucks for a one-song lap dance, and they kept doing it. I asked them how come they had so much money and that guy," Ginger pointed at the picture, "he told me how he ran the money for this mammoth public company — Global Components — like he owned it himself. The other guy slapped him on the back and started bragging about how they'd created billions of dollars of phony earnings out of thin air and nobody knew about it but them. How they were keeping all these expenses in something they kept calling a shadow account in Minneapolis. And how the two of them were the smartest executives ever to hit corporate America. They told me they were senior executives at Global Components a couple of times. And they told me I ought to buy the company's stock because it was going to keep going up."

"You figured there might be an angle," Conner said calmly.

Liz nodded.

"And you called Paul Stone. You were the one who had met him, not Ginger. He put you up here and let Ginger live with you."

"That's right." Liz's voice was barely audible. "Ginger's just my roommate. She doesn't know anything. I told her I was dancing at a club in New York City for the last few months. She didn't question me, because the people who run these clubs have us move around every once in a while. So we don't get too friendly with the regulars."

"You talked to Stone because you figured he would know what to do with the information about Global Components?"

"I figured there was money to be made. But I didn't know how to do it. I thought Paul would."

"Did Stone get you the job at Merrill Lynch?"

"Yes. I needed spending money while I was in New York, and he knew someone over there. All I had to do was take people to lunch and walk their dogs. It was easy."

"Until that guy from Miami showed up a few weeks ago in New York. Then you had a problem."

"Yeah, right."

Conner shut off the water. The tub was almost full. "Why did you tell me that Ginger worked with you in New York?"

"When she called your apartment that first night back in May, you asked me about her. I blanked. I couldn't think of anything else to say. It was stupid, but you'd promised not to come to Merrill, so I wasn't that worried about it."

Conner watched as a drop formed at the end of the faucet, slowly growing larger until finally it fell into the tub. "So a couple of guys come into the club one night drunk off their asses and start telling you to buy their company's stock. Just to impress you."

"Men try to impress me all the time. They want to think that somehow they're different from all the others. Most of the time they're lying." She hesitated. "This time, they weren't."

"And that's how it all started," Conner said quietly.

"Yes."

He shook his head. "For some reason I think you're finally telling me the truth."

Conner slipped behind the steering wheel and checked his watch. It wasn't even seven. He was going to make that nine o'clock flight to Washington with plenty of time to spare.

He slid the key in the ignition and turned the engine on. He'd call the Miami police and tell them about the young woman who was bound and gagged on the floor of the walk-in closet upstairs when this thing was over. Which ought to be by this time tomorrow, he figured.

"You're doing the right thing."

Brenda glanced up at her managing partner. She didn't have a choice. She'd missed the statute of limitations on a personal injury case for the second time in three months. Both clients had lodged complaints with the D.C. Bar Association, and she was looking at a bad situation. Maybe even disbarment.

"Just take care of the complaints for me," she said. "Please, Hootie."

James "Hootie" Wilson was one of the most well-connected attorneys in Washington. A white-haired sage who spoke with a soft southern accent and seemed to know everyone in town.

"Call the people you know at the association," Brenda continued. "I can't have this on my record."

Wilson looked down at the marble notebook lying on his desk and smiled. Perfect. It was exactly as Bennett had explained. "Don't worry that pretty little head of yours one more second," he said comfortingly. "Consider it done."

Brenda hesitated. She shouldn't ask this. She shouldn't care. This was all about saving herself. But she couldn't help it. "Hootie, what's going to happen to Lucas?"

Wilson picked up the marble notebook and slipped it into his briefcase. "Don't you worry about that either, sweetie."

CHAPTER 22

Cheetah picked his way carefully through the tombstones of the vast graveyard. He'd never met his contact here before, but that wasn't what concerned him. They were constantly changing the locations of these rendezvous points. What concerned him was that they were meeting in broad daylight. That had never happened before. There must be an emergency, particularly since the order to meet had such a short fuse.

He spotted a mausoleum down the hill near a tree line and headed for it, making certain to give a crew of men excavating a fresh grave a wide berth. The mausoleum was the rendezvous point, and he didn't want the workers getting suspicious and interrupting the meeting.

Cheetah trotted the last few yards to the marble structure, past two matching headstones, putting the building between himself and the workers as he slipped around one corner. He didn't like graveyards. Never had. Not because he harbored some irrational paranoia about specters or was uncomfortable with death. He just hated such a blatant waste of good real estate. He'd already given his father strict instructions to have his corpse cremated — if there was one.

Cheetah's contact was waiting, leaning casually against the mausoleum wall.

"What's going on?" Cheetah demanded. "And why was I given so little notice?"

"Our source believes Conner Ashby may be getting close to something."

"So?"

"What information do you have on Ashby?"

That was a ridiculous question. "How would I know anything about him? You guys at Justice are the ones all over that." He snorted, mad as hell that they'd dragged him all the way out here. "Listen, I —" Cheetah interrupted himself. Suddenly it all made sense. Franklin Bennett was covering his tracks. Destroying all evidence of the operation as the pieces became unnecessary.

Cheetah turned to run, but the heavy rope slipped over his head from behind before he could take a step. It snared tight around his throat, and the garrote rod spun quickly. Suddenly he couldn't breathe and his eyes felt as if they were going to explode from his skull. He clawed at the rope, gazing at his contact, who was staring back, expressionless. He reached out with both hands, as though that pitiful gesture might have an effect.

Then his knees touched the ground, and he gasped for one more precious breath. But it didn't come, and everything faded to black.

Lucas checked up and down the darkened street, then knocked on Glen Frolling's front door for the third time. It was almost eleven thirty and the report he'd gotten from Bennett claimed that Frolling had gotten home around ten. Frolling's wife was visiting a relative in California and they had no children. The house ought to be empty except for Frolling.

Bennett was in contact with Lucas constantly now. Supplying him with many things, including the report and the two "associates" accompanying him tonight. One of whom had gone around the side of the house to make certain Frolling didn't try to escape through a back door. Bennett was acting almost friendly now. It was odd, but Lucas wasn't going to kid himself. Bennett's new attitude was coming only as a result of his fear of what was in the marble notebook.

Lucas hesitated, thinking about Brenda. How she'd promised to keep the notebook safe. To open the envelope taped to the inside of the back cover of the notebook only if she didn't hear from him within the next forty-eight hours. How she'd slipped her arms around him and hugged him tightly as they stood beside the bench near the Washington Monument. Begging to know what was going on. Pleading with him to take care of himself, a worried look creasing her face. He glanced at a streetlight. It was strange how much older she'd looked this afternoon.

Lucas pointed at the knob. "Go on."

The other man moved to the door, slid a pick into the lock, and popped it open. That quickly they were inside Frolling's house.

Lucas had permission to do whatever was necessary to get Frolling's cooperation. Frolling had been secretary to the Global Components board of directors for over a decade. If there was anyone who knew whether there had been a quid pro quo when Alan Bryson and the AB Trust had received the option grants, it was Frolling.

"Get the other guy in here," Lucas ordered, turning on a hall light. They had to be in and out fast so the neighbors didn't suspect anything. "Then check upstairs."

"Yes, sir."

Lucas's expression turned steely as he watched the other man obey his order. He liked giving orders. And being called *sir.*

There was light coming from beneath a door in the kitchen, and he pulled it open. Behind it were steps leading down. "Hey," he called over his shoulder softly.

Instantly, the man was back. "Yes, sir?"

"Forget the other guy," Lucas said. "Come with me."

The other man pulled a pistol from his shoulder holster and followed Lucas down the stairs.

As they reached the basement, Lucas smelled smoke — then saw Frolling. He was hanging from the ceiling by his neck, his stocking feet dangling a foot off the floor. Behind him was an overturned chair and his shoes.

The other man slipped past Lucas to Frolling, touching the man's wrist. "He's dead."

Lucas gazed at Frolling, who was still swinging slightly from side to side. It occurred to him that he'd never actually seen a dead body, and he stared at the noose around the neck, then up to the open eyes, thinking about the time a few years ago he'd considered this option. "What are you doing?" he asked. The other man had picked up the overturned chair and was about to climb onto it.

"I was going to get him down."

"Leave him," Lucas instructed, moving to a pile of smoldering papers he'd spotted in one corner of the room. "Call the police when we're gone. Tell them you're a neighbor and you heard something." He knelt down and sifted through the pile, picking up a piece of paper that was only half-burned.

"You find something?"

Lucas nodded. "Yeah. Looks like our next stop will be the accounting firm of Baker Mahaffey. Specifically, Victor Hammond's office."

"Mr. Reeves?"

The baby-faced, red-haired young man in the plaid bathrobe squinted, then shielded his eyes against the brilliance of the porch light. "Yes?" His voice sounded like metal scraping against metal. "What time is it?" he asked angrily.

"Mr. *Phil* Reeves?"

"Yes, but —"

"Honey, what's going on?" A young woman appeared in the hallway behind Reeves. She was holding a baby. "Is everything all right?"

"Everything is fine," Reeves assured her. "Go back to bed." He turned to the man standing on the stoop. "Who are you? What do you want?"

"My name is Greg Adams. I'm with the office of the United States Attorney General."

Reeves looked off into the distance for a few moments, then turned his head slightly to the side. "Let me see your credentials."

"They're in the car."

"What is this?" Reeves demanded angrily.

Conner had driven to Reeves's Virginia town house after landing at Dulles Airport thirty minutes ago and renting another car. Paul Stone could track Conner by his credit card activity, but he wasn't planning on staying in one place long enough for Stone to catch up. But he'd be heading straight into the lion's den itself if everything worked out. Then it would get tricky.

"Okay, I'm not with the AG's office," Conner admitted. "But if you don't cooperate with me, Mr. Reeves, I'll call the AG's office and tell them everything I know about what's going on at Global Components. I'll tell them about Minneapolis, and how people at Baker Mahaffey are in on it. People like you."

Rusty stared back at Conner silently.

Conner glanced down. The other man's hands were shaking badly. "Listen to me, *Rusty*. You and I are going downtown to your office right now, and you're going to turn over everything to me. All the documents that prove fraud at Global Components. I know you have them. For some reason you accounting guys have this need to document *everything*. Even if it's bad stuff." He remembered Jackie telling him that. "Like I said, if you don't cooperate with me, I'll call the authorities and you'll have less than thirty minutes left with your wife and that beautiful little baby."

"Sounds like that's all I'll have, anyway," Rusty mumbled. "If I turn over everything to you, there will be people pounding on my door a few minutes later."

"I'll give you a twenty-four-hour head start." Conner saw indecision on Rusty's face. "Listen to me," he said quickly, "this is your best shot. I'm a better risk than the people who will come next. And

I promise you, they will come."

Rusty gazed at Conner for several moments. Finally he nodded. "Okay."

Conner followed Rusty inside the two-story town house, not letting the man out of his sight the entire time. Worried the young accountant would call Vic Hammond, or that his wife would call the cops. But Rusty had convinced his wife that Conner was an old fraternity brother who was in trouble and needed help. She'd patted Conner on the shoulder and asked if there was anything she could do.

Fifteen minutes later, Conner and Rusty were headed east on Interstate 66 toward downtown Washington. Conner sat in the passenger seat while Rusty drove.

"What's the deal in Minneapolis?" Conner asked.

Rusty glanced over. "You mean you don't know?"

"I know there's fraud going on out there. I know that if an SEC SWAT team went in, *they'd* find it."

"Yeah, they would," Rusty agreed. "How do you know something's wrong out there?"

"Can't say."

"If you aren't with the AG's office, who are you with?"

"It doesn't matter. What matters is that I'm giving you a chance. You should appreciate that."

"I guess I do. Although twenty-four hours isn't much to work with."

"Too bad. It's all you're getting."

The Washington Monument appeared in front of them across the Potomac River. It was brightly lit, a stark white tower set against the black night.

"I assume your name isn't really Greg Adams."

"No, it isn't," Conner confirmed. "Now, give me specifics on Minneapolis."

Rusty tapped the steering wheel. "A while back Global Components set up this tiny little company out there. Two offices and a receptionist desk. Just three people, and they don't really do anything all day. It's called Fargo Lease Management, and ultimately it's owned by Global Components. But there are twenty-six other subsidiaries stacked between Global and Fargo. All incorporated in different countries around the world. All with names that don't have the words *global* or *components* in them. Even in the local language. In other words, if you weren't Jim Hatcher, Global Component's CFO, or Phil Reeves, accountant at Baker Mahaffey, or a couple of bankers in New York who are on the take, you'd never figure out who owns Fargo."

"Don't forget Vic Hammond."

"How do you — ?"

"Don't worry about it," Conner interrupted as they pulled to a stop at a red light where I-66 met Constitution Avenue. "Come on. Tell me about Fargo."

"A few years ago Global hit a bad streak. Foreign competition got nasty, and, at the same time, senior management let internal manufacturing costs get out of control. Global had to take on a lot of debt just as earnings tanked. So the stock market pounded the company's shares. The price dropped from the upper fifties to the low thirties in less than a month."

Conner nodded. He'd read about the stock's nosedive while researching the company.

"It was a bloodbath," Rusty continued. "The senior guys at Global had their nuts in a vise. Shareholders were making a big stink about the terrible financial results, *and* about a bunch of big-dollar loans the executives had made to themselves using corporate funds. A couple of important institutional investors threatened to take drastic action unless something happened fast."

"Like the stock price going back up."

"Exactly. If that didn't happen, the senior executives were going to have their asses handed to them. And there were gonna be lawsuits. So they came up with a plan."

"With the help of their accountants, I assume," Conner said as the light turned green.

"Yeah," Rusty agreed, his voice dropping. "With Baker Mahaffey's help."

It was exactly as Jackie had described. The accountants had been in on the fraud right from the start.

"In fact," Rusty continued, "that's how we won the business away from the firm that was auditing Global Components at the time. I think it was Deloitte and Touche."

"What do you mean?" Conner asked, aware that Rusty seemed strangely relieved to be spilling his guts. Like talking about this was cathartic. *"You mean you proposed fraud to get the business?"*

Rusty looked over as they passed the White House. "Vic Hammond proposed it. Not me."

As if that made Rusty any less guilty, Conner thought to himself.

"Vic had just lost a couple of big clients," Rusty explained, "and he was desperate for a win. The managing partners in New York were coming down on him hard. I had just joined the firm." He paused. "I work for Vic, but somehow I get the feeling you know that."

"Yes, I do," Conner said. "*So give me the specifics.* What goes on at Fargo Lease Management? Why is it so important?"

Rusty turned left onto Seventeenth Street. Baker Mahaffey's offices were only a few blocks away.

"So Global ended up selling a huge chunk of its capital assets, you know, its plants and equipment, to this tiny little company out in Minnesota. Then leased it all back at a nothing rate. They took the cash from the sale and paid off a bunch of debt. That transaction had the effect of cutting Global's capital expenses by almost two billion dollars a year, thereby increasing earnings by the same amount. The minimal amount Global pays Fargo to lease the capital assets back barely even shows up on the income statement. It's just enough to cover the interest on the loans a couple of banks made to Fargo, quietly guaranteed by Global, of course," Rusty added. "Anyway, earnings per share shot back up and the stock market was ecstatic.

The share price shot up as well. Over the next two years senior management got manufacturing costs back in line and developed several new products. Suddenly everything was beautiful again. But the executives liked that two billion dollars a year of cost cuts, so we had to keep giving it to them."

"Wait a minute." Conner shook his head. "A couple of banks loaned Fargo all that money to buy Global's assets?"

"Yup," Rusty answered, pulling into an all-night parking garage just down the block from Baker Mahaffey. "Like I said, with Global's guarantee."

"But what about year-end consolidation? Intercompany transactions are always netted out on the financial statements. That parent guarantee would reverse everything you structured for them, wouldn't it?"

"First of all, there are twenty-six subsidiaries between Global and Fargo. No one's going to figure out that there's any ownership relationship between the two entities. No one but us, because we structured it. And we're not going to tell anybody. And the banks didn't tell anybody about the guarantee." Rusty snagged a ticket from the electronic dispenser and headed down into the garage. "Remember, almost anything is possible if your accountants comply," he said, swinging into a parking spot. "You know?"

"You're the accountant. I'll take your word for it."

Rusty turned off the car. "Fargo is Global's shadow account."

Conner had been about to reach for the door handle, but he turned in his seat to listen.

"Fargo operates in the dark," Rusty continued. "That can happen because only a few people know about it. It has to be that way," he murmured. "That's the rule." He shook his head. "The other rule is that, ultimately, the light moves and so does the shadow. If you don't move with it, you get caught."

"Well, the light moved, Rusty," Conner said, pointing at Rusty's hand. "Give me that parking ticket."

Rusty forced a wry smile. "You don't miss much, do you?"

Conner kept Rusty ahead of him as they walked out of the garage and into the lobby of the Baker Mahaffey building. He was looking around constantly, watching for anything suspicious, even as they stepped into the elevator Rusty activated with a magnetic card. Conner hadn't been more than five feet from Rusty since knocking on the guy's door thirty minutes ago, but Rusty might have still somehow gotten a message to somebody.

"This way," Rusty called over his shoulder as he stepped out of the elevator onto the fourteenth floor. "I'm going to make this easy for you."

Conner followed Rusty through the floor's familiar lobby. He'd waited out here for Vic Hammond a few days ago. At eleven in the morning, it had been a bee-hive of activity. Now, after midnight, it was eerily silent.

Rusty headed down a long corridor, then turned into a small office, pulled a set of keys from his pocket and inserted one into the lock of a file cabinet behind his desk. He hesitated and looked back at Conner, who had stayed near the door. "If I give you this, are you really going to let me have a twenty-four-hour head start?"

Conner nodded. "Yes."

"I want to see my baby grow up," Rusty said, his voice cracking.

It had suddenly become real for him, Conner realized. The consequences of his actions were setting in. But he should have thought of those consequences before agreeing to help Vic Hammond. "I understand."

"I have relatives in another country. I might actually be able to make this work."

"I told you," Conner said firmly. "Twenty-four hours. I can't promise you any more than that. Now, *give me what you have*."

The file cabinet lock clicked open, and Rusty removed a large three-ring binder. For the next ten minutes he went through the file that detailed the fraud at Fargo Management and Global Components. There were original communications back and forth between Vic Hammond and Jim Hatcher, and handwritten notes from Hammond to Rusty. Even memos from several bankers who'd agreed to fund Fargo and keep it quiet — in return for millions of dollars of fees.

"Is this the only file?" Conner asked.

"Yes." Rusty had moved to the office window and was staring out into the night.

Probably wishing he could rewind the tape a few years, Conner thought to himself. "Why did you do this?" Rusty seemed like a capable enough guy. Not someone who needed to cheat to get ahead. Now he was going to be looking over his shoulder until the FBI inevitably tracked him down, even if he did make it to that foreign country.

Rusty was silent for a few moments. "My wife was about to give birth to our first child. I had fifty thousand dollars of school loans and nothing in the bank. And my mom was sick. She didn't have health insurance. Vic Hammond gave me a hundred thousand bucks out of his own pocket, and suddenly I was okay. Except that I was in his debt," Rusty said softly. "I made a deal, and I had to live with it." He took a deep breath. "Down deep I suppose I knew this day would come."

"Why did you put this book together?" Conner asked.

"There's a lot of evidence in there *proving* that I was coerced," Rusty said, bitterness in his voice for the first time. "I wanted to make certain if things ever got nasty that it was all in one place. I thought it might give me a better chance to negotiate."

Conner gazed at Rusty for a few moments, then glanced back down at the notebook. "What is this?" he asked. There was a section at the back of the binder set off from the rest of the pages by a bright red divider.

Rusty laughed harshly. "This is the

smoking gun, my friend. The ultimate smoking gun. Those pages at the back detail how a man named Alan Bryson, a member of Global Components's board of directors and the chairman of the board's audit committee, forced Global to grant him five hundred and fifty thousand in-the-money call options to look the other way when they hired Baker Mahaffey and structured the Fargo Management transaction. As chairman of the audit committee he should have stopped that transaction, and the hiring of Baker Mahaffey. Instead, he made money on it."

Conner's brain began to pound. He'd just stepped into some very bad shit. Paul Stone was one thing. Alan Bryson was quite another. "How much money did the treasury secretary make?"

"The options were worth about twenty million dollars at the time of the grant. I think they're worth almost twice that now."

"Oh, Christ."

Rusty nodded. "Yeah, if you intend to use this binder for personal gain, you better think very carefully. Before you tell anybody about what's in that binder, you may want to get out of this country, too."

They both heard the front door open far down the corridor.

Conner hustled to the office doorway and peered out. Three men stood in the lobby. A tiny, balding man and two bigger men in dark suits. Conner signaled for Rusty to take a look. "You know them? Are they Baker Mahaffey people?"

"No," Rusty said, shaking his head. "I've never seen any of them before."

"We better get out of here," Conner said, bolting to the desk and snatching the binder. "Where's the nearest stairway?"

"Back down the corridor. About halfway to the lobby."

Conner stopped at the office doorway, then leaned slowly out and peered down the corridor again. The men had disappeared. "All right, let's go," he ordered, bolting from the office. "Where's the door?" he called over his shoulder as they ran.

"Another fifty feet," Rusty answered, trying to keep up. "On the right."

As they headed for the stairway, the little bald man emerged from an office down the corridor.

"Stop!" Lucas shouted, spotting Conner and Rusty. The two other men appeared behind him. "Don't let them out of here!" he yelled. They dashed past him, racing toward Conner and Rusty.

Conner glanced over his shoulder. Rusty

had fallen way behind. "Come on!" he yelled. "Run!"

Hootie Wilson settled into the back of his limousine as the driver closed the door. He was exhausted. He was sixty-two years old and the pressure of running one of Washington's most prominent law firms was wearing on him. He should have retired by now with millions in the bank, but the divorce from his wife of forty years had set him back. *Way back*. And all because of that one night of indiscretion.

Wilson sank into the leather seat, thinking about the marble notebook safely stowed in his briefcase. Franklin Bennett was going to be very happy about that. In return, Wilson would have unlimited use of all of those assets the party controlled. Assets his ex-wife's divorce attorney would never know about.

Lucas stood a few feet away as the two men went to work on the accountant. He cringed as the one wearing leather gloves delivered a wicked right to the accountant's stomach, while the other one held him up. Then there was another awful thud as the accountant's internal organs bore the brunt of a second, swift punch.

"Oh, God!" Rusty clutched his stomach and dropped to the cement floor of the deserted Metro station in a tight ball.

"Try now," the man wearing the gloves said.

Lucas walked to where the accountant lay, and knelt down. He couldn't imagine what this man was going through. In his entire life, the only real pain Lucas could ever remember enduring was a twisted ankle. "You work for Victor Hammond, correct, Mr. Reeves?" he asked, his voice low.

"Yes," Rusty gasped, blood trickling from one side of his mouth.

"Who was the other man with you tonight?" The other one had barely eluded them, scaling a tall fence like a big cat going straight up a tree — even as he clasped a huge binder — just as they were closing in on him.

"I don't know."

"Answer me!"

"I swear I don't know."

Lucas hesitated. "What was in the binder he was carrying?"

Rusty said nothing.

"Mr. Reeves, do I need to have my associates come back over here?" Lucas asked. "I don't want to, believe me. But if you don't start giving me answers soon, I will. Now, what was in the binder?"

"Information about a company named Global Components."

Now they were making progress. "What kind of information?" Lucas asked.

"Information about fraud Global has been committing over the past several years." Rusty could barely speak his stomach hurt so badly.

"Anything else?"

"Yeah."

"What?"

"Information about Alan Bryson."

Lucas leaned down very close to the accountant's ear. "From now on, I want you to answer so only I can hear. Speak only after I squeeze your right hand. Do you understand?" He put his ear next to Rusty's mouth and squeezed the man's hand.

"Yes," came the faint reply.

Lucas put his lips back to the accountant's ear. "What information was in that binder concerning Secretary Bryson?" He moved his ear to the other man's lips and squeezed.

Thirty minutes later they tossed the accountant onto the Metro tracks, a blindfolded, moaning heap. The man wearing the black gloves had delivered one last howitzer to the stomach, then they'd sprinted away. There was no reason to do anything else to him. The accountant had no idea who they were, and he'd have enough problems when the Global Components scandal broke. If he was able to get himself off the tracks before a train came through the station.

Lucas glanced back through the car's rear window at the Capitol. The brightly lit dome was disappearing behind them. Next stop, New York.

An hour ago, the "Paul Stone Cell" had reported in to Franklin Bennett. Now Bennett wanted Lucas and the two other men to get to Queens as quickly as possible. Bennett had given that order to Lucas after Lucas had called to report that he had come within a hair of obtaining the binder. It was then that Bennett had explained in detail what was going on with the other cell.

Lucas smiled to himself as he turned his back on the Capitol. Threatening Bennett with the marble notebook had been pure genius. Suddenly he was on the inside. Suddenly he and Bennett were pals. Which would last only as long as Bennett was scared. But he had a plan in place to keep

Bennett away from the important things he'd recorded. Brenda was phase one of that plan.

The Paul Stone Cell had begun as a legitimate insider trading investigation, Bennett had explained. The Justice Department had Stone dead to rights for buying put options on two thousand shares of a small publicly traded biotech company just ahead of very bad news about a product liability lawsuit that was about to be filed against it. News that Stone had released himself onto the company's chat board. As the share price dropped when the bad news was released, Stone had made thirty bucks on each share he controlled, pocketing sixty grand in an afternoon. But he'd been sloppy about how he'd released the bad news. And the Justice Department had tracked him down.

When investigators had questioned Stone under the bare bulb, he'd broken. And, in an attempt to cut a deal, had admitted he was planning another insider trading scam. But this time the stakes were bigger. And he claimed to have a partner. A man named Gavin Smith. Somebody in the room had gone ballistic at the mention of Smith's name. Seems a few years before, Smith had fired the guy from an investment bank named Harper Manning for no reason at all. And the guy had vowed revenge.

But the guy never had a chance to exact that revenge. Through his senior-level contacts at the Justice Department, Bennett had heard about *why* Paul Stone was targeting Global Components for his insider trading scam. Stone suspected that the senior executives at Global were committing fraud, and Bennett knew that Secretary Bryson had been on the board of directors of Global Components. That this was one of those forty-three combinations he'd originally instructed Lucas to investigate. So Bennett had taken control of the Paul Stone insider trading investigation himself. The lower-level people who'd been in the room when Stone was trying to cut his deal and had mentioned Gavin Smith, had been removed from the investigation completely and been replaced by Bennett's men.

Control of the Stone investigation provided Bennett with critical information. And when Lucas called to tell Bennett that he and the two associates had come within a hair of getting a binder that would have given Bennett proof of exactly what they were looking for — incriminating information on one of the jewels — Bennett had ordered Lucas to get to New York because that was where the binder was headed. Paul Stone had reported to his contact at the Justice Department, and that contact had reported to Bennett, through Sam Macarthur. It was all coming together.

Bennett had explained all of this to Lucas as the young accountant from Baker Mahaffey was first beginning to cough up blood.

When Lucas was at Exit 8 on the New Jersey Turnpike, an hour outside New York, Bennett had called again to tell him that it had been Conner Ashby who had escaped from Baker Mahaffey with Phil Reeves's binder. There was a surveillance camera at the accounting firm's office, and they'd taken possession of the tape to make certain no one at the firm saw footage of Lucas and the other two men breaking in. From that tape they'd also identified Conner Ashby.

It was four o'clock in the morning when Lucas and the other two men pulled up in front of 662 Greenport Avenue. Amy Richards was waiting on the sidewalk, as Bennett had assured Lucas she would be. The man in the front seat got out and opened the rear door of the sedan for her.

"Thank you for meeting with us, Ms. Richards," Lucas said politely as she slid onto the seat next to him and the car accelerated away from the curb.

"No problem," Amy answered. "I'm happy to do anything to help you get Conner Ashby. I had no idea he was a criminal. Just another Wall Street insider trading thug, huh? At least, that's what Paul told me."

"Mr. Stone is exactly right," Lucas agreed, acting as if he actually knew Stone. "Conner Ashby is a criminal." She'd bought the story about Ashby so easily. Because she wanted to, Lucas realized. Less than thirty-six hours ago she'd called Stone from a cab outside a Manhattan restaurant to tell him that she'd do anything to take Conner down. In turn, Stone had called his contact at Justice. Five minutes later, Bennett had known about it, too. "Stealing hundreds of thousands of dollars from ordinary people like you and me."

"I hate him," she snapped. "He's a snake."

"So you'll help me find him?"

"Yes, I will." Amy smiled. "And I know just how to do it."

Amy Richards ended up in the East River. Her body was never recovered.

Chapter 23

Conner trudged across the terrace toward the table. He'd driven all night on the back roads of Maryland, Pennsylvania, and New Jersey. Wary of using Interstate 95 or the New Jersey Turnpike to get to New York. It seemed obvious that they would cover the major routes to try and intercept him. Once through New York, he'd followed the same procedure on Long Island, staying off the LIE and the other primary roads. It had added a couple of hours to his trip, but greatly increased his chances of getting here — and surviving.

"Good morning, pal," Gavin said cheerfully, putting down his newspaper. "How are you?"

"Okay," Conner answered. He ought to be exhausted. Strangely, he wasn't. Once he'd made it past Manhattan, he'd caught a second wind. He eased into a chair opposite Gavin, taking in the scents of the ocean and the freshly mown grass. "Always on Wednesday," he murmured, gazing down the terrace at the waves breaking onto Gavin's beach. They were small, nothing he'd bother surfing. Suddenly, he wanted to go to Hawaii.

"What was that?" Gavin asked curiously.

"They always cut your grass on Wednesday. It's Thursday morning and it smells like they just cut it. It was the same last week."

Gavin chuckled. "I think you're right, pal. I think they do cut it on Wednesday."

Conner began to recline into the chair, then forced himself to sit back up. He couldn't allow himself to get comfortable. He could feel exhaustion coming on again, and he needed to stay alert. "It's nice out here."

"Yes, it is. I love it." Gavin folded his hands in his lap. "Well, you've had yourself a hell of a few days."

"Yeah, I have." He'd called Gavin after making it out of Washington and relayed what he'd uncovered over the last twenty-four hours about Global Components — and Paul Stone.

"Two billion dollars a year of buried expenses in Minneapolis," Gavin said softly.

"Thanks to Global's accountants at Baker Mahaffey."

"It's incredible. Global has always been such a great company. I never did any business with them during my career at Harper Manning, but I always admired the numbers they put up." Gavin paused. "Except for that one time a few years ago. I guess we know now how the execs were able to get the numbers back on track." He shook his head. "Still, it's going to be terrible watching the company crash and burn when word gets out."

"Just another example of corporate executives taking advantage of their positions," Conner observed. "Defrauding shareholders for their own gain."

"I can't believe all those things about Paul," Gavin said sadly. "The insider trading. Allowing those two women to stay at my place in Miami. Setting you up by using one of them." He glanced over at Conner. "Did you ever have any idea that Liz Shaw was working with Paul?"

"Not until yesterday."

"I ought to be pissed off that you found out about my place in Miami by snooping around my apartment. But, under the circumstances, I guess it's a good thing you did. If Paul had been able to follow through with this Global Components scam, there's no telling what might have happened to Phenix Capital. If he'd been caught, and I'm sure he would have been,"

Gavin said, interrupting himself, "the SEC might have shut us down. At minimum, we all would have been caught up in the proceedings against him."

"I wasn't snooping around your apartment," Conner replied. "I told you, I was just looking for a —"

"It doesn't matter," Gavin cut in. "Jesus, what an idiot I am. No wonder Paul wanted to know where I was all the time. He was afraid I'd go to Miami without him knowing and find out he was keeping strippers in my condo."

Conner looked up. "You really had no idea Paul was letting those women stay there?"

Gavin shook his head. "No. I'd given him the keys to the place a few years ago because he said he wanted to take Mandy down there for a romantic weekend. He must have made copies of the keys then." Gavin banged the table. "You think you know someone, pal, but I guess you never really do."

"You know me," Conner said firmly.

Gavin nodded. "Yes, I do," he agreed quietly.

Conner glanced toward the ocean again. "What are you going to do?"

"The only thing I can do. Turn Paul in."

Gavin sighed. "This will present quite a challenge for Phenix Capital, Conner."

"Actually, it will present a *problem,* Gavin. Not a challenge."

"Right, a problem." Gavin hesitated. "Will you stay on at Phenix?"

"If you want me to."

"Of course, I do," Gavin said firmly. "In fact, I'm going to need you to take on more responsibility. This weekend we'll discuss your equity stake in Phenix. And how I'm going to get Paul's back," Gavin muttered under his breath.

"Thanks. I appreciate that."

"You deserve it." Gavin rubbed his eyes. "How could I have been so stupid? I'm usually a better judge of character. I should have listened to you before."

"Don't be so hard on yourself," Conner said gently, standing up.

"I'm sorry I lied to you about Pharmaco," Gavin offered. "That was wrong. But I knew you were very worried about our financial condition. Look, this other mandate is real," he said firmly. "It'll be at least a twenty-million-dollar fee."

"Great."

"I'll let you talk to the CEO yourself."

"Okay."

"There will be at least a couple of million in it for you."

"It's all right, Gavin. I know you'll take care of me." Conner nodded across the terrace at the mansion. "I'm going to catch a few hours of sleep. Can I use the same bedroom I did last time?"

"Sure. And help yourself to whatever you want. Grab a bite to eat before you go upstairs. There's plenty of stuff in the kitchen."

"Thanks." Conner took a couple of steps toward the mansion, then stopped and turned around. "There is something I want to talk to you about."

The old man was about to pick up the newspaper. "Oh? What's that?"

"Remember when you told me that senior guy from Baker Mahaffey called you the other day?"

"Vaguely."

"That was how you knew I was in Washington."

"Oh, right," Gavin said, snapping his fingers.

"What was his name?" Conner asked.

"*You* met with him."

"I know, but I can't remember. How did he introduce himself on the phone?"

"Victor Hammond."

"Did the conversation go well?"

"Very well. We spoke for at least ten minutes. He's a good man. I think there's a lot of business we can do with him."

"Did he ask you to call him anything else during the call?"

"No."

Conner looked off toward the ocean. If they'd spoken for ten minutes, Hammond would have asked Gavin to call him Vic. "Did Hammond really call you, Gavin?"

"What? Of course," Gavin retorted angrily. "Why would I lie about something like that?"

"I don't know."

"You're being ridiculous, Conner. Go get some rest. You're just tired."

"Yeah, maybe. One more thing."

"What now?" Gavin snapped, his irritation boiling over.

"About a year ago you bought your wife a one-way ticket to Miami. Why did you do that?"

Gavin's eyes flashed to Conner's, a strange smile playing across his tanned face. "What?"

"Last July, you bought Helen a one-way ticket to Miami. You booked her on a United flight from LaGuardia to Miami. But you didn't buy a return ticket. You bought yourself a return ticket, but you didn't buy her one." Conner spotted Gavin's fingers curl tightly around the arms of the chair.

"What are you talking about?" Gavin asked nervously. "I didn't do that."

"Yes, you did. I checked your expense files at Phenix. It's very clear."

"I must have put the return trip on another credit card."

"I suppose you could have. But that would seem like a strange thing to do. Don't you think?"

"What's this all about?" Gavin demanded, standing up.

"It's just that I had a long time to think about this thing while I was driving up here from Washington."

"Yeah. And?"

Conner hesitated. "It's hard for me to believe Paul Stone could pull it off by himself. Without you at least figuring out what he was doing."

The veins in Gavin's neck began to bulge. "Conner, you better be careful what you —"

"Then I remembered something Liz said to me yesterday. She said that a couple of times over the last year and a half she and her roommate had to clear out of the apartment because Paul had warned them you were coming down to Miami."

"So?"

"But then I thought about your expense files again. You've been going to Miami at least once every few weeks since about six months before Helen died. Sometimes more often than that. That's a lot more than *a couple* of times in the last year and a half."

"I have no idea what you're talking about."

"And I thought about how it didn't bother you that Paul was having an affair with Rebecca. How you blessed that affair, so to speak. 'Got Rebecca for Paul,' I think you told me. So I couldn't understand why you'd care if he was keeping a couple of strippers in Miami. It didn't fit." Conner stared straight at Gavin. "Then it hit me. Paul didn't set up this thing with Global Components. You did. You saw it as a way to make a lot of money fast. A way to get yourself out of a financial hole you dug by starting Phenix Capital." Conner's eyes narrowed. "How long have you been seeing Ginger?"

Gavin gritted his teeth. "You son of a bitch. You don't know what you're talking about. How can you accuse me of this?

After all I've done for you?"

"Don't deny it, Gavin. I know everything. Liz told me."

It had become clear to Conner as Liz was telling him how men were always trying to impress her at the club. Trying to make themselves seem different from all the rest. It was Gavin who was behind everything, not Paul. Paul was just the errand boy.

Liz had denied it at first. So Conner had forced her face down toward the scalding water again. With no intention of actually pushing her head beneath the surface, but Liz hadn't known that. All she knew was that she'd screwed him. And she was petrified.

She'd admitted everything as he'd held her face two inches from the water's steaming surface. Gavin had met Ginger one night at the Executive Suite about eighteen months ago, and they'd begun a torrid affair. Gavin had lavished her with gifts, then encouraged her to move into his condominium. And allowed Liz to move in as well when Ginger had asked. When Conner let Liz up from the tub, she'd shown him the love letters Gavin had written Ginger, stashed in a shoe box in Ginger's closet.

A few months after Gavin and Ginger had begun seeing each other, Liz had overheard the Global Components executives bragging about the fraud while she was with them at the Executive Suite. And she had approached Gavin about it on one of his trips to Miami. Gavin and Liz had hatched the plan to manipulate Conner into finding out exactly what was going on at Global. Not Paul and Liz.

"You've been having an affair with Ginger for more than a year," Conner said quietly. "I saw the letters you wrote her. Liz showed them to me. Which is why you murdered Helen. Helen wasn't going to just step aside and let you have your fun. Not after all those years. She suspected something. She didn't know where or with whom, but she had a feeling."

Gavin stared intently at Conner for several moments, then sank slowly back into his chair and ran his hands through his gray hair.

"Liz Shaw overheard those executives from Global Components talking about the fraud they and the accountants were committing in Minneapolis. They were bragging their asses off because they were drunk and they wanted to impress a beautiful woman, even if she was a stripper. They never thought a stripper would be able to take advantage of what she overheard."

"No, they didn't," Gavin agreed, his voice barely audible.

"They had no idea her roommate was having an affair with one of the biggest names on Wall Street. Even if they had, they would have had no idea how far that man would go because they wouldn't have known what sorry financial shape he was in." Conner shook his head. "But that's what made you such an incredible investment banker. You'd do whatever you had to do to get a client. So executing this scam involving Global was nothing for you. Even if it involved screwing a young guy who thought you walked on water," Conner said bitterly. "You convinced Liz to seduce me. You faked her murder. Then you sent one of your ex-FBI boys in to chase me through the subways of New York, even shooting me in the arm just in case I had any doubts about how real the whole thing was. Then you sent a man who claimed to be a private investigator to scare the shit out of me. To make me take action to save my own ass. You even brought back Amy Richards to really throw me off my game. Had Paul tell her I was having an affair with Mandy so she'd watch me every minute of the day. All to get me to find out what was going on at Global Components."

Gavin nodded slowly as he stared down at the grass. "Yes."

"How did you kill Helen?" asked Conner directly. "Did you take her out on a pleasure cruise under the guise of reconciling, then push her overboard? You feed her to the sharks?"

Gavin dropped his face into his hands. "Yes," he admitted.

"Then Ginger and Liz could live in the condominium and not have to worry about a surprise visit from her."

"Helen was going to divorce me. I couldn't have that."

"So you made up a phony story about a sailboat accident off Shelter Island for the cops. But why did you tell me about it? I would never have asked about it. But *you* brought it up."

"I thought you'd relate to it because of everything that had happened to your mother," Gavin mumbled. "I didn't think you'd check it out."

"You probably didn't think I'd check out your expense statements either. Buying that one-way ticket for Helen was so stupid, Gavin. You're usually much smarter than that." Conner shook his head. "But why me, Gavin? Why didn't you have Stone go down to Baker Mahaffey himself? Why didn't you have him go see Glen Frolling?"

"We wanted to keep our distance from the situation in case something went wrong." Gavin looked up at Conner, glassy-eyed. "I knew you would figure it out if I gave you the right incentive. You're one of the most capable people I've ever met."

"Then you should have known I'd figure out what you and Liz were doing. What was really going on here."

"Yes," Gavin agreed, beginning to sob. "I should —"

"You have no idea what's *really going on,*" a voice behind Conner said.

Conner spun around. Paul Stone stood a few yards away, aiming a revolver at him.

"Hello, Conner," Stone said calmly.

"Put the gun down, Paul!" Gavin shouted, standing up. "It's over. I can't take it anymore. Put it down."

"No," Stone snapped. "I think Conner got what we needed when he was in Washington. Didn't you?" he asked, nodding at Conner. "Where's the binder?"

How could Stone possibly know about

the binder? "What the hell are you talking about? I don't know anything about a binder."

"Don't lie to me."

"They were going to throw you to the wolves, Paul," Conner said quickly. "Gavin and Liz were going to pin the insider trading rap on you if things got tough." That was why Liz had protected Gavin right up until she thought Conner would actually push her face into the steaming water. She assumed Gavin was a better risk than Paul in a tight situation. She had it all figured out. "They were gonna throw you out like yesterday's garbage."

"That's not true," Gavin spoke up. "I would never do —"

"Shut up, Gavin," Stone snapped. "I know exactly what you're capable of. Remember, I've been with you for a long time. I've seen you in action. You're a cold son of a bitch." He smiled. "Fortunately, I've picked up a few things along the way. I have my own escape hatch."

Conner's eyes flashed to Stone's. Suddenly he realized how Stone could know about the binder.

Stone closed one eye and held the gun out, both hands wrapped around the handle. "You know what it is, Conner? You know what it all really boils down to?"

Conner glanced at the gun. It wasn't shaking at all. Stone was dead calm. A bad sign. "What?" he asked, taking a step back, worried that he'd underestimated the man.

Stone stepped forward. "The fact that I just can't stand you," he said, squeezing the trigger.

The bullet entered Stone's head behind the right ear, shattering his skull. He toppled forward, dead before he even hit the ground.

"Oh, Jesus!" Gavin shouted, taking cover behind a chair. "What the hell is going on?"

Conner saw the three men spill out of the mansion, one right behind the other. The little bald one, then the two bigger ones. The two bigger men were carrying rifles. They were the same men Conner had seen at Baker Mahaffey a few hours ago. He bent down and quickly grabbed Stone's revolver, then took off toward the ocean.

"Stop!" Lucas yelled as he reached the spot where Stone's body had fallen. "Stop!"

The two bigger men were racing toward the dunes, going after Conner.

"Don't bother," Lucas called to them as they looked back. "We have what we need."

Hootie Wilson handed Bennett the marble notebook as they sat on the porch of the Middleburg house. It was going to be nice living in splendor again, Wilson thought to himself. Not in the one-bedroom, starkly furnished apartment he'd been forced to go home to since the divorce had become final. "I think this is what you want."

Bennett grabbed the notebook. "What about the woman?" he snapped.

Wilson shook his head. "She's got a big problem with the D.C. Bar Association. Which I'm taking care of. Besides, she doesn't really give a shit about this Lucas character, anyway."

Bennett stared at Wilson for a few moments, unconvinced. Then he glanced down and rifled through the notebook, his blood pressure rising as he reached the end. "Goddamn it!" he roared.

Conner moved into a grove of trees, sucking air. That was the fastest two miles he'd ever run. It seemed like he'd lost them. Now he needed to find help. He was about to start moving again when his cell phone rang. Jackie's cell number appeared on the screen.

"Jackie?"

"Conner Ashby?"

Conner's eyes narrowed. It wasn't Jackie. "Who is this?"

"Doesn't matter. What matters is that you need to get your ass back to Gavin Smith's place right away."

"Why would I do that?"

"If you ever want to see Jackie Rivera alive again, you'll get back here."

"What the —"

"You can thank your old friend Amy Richards for giving us Jackie. We sure did."

CHAPTER 24

Jackie sat on the couch of the mansion's living room. The same couch Mandy Stone had been sitting on when Conner had gotten to the mansion early last Thursday morning. Jackie was staring straight ahead, her lower lip trembling. They'd gotten her at seven o'clock this morning. Forced her into their car as she'd been coming out of her apartment to go to work.

"Let her go," Conner demanded. He was sitting beside Jackie on the couch. "She doesn't know anything."

"I understand that," said Lucas calmly, standing a few feet away. One of the other two men stood beside him, pistol drawn. "I want the binder you took from Baker Mahaffey."

"What does she have to do with a binder?" Conner asked, wishing they hadn't frisked him and found Stone's revolver.

"Nothing."

"Then why is she here?"

"I want the binder," Lucas repeated.

"You give it to me and she goes free."

"I don't have the binder," Conner said truthfully. On his way from Washington this morning, he'd stopped at the Harrisburg, Pennsylvania, Greyhound bus station. He'd rented a small locker there and stored the binder inside.

"Where is it?"

"I don't know."

Lucas nodded at the other man. He yanked Jackie off the couch by her wrist. She screamed as the man spun her around, wrapped one forearm tightly around her neck and put the gun to her head.

"Conner!" she yelled.

Conner leapt up off the couch, but the man turned the gun on him.

"Sit down, Mr. Ashby!" Lucas ordered.

Conner sank slowly back to the couch. He could see the terror in Jackie's eyes, but there was nothing he could do.

"Now," Lucas said deliberately. "Where's the binder?"

Then Lucas's cell phone rang.

Lucas glanced at the phone's tiny screen. It was Brenda, calling from her cell phone. He'd seen the number yesterday afternoon when she'd called to ask him to meet her at the Washington Monument. He turned away from Ashby, Jackie Rivera, and the man holding the gun. "Hello."

"Lucas! Lucas!"

"What is it, Brenda? Calm down."

"Lucas, I gave that notebook you asked me to keep to the managing partner of my law firm. Somehow he knew about it. He wanted it. He made me give it to him."

"It's all right, Bren. Don't worry." It was exactly as Lucas had anticipated. Franklin Bennett had coerced her. Bennett had something on her and she'd been played. But it was just like a chess match, and, fortunately, Lucas had expected this. And done something about it.

"I'm sorry, Lucas!" Brenda cried at the other end of the line. "Don't hate me, please don't hate me."

"I don't hate you." How could he? She was calling to warn him of what she'd done. And she was riddled with guilt. She cared after all. "Everything's going to be all right."

"Lucas, I — Oh, Jesus Christ, I — Please don't —"

Lucas heard a blast at the other end of the phone. Then silence. Then muffled voices in the background.

"Brenda! *Bren!*"

Then the connection went dead.

The world turned red in front of him. He never should have done this. He should have stayed in his quiet little world. He never should have listened to Cheetah. He should have known better. He should have tried to avoid disaster one more time. But now it was too late.

He'd outplayed Franklin Bennett, but maybe that didn't matter. Maybe there were only degrees of losing in this match. Lucas snapped the cell phone closed and slipped it back in his pocket. There was only one thing left to do.

Conner watched the little bald man slip the cell phone back in his pocket.

"What now?" the man holding Jackie demanded.

"We kill both of them," Lucas responded. "That was the order."

"But we don't have the binder yet," the man protested, dropping the pistol from Jackie's head for a moment.

Lucas lunged at the man just as he lowered the gun.

Conner was off the couch instantly, racing toward the struggle. Reaching them just as the gun exploded. Lucas and Jackie tumbled away, falling to the floor.

Then Conner was on the man with the

gun, grabbing his wrist and pointing the gun toward the ceiling. It exploded twice in rapid succession, showering the room with plaster as the bullets slammed into the ceiling. Conner nailed the man with a quick right to the chin, and he tumbled to the couch. He tried to get up, but Conner was on him again immediately. Delivering two more wicked blows to his face. The man collapsed, unconscious.

Instantly there was the explosion of another gunshot and the whine of a bullet. The second man who had accompanied Lucas from Washington stood in the living room doorway, aiming. Conner dived for the gun on the floor, grabbed it, raised up, and fired twice. And the man in the living room doorway tumbled backward.

Conner raced to where the man lay, clutching his stomach and moaning. He picked up the second gun and turned around just in time to see the little bald one pull himself to his feet and stagger forward, his white shirt covered with blood. After a few steps, he collapsed to the floor.

Conner crawled quickly to the little man's side. He'd saved Jackie's life. Conner had no idea why. But he had, and that was all that mattered. "Stay still, I'm going to get you an ambulance."

Jackie was just picking herself up from the floor. "I'll call one, Conner," she said, hurrying to a phone on a table.

"You've got to get out of here," Lucas gasped. "More people will be here soon." He reached into his jacket pocket. "Take these," he murmured.

These were the last ten pages of the marble notebook. Pages Lucas had ripped from the notebook before giving it to Brenda. In the end, he'd outplayed Franklin Bennett — but died doing it.

"Those pages are important," Lucas whispered, feeling his life ebbing away.

Conner took the bloodstained pages from the little man's trembling hand, then clasped the small fingers tightly.

Moments later, Lucas was gone.

EPILOGUE

Jackie picked up a glass of wine off the table and took a sip. "All right, I want an explanation." It had been a week since the episode at Gavin's mansion. A week since they had climbed frantically into Conner's rental car and raced to the East Hampton Police Station ahead of any more of Franklin Bennett's men. "What happened out there?"

"Oh, you want an explanation, do you?" Conner asked, grinning as he sat beside her on the couch.

"I think I *deserve* one."

Conner tried to look puzzled. "Why? Just because you were held at gunpoint and almost killed?"

"I think that qualifies me."

Conner laughed. "Yeah, I guess it does." He took a sip of wine before he started. "Paul Stone had committed insider trading a while back. After he heard about a lawsuit involving a little biotech company in Massachusetts before the rest of the world did. He found out about the suit from one of the company's senior executives and made around sixty grand shorting the stock. But Stone was sloppy with the way he went about releasing the information concerning the lawsuit. He did it on the company's chat board directly from his own computer. The Justice Department nailed him right away.

"While people from Justice were interrogating Stone, he communicated the fact that he was planning to do the same thing with Global Components. But this time he had a partner."

"Gavin Smith," Jackie spoke up.

"Right. Now, it turns out one of the guys from Justice who was interrogating Stone used to work at Harper Manning and had been fired by Gavin Smith a couple of years ago. Gavin had fired the guy to cover up for his own mistake, so the guy was looking for revenge big time. When he heard Gavin's name, he couldn't believe his luck."

"And, of course, Justice always wants to nail the biggest dog they can," Jackie pointed out.

"Always," Conner agreed. "Which Stone knew and was probably why he told the guys interrogating him."

"They would have been all over that opportunity right away. Even if the one guy wasn't looking for revenge."

"That's right. So they decided to set up a sting to get Gavin," Conner continued, "simply by letting the Global Components situation play out. In return for his cooperation, Paul Stone was supposed to be able to stay out of jail when the thing was over."

"And Gavin Smith set you up to do all the dirty work on Global."

Conner nodded. "Because he didn't want to take a risk in case something blew up along the way."

"But how did Gavin find out there was something going on at Global in the first place?"

"Liz Shaw, the roommate of the woman in Miami that Gavin was seeing, had overheard two Global Components senior executives bragging about what they were doing. How they were creating billions of dollars of earnings out of thin air because they were the smartest guys in town. But Liz hadn't heard enough for Gavin and Stone to make such a huge bet. They had to be absolutely sure the fraud was being committed, *and* they had to be able to control when the existence of the fraud was exposed."

"So they could get in and out of the market quickly."

"Yes." Conner nodded approvingly.

"But who was the little guy who died at the mansion?" Jackie asked. "The guy who kidnapped me that morning, and handed you those pieces of paper at the end."

Conner had been debriefed by the FBI. He wasn't supposed to tell anyone what they'd said, but Jackie deserved to know. "His name was Lucas Avery."

She shook her head. "I don't know any Lucas Avery. Why did he come and get me?"

"Amy Richards."

Jackie raised both eyebrows. "You mean that psycho woman you dated last winter?"

"Yeah, she told Lucas about us."

"I don't understand."

"Amy knew that I cared for you," Conner said softly. "Apparently, she's been stalking me for quite some time. She's seen us out together a few times and she told Lucas that was the way to get to me." He ran his fingers over Jackie's cheek. He hadn't realized how much he cared about her until he'd seen the gun pointed at her head. He smiled. "Amy was right. That *was* the way to get to me. I came back to get you."

"I know," she said, leaning forward to kiss him. "Thank you."

"Don't thank me. I don't know what I'd do without you. Besides, it was because of me that you were there."

Jackie kissed him again, this time more deeply. "But how did Lucas find Amy?" she asked, pulling back.

"Paul Stone."

She took another sip of wine. "So who was Lucas Avery?"

"He worked at the West Wing of the White House. Until the president's chief of staff gave him a special assignment."

"The president's chief of staff," Jackie repeated, wide-eyed. "You mean Franklin Bennett?"

"Yes."

"What was the assignment?"

"Lucas was supposed to make certain there wasn't any bad stuff floating around out in the ether about top members of the president's administration, specifically the vice president and the secretaries of treasury, state, defense, and energy."

"You mean the Beltway Boys," Jackie said.

"Yup. But apparently Bennett had another agenda. And Lucas figured it out."

"What was that other agenda?"

"Bennett really wanted the information so he could take the president down."

"Why would he want to do that?"

"Project Trust."

"You mean the subject of the speech the president made last week? Nailing all of you Wall Street types to the wall."

Conner grinned at her. "Yes. I guess some very influential people inside the president's party didn't care much for Project Trust. He was going to propose a seventy-five percent tax rate on all income over a million bucks. And some kind of net worth tax, too."

Jackie whistled softly. "Jesus. I've got some clients who'd be pretty upset about that."

"Lucas figured out what Bennett was really up to, and he found out something very bad about one of the Beltway Boys."

"Which one?"

"Let me come back to that."

"Okay."

"So Lucas figures out everything, but he horse trades. He won't tell Bennett who the bad guy is or what he's done until Bennett promises a big career in the party. Money, perks, the whole nine yards. Bennett agrees, but crosses his fingers behind his back. Thing is, Lucas had an insurance policy."

"Those pages he handed to you at Gavin's."

Conner nodded. "Yes. He'd written every-thing down."

"And what was the binder Lucas kept asking you about?"

A few days ago Conner had accompa-nied FBI agents to Harrisburg to retrieve the binder at the Greyhound bus station. They were going to use it as evidence against Franklin Bennett, Alan Bryson, Sam Macarthur, and Vic Hammond, as well as the Global Component executives. As Phil Reeves had said, it was the ulti-mate smoking gun.

"It was a binder an accountant at Baker Mahaffey put together in case he ever had to negotiate with the authorities. It detailed the fraud at Global Components as well as what the Beltway Boys had done. It showed that he had been coerced. Not that it's going to help much," he said, thinking back on the news of Phil Reeves's violent death.

"No, it won't," Jackie agreed somberly. "Was this Beltway Boy a director of Global Components?"

Conner clapped several times. "Damn, you're good."

"It's my business, Conner. I have to be good." She paused. "But what does Lucas have to do with Justice? How did he know about you?"

"Franklin Bennett found out about what was going on at Justice with Paul Stone and Gavin Smith, and the fact that they had uncovered something nasty about Global Components."

"So he figured he might be able to find out about the Beltway Boy that way as well," Jackie reasoned.

"Yes."

"And that's the connection from Lucas to Paul Stone."

"Right." Conner slid his hand behind Jackie's neck and pulled her mouth gently to his. He was going to take her to Hawaii and propose to her while they sat on a surfboard in a quiet lagoon on top of the turquoise water. In fact, he knew exactly which lagoon it would be. He'd found it one day by himself when he'd been to the Islands surfing the Banzai Pipeline. He chuckled. He might even find his way out onto the Pipeline once or twice while he and Jackie were there.

"What are you laughing about?" she asked, poking him in the ribs.

"Nothing, nothing." He wanted to tell her so badly how he was going to propose.

"So?"

"So what?"

"So which one of the Beltway Boys was

it and what did he do?" Jackie asked.

"Oh, right." Conner picked up the remote and flicked on the television. "Check it out."

They watched for a few moments as a commercial ended. Then a reporter appeared on the screen.

"Back to our top story," the reporter said excitedly. "Shares of Global Components have plunged to three dollars and ten cents in the last hour of trading due to the massive financial fraud uncovered this morning at the *Fortune* 500 giant. In a related story," the woman continued, "Treasury Secretary Alan Bryson has been implicated in the exploding scandal."

ABOUT THE AUTHOR

Stephen Frey is a principal at a Northern Virginia private equity firm. He previously worked in mergers and acquisitions at J. P. Morgan and as a vice president of corporate finance at an international bank in Midtown Manhattan. Frey is also the bestselling author of *Silent Partner*, *The Day Trader*, *Trust Fund*, *The Insider*, *The Legacy*, *The Inner Sanctum*, *The Vulture Fund*, and *The Takeover*.